Also by R.W Peake

Marching with Caesar-Conquest of Gaul

Marching with Caesar-Civil War

Critical praise for the Marching With Caesar series:

"Fans of the author will be delighted that Peake's writing has gone from strength to strength in this, the second volume...Peake manages to portray Pullus and all his fellow soldiers with a marvelous feeling of reality quite apart from the star historical name... There's history here, and character, and action enough for three novels, and all of it can be enjoyed even if readers haven't seen the first volume yet. Very highly recommended."
~The Historical Novel Society

"The hinge of history pivoted on the career of Julius Caesar, as Rome's Republic became an Empire, but the muscle to swing that gateway came from soldiers like Titus Pullus. What an amazing story from a student now become the master of historical fiction at its best."
~Professor Frank Holt, University of Houston

Marching with Caesar

Antony and Cleopatra

Part 1 Antony

Volume Four

By R.W. Peake

Marching with Caesar –Antony and Cleopatra by R.W. Peake

Foreword

As the Marching With Caesar series continues and grows in popularity, so too does my need for a solid team of people to help me continue this dream journey that I'm on. What you see in Marching With Caesar-Antony and Cleopatra Parts I and II, the third and fourth book in the series, is even more a collaborative effort than the first two books combined. This is because of a group of unselfish, excellent people who have taken Titus' story into their hearts and minds, and have become invested in helping me make these books the best they can be.

As always, I owe a deep thanks to Beth Lynne, my outstanding editor who's willing to put up with what I freely admit are moments of OCD combined with my own streak of perfectionism, with just a dash of paranoia thrown in. She does what I believe is a remarkable job at not only understanding the structural aspects of the craft of editing, but the underlying intent of the author.

To my cover artist, the superlative Marina Shipova, who I believe outdid herself with these covers, she too is easier to work with than I imagine I am! She has not only managed to make Titus come alive with her first cover, she tells the story of all that Titus endures and how the ravages of time catch up with all of us. Through her covers you can see Titus age and progress, in a way that not even my words can convey as well.

Perhaps the biggest change from the first book to this one is the addition of my team of advance, or beta if you prefer, readers. This small group of fans has given me input that is so valuable that just saying something here seems to be a paltry way of thanking them for their help. Specifically, and in no particular order, Stu McPherson, Joe Corso (who is an author in his own right and whose wonderful books you can find at http://www.corsobooks.com), Curtis Graham, Margaret Courtney and Jim Zipko. Between their keen eyes, thorough understanding of the previous books and insights into the characters, they provided me with advice and guidance that there is no way to put a price on its value.

Finally, perhaps the nicest surprise benefit from the books has been in enabling me to reconnect with Marines with whom I served, along with the chance to connect with other veterans, who have apparently found something that resonates with them in Titus' story. That in itself has made all of this worthwhile.

Historical Note

With this, the third installment of the Marching
With Caesar series Titus Pullus, his surviving friends
and comrades, and I venture into exotic, little-known,
and dangerous, territory with Marcus Antonius'
doomed expedition into the wilds of Parthia. What
today covers Turkey and Iran in many ways is as
remote and mysterious to most Westerners as it was
when the general launched what was the largest such
campaign up to that point in history.

Although the physical dangers and hardship were
borne by Antonius and the men who marched for him,
I am fully aware that I am also stepping into my own
version of dangerous territory because there are so few
extant sources existing for Antony's attempt to exact
revenge for the defeat of Marcus Publius Crassus and
his army at Carrhae years before. At least, that was the
goal according to the Triumvir, although there is more
than one historian who has posited that it was more to
enhance his own prestige in the ongoing battle with his
rival Gaius Octavius. It is not my goal, or my concern
frankly, to examine the motives of Antonius, simply
because his real reason for launching this campaign
would not have meant anything to Titus or his
comrades. No matter what the reason the Legions were
on the march, and the fact that the order was given by
a lawfully appointed Legate was the only reason that
was needed.

There has been much written about the
composition of the Legions composing Antonius' army,
but the truth is that with a couple of exceptions,

nobody knows for sure. From my research, it seems to be accepted that the 10th Legion was with Antonius, so it was easy to tell the story from that perspective, with Titus and the 10th part of the army. And while I have endeavored to hew as close to the historical record as possible, there are indeed places where I diverge, at least by design. One thing I have learned from the first two books is that no matter how deeply you dive into what is available as primary source material there will always be someone who insists that you got it wrong. Fortunately, those who hold this view seem to be a very small minority, no matter how vocal they may be.

Specifically, in the only successful campaign against the Parthians the Romans ever conducted, when the army was led by Aulus Ventidius in Antonius' stead, the "Muleteer" began an investment of the city of Samosata on the Euphrates River, where the modern-day city of Samsun is located. According to some sources, Antonius showed up before the city fell and Antiochus, the king of Commagene came to a financial arrangement with the Triumvir. In this story, Titus and the army conduct a siege and take the city by assault but reach an accommodation with Antiochus before they take the palace complex itself. I did this to further increase the tension between Ventidius and Antonius, who believed that his general was deliberately trying to outshine him. The fact that, at least militarily, this was not that hard to do is made apparent when Antonius conducted his own campaign. Whatever the case, Antonius was clearly displeased, whether the city fell before he arrived or not. I chose for dramatic purposes to have Ventidius and his army take the city, to add "fuel to the fire" for Antonius' actions towards this older but loyal lieutenant.

Speaking of Ventidius, I would like to take this time to clear up something that I personally found very confusing, but thanks to the superlative (and expensive!) *Barrington Atlas Of The Greek And Roman World*, I now understand, and that is the location of the Cilician Gates. When I was reading the source material, particularly Plutarch's account and he mentioned the Gates and the Taurus Mountains, that confused me, since the location of the Gates is along the coast. Besides the fact that there was apparently a real gate there, when "walking" the ground thanks to Google Earth, the nearest thing that could only charitably be called a mountain is a little more than a mile inland from the coast, and is barely three hundred feet high. It wasn't until, after something of an odyssey in itself, I finally received my Barrington Atlas that I was able to determine the reason for the confusion. Located on the southern slopes of the Taurus Mountain, at roughly Latitude 37'15"N and Longitude 34'40"E is the PASS of Cilicia, while the gates are located at roughly Latitude 36'50"N and Longitude 36'05"E.

One of my goals for this entire series of books has been to cleave as close to the historical record that I can. To that end, I did my best to lean on those scholars who have made the study of Rome and this time period in particular their lives' work, in conjunction with the advantages modern technology has to offer, like the aforementioned Google Earth. Particularly vexing, for me anyway, was the mapping of Antonius' Parthian campaign, particularly the point at which he leaves the Euphrates River behind. I have placed in the book the map that T. Rice-Holmes claimed was Antonius' route, but I confess I have major reservations about its accuracy. The source of this confusion comes from his labeling of the modern Turkish town of

Erzerum as Karana. However, as I was in the process of fact-checking I kept running into an issue because, since the maps in the atlas are arranged for the most part on an east-west axis, they naturally can't be aligned along a north-south axis. So I was left trying to piece together the maps in a way that would match up in a way where I could look at the entire route as described by Rice-Holmes. That's when I discovered there is a discrepancy between what Rice-Holmes labels as Karana, and where it's located in the Barrington Atlas. Where Barrington's places Karana is much farther west than would make sense for Antonius, who had turned east south of Satala. Using Rice-Holmes' reference point of Erzerum for physical location but Barrington's for a place name, the nearest point I could find was Calcidava. However, there is no current evidence that suggests that any settlement with the name Calcidava was even in existence when Antonius and his army, with Titus, marched through. Therefore, I refer to it in the book only as a reference point to help the reader understand the route that Antonius most likely took.

Table of Contents

Prologue

*(**Note by Diocles:** I confess that I was snooping when I found this. My former master and now-friend has not been sleeping well lately, and I can see that telling this tale of his is putting more strain on him than he lets on. But two days ago now, he closeted himself away one night, barring even me from his presence. That did not prevent me, however, from keeping a careful eye on him, even if it was through a keyhole, as I watched him scratching feverishly on a scroll. Or more accurately, a series of scrolls. For a day and into the night, he scribbled away, and now he is sleeping, well past his normal time to rise, prompting me to go poking about in his desk, equipped with a number of cubbyholes specifically designed for such scrolls as the one here. This is what I found; even with his adoption of Caesar's practice of placing a dot above the last letter of a sentence, his handwriting is almost impossible to decipher! What I do not know is whether he plans on including this in his account of his extraordinary life; I will have to ask him, but only when the time is right.)*

Every man, or woman I suppose, has a favorite time of the day. For some, it is as the sun is coming up, the rays of light chasing the dark away as the watches of daylight time lay before them, fresh with promise and possibility. For others, it is the opposite: the sight of the sun sinking down over the horizon, a signal that the day's labor is over and those delights that the night will bring are before them. Neither of those appeals to me. No, despite spending 42 years under the standard, where I started almost every single day before the sun made its appearance, I have never particularly enjoyed that part of the day. At least not for the sun coming up, although I must say that once I made the Centurionate I became rather fond of putting a boot up the backside of Publius for moving too slowly and the resulting organized chaos of a Legion waking up. No, for this old soldier, I enjoy the quiet time of the night, just before I retire, after all the servants have retired and only my old friend Diocles is still up, despite the fact he has long since surpassed the status of body slave and no longer needs to attend to me. I must admit I find it somewhat humorous that here in my 61st year, for the first time in many years, I am putting myself to bed. It is especially nice now that I can rise whenever I choose, and I find that I rather enjoy the slightly sinful feeling of sleeping well past the rise of the sun, which in turn fuels my ability to stay up even later. Usually, I try to read as I sit in my favorite chair, but over the last few months, I have found that increasingly difficult, as I squint and turn the scroll this way and that, putting it so close to the lamp that I have been scolded by Diocles on more than one occasion for the scorch marks on the edges of his precious manuscripts. That is when I remind him that it is scandalous for a slave to own a library as extensive as that of his master, but he is just as quick to remind me that I freed him long before and that the only reason he is still around is because he takes such pity on me for my age and decrepitude. Truly, we are like an old married couple in many ways, only genuinely happy when we are squabbling.

Now, instead of reading I spend most of my time in quiet reflection, a curious habit I have formed, given that I have come to this practice so late in life. When I was younger, I was possessed with very little self-doubt and was never inclined to look back on events and actions that I took with any kind of critical examination. While that made me very good at my job, it is only now in these waning years of my life that I realize how ill this trait served me in every other aspect of my life. So I suppose I am making up for lost time as

I reflect back on the twists and turns that my life has taken, because of the choices that I have made. At one point in time, like most of my friends and contemporaries, I ascribed all that happened to me as being the will of the gods. Now I, for one, no longer carry that belief; in fact, I think it is an illusion that we use to excuse our actions. But I have not worshiped the gods for some time now nor do I intend to start as I feel my string playing out, as it does for all of us. Consequently, I lie back in my chair, with my feet propped up because they tend to swell now, and stare into the fire. The fireplace itself is an oddity, not so much for its presence but its location, because I had it specially built for my private chambers. I do not boast when I say I am more than wealthy enough to have every convenience in my villa here in Arelate, and I do have the same hypocaust heating that is present in the finest homes in Rome. But I am a soldier who spent more nights than can be easily counted sitting with my friends by a fire, and there is something so comforting about the sight and feel of the dancing flames. I am sure that my face carries the same expression as I gaze into the cleansing flames as it did when I was a young *tirone* on my first campaign in Hispania.

But instead of solid, corporeal forms sitting around me, there are nothing but ghosts, of both friend and foe, especially since I was destined to live during a time when a Legionary of Rome was as likely to look over his shield at another Roman as a Gallaeci, Gaul, or Parthian. And some of those Roman foes, even in the civil wars that threatened to rip our Republic apart, were ostensibly on the same side as I was, and I shared more than one fire with them, yet that did not make them any less deadly an enemy. These are the deaths that trouble me the most, whose faces are the most commonly seen in my dreams, making me wonder if it was all worth it.

What I am about to relate is not as much of a dream as it is, well, I do not know what to call it. I suppose it is possible that I was dozing in my chair next to the fire, but in my recollection, I was wide awake when I became aware of a presence beside me. Thinking it was Diocles, who had the habit of appearing at about this time every night, rousing himself from his own slumber to ensure that I had put myself to bed, I turned away from the fire to assure him that I was about to do that very thing. However, the figure who was somehow seated next to me, despite the fact that under normal circumstances there was no extra chair in that spot, was both familiar and foreign to me. Familiar because it was a face that I had gazed down upon more times than I could easily count, but foreign because this face, and the body along with it, was consumed and cleansed by fire many years ago.

Yet, somehow, I was not surprised; at least, my voice did not sound like it as I said, "*Salve*, Caesar."

"*Salve*, Titus Pullus," Caesar, or his shade, replied in a genial tone, as if we had somehow just bumped into each other on the street.

For his part, he looked essentially unchanged from the last time I laid eyes on him, in his *Praetorium* tent in Hispania, where he, the young Octavian, and I dealt with the allocation of Centurions for the new enlistment of the 10th Legion Equestris, a Legion that no longer exists. Even as my mind struggled to comprehend the portent and meaning of what had to be an apparition, there was a part that registered that of course he would not have aged, because he was dead.

"Are you here to take me with you in Charon's Boat?"

As was and is my habit, I blurted out the first thing that came to my mind, but much to my own surprise I realized even as I asked the question that if he answered in the affirmative, I was not all that upset about it.

But in response, Caesar threw back his head and laughed, saying, "No, Pullus. It's not your time yet. No," he continued once he had regained his breath. "I've just come to visit."

Struck by a sudden impulse, I leaned over out of my chair and reached for Caesar's right arm, the appendage nearest to me. I do not know exactly what I was expecting, although I had told myself that I would not be surprised if my hand went right through him, but it certainly was not the feeling of solid flesh and muscle, even if his skin temperature was a bit cooler than normal, as if he had just come in from the cold. That was not likely; although it was nighttime, this was the height of summer and we had been experiencing a bit of heat for the past several days. Caesar's only reaction to my sudden test of his corporeal form was to look down at my hand with a raised eyebrow, before looking at me with that quirk of the mouth that I knew so well, the sign that he was fighting off the urge to laugh.

"You were expecting . . . what, exactly?" he asked, his tone matching his expression.

I was struck by a sudden irritation that he found this so amusing, but I tried to keep from sounding defensive.

"I'm not sure," I admitted. "I suppose I was hoping that my hand would go right through you. That would mean this is just a dream."

"And now that you've felt my arm and see that I'm as real as you are, what now?"

"Why are you here? What's your purpose?"

[16]

"As I said, I just came to visit." Now he sounded a bit peevish to me, but as surprised as I thought I was, I was even more unprepared for what he said next. "And to answer the questions you've been asking yourself."

I believe it was at this point in our conversation that I slapped myself, with as much violence as I could muster, in the hope that it would awaken me from what I was sure was a dream. Yet, despite the sting bringing tears to my eyes, when my vision cleared, there sat Caesar. And this time there was no mistaking his impatience as he regarded me with folded arms, shaking his head at what he undoubtedly thought were my foolish attempts to send him back to from wherever he had come. Taking a deep breath, I remember thinking to myself, very well. If you are so insistent on me asking you questions, I will make it worth your journey.

"So was it worth it?"

I had hoped to catch Caesar off-balance, but he did not seem the least bit surprised, and in fact, I suppose he was expecting such a question. Even so, he was still Caesar, and what I had learned was that he enjoyed nothing more than rattling the people around him.

"Was what worth it?"

"All the deaths, all the killing, all the turmoil." I am afraid my exasperation got the better of me. "Do you know how much those of us who followed you had to suffer because of your actions? Do you know how much some of us have lost?"

By the time I was finished, I knew that my voice was raised to a level guaranteed to arouse the rest of my household, and in fact, I imagine that was my hope, that Diocles, Agis, and the others would come running and send this version of Caesar back to where he came from. Although it was not my intent to do so,

Caesar appeared completely unruffled by my outburst, as if this was nothing he had not heard before. Unbidden, the thought came to me that perhaps he had appeared to others who had survived this long, as few of us left as there were, and so had heard all of this before. And while I cannot say for sure, I believe that I was at least looking for an apology, but I was to be disappointed.

"Lost?" Caesar made an exaggerated show of looking around at our surroundings. "It seems to me that you've done very well for yourself. Of course, you earned it on your own merit, but I'm hard put to see how you're a loser because of the changes I endeavored to bring to Rome. If it weren't for my actions, you would hardly be a member of the equestrian class."

If Caesar's goal was to anger me, I must say that like everything he did, he was doing a thorough job of it.

"There's more to life than position and advancement," I shot back. "I lost my best friend that day at Pharsalus, all because you were too stubborn to admit that your men had a legitimate grievance, that they were tired and just wanted all that you had promised them."

I saw Caesar's lips thin down and his eyes narrow, which was always a sign that a Caesarian volcano was about to erupt. This time I was not cowed, although I freely admit that a large enough part of my mind was sure that this was a dream or hallucination of some sort. However, he surprised me because when he replied, his tone was still as calm and even as when this conversation started.

"Do you really believe that, Pullus?" he asked quietly. "That I was responsible for the falling out between you and Domitius?" Suddenly he leaned forward, and placed a hand on my arm as he gave me that penetrating gaze that could inspire and terrorize, sometimes at the same time. "Think back to that day, Titus. Search your memory; search your feelings. Did you *really* almost strike Domitius down because of your loyalty to me? Was that *really* the only reason?"

Looking down at his hand on my arm, I was struck by how smooth and white it was, as if Caesar had not been in the sun for some time, which I suppose is accurate. I felt my mouth pulling down into a frown as I stared at Caesar's hand, my mind flying back through the years, and the battles, and the deaths. I do not know exactly how it happened, but it seemed as if I only closed my eyes for an instant longer than a normal eye blink. When I opened my eyes again, Caesar's hand had changed, instantly becoming brown and dirty, the nails caked with grime, the fingers stubbier and wider than Caesar's long, slender ones. It was a hand I still knew very well, even after so many years, because it belonged to Vibius Domitius, my friend and comrade from my childhood and early days in the Legion. We had been as close as brothers were; in fact, Vibius had remarked on many occasions how much closer he and I were than he was with any of his other brothers. We had both held the dream of being in the Legions from the time we were about 11 years old, and had sought out the tutelage of a man known locally as Cyclops, who had served under the standard in Sertorius' army during his rebellion in our home province of Hispania. But a rift had developed that gradually grew wider, the result of Vibius' opposition to almost every action taken by Caesar. Vibius was a strict Catonian in sentiment, and our disagreement grew until that day at Pharsalus, when Vibius, and most of the 10th Legion, it must be said, chose to mutiny rather than continue to follow Caesar in his pursuit of Pompey after the older man's defeat.

Now, in that moment, I somehow found myself back on those dusty plains as I remembered that in our final confrontation, Vibius had done the exact same thing as Caesar, placing his hand on my arm as he pleaded his case with me. And he was very persuasive, because I had not even realized that I bore the same kind of anger towards Caesar that Vibius was expressing at that moment. Truth be known, I was perilously close to agreeing with my friend and joining the mutiny. But then, something inside me stopped me, and over the years I suppose I have convinced myself that my decision was based in the purest of motives; devotion to my general and trust that he was doing what was best for Rome. Yet, every time I thought about, or told this version of my history to others, I was aware of a very tiny, timid voice inside my head that whispered to me that I was speaking a lie. If not a lie, then at the least not the complete truth. What tipped me back from the edge of the precipice that was represented in Vibius' hand on my arm was a simple, but brutal calculation. Who was likely to win in this battle of wills between Caesar and his Legions? I had been marching for Caesar for my entire career to that point, and had seen him snatch a victory when all seemed lost on a number of occasions. Caesar was fond of saying that he never suffered a defeat, only a setback, and I know now that I had taken this philosophy as my own. In short, while I did not believe Caesar would win every battle, I had the utmost faith that he would find a way to win every war in which he was involved, if only because he had always done so before Pharsalus. By siding with Vibius and the rest of the 10th, I would preserve the relationship with my longest and best friend, but it would do harm to my career, which in turn would damage my chances of reaching my ultimate goal of becoming an equestrian.

Granted, it might not have been irreparable; even by this point Caesar had become well known for his clemency. However, I was not blind to the fact that his clemency was almost always reserved for the men of his own class, and I was not willing to count on him extending that to one of his Centurions, even if I was one of his personal choices to be elevated to the Centurionate. That was simply a risk I was unwilling to take with my career.

So in that moment at Pharsalus, as I revisited it sitting here with the shade of Caesar, for the first time I was able to see into my heart clearly and without excuse, and I recognized that it had come down to a simple choice of my career over my friendship with Vibius. In the space of no more than a dozen or more heartbeats, I had made the calculation that my ambition meant more to me than my friendship with a man who had been at my side for more than 20 years at that point. In the end, that was all that Vibius was worth to me: a dozen heartbeats before I threw our friendship onto the flames of my desire for success. I was still staring down at Vibius' hand, but it suddenly began shimmering and after a moment, it was completely obscured as the tears flooded my eyes. Blinking them away, my vision cleared just in time to see one of my tears drop onto the back of the hand, still on my arm. But now it was Caesar's hand again, and I was horrified at this show of emotion and shame in front of him, shade or no. Looking up, it was only through a force of will that I returned his gaze, but his expression was not what I was expecting. He had a smile, but one that was so sad, and so revealing at the same time, and while I could not be sure, it seemed as if his eyes were shining more than they had been a moment before.

"Do you still want to know the answer to that question?" he asked quietly.

I thought for a moment, then shook my head.

"I didn't think so," he said with that same sad smile.

"What would you have done differently, then?" I again blurted out a question before thinking, but this did seem to catch him by surprise.

Regardless, he considered the question a moment before answering.

"Actually, Pullus, I don't think I would have done anything differently," he replied.

Then, he looked me directly in the eye.

"Would you?"

Instead of answering, I turned away to gaze into the fire, hating myself because I not only knew the answer, but understood that he did as well. I became lost in thought as I stared into the flames, thinking all the thoughts that had been lying dormant for so long until this unexpected and uninvited visitor had arrived. I am sure that I was awake for the entire time, but when I felt a tap on my shoulder and turned my head to resume my conversation with Caesar, I was so startled that I jumped from the chair, knocking it over.

"M-m-master?" Diocles' expression was alarmed as he held his hands out, trying to help me avoid tripping over the overturned chair. "I'm sorry to disturb you! Please forgive me, but it's very late. I think you should go to bed."

I did not answer him, mainly because I was trying to allow my heartbeat to slow enough so that I did not sound as if I had just run a furlong. He looked puzzled as I peered over his shoulder, staring at the spot where Caesar had been sitting, but neither he nor the chair were there any longer. I allowed Diocles to take me by the elbow as if I were decrepit and lead me from the room as I tried to comprehend what had just taken place.

"Was I asleep when you came in?" I asked Diocles.

"Well, I didn't think so. Your eyes were open and you were staring into the fire. But judging from your reaction, I guess I was wrong."

I did not reply, and I am somewhat ashamed to say that I allowed Diocles to more or less undress me and help me to the bed, but truthfully, my mind was not up to even that simple task at that moment. Bidding me goodnight, I was quickly left alone with my thoughts, and I knew that sleep was not going to be coming this night as I mulled over what seemed to me to be as real an event as Diocles putting me to bed. However, gentle reader, you may be surprised to know that my thoughts were less consumed with the apparition of Caesar appearing in my study than the revelation that he had forced me finally to face. For the rest of that night, I was absorbed with the question of what it said about me; that I could so quickly and easily destroy a friendship that I had always accepted was the dearest relationship to me in the world? Was this the real cost of my ambition, being forced to recognize this truth about myself, that I was truly no different than Caesar, for whom everyone else was a piece to be used as he saw fit in the game that he was playing to become the First Man in Rome? For most of my life, I had accepted as fact that I was different from Caesar and the men of his class, at least in the ways that mattered, holding my honor, my integrity, my word as something purer than those of the upper classes. Now I was forced to face the fact that this was not the truth, that while the stakes may have been lower, at least when compared to those that Caesar and the others of his class played for, I played the game in the same manner as those men I despised for doing the same thing.

This, I suppose, is the true price that one pays to reach one's goals, that sooner or later you are forced to confront what you really are when stripped of all else. These are the thoughts that disturb my sleep now, and I long for a day when I am no longer troubled by all that I have gained, and lost, because of the choices I made while I was marching with Caesar.

Chapter 1- Prelude

After an exceedingly busy spring and summer, at least as far as events in Rome were concerned, things calmed down for a bit, since there was no longer the steady stream of dispatch riders coming into camp. In retrospect, that could have had more to do with Pollio's absence than anything else, because as we would learn later, the sparring between Antonius and Octavian continued. Sometime in October, Antonius left Rome for Brundisium to meet with the Legions in Macedonia, which Antonius had sent for as part of the force that he was going to lead to expel Decimus Brutus. While Octavian had returned to Rome after his own initial trip down to Brundisium, he had left behind a number of agents to conduct a whispering campaign in favor of Octavian and against Antonius. Therefore, when the Legions from Macedonia arrived, they were subjected to the blandishments of Octavian's men. Octavian himself went back to Campania, to continue his efforts in raising his own army from Caesar's veterans, which he was more successful at than Antonius ever was. There has been much speculation about what was really going on between the two of them, but I believe that Scribonius had the rights of it.

"Antonius doesn't want that army to crush Decimus Brutus; he wants it to cow the Senate and crush Octavian. That's why Octavian went running to Campania as soon as he heard that the Macedonian Legions had landed in Brundisium and Antonius was going to them. He's trying to raise enough of an army that Antonius will think twice about attacking him."

Scribonius, Balbus, and I were sitting in my tent one evening when he made this statement, and it had the ring of truth to it.

"I heard that he's giving the men 2,000 sesterces in cash, and promising them 20,000 more," Balbus remarked.

"Then it shouldn't take him long to raise at least a Legion," I said, thinking how most of my former comrades blew through money and that many of them were probably already broke.

"He already has," Balbus replied flatly, reaching for a chunk of bread.

I raised an eyebrow. "And you know this, how?" I asked.

Balbus grinned, his mouth still full of bread. "I have my sources, just like you, though mine aren't generals like Pollio; they're just lowly born scum like us. But they know what's what."

"I wonder where Octavian is getting the money to throw out more than a million sesterces in cash?" Scribonius mused, and once again, I marveled at his ability to calculate sums so quickly in his head.

"Where do you think?" Balbus put his finger on the side of his nose and winked. "That war chest, no doubt about it."

"You don't know that for sure," I protested, though I admit that it was only half-hearted, for I believed that was where it came from as well. In these early days, something made me cautious about being too critical of Octavian. I cannot help thinking that some instinct in me was triggered during my short exposure to Octavian, though that might be hindsight.

"Where do you think it came from, then?" Balbus retorted. "Antonius has locked up the boy's inheritance tighter than Juno's *cunnus*. He has to be getting it from somewhere, and that's the only place."

"Not really," Scribonius interrupted. I looked at him in some surprise, and then saw his thoughtful frown. "The plutocrats could be lending him the money, if they thought that he was a good bet to come out on top."

Balbus snorted. "Fat chance of that happening. Oh, he's clever; I'll grant you that. But he's still a shade compared to a man like Antonius, who's been around in every way imaginable. There's no way he would come out on top against Antonius."

I shook my head.

"No, Balbus, he's far more than clever. Remember, I met him. There's something about him that makes him seem much older than he is. I think the plutocrats, if they indeed did lend him the money, saw the same thing that I did." I looked over at Scribonius and grinned, finishing. "But I agree with Balbus. I think he stole the money."

I just ducked the cup that Scribonius threw at me.

As successful as Octavian had been, Antonius was as unsuccessful in his attempts to ensure the loyalty of the men in Brundisium. He offered them all of 400 sesterces at the same that Octavian's agents had been offering the 2,000, so men laughed in Antonius' face, which probably cost some of them their lives. Antonius was so infuriated that he ordered some of the men to draw lots. Then, in front of him and his wife, Fulvia, he had them executed, citing his authority as a Consul of Rome in making the sentence stick. It was a classic case of winning a battle but losing a war, for while Antonius was successful in enforcing his will, he lost what little respect he had left among the Legions. They would obey him, but only sullenly, while their attention to their duties would border on unacceptable, doing only the bare minimum. I have no doubt that the

Centurions turned a blind eye to this laxity and in fact encouraged it. Antonius had seriously overestimated his hold on the troops by virtue of his status as Caesar's man and his own personality, so I have to believe that the word of what happened in Brundisium encouraged Octavian to take his next step of marching on Rome with the men he had recruited in Campania. Not only did he have a head start on Antonius, the men marching for the Consul did not exactly move with the same speed that they had under the real Caesar. Meanwhile, Octavian's troops would have done their late general proud with the speed at which they moved. Octavian reached Rome, marching up the Via Latina, entering the Forum before anyone in the Senate, or Antonius for that matter, could do anything to stop him. Octavian was now master of Rome for all intents and purposes, but it would be short-lived.

The courageous men of the Senate did not stick around to see exactly what Octavian's intentions were once he reached Rome, all of them fleeing for their miserable lives. Of course, this actually played into Octavian's hands in one way, because it gave him the opportunity to orate in the Forum to the people, making his case to win their hearts further. He railed at Antonius for being so lenient with The Liberators, then described in detail Antonius' denial of his patrimony. Apparently, he proved to be an effective orator, winning even more of the people for himself while, more importantly, turning them against Antonius. Antonius himself came barreling into Rome, though he was in enough possession of his senses to keep the 5th Alaudae, the one Legion he had brought with him, camped on the Campus Martius. Nevertheless, he insisted on bringing his bodyguard, which was still a violation of the law. Despite Antonius' blunders, things did not go completely Octavian's way, as the men who came with the younger man made it clear that they had no plans of fighting against the duly appointed Consul, whether they hated him or not.

Despite winning over most of the people, Octavian was forced to flee to Arretium to await further developments. Fortunately, for the young Caesar, when Antonius appeared before the Senate, those mice masquerading as men that returned once Octavian left, that is, and the Consul demanded that Octavian be declared *hostis*, they refused him, at least the first time. It is hard to say how long they would have continued to reject his demand, but there was a development that was a serious blow to Antonius when the 4th Legion, who was at Brundisium and ordered to join him at Rome, suddenly veered off the road to Rome and headed for Arretium, declaring instead for Octavian. Antonius was in the middle of his second attempt to declare Octavian *hostis*, this time trying to load the dice in his favor by banning the Tribunes of the Plebs so that they could not exercise their veto, which they had made clear that they would do.

When he was informed of the 4th's change of heart, Antonius flew into a rage, abandoning the Senate floor to lick his wounds and to decide what to do next. By this point, Octavian had gathered enough men to form two Legions, plus the 4th, and three Legions were too formidable a force for Antonius to subdue easily, at least without shedding a lot of blood. It had to be in the back of his mind that there was also a good chance that his men would turn on him if they were forced to fight Octavian. In response to this new reality, Antonius decided to turn back to his original plan of ousting Decimus Brutus from Cisalpine Gaul, who still refused to vacate his post as governor.

Before he left Rome, Antonius intimidated the Senate into reassigning the governorships of the many provinces, not only including the provinces of Crete and Cyrenaica originally assigned to Brutus and Cassius, but their newest choices, Macedonia and Syria respectively. Antonius gave Macedonia to his brother Gaius while confirming Dolabella for Syria, who was already there anyway. There was also a matter that impacted us, when Antonius enacted a decree declaring a public thanksgiving to none other than Marcus Lepidus for convincing Sextus Pompeius to reconcile with Rome. Lepidus had conveniently explained away the fact that Sextus' supporters were still up in the hills as local bandits. Since young Sextus was having all of his father's fortune restored to him, minus his house in Rome that Antonius lived in, of course, he had no reason to dispute Lepidus' version. When the announcement was made at our morning formation, I wondered what Pollio would think of all this as he ate short rations and lived in a tent in the hills.

By this point, it was late in November in the first year after Caesar reformed the calendar, so that the seasons were finally in alignment with the date, meaning there was not much time left to Antonius before winter set in and the campaigning season came to a close. Antonius decided to invest the city of Mutina, the provincial capital of Cisalpine Gaul and, while he did, issued a number of edicts that we Primi Pili were required to read at our morning formation as soon as they arrived. Almost all of them concerned Octavian, starting with his supposedly illegal raising of a private army, which Antonius likened to that of Spartacus, insinuating that the men who chose Octavian were slaves and rabble. This did not sit well with either the Centurions or the veterans in our ranks, since most of us knew or were related to men who were marching for Octavian. Antonius did not stop there, though. As the weeks passed, his edicts became more and more scurrilous and sordid, many of them aimed at Octavian's supposed unnatural love for Marcus Agrippa and Gaius Maecenas, two of Octavian's closest friends and supporters. Even Lepidus began looking distinctly uncomfortable, but nothing could be done because Antonius was still Consul for the rest of the year. This was how the year closed out, with a war of words between Antonius and Octavian, while most of us held out little hope that it would stay bloodless for much longer.

We spent the winter months instructing the men in the art of making a winter camp, building huts in place of tents, which had almost worn out by this point anyway. The tents would have to be replaced before we marched in the spring, yet another headache in the form of a mountain of forms that had to be filled out. The men were about as well trained at this point as we could make them without actually going into combat, and I was cautiously optimistic that they would acquit themselves well when the time came, though it was impossible to know for sure until it happened. We were almost at full strength, having lost a handful of men to injuries and deaths while training, along with a few to illness. However, it seemed as if my practices in terms of sanitation and hygiene were paying off, something that the veterans in the Legion were quick to point out to the new men. Normally, in winter camp there would almost always be an outbreak of some sort of sickness, but the combination of mild winter and the men bathing regularly, at least in my view, meant that we survived the winter virtually unscathed by disease.

It was the year of the consulship of Caesar's old lieutenant Aulus Hirtius and Gaius Vibius Pansa.

Meanwhile in Rome, Octavian somehow managed to turn the tables completely on Antonius, getting himself entered into the rolls of the Senate, despite being many years too young. Antonius was no longer a Consul, but Proconsul, a subtle difference perhaps, but in the political currents of Rome, it is akin to a swimmer suddenly unable to use his legs to help him paddle across a swift river. Much of Proconsular authority is based in tradition, and as we were seeing, while Romans paid lip service to the revered past, if a practice based in antiquity got in the way of an ambitious man's goals, it was either simply ignored or modified in some way. Such was Octavian's selection for the Senate, and such was the basis for his attack on Antonius' status. Traditionally, governorships went to men who had been Consuls, with the new Proconsul having the choice of what province he was to govern, but as with everything in Rome, there is a certain way things had to be done, and Antonius had flouted tradition by having his post confirmed by the Tribune of the Plebs and not by the Senate. I did not pretend to understand the finer points as described to me by Scribonius, whose knowledge of the political ins and outs of Rome was astonishing, but I understood the essence; Antonius was now the odd man out in the power struggle. Octavian did not achieve this result on his own; he had a powerful, if somewhat surprising ally in Marcus Tullius Cicero.

Despite being an avowed enemy of Caesar, Cicero had, for whatever reason, decided that his former enemy's namesake and heir was the horse to back in this race that was rapidly dwindling down to a field of two serious contenders. The famed lawyer and orator commenced a series of attacks, using a pen and his words on Antonius, which did incredible damage to the former Consul's prestige and status. As Scribonius explained to me, Cicero was as much a master of the Senate floor as Caesar had been on the battlefield. Therefore, it was a matter of just a few meetings of the Senate that saw Antonius vilified by Cicero in a series of speeches that have already been copied into books that are quite popular, especially given the outcome.

Cicero was pushing at every meeting to get the Senate to declare Antonius *hostis*, which they refused to do, as there were enough of Antonius' creatures on the benches to keep the motion from carrying. Instead, an embassy was proposed to approach Antonius to call off his siege of Mutina, confirm Decimus Brutus as governor, and to submit to the authority of the Senate and People of Rome. Of course, there was no way that Antonius could simply acquiesce; it just was not in his nature to do so, as the harm to his already-battered prestige would have been too much for him to take. He supposedly made a counter-proposal where he would allow Decimus Brutus to retain Cisalpine Gaul, while he would take Transalpine Gaul instead, and hold that post for four years. He in fact had precedent for asking for such an extended period of time; our old general had done much the same in his command of Gaul and Illyricum. However, Antonius was no Caesar, and the Senate refused him. The Senate then declared a state of *tumultus*, meaning that a civil war now existed, while declaring Antonius *inimicus*, which is not as serious as being declared *hostis*, so that it was not a complete and total victory by Cicero, but it was close. A decree of *Senatus Consultus Ultimum*, or the Ultimate Decree, was issued, naming Octavian and Hirtius as co-commanders of the Senatorial army that was ordered to march to Mutina to engage Antonius and defeat him in the name of the Senate and People of Rome. Since it was early in the year and the passes were still snow-bound, the confrontation between Antonius and Octavian and Hirtius was not to be for a few weeks. It was about this time that the 10th was called on to enter the latest act in the drama unfolding about us.

"We're marching to Narbo," I announced to the Centurions, coming straight from the meeting with Lepidus, who had informed me himself.

He had also ordered that we would be marching the next morning, a pronouncement so absurd that I almost burst out laughing in his face. I pointed out that it was as close to impossible to order a Legion that had been in garrison for almost a year to be ready to march on such short notice as one could get.

"Your primary job is to keep this Legion ready to march, Primus Pilus," Lepidus sniffed. "It would seem that you have failed yet again in your duty."

"Governor, if you think that you can find someone to do a better job, by all means please relieve me." I made sure that my tone was as formal and polite as circumstances allowed.

I had learned by this time that Lepidus was an empty uniform, his threats having no teeth because he was acutely aware of the precarious hold he had on the Legion. If a man like Antonius could be turned upon by his troops, Lepidus was smart enough to know that he was even more vulnerable, so we had gotten to a point where we tolerated each other. I was willing to let him bluster and strut about while making the kind of sneering comments he had just made, while he did not attempt to do anything silly like actually discipline the men. I also found that I had an unexpected ally, the

Tribune who I had bribed those months before, who stepped in now.

"Excuse me, Governor, but the Primus Pilus is correct, whether or not it's due to any negligence on his part is for you to determine, of course," he said smoothly, giving me an almost imperceptible wink. "But as he pointed out, we have been in garrison for many months, and the type of preparations that must be made for a march of many days or weeks is different from what we've been doing in training."

Lepidus was not happy about this, but as I had learned from observing him, he was not a particularly smart man, though he was intelligent enough to know that he was lacking in most areas.

Waving a hand in exasperation, he said, "Fine! Then tell me how long it will take to get underway."

"A week, at the minimum," I responded instantly.

The truth was that it would not take that long, but I had long since learned the value of under promising and over delivering, especially to empty uniforms like Lepidus.

"Very well, but it better not be a day over a week, or I will not be happy." He glowered at me, showing me his teeth like he was a wolf.

I saluted, then went to tell the Centurions. Now I was standing in front of them as they gathered in the forum, waiting for the buzzing of talk to die down as the men talked excitedly about the prospect of Narbo. Because almost all of these men were Caesar's veterans, having marched with the 10th since our *dilectus* now 18 years before, they had fond memories of time spent in Narbo. I knew that it was best to let them chatter like a bunch of women about the whores and wineshops that lined the city streets for a few moments. Finally, I told them to shut up before proceeding to give them the details that they needed to know to make their men ready to move. As soon as I dismissed them, I was gratified to see the blur of movement accompanied by the sudden outburst of noise as each Centurion hurried to their respective area to start kicking in hut doors, bellowing at the men to get moving. I turned to head to my own Century to begin the process, smiling at the inventive cursing and yelps of surprise that I heard up and down the streets. The next few days would appear to the outside observer to be pure chaos, with no discernible pattern that made any kind of sense. In reality, it was a carefully rehearsed dance that would find at the end a fully loaded and prepared Legion, ready to step out of the gates of the camp at exactly the moment that I decided that we would. It was moments like this that I loved being a Primus Pilus more than any other, I decided, stopping at the door to the first section of my Century. I took a breath, then reared back with my foot to kick the door open with a huge crash.

"All right, ladies," I roared. "Your days of lying about and sucking up Rome's money are over! You're about to earn your pay."

"Governor, the 10th Legion will be ready to march in the morning," I announced to Lepidus, enjoying the look of surprise and a little panic on his face.

It was the third morning since I had been given the order to march.

"Tomorrow?" he spluttered, almost dropping the cup of wine he had been sipping from, shooting a look at the Tribune, whose face remained carefully blank. "Why wasn't I informed that you'd be ready earlier?" he demanded of both of us.

The Tribune raised an eyebrow in my direction, a silent signal that I should provide the answer that we had already rehearsed.

"Why, Governor," I said with as much surprise in my voice as I felt I could get away with and still be believable, "I was just acting on your orders to make the men ready as quickly as possible."

"I didn't say that," he protested, then his brow furrowed as he remembered our conversation. "Well, er, not exactly that," he amended.

"Sir, you made it clear that when I told you that it would take more than a day to be ready to march that this was not acceptable. The men have been working through every watch to make themselves ready to meet your expectations." This came from the Tribune, again as part of what we had discussed before approaching Lepidus.

As it turned out, the Tribune loathed Lepidus as much as the rest of us, and was more than happy to do whatever he could to make Lepidus look like the fool that he was.

"Well, I don't know that I'll be ready to march in the morning." Lepidus actually had the grace to look embarrassed. "I was expecting that we wouldn't be marching out for another few days, so my household hasn't been broken down yet. I'm hosting a dinner party tonight with some of the prominent citizens of the area as my guest, and we won't be through until dawn at the earliest."

The Tribune and I looked at each other in mock dismay.

I cleared my throat, asking Lepidus, "Governor, might I ask when you would be ready to march?"

"Not until the day after tomorrow, at the earliest," he finally said, refusing to meet my gaze.

"Then may I ask the Governor if he'd agree to give the men the day off tomorrow, seeing as they're ready to march now?" I asked, for this was the real purpose behind the whole act between the Tribune and me.

My hope was that Lepidus would feel guilty enough about making the men wait that he would relent and give the men the day off. If he did not, then the Tribune and I had another pair of dice to throw that the Tribune was sure would come up Venus, but it was not needed.

"I suppose that they've earned it," he said grudgingly. "Very well, but I expect them to behave themselves in a manner worthy of Legionaries of Rome," he said severely.

I saluted him, assuring him that I would personally guarantee that they would, then exited his office. What I did not say was what our respective opinions about how a Legionary on liberty should act were, and how they probably differed dramatically, but I reasoned there was no need for him to know that.

As at least I expected, the men debauched themselves in a manner completely fitting for a Legionary of Rome, so that when we were set to march out two days after our meeting with Lepidus, the groans of the men could be heard a mile away. As heartily as I had been toasted by the men for securing the day off for them, now I was as roundly cursed for my inhuman cruelty in making them march, and that was just from the Centurions. For my part, I was all smiles and good cheer, slapping wincing men on the back while making much of the fine morning for a march, for this was part of my plan as well. I knew that the men would love me for getting them the day off, though I also knew that they would curse me for what I was about to put them through, but there is nothing quite as instructional or bonds men together more than shared misery and a hatred for someone. I was about to make them miserable, because I was going to set a blistering pace worthy of a Legion raised by Caesar, and most of the veterans and all of the Centurions knew it. We stepped off, and it did not take long for the cursing to stop, replaced by ragged breathing, and punctuated by sounds of retching by a Legion full of men suffering from hangovers. Lepidus, of course, rode, not realizing, or caring I suppose, that Caesar had always walked with us. That first day was one of torture and misery for the men, but they grimly marched on, some of them stopping to vomit before running back to take their places in the formation. As was my habit, I had not partaken of much wine the night before, so I presented exactly the image I wanted as I strode up and down the column, seemingly impervious to the pace I was setting, which even Lepidus and his party were having a hard time matching on horseback.

"Doesn't that bastard ever get tired?" I heard someone mutter as I trotted down the column to smack a man, who looked as if he were about to fall out, with my *vitus*, to encourage him to try a little harder.

"No," someone replied. "To get tired means you have to be human, and he's some sort of beast sent from Hades."

I did not let them see me smile as I ran by, just snapping at them to shut their mouths instead.

As expected, the first three or four days on the march were the most difficult, and we had stragglers staggering into camp until well after dark. I believe that if Lepidus had not been so tired himself he would have tried to have the stragglers flogged, which for once I might have agreed with, though I still would not have done it because I did not want men riding in the wagons. It was somewhere along the way when a dispatch rider came galloping in carrying the latest news from Rome, and this was news indeed. The

Tribune found me during a break, squatting down by me as I sat sucking down the contents of my canteen.

"Trebonius was murdered by Dolabella," he said quietly.

I looked at him in shock; Trebonius had been a governor of Asia. While Dolabella was Proconsular like Antonius, it was still a huge risk for him to kill a governor, even if he was one of The Liberators, particularly since Cicero wielded so much influence and was an avid supporter of Brutus, Cassius and the rest of The Liberators.

"How? When?" I asked.

The Tribune shrugged. "I don't have many details, but apparently Dolabella was convinced that Trebonius had a lot of money locked in the vaults of his residence in Asia, and Dolabella came looking for it on his way to Syria. He took Trebonius prisoner and tortured him to find out where the money was, because it wasn't in the vaults."

"I doubt that worked," I commented, because as much as I loathed Trebonius for his role in Caesar's murder, he was a tough man.

The Tribune nodded in agreement. "You're right; it didn't work. So Dolabella got angry and sawed off Trebonius' head, supposedly very slowly. Then he nailed his head to a post in the forum of the town."

I sat, digesting this news. This was the first of the assassins to die, out of the 23 who either had stepped forward to claim responsibility or had been named by others, and I took some satisfaction in that knowledge.

"That's not all," the Tribune continued. I looked at him, waiting for more. "Brutus took Gaius Antonius prisoner as soon as he arrived in Macedonia, and he's staying put, saying that Antonius had no right to strip him of the governorship appointed to him by Caesar."

I could only shake my head, it no longer being possible to surprise me at the duplicity of the upper class in their fight for power. Here was Brutus, claiming legitimacy to his governorship because the man he helped to murder, indeed Brutus was the one who delivered the killing blow if some people were to be believed, had appointed him. It was this kind of thinking that I found positively baffling, because it seemed that only the upper classes were capable of the kind of mental gymnastics that such thinking required.

We made it to Narbo, where we marched to the permanent camp there, which by this time had grown into a place with stone walls and sturdy wooden huts, a far cry from our first winter there, when Narbo was still a frontier town where everything was raw wood and rawer people. There were still the operators and tricksters, the whores, the wineshops selling stuff so raw that you were hoarse if you drank it, all of them cheering the sight of a bunch of youngsters marching through the gates of the camp, excited at the prospect of plumping up their purses. The night we arrived, I called a meeting of the Centurions and Optios, reminding them of what it was like when we were youngsters, much like the men now. Although we had been blooded by the time we came to Narbo, we were still all raw country boys, and many of us, including me, had been taken in one sham or another.

"Watch the men for the first couple of weeks until they learn what it's like to be in a big military town," I reminded the Centurions, and there were a few chuckles at the memories. "We're going to be busy keeping the boys out of trouble," I continued. "And I don't have to remind you that Lepidus will look for any excuse he can find to flay a man. So be alert, and don't let the men get too far out of hand."

With that admonition, I waited to see what kind of mayhem and havoc the men would wreak, but fortunately, Narbo was by then an old military town. Its inhabitants were accustomed to dealing with Legionaries of all stripes. They had to contend with us after a few years in Gaul, so the raw youngsters that composed the 10th at this point did not pose them any problems. There were the usual transgressions, and we had a few men flogged, but fortunately there were no incidents like what happened with Atilius those years ago, for which I was thankful, even if none of the rankers were close friends except for Vellusius and a couple of others. It was certainly not anything that required me to make trips into town with a full purse as in years past, and I was happy about that as well, though it was not destined to last.

In the larger world, the junior Consul Pansa raised another three Legions then marched to join Octavian and Hirtius who were slowly but methodically working their way north to confront Antonius, who still besieged Mutina and Decimus Brutus. While we had marched with Lepidus, he had also sent for the other Legions in Hispania, and they were arriving in Narbo, ending the interlude of relative peace for the Centurions. Over the next two or three weeks, Narbo saw another six Legions arrive, which is when trouble really began for us, since it is inevitable when Legions get together and there is no enemy directly in front of them that they will turn on each other. The status of the 10th as a new Legion guaranteed that the men of the other Legions would mark our men as fresh meat for any variety of mischief, from games of "chance" to wineshop brawls, whereupon the Centurions would find themselves fully occupied trying to keep the men separated and not killing each other.

It was at the end of April when a dispatch rider came pounding into camp on a lathered horse, heading straight for the headquarters building. Within moments, the *bucina* call for all Primi Pili to assemble sounded, and I hurried over to the *Praetorium*. Lepidus was waiting, holding a scroll in his hand, and as soon as we were all there, he gave us the news he had received. It was a sign of his agitation and excitement that he did not start with his usual barbed comments about tardiness on the part of Centurions.

"There's been a battle at Mutina," he announced, "and Antony has been soundly defeated and forced to retreat. He's heading for Transalpine Gaul now with what's left of his Legions. According to this," he waved the scroll, "he lost half of his force. Since he's heading in this general direction, I've been ordered by the Senate to head him off if possible."

There was a complete silence as we digested this then waited for actual orders. He looked back down at the scroll again, frowning as he seemed to remember something.

"Oh yes. There's more. While the forces of the Senate and People were victorious, it was not without cost. Both of the Consuls Hirtius and Pansa died in the battle, so Octavian is in command."

As he spoke Octavian's name, his lip curled up, his distaste for the young Caesar plain for all of us to see.

"Be prepared to march in the morning," he said, but he was stopped short by the protests of the Primi Pili, with my voice among them.

Will he never learn? I wondered. Now that we were marching into probable battle, we would need even more time to prepare, and this time when he was told that it would take a week, it was going to take that long to get everything ready. He relented with his usual snarling bluster, then turned and stalked off, leaving us to our business.

The week flew by as we prepared to march to what we thought would be some sort of fighting. There did not seem to be enough watches in the day to get everything done. Rations had to be drawn, and things like the torsion ropes of the artillery had to be examined, while the artillery itself had to be checked to make sure that the wood had not cracked. Gear had to be mended and strengthened for the march, all the myriad tasks that men like Lepidus seem to think just magically take care of themselves but are actually only seen to by hard work and attention to detail. However, as promised, the army was ready to march at the exact moment we had told Lepidus it would be. We stepped out of the gates of Narbo heading east, in the general direction of where Antonius was last sighted. It was on the march that the talking began around the fires about what would happen when we finally came face to face with Antonius. It was quiet, at least in the beginning confined to the lower ranks, but it did not take long for what they were saying to reach my ears, and it was disturbing to say the least.

"I don't want to fight Antonius or his men," they were saying. "And I hate that bastard Lepidus. I'd rather fight for anyone else but him."

As unsettling as that kind of talk was, the worst part was that I agreed with them. I was not any more willing to risk the lives of my men for Lepidus against Antonius than they were to do it, so for the first time in my career, I was not sure what I was going to do if the moment came. It soon became clear that the other Centurions felt the same. Further complicating matters was the news that Antonius was being reinforced by a man named Bassus Ventidius, who had served Caesar as quartermaster, master of the livestock and rolling stock of the army. He was a tough old bird, coming to a military career relatively late in life yet nonetheless excelling. Ventidius was the kind of man that a Lepidus would have no use for, but Caesar saw the potential in, and now he was joining forces with Antonius.

"Do you think we're on the wrong side in this?" Balbus asked me one night, finally saying what I had been thinking for some time.

Still, I had a duty to perform, so I looked at him for a moment before I said sharply, "We're on the side that the Senate has deemed to be the right side, Balbus."

Balbus was not cowed, and he knew me too well.

"Don't give me that, Titus. I asked you a question."

I sighed. "Well, the men certainly think so, and I for one think they might be right. It wouldn't be as much of a question if it weren't for Lepidus."

"So what are we going to do?"

All I could do at that moment was shake my head and say I did not know, that we would have to ford that river when we got to it.

Ironically, it was at a river that we could no longer put off a decision. We came to the river that serves as the border between Transalpine and Cisalpine Gaul, with us on one side and Antonius' army on the other. By the time we arrived at the spot we were currently occupying, I had learned through contacts of Scribonius that Lepidus had not been ordered by the Senate after all, that he had taken it upon himself to move closer to the action. As a result, he was made *inimicus* like Antonius, which took away the last little hold he had over all of us because he carried the same status as the former Consul. Since it seemed that we would not win either way we went, it became a much easier decision to choose Antonius. Now the question was how we did it. Fortunately, the river was more a stream so it did not take much to send men across who were known to Antonius and make overtures to him, to which he was extremely receptive. I had sent Diocles to the other Primi Pili of Lepidus' army, and I was not surprised to learn that they were doing much the same thing, albeit each in a slightly different way.

By the time the sun rose on our second day next to the river, the transfer was complete. Antonius sent a messenger telling Lepidus that he no longer had an army who would fight for him, so he might as well join Antonius, which of course Lepidus did, though he was none too happy about it. Lepidus avoided the Centurions of his former army as if we had the plague, absenting himself from every meeting held with the command group. I do not believe that it ever occurred to him that it was his actions and attitude towards the men that led him to be in the predicament in which he found himself, but given how things turned out, he deserved everything he got.

One happy event, at least as far as I was concerned, was the appearance of Pollio, with the two Legions he had been dragging through the hills of Hispania. Now that Sextus Pompey was forgiven, Sextus was given command of the Roman fleet in Our Sea, all while keeping his partisans on the payroll in the event that things turned sour in his relationship with the Senate. Now, with hostilities ceased, Pollio was getting bored sitting in Hispania, so one day he and his Legions showed up in our camp. I for one was happy to see a friendly face. While the men, both rankers and Centurions preferred Antonius, I had never warmed to him the way they had, viewing Pollio as more of an ally and a man worth following than Antonius, who I thought to be fickle and too changeable from one day to the next. Oh, he was brave enough, yet both his generosity and his cruelty did not seem to have any reason behind it. Instead, he seemed subject to some whim that I could not see any sense to, and for that reason, I did not care for it. Do not mistake me; as many misgivings as I may have had about Antonius, I had no regrets about choosing him over Lepidus, but in my mind neither was a great choice; it was just that Antonius was the best bad choice facing us. The final blow to Decimus Brutus, and by extension to the Senate, who was backing him, was the defection of Munatius Plancus. He had been marching to join Brutus when he received a letter from Pollio inviting him to join Antonius' forces. Plancus immediately accepted, changing his course, joining us at the river, now giving Antonius a huge army of 23 Legions. With all these developments, Decimus Brutus threw up his hands. Leaving his bewildered Legions with no commander, he decided to leave and join up with Marcus Brutus in Macedonia. However, he did not make it, being captured by Camillus, the chief of the Brenni, who sent to Antonius asking for instructions as to the disposition of his prisoner. Not surprisingly, Antonius sent a fat purse of gold coin along with the instruction to execute Decimus Brutus, which Camillus was more than happy to do. It was in this way that the second of Caesar's assassins died. The third to perish was Lucius Minucius Basilus, a minor player in the assassination. However, he died at the hands of his own slaves, who finally had enough of his habit of torturing them for his own pleasure, tearing him to pieces in his own home.

For the time being, Antonius was content for us to sit in place as he waited to see what would happen next, and it was early in the month now named for Octavian, or Augustus as he is better known now, that word came that the young Caesar had marched on Rome again. This time, there was nobody to oppose him. Actually, he had been preceded by a large number of his Centurions and Optios, who surrounded the Senate building while the senior Centurion, a man named Barbatus entered the Senate to inform them of Caesar's demands. When he told them what Octavian wanted, a Consulship for himself along with the money for the bonuses he had promised his troops, the Senate told Barbatus a flat, unequivocal no, asking Barbatus by what right Octavian made demands of the Senate of Rome?

Supposedly, Barbatus tapped the hilt of his sword, replying, "This is what gives him the right, and it's this that will give him what he asks, one way or the other."

I do not know that this actually happened, but it made a good story to tell around the fire at night. However, the Senate still refused, until Octavian called their bluff, actually marching on Rome, arriving at the gates of the city on the 17th of August, whereupon the Senate panicked, immediately giving in, promising Octavian that he would be Consul, and the troops paid their bonuses. Two days later, the young Caesar was made the senior Consul, with his cousin Quintus Pedius the junior.

Once Octavian was in power, it did not take him long to move against the two men he perceived to be the principals among The Liberators: Brutus and Cassius. It would not be accurate to say that Octavian was without a blemish, however. After the battle at Mutina, where Antonius had been soundly defeated, word began to circulate through all of the Legions, on both sides. The talk was that it was Hirtius and Pansa, both now dead, who were the true architects of the victory, and that Octavian had been too frightened to participate, choosing instead to hide in his camp. I do not know how much truth there is in this tale. The time we talked, Octavian had been forthright in his lack of martial ardor, at least compared to his adoptive father, but I never got the sense that he was a coward. Whatever really happened, that tale would dog him for years, with Antonius the prime mover behind the tale, making sure that his own agents kept it alive for all the years that they were contending with each other. Once Octavian was in power, the *lex curiata* confirming his adoption by Caesar was quickly ratified, removing the last obstacle for taking his inheritance. His next step was just as predictable; through his confederates, trials were held, where Brutus, Cassius, and the rest of the conspirators in Caesar's assassination were found guilty of murder in absentia, with sentences of death confirmed for all of them, and all their property confiscated. Also, the fortunes of Sextus Pompey took yet another reversal, as Octavian made it clear that he was to be considered *nefas*, an outlaw. The problem was that it was one thing to declare him an outlaw, quite another to actually capture him, since he had a firm control of the fleets in Our Sea, and of Sicily. Finally, Octavian made sure that the men in his army were paid a part of their bonuses, which ordinarily would have not made the men happy, since they were expecting to be paid every sesterce that they had coming to them, but it was here that Octavian demonstrated his true genius. By promising that the remainder of their bonus would be paid, with 10 percent interest, Octavian guaranteed the men a future income. Given most men's propensity to blow through their money on gambling, whores, and wine, the lure of that guarantee was too much for them to resist, so they sang Octavian's praises to the skies. The news of this development caused Antonius untold problems, as the men were already unhappy at the parsimony of Antonius when compared to Octavian. It was a sign of his arrogance that he refused to match Octavian's generosity, either with the amount or the conditions of what he was paying. Once Octavian disposed of the most pressing matters in Rome, he gathered his army, now 11 Legions strong, then headed in our direction.

"Are we really going to be fighting the young Caesar?" Vellusius' voice was filled with anxiety as he stood next to me, watching the dust cloud that signaled the approach of Octavian's army just a few miles away.

While the rest of the youngsters of the Legion were naturally apprehensive at the idea of facing battle for the first time, their focus was not on the prospect of facing the adopted son of the father of the Legion, just on fighting for its own sake.

Despite understanding why Vellusius was asking me this question, I could not allow my personal feelings to prevent me, or any of the Centurions for that matter, to do our jobs, so my tone was sharp as I replied, "We'll be fighting whoever we're told to fight Vellusius, whether it's young Caesar, or Mars himself."

"Yes, Primus Pilus, I know that," Vellusius protested defensively. "But it's just that . . . he's Caesar, isn't he?"

The look he gave me softened my heart because his anguish was very real, causing me to give him an awkward pat on the shoulder as I said softly, "Well, let's hope it doesn't come to that."

The fact was that I was almost positive that it was not going to come to battle, because I had been using

Diocles and his network of slaves to keep me informed of what was going on in Antonius' headquarters tent, as he, Lepidus and Plancus were huddled together for watches at a time. It was through Diocles that I learned that the emissary from Octavian that rode into the camp had not been there to deliver an ultimatum or some sort of challenge, but an offer of a parley to discuss a possible alliance. However, I was not about to tell Vellusius, or anyone else other than Scribonius, Balbus and a couple other men about this development, in the event that talks fell through. We had been marching back in the general direction of Mutina, heading towards Octavian as he was heading for us. When our scouts spotted his army, we had stopped on the west side of the river Lavinius (Lavino), waiting for the situation to develop. Over the next few days, riders came galloping into camp, then went galloping out, carrying dispatches between Antonius and Octavian, before the two of them finally agreed to a meeting. For appearance's sake, Lepidus was included in the meeting, which took place on an island in the middle of the river. Both armies stood on their respective sides of the river in formation, so naturally I had a front row seat at the head of the 10th. We could only hear snatches of conversation, when one of the three of them raised his voice, and it did not take long to see that invariably, Antonius did the yelling. Octavian's body language was the model of restraint, as he struck a perfect orator's pose, gesturing first to his army then to ours. Of course, it did not take long for the wits in the army to start providing their own dialogue, reminding me of that day in Hispania when Caesar met with Afranius in front of the armies when the Pompeian general surrendered.

"I'm Caesar's heir and you're not," a voice that sounded startlingly like Octavian said somewhere in the ranks behind me.

"That may be, but I have a bigger cock than you'll ever have," a deeper voice growled, again sounding much like Antonius.

"Ooooohhhh, can I see it?" the Octavian voice asked, followed by a wave of muted snickering rippling through the ranks.

"No, you can't see it. Not unless you pay me 10,000 denarii," the mock Antonius said.

"I don't want to see it that much. Now bow down before me, for I'm Caesar!"

"I'll bend you over and ram my…"

"Enough," I snapped, turning my head to glare at the men, wondering why every time we were in this situation things always degenerated into jokes about buggery.

Sighing, I turned back to see Antonius pounding a fist into his other hand, then point back at us, obviously making the point that he thought he could crush Octavian and his army. As for me, I was not so sure. Octavian was certainly not in the same league as Antonius, yet his army was more veteran than ours was, since Octavian was much more successful in luring Caesar's veterans to his banner than Antonius was. I think it was at this moment that the first seed of doubt that I had picked the wrong side was planted in my mind as I watched the two of them bicker back and forth. To my eye, Antonius was full of bluster, while Octavian was calm and in total control of himself, reminding me of the short amount of time I had spent with him. At the time of this parley, the gamblers in the army were still betting that Antonius was the sure wager, that Octavian was too raw a youth. Nonetheless, what had always stuck in my mind was the fact that Caesar himself had chosen Octavian over Antonius, and having had more contact with Caesar than the rankers, I had to believe that he knew what he was doing.

The meeting took all day, but with nothing more concrete accomplished than the agreement to meet the next day. The camp was abuzz with speculation of how things would turn out, as very few men got any sleep that night, all the various possibilities being discussed around each and every fire.

"I think there's going to be an accommodation," Scribonius said as we sat in my tent. Balbus had the duty that night, so Servius Metellus, the Tertius Pilus Prior and Glaxus, my old Pilus Posterior, were there instead.

Metellus looked surprised, exclaiming, "After the way those two carried on today? I doubt it. Did you see the way Antonius was jumping all about and roaring like a gored bull?" He shook his head. "Sorry, Scribonius, I don't see it."

"Theatrics," Scribonius replied. "For our benefit. He can't be seen to just fold up his tent, but the reality is that he's in the weaker position."

Now it was my turn to look at him in surprise, though not in disbelief. I knew that Scribonius had a good reason to say this, so I wanted to hear it. The other two were having none of it, forcing me to wave them to silence before I asked Scribonius to continue.

"Octavian is young, that's true. But he also has Caesar's name, his money, and more importantly than anything, the bulk of his veterans," Scribonius explained, and I saw the glimmering of doubt show in the faces of the other two. I understood how they felt; every successful soldier has a great deal of pride, meaning that it did not sit well to think they were on the weaker side, but when Scribonius explained things, it suddenly seemed to be more feasible that this was the case.

"Antonius, on the other hand, is more experienced, that also is true. But he's made many more enemies, at all levels of society," Scribonius continued. "In fact, you could say that Octavian's youth is actually working in his favor because he hasn't been around long enough to make the kind of enemies that Antonius has. Given time, he may, although I have to say that so far he hasn't made any huge mistakes. Maybe his first march on Rome was a little premature, but he recovered nicely."

"So what are you saying?" Glaxus asked, clearly confused, for deep thinking had never been Glaxus' strong suit.

"I'm saying that all the jumping about on Antonius' part is theatrics, that he's in a corner and that there will be some sort of accommodation made, where the two of them share power equally."

This made sense, at least to me, but then he threw out something that caught me completely by surprise.

"Of course, they'll probably have to include Lepidus in some way," he sighed.

I sat up in my chair, shocked to my core.

"Lepidus? That...that worm?" I gasped. "How could that be? He's about as useless as any man I've ever met. Surely they see that," I protested.

Scribonius gave me a smile that I had seen him give before which I found infuriating, a smug little smile that seemed to say, "Poor Pullus, you just don't understand these things."

Which I suppose I did not, at least not to the level that Scribonius did, as he went on to explain. "I have no doubt that both of them know exactly how useless Lepidus is," Scribonius agreed. "But unfortunately, because of Lepidus' birth, he's important to the both of them, because he's nobler born than either of them. And that's still important in Rome. So," he finished, "don't be surprised if things work out with Lepidus being named as one of the big bosses, although I think it'll be more in name than deed."

With that pleasant prospect, we all sat gloomily, waiting for what the next day would bring.

The next day, at least starting out, seemed destined to be a repeat of the first day, with much gesturing and pulling of hair by Antonius, placating gestures and soothing tones by Octavian, while Lepidus slumped in a chair seemingly oblivious to the histrionics going on around him. Just as the day before, both armies stood in formation, the sun beating down as we watched our future being decided. By midday, when the three were rowed to their respective sides to take a break, things seemed to have calmed down, so I sent Diocles to find out what he could from his network.

When he came back, he whispered to me, "I think they're close to making a deal."

Diocles was right; shortly before the end of the day, the three of them suddenly stood, then walked to the center of the island, where both sides could clearly see what was about to take place, whereupon the three men clasped hands in a three-way handshake. Immediately both sides erupted in cheers, the knowledge that we would not have to fight each other hitting all of us.

Of course, it was not that simple; the details still had to be worked out, so we spent another couple of tense days as Antonius and Octavian hammered out how this new Triumvirate was going to work. Finally, it was announced that Antonius would govern Transalpine and Cisalpine Gaul, while Lepidus governed Narbonese Gaul and both Hispanias. Octavian would govern Italia, Sicily, Corsica, Sardinia, and Africa. On the face of it, it sounded like Octavian got the better of the deal, but the reality was far from it. The governors of the African provinces were waging a private war with each other, while Sextus Pompey was in actual control of Sicily. Both of those provinces provided, or were supposed to provide the bulk of the grain to feed Rome. In short, Octavian had inherited most of the headaches of the three of them, but he was now a major player in the game, so I suppose that he thought that it was worth the ordeal. The final argument came over who would enter Rome first, a battle Octavian won, mainly because he had the law on his side. Because both Antonius and Lepidus were declared *hostis*, they could not legally enter Rome before their status was changed and only Octavian could do that, being the senior Consul. Once he made the change, he would lay down his Consulship and the Triumvirate would then begin.

There was one more component to this thing that was officially named the Committee of Three for the Ordering of the State, but was more commonly known as the Second Triumvirate, after the original of Caesar, Pompey, and Crassus. The state was bankrupt, for a variety of reasons, from the civil war to the bonuses that had to be paid to the men who re-enlisted, meaning that money had to be raised in some way, so the method chosen by the Triumvirate were the proscriptions of wealthy citizens. The idea of proscriptions started with the dictatorship of Lucius Cornelius Sulla, who had initiated a reign of terror and bloodletting that people still talked about in hushed tones. Those proscriptions paled in the scope and depth of those ordered by the new Triumvirs, and they began almost immediately. It was also a way to eliminate political enemies, so it should be no surprise to know that Cicero's name was at the top of the list, after his series of speeches against Antonius in the Senate and the Forum. Cicero's demise was particularly brutal, with his head chopped off, his hands nailed to the Senate door at the order of Antonius, and a stylus run through his tongue. By this point in time, we had marched from Narbo, and were living on the Campus Martius, and while the rankers were strictly prohibited from entering the city, word of what was happening was quick to reach our ears. The streets were almost deserted, at least of the upper classes, who, as they had in the time of Sulla, lived in fear that their name would suddenly appear on a list nailed to the Rostra. Men were turned in by their slaves, or in some cases by other family members, while the roads were filled with men fleeing for their lives in the night. A growth industry sprang up again as men made tidy sums of money hunting down those who had not been turned in, bringing their heads back to claim their reward. Unlike during the time of Sulla, few of the heads were displayed publicly, Cicero being a special case, along with a few others who for one reason or another had earned the enmity of the Triumvirs. However, each of the Triumvirs was forced by their counterparts to give up someone close to them. In the case of Octavian and Antonius, it was their mutual kinsman Lucius Caesar, one of the great man's most steadfast allies. Lepidus gave up his brother, although neither man lost his life, just his fortune. All in all, it was a bad business. The only people with a lot of money that were not touched were either closely allied with one of the Triumvirs and considered indispensable, or that class of men called plutocrats, who were in effect the bankers of the Republic. I did not understand why such an obvious source of wealth would escape with their fortunes, if not their lives intact, but as usual, I looked to Scribonius for an explanation.

"If that happened," he explained, "all the hard cash would dry up."

I looked at him helplessly, still not understanding. If I was trying his patience, Scribonius was graceful and smart enough to hide it from me. I was, and still am, particularly sensitive about my lack of education, and the perception that stupidity goes hand in hand with that lack.

"Every one of the plutocrats was in one camp or the other of one of the Triumvirs," he went on. "And let's say that Antonius demanded that Atticus, who was one of Caesar's men and has transferred his loyalty to the young Caesar, be one of the men proscribed."

He gave me a questioning look, and I nodded that I was following him.

"If that happened, then Octavian would be both honor-bound and politically required to demand that one of Antonius' men go, like Oppius."

I again nodded, this time thoughtfully as I was beginning to see where he was going.

"Now, Lepidus being Lepidus, would probably want to get in on the game, and suddenly none of the plutocrats are safe. So what do they do?"

"They take their money and run for their lives," I answered, now seeing the wisdom of leaving these men alone, as Scribonius finished.

"And in hard times, the one thing that's needed is hard cash, to pay greedy bastards like us."

He grinned, and I grinned back.

Aside from watching the game that was politics in Rome, a particularly bloody one in those days, there was not a lot for us to do. The Campus Martius is a huge area, yet it was positively crammed full of Legions at this point, so there was hardly any room to do much training on anything larger than a Cohort-sized scale. Because of what the 10th had done during my time away when I was in Alexandria with the 6th, when they had gone rioting through Campania, the army was prohibited on doing any marching out into the countryside, for fear that the men would see some villa belonging to one of the proscribed and help themselves to the contents. A valid fear, I suppose, but one that did not sit well with me, since it was because of the old 10th, and not the youngsters who were marching at that point in time. Still, it was a problem having so many men basically doing nothing, meaning that the Centurions and Optios in every Legion at this time, mine included, were busier than we had ever been before trying to keep the men out of all sorts of trouble. I was at my wits' end trying to come up with clever ways of occupying the men or tiring them out sufficiently to keep them from killing someone or each other. At this point in time, there were a total of 43 Legions marching for Rome, though not all of them were on the Campus Martius. When Octavian and Antonius had combined the two armies, there were thirty-odd Legions, many of them full-strength, and while some of them were sent to Brundisium, there were still more than 50,000 men crammed into close proximity to each other. Given that, I suppose it was inevitable that there would be trouble sufficiently serious that the 10th suffered its first deaths in some sort of combat, although it was certainly not the way either the men who died or I would have wanted them to go out.

As it is with most disputes of this nature, this affair started over a woman, one of the camp followers. Apparently, my men, youngsters from the Tenth Cohort, had mistaken her for a common whore, one of them trying to buy her services. This may sound like a trivial matter to you, gentle reader, but the difference in status between a woman like Gisela, who took a man to be her husband for all intents and purposes, living with that man only, in theory anyway, and the woman who chose to ply her trade on her back, was huge and jealously guarded by the women of the former sort. To even insinuate that she was a whore was a huge insult, so under the best of circumstances; say, if the woman in question had belonged to a man from the same Legion as the one approaching her, there would still be some sort of altercation. The fact that this woman belonged to a veteran of the 4th Legion meant that it was the worst of circumstances, and to whom the youth and inexperience of my boy from the 10th mattered not at all, and in fact, contributed to his demise, because he had no idea he had done anything wrong. According to witnesses, he had approached the woman, who worked in the wineshop that the youngster and his friends liked to frequent. She had rebuffed him, then prevailed on the owner to throw him and his friends out. Things like this happened all the time, usually being of no moment, but on this evening, she ran to her man and I imagine that in her recounting, what was a relatively innocent exchange became a brutal attempt at raping her. At least, that is what the comrades of the Legionary from the 4th claimed under questioning during the investigation. Whatever the case, the man from the 4th gathered some friends, then went looking for the youngster, whose name I cannot remember for the life of me. They found him along with his close comrade sitting in another wineshop where, according to witnesses, the man from the 4th did not go storming up to my boy or in any other way alert him that there was something amiss. In fact, the man from the 4th and his comrades acted as if they had just happened into the wineshop, striking up a conversation with my two boys, even standing for a round of wine. All seemed well; newly found friends, much joking about their Centurions and how stupid they were, the usual things that Legionaries talk about. Then, according to the witness, a man who was tending bar, the Legionary from the 4th asked what seemed to be a casual question, about whether my boys had ever frequented the wineshop where his woman worked. Of course, neither of my two knew his real purpose behind the question, nor that they were in the last moments of their lives. My boy said yes, that they had indeed just come from the very place. The Legionary from the 4th then asked what they thought of the barmaid in the place, whereupon my boy said something that the witness could not make out, though I seriously doubt that it mattered at all what he said. His fate had been sealed when the camp follower went to her man, probably saying something along the lines of, "If you don't avenge my honor, you're not lying in my bed again," or something to that effect. Whatever he said, it was barely out of his mouth when the Legionary from the 4th whipped out his dagger, plunging it into the eye socket of my youngster. According to the witness, his comrade was so overcome with shock that he made no attempt to defend himself when one of the men who had accompanied the murderer did the same thing to him, except that he was stabbed in the throat. Their bodies were found in a pigsty, which is fairly common practice when there is a hope that the pigs will destroy the evidence before the body is found. However, in this case, the men's absence was noticed immediately, as they missed the morning formation, with neither of them having a history of such behavior. It was at this point that things could have and should have taken an official turn, the first of many opportunities, so I have to assume my share of responsibility for what happened next, which was anything but official.

Many weeks before, I had led my men out of camp in relief of their comrades who were involved in the off-duty brawl. In doing so, I had set a tone that sent a message to the men, encouraging the belief that the 10th took care of its own, and would exact retribution for any wrong done to a member of the 10th, no matter what the circumstances. That is what happened now. The Centurion of the Fourth Century of the Tenth Cohort to whom the two belonged, whose identity caused me additional heartache, albeit for personal reasons, called his men together, asking for volunteers to go hunting. Despite the resulting consequences, I am proud to say that every man volunteered, so the next evening, after the final formation, a full Century of men from the 10th went looking for the murderers of their comrades. They were smart about it; they did not go out in one group, instead breaking down into sections, spreading themselves out over the neighborhood outside the Campus Martius. Unlike the shantytowns that surrounded our marching camps, the community around the Campus Martius was substantial, at least in the sense of the quality of the buildings, if not the people, who were basically the same sort that followed us around, except there was a much higher percentage of Roman citizens. The densest section of the surrounding neighborhoods was along the Via Flaminia and Via Recta respectively, so it was to these two areas that our men went, dropping coins into hands rather than bashing heads in an attempt to find out what happened to their friends. A small point perhaps, but one that saved me quite a bit of money, if not headaches, with the inevitable line of angry and injured people claiming they were roughed up at the hands of the 10th. It was not long before the wineshop that the two youngsters had been thrown out of was found, though from what I gathered the woman who started the whole affair was not there. Next, the shop where they were murdered was located. Since the first shop was the home turf of the 4th, at least of the bunch that our men were looking for, the people working there were not as forthcoming or willing to help as in other places, so this is when things got a little rough. After some physical persuasion, the identities of the murderers were given up to the men of the Fourth Century.

Things could have more or less ended here, if their Centurion had made his report to his Pilus Prior, who would have come to me, whereupon I would have gone to Antonius or Octavian, there being no such post as Camp Prefect at this point. I would never have gone to Lepidus under any circumstances. However, that is not what happened, because neither the Decimus Princeps Posterior nor the Decimus Pilus Prior thought that is what I would have wanted, given my previous example. Instead, once it was learned that this was the wineshop the murderer frequented, the Centurion decided to set an ambush using his most experienced men. Nobody was allowed to leave the wineshop to warn the men of the 4th, while the rest of the men of the Fourth Century were sent back to camp, no doubt disappointed, though it ultimately saved them a considerable amount of pain.

I do not know if the Legionary from the 4th thought he had gotten away with it, making the ambush a complete surprise, or if he was suspicious and alert. What I do know is that he entered the wineshop with three other men, whereupon the men of the 10th who were selected for this mission, led by their Centurion, burst out of hiding, taking the four as prisoners. Moving quickly, while leaving behind a couple of men to keep anyone from running to the 4th for help, they dragged or carried the men to the scene of the murder, where other men from the Fourth Cohort of the 10th were waiting with the shopkeeper who had witnessed the murders. When he saw the prisoners, he identified three of the four as being involved, indicating the man who had struck the first blow, and another as the man who had killed the second youngster. Once identified, the three men were then beaten to death by the men of the Fourth, who used cudgels in much the same manner as an execution, while the surviving man was forced to watch, spared instead to be given a warning to take back to the 4th that to assault anyone of the 10th was the same as being sentenced to death. As I was to learn when I questioned the Princeps Posterior, the use of the cudgels was calculated, as a signal and to give the whole affair quasi-legality, since this would have been the sentence imposed under regulations. Naturally, the men of the 4th did not heed this warning. It was only after they retaliated, catching some men from the Fifth Cohort a couple of nights later and beating them so badly that one of them was crippled and had to be retired from the Legion, that I became aware of what the Princeps Posterior had done.

"Tetarfenus, what by Pluto's thorny cock did you do?" I demanded of the short, wiry Centurion standing in front of my desk, his Pilus Prior, Gnaeus Nasica, at *intente* next to him.

I had first met Quintus Tetarfenus when I was the *de facto* Primus Pilus of the 6th Legion, plucking him from his post as Optio when his enlistment was up, so he and his brother Gaius had joined the 10th when we re-formed the Legion, although Gaius never became more than a Sergeant. Tetarfenus was promoted to Centurion and placed in the Tenth Cohort, one of my veterans whose fighting quality I knew from firsthand experience. Also, during our time in Alexandria together I had been impressed at his resourcefulness and initiative. In fact, this was not the first time he had taken matters into his own hands. I cursed myself for forgetting about the incident in Alexandria, when Tetarfenus was involved in beating the ringleader of a planned defection, from the 28th Legion to the Egyptians, putting me and the Primus Pilus of the 28th, Gnaeus Cartufenus, in a tight spot. It was a detail that had escaped me, and in hindsight the moment I learned the identities of the murdered men and who their Centurion was, I should have put two and two together, stepping in immediately. Now, here we were, except that it was much more serious than just the beating of a single man, and the circumstances were not as extenuating this time as they were in Alexandria. Tetarfenus' face was expressionless and his tone flat as he answered what had in effect been a rhetorical question.

"Just doing what I thought was right, Primus Pilus; taking care of my men."

"If you had been taking care of your men in the proper way, their ashes wouldn't be on the way to their families now," I snapped, immediately regretting the words, because I knew how unfair and how wounding they were.

Tetarfenus' face flushed, though his tone remained under control. "Yes sir. I know I failed my men. I was hoping that I could do something that would at least appease the spirits of the men who were murdered."

"And send a message?" I asked, in what I hoped was a milder tone.

Right then, I had to get more information from Tetarfenus, to find out if there were any more reprisals planned, because this was spiraling out of control rapidly. Making him even more defensive than he was would not help anything.

Tetarfenus hesitated, then nodded. "Yes, sir. That too. Like you did that time a few weeks ago," he finished.

I stared at him hard, trying to determine what was behind the words, if there was some sort of implied threat in them, but I could not tell. Titus, old man, you are getting too suspicious for your own good, I chided myself. I sighed as his words sank in, realizing that no matter what his intent was, there was truth in what he said, and this was the moment when I first realized my role in what was happening.

I rubbed my face as I tried to think, finally saying, "Tetarfenus, you and your entire Century are restricted to your Century area until further notice. We have to see how things play out. Hopefully, Primus Pilus Corbulo knows enough of the full story that he won't want to pursue the matter any further. In case he does, we need the man who witnessed the original murder under lock and key, so go get him now."

I looked at Nasica as I said this, my stomach twisting at the look of guilt on his face as he shot a glance at Tetarfenus, who looked as distressed.

"Er, actually, Primus Pilus, we already thought of that and I personally sent my Optio and a section to go get him."

I could tell this was not going to end well, but I had to ask. "And?" I demanded.

Nasica grimaced. "He's disappeared. We tore the shop apart, and asked the neighboring shopkeepers, but nobody has seen him."

All I could do was curse.

"He's probably in a pigsty too," I said bitterly. I turned back to Tetarfenus. "Tetarfenus, I can't say that I'm surprised, but I am disappointed. This isn't Alexandria, and the circumstances aren't the same either."

He looked at me with a mixture of defiance and contrition. "Someone killed my men, Primus Pilus. They had to pay."

"They did," I agreed. "But it's neither your place nor is it mine to make those men pay."

I could see that Tetarfenus was not convinced, but it did not matter, so I dismissed him, then turned to Nasica.

"When did you know about this?"

I kept my tone as controlled as I could, knowing that venting my anger would not help matters, as much as I wanted to. Nasica opened his mouth to say something, then seemed to change his mind before he spoke, so I do not know what was going to come out of his mouth originally.

"Not until after the deed was done," he said, not terribly convincingly, but I could tell I was not going to get anything more out of him on this subject.

"Well, this doesn't speak well of your hold over your Centurions, Nasica."

He flushed, but said nothing, waiting for me to continue. I tapped my fingers on the desk as I tried to think what to do. Finally, I called for Diocles.

"Pass the word that the Legion is restricted to camp until further notice." He turned to leave, then I added, "And extend that restriction to the 4th's part of camp as well. In fact, I don't want them on that side of the *Praetorium*."

Fortunately, we were located on opposite sides of the camp, but men being what they are, I knew there were some of them whose heart's desire would now be to go to that side of the camp, simply because it was forbidden. I just hoped that they would be sufficiently aware that they would probably end up the way the other men of the 10th had, if not worse, if they did.

Turning back to Nasica, I finished with him by saying, "I took a chance on you, Nasica, and now I'm beginning to worry that I made the wrong bet. I'll be keeping an eye on you, and all we can hope now is that this blows over."

With that, I dismissed him, and I could see that he was visibly shaken, which is exactly what I was intending. I made a mental note to make an offering of a kid goat that this would indeed blow over, but I just wasted my money, because it was before the end of that very day that I received a summons to meet with Lepidus, of all people.

In retrospect, I suppose it was a good thing that neither Antonius nor Octavian thought that the drama that was unfolding on the Campus Martius was worthy of their attention when compared to the larger events in Rome itself. Dealing with Antonius would have been straightforward but costly. His greed had gotten out of control, I suppose in line with his ever-mounting debts, something that dogged him for most of his days. He would have demanded some exorbitant sum from both sides, promising each of us an outcome that we found agreeable, then would have decided by whatever whim moved him at the moment. Octavian was another matter entirely; there was not an ounce of whimsy in the man. Everything was cold calculation, which to my mind made him equally unpredictable as Antonius, because his decision would be based on some internal judgment that I could not divine, at least until I knew him better. Lepidus, I knew. I despised him, but I knew him, so I held onto this as my best hope of at least seeing what was headed my way before it happened as I made my way to the *Praetorium*.

When I was announced, nobody, not even Lepidus could fault the perfect parade-ground entrance and salute I gave him, nodding at an obviously unhappy Primus Pilus of the 4th Legion, a man slightly older than me named Corbulo. I had not had much to do with the man, since he was a Pompeian in the first civil war. Then his Legion had been shuttled back and forth from Macedonia to Brundisium. It was the 4th who had defected to Octavian en masse, which in the past may have made him and his men suspect, but Legions jumping from one side to the other had become the norm. Now that I had been involved in doing the very same thing, I did not feel right judging anyone. He returned my acknowledgement with a curt nod, his lips thinned into a frown. My first hint that things would not be going my way was when I noticed that while he was seated in front of Lepidus' desk, there was not a chair for me. Fine, I thought grimly, if you want to play it this way, then that's what we will do. I stood stiffly at attention, while Lepidus busied himself with a scroll, pretending to study it with great interest. Rather than get angry, I had to suppress a chuckle because he had obviously forgotten that given my height, I was in a position to look down to see that it was blank. That fits, I thought to myself, that's about as complicated a document as he's capable of reading. Corbulo was not willing to indulge him, however, as he noisily cleared his throat, forcing Lepidus to drag his attention away from his important document.

"General, if we could . . ." Corbulo began, but Lepidus cut him off.

I smothered the smirk that threatened my mouth, knowing what was coming.

"That is 'Triumvir,' Primus Pilus, if you please," Lepidus corrected him, showing his teeth in what passed for his smile. "After all, you wouldn't like it if I called you 'Pilus Prior' or some such nonsense, would you?"

"Forgive me, Triumvir." Corbulo recovered well, I will give him that. "It's just that we have a situation that I'm afraid is in danger of escalating out of control if we don't act quickly."

So far, I could not fault anything he was saying; he was indeed correct that the situation was serious. I waited to see what else he had to say before I opened my mouth.

"And what situation is that, Primus Pilus?" Lepidus asked with feigned interest.

It was plain to see that they had rehearsed this bit, making it clear that was why Corbulo had been sitting here waiting for me, because he had been here for some time. I felt my stomach tighten, while there was a tingling sensation in my hands and feet that always happened when I sensed some sort of danger lay ahead.

"There has been a murder, Triumvir. Three murders in fact, and I'm afraid that it involves men from our respective Legions. Sadly, the victims are

[70]

from my Legion, while the murderers are from the 10th, at least that is what our witnesses say."

Both sets of eyes turned towards me as my mind raced, trying to determine what the real objective of this assault was. I did not know Corbulo, so I could not imagine that he had some sort of personal vendetta against me. Lepidus was another matter, the memory of our initial clash popping into my mind. Could Lepidus be behind whatever was happening here, at least in the sense of using the situation to his advantage to even a score with me? I could not give it the thought it deserved, because they were obviously expecting an answer, so I replied with a tone that I hoped balanced respect with indignation.

"That's not exactly what happened, Triumvir. In fact, two of my men . . ."

"So you're saying that your men did not kill three men of the 4th," Lepidus interrupted.

"Yes, but . . ."

"There is no 'but,' Primus Pilus," he snapped, and I could feel the dangerous rush of heat rising to my face as I thought, careful, Titus, you're in dangerous waters here.

"You just admitted that your men killed three men of the 4th Legion, without provocation," and as soon as he said it, he knew he had made an error.

I was not about to let that opportunity pass without pouncing on it.

"That's where an error has been made, Triumvir, in the last part of your statement. In fact, men of the 10th did *execute*," I emphasized the word as I looked at Corbulo, pleased to see that it was his turn to flush red, "not *murder* three men of the 4th, who were identified by witnesses as having been the ones who committed murder, when they stabbed two of my men to death."

"So you say," Corbulo snorted.

I wheeled on him, glad now that I was standing and he sitting, as it gave me command of the high ground, so to speak.

"I hope that you're not insinuating that I'm lying, Primus Pilus Corbulo," I said quietly, but I was glad to see that he did not mistake the menace in my tone, the color that had been in his face suddenly fleeing.

"I...I meant no such thing, Primus Pilus Pullus," he stuttered. "I spoke in haste, forgive me. It just seems that there are two different stories."

"There usually are in matters like this," I responded coolly. "And I have the ashes of two of my men, whose bodies were found in a pig sty, I might add, and we both know that's a favored method of disposing of bodies by men who are trying to hide the evidence. I also have their deaths entered in the Legion diary."

"That doesn't mean that it was my men who were responsible," Corbulo protested, but I was pleased to see that I had him on the defensive.

Before I could continue the pressure, Lepidus, seeing the same thing, reasserted himself.

"Enough," he snapped. "Primus Pilus Pullus, I suppose that you can produce this so-called witness to corroborate your version of events?"

The sight of those damned teeth shining at me as he made no attempt to hide his triumphant grin told me why we had not found the witness.

Oh, he had done me neatly, and we both knew it. I could see the malevolence in his smile as he waited for the answer that he knew was coming, his expression saying to me, "Did you think I forgot how you humiliated me?"

I did not speak. My mind raced as I tried to determine how badly this would go. I had no doubt that part of the motivation, at least on Lepidus' part, was some sort of twisted determination to see the floggings that he had been cheated out of. What I could not easily discern was how determined he was to punish me along with the others.

Finally, I replied, "We've been unable to locate the witness. But you already knew that, didn't you, Triumvir?"

The smile faltered, and I saw his face redden, but my gibe was not for him; it was for Corbulo because I wanted to see how deeply he was involved in Lepidus' plan. I was rewarded by a look of confusion on Corbulo's face as he looked from Lepidus to me then back again, trying to determine what undercurrent was threatening to sweep him away.

"I don't know what you're talking about I assure you, Primus Pilus, and if I were you I would be careful making accusations." Lepidus glowered at me, and as much as I despised him, I had to recognize that his status as Triumvir, even as the weakest of the three, made him a dangerous man.

"Forgive me, Triumvir," I said through clenched teeth. "I was asking a question and didn't mean for it to be construed as an accusation."

Nothing was said for several heartbeats, then Lepidus waved a hand, which I took to be his version of a magnanimous gesture.

"So I must deliberate on this matter carefully," he said, though again he could not completely contain his smirk. "You'll return to your quarters and wait to hear from me."

It took every bit of discipline in my body to keep my face impassive and my manner impeccable as I saluted, then executed the proper about-face, marching out of his office. Before I reached the door, Lepidus called out to me.

"Oh, and, Primus Pilus, do I have your word as a Centurion of Rome that you will not suddenly decide to take leave?"

I turned slowly and with as much defiance as I thought I could get away with, I replied, "Triumvir, I have never, ever run from a fight yet."

"Just see that you don't this time," he sneered. Then, I turned my back on him, thinking, You're going to wish I had, you little prick, though I had no idea how I was going to best him this time.

Corbulo was standing outside the *Praetorium*, and we approached each other awkwardly, neither of us seeming to know what to say.

Finally, he jerked his head in the direction of the *Praetorium*, asking, "What was all that about?"

"Payment of an old debt," I said shortly, not really wanting to have this conversation at this moment, but then I stopped.

I needed friends and allies as I never had before. If it was too much to expect Corbulo to be counted as either, given the circumstances, neither could I afford to make more enemies. I briefly explained the beginnings of what I now recognized was a feud between Lepidus and myself; even if I had never thought about it that way before, Lepidus obviously had. After I explained, Corbulo nodded thoughtfully.

"I had heard that about him," he said. "He really has it in for you, then?"

"I suppose he does, though I never thought about it before," I replied honestly.

"Oh, I know those types." Corbulo spat on the ground. "They're as touchy as a Vestal about the flanks when it comes to their exalted status, and if someone that they think of as inferior to them gets the better of them, they won't rest until they even the score. And you," he suddenly grinned at me, catching me by surprise, "are about as inferior to him as one can get." He chuckled. "Yes, I can see how you were a rock in his boot, all right."

I was not sure that I liked how he seemed to be taking pleasure in my predicament, but I could see that he held me no malice, nor I to him. We were two men who got caught up in the actions of our respective subordinates, so now we had a mess to clean up, though it looked very much as if I was actually part of the mess now.

"You know." I do not know what prompted me to say this, but it was suddenly important to me that Corbulo hear the truth. "We did have a witness who saw everything."

He nodded again, then looked away as he spoke. "I thought as much, just from the way Lepidus reacted. He looked too pleased with himself for there not to be a witness. How do you suppose he knew about him?" he asked suddenly.

I had been turning that very question over in my mind as we had been talking. There was only one conclusion I could draw.

"He obviously has spies in the ranks," I replied. "It makes sense, I suppose. After all, Octavian certainly has men working for him. You should know about that." I could not help myself, and I felt a momentary satisfaction as his face turned red.

He opened his mouth, clearly about to make a sharp retort, then snapped it shut.

"I suppose I deserved that," he said grudgingly.

I found myself liking and respecting Corbulo more with every passing moment.

Turning back to the more pressing matter, he asked me, "So what happened exactly? Just between you and me, one Primus Pilus to another, off the record. You be totally honest with me, and I'll do the same with you."

I could not refuse such an offer, even if I had been so inclined, so I told him what I knew at that point. When I had finished, he heaved a great sigh, shaking his head in disgust.

"Figures. That bastard," he gave the name of the man who murdered my boy, though I forget it now, "was tied to that woman's apron strings, and she was bad business. Her first two men died, one in battle, but the other under almost identical circumstances. I don't know what she has between her legs, but I'm going to have to do something about her." He turned to look me in the eye. "And if you ever repeat what I'm about to say, I'll deny it and I'll never speak to you again, understand?"

I nodded, then he continued, "The fact is that as much of a pain in the ass as that woman is, her man was worse, and I'm plain glad to be rid of him because I know that sooner or later I'd have had to do something permanent about him."

He did not elaborate. He did not need to; the Legionary in question would have had a training accident. Executions may be necessary at times, but they are bad for morale, and while every Primus Pilus had men who they wanted to be rid of in a permanent way, doing so in an official manner is always the last resort.

He went on. "The other two were bad ones too, but they were followers. He was the leader, and if he had been removed, I think those two would have been all right, given the proper motivation."

He smiled grimly at this inside joke, and I returned the smile.

Shaking his head, he finished. "But what your men did was wrong, even though I understand it." He gave a snorting laugh. "Who knows, a few years ago I may have done the same thing as your Princeps Posterior. Still, I'm afraid that Lepidus is going to have his way on this one."

We stood there then, as a misting rain began, the leaden skies matching my mood. I wish I could say that my main concern at this point was the fate of Tetarfenus, but I had recognized that for all intents and purposes his career was over, with the only real question being if he would be executed. I also regret to say that I did not have a thought for Nasica either, as I was seeing all my hard work, all that I had achieved about to blow away like a puff of smoke at the whim of a man like Lepidus. I suppose that it was this thought, threatening to overwhelm everything else crowding in my brain that prompted me to turn suddenly to Corbulo.

"What should I do?"

If he was surprised, he did not show it. His answer was instant.

"You need to see Octavian. The only one who can get you out of the mess you're in with Lepidus is another Triumvir."

I sat in my quarters the rest of that day and night, only seeing Diocles, not even seeing Scribonius when he came to call. I needed time to think and to decide my next move. I recognized that Corbulo was right, that my only hope of escaping Lepidus' revenge was to go to Octavian and hope that my status as his adopted father's man would be enough to convince him to intercede on my behalf. I think that in those thirds of a watch I was harboring the belief, delusion is probably more accurate, that I would be able to reach an accommodation with Octavian without selling my soul. I remembered the bright-eyed youth who seemed to hang on my every word, and seemed a little in awe of my reputation. I say this now with the brutal clarity of someone who is about as wrong as it is possible to be, while still being alive to tell about it. One decision I came to was to wait until I heard exactly what Lepidus had in mind, which was a huge risk. However, as I thought about it, I realized that I was not in a completely weak position, despite appearances. Of all the segments of Roman society at this point, the one with the most power was the army, so my status as Primus Pilus of the 10th gave me quite a bit of influence, not just with my Legion, but throughout the army. While I would have liked to think it had everything to do with all that I had accomplished, I was realistic enough to recognize that it had more to do with the idea that a threat to one Centurion, even from a Triumvir, was a sign that none of us were safe. There was an atmosphere of suspicion and paranoia with the proscriptions, which had not been generating the amount of income the Triumvirs thought, for a variety of reasons. Now they were dipping deeper into the rolls of citizens, so it did not take long for the fear to develop among the first grade Centurions that we would be next. It was no secret that those of us who had marched with Caesar were now wealthy men, though I believe that if how much some of us actually had was known, we would have been prime targets for the list. However, that was a dangerous game for even Triumvirs to play, the Legions demonstrating this on more than one occasion, when we switched allegiance to one or the other. The more I thought about it, the more I became convinced that Lepidus' actions against me were less about me stopping him from getting his enjoyment from striping men bloody than how we had emasculated him by defecting to Antonius. He had thought himself to be as important a player as

Antonius and probably more important than Octavian. But in one stroke, he lost his position, thanks to the actions of the Legions, the 10th in particular, so I suppose it made sense that I was the focus of his rage. It did not particularly help matters, though I suppose it was better to comprehend the true nature of the problem.

Finally, at dawn on the second day, I heard the tramping of boots, for some reason knowing that they were headed for my door. I had already dressed myself, wearing my full uniform with decorations, Diocles taking extra care with the phalarae so that they gleamed like silver fire. The pounding on the door started my heart hammering, and I could not remember ever being as scared as I was at that moment. Before, in every battle I had ever fought, the situation was clear-cut; either I would live, or I would die. If I died, I could at least control the manner of my death in some way: dying on my feet, facing the enemy. Now, I was facing the destruction of something more important to me than my life, my reputation, my own fragile *dignitas*, such as it was. Caesar had rubbed off on me even more than I thought, I realized, as Diocles opened the door to a hard-faced provost, the man's face betraying no emotion.

"Primus Pilus Pullus, you are summoned to meet with the Triumvir Marcus Aemilius Lepidus immediately. We," he indicated the squad of men behind him, "are to escort you to the *Praetorium.*"

He did have the grace to look a bit embarrassed at the heavy-handedness of Lepidus in providing what was in effect an armed guard, as if I were a ranker caught trying to desert. I was about to make an angry remark to the provost, but I appreciated he was just doing his job, so I gave a curt nod, indicating I was ready to go.

I turned to take my helmet from Diocles, whispering to him, "You know what to do."

"They'll be there," he assured me in the same soft voice.

If the provost heard, he gave no indication as I left my quarters, wondering if I would be sleeping in my bed that night.

Lepidus was sitting at his desk in much the same posture as when I had seen him last. Marching up to stand the prescribed distance away, I came to *intente*, then saluted, which he did not bother to return. The only other men present were slaves acting as scribes, along with four Romans of obviously noble birth who were always hanging around Lepidus, laughing at his jokes and fawning all over him. I was disappointed but not surprised to see that the Tribune who had been my secret ally was absent; I suspect that Lepidus finally learned of the man's true feelings for him and dismissed him.

"Primus Pilus Pullus, after deliberating on this manner carefully, I have reached the conclusion that your leadership of the 10th Legion is so inept and weak that a situation was allowed to develop that you should have stopped before any of this happened. You're hereby relieved of your command, you'll be reduced to the ranks, and you'll be flogged." He had been looking down at what I was sure was another blank scroll, but he now looked up at me, his eyes gleaming with triumph and hatred. He added, "With the scourge, to the count of 30 lashes."

He turned to the provosts, who had been standing in the corner while waving at me.

"Take him to the holding cell."

You might think, gentle reader, that I would be reeling with shock, or at the very least be so riveted by what he was saying that I would have given him some sort of reaction. The truth is that I was only half-listening to what he was saying, because most of my attention was focused on listening for another sound, and I was rewarded by the first rumbling of what I was waiting for. Hearing it, I turned to Lepidus and I smiled at him.

For several heartbeats, he sat there, clearly unable to comprehend my seeming lack of fear. What men like Lepidus never realize about men like me is that fear is a constant companion that we have learned to accept and, in fact, make our servant. I doubt that Lepidus had ever actually faced a man in combat, no matter how much he liked to strut about in his uniform, wearing medals that he had never earned. Now his jaw went slack in shock at the sight of my smile, but he had not yet heard what I had, to my ears distinguished as the sound of tramping boots on the cobbles outside. That sound meant that I was content to watch him as the noise grew louder and more recognizable. Then, recognizing the racket for what it was, he jumped to his feet, shooting a panic-stricken glance first at his minions, then at the provosts, who seemed rooted to the ground in shock themselves. Despite being prepared for it, the booming sound of someone banging on the door to Lepidus' office almost made me jump, while it certainly had that effect on Lepidus and the rest of the men in the office. I felt a twinge of pity for the slaves, who were now cowering in terror, looking for any nook and cranny to hide in, though from the way it looked, Lepidus was going to beat them to it.

"Excuse me, Triumvir," I said as I turned to walk to the door, pulling it open.

Standing there was Scribonius, his face a mask, and as soon as I opened the door wide, without a word being said, he filed past me, followed by every Centurion and Optio of the 10th Legion, all of them wearing their full uniforms, and most importantly, their weapons. The office was very large, yet even so, cramming 120 men into it was impossible, so a number of the men waited outside. Lepidus finally found his voice, and while I am sure that he wanted his words to come out a thunderous roar, what everyone in the room heard was more of a spluttering squeak.

"What do you mean by this? You're here to assassinate me."

The idea was so ludicrous that I burst out laughing, which I admit seemed incongruous given the seriousness of what was taking place.

"Not at all, Triumvir," I assured him. "We're all loyal and obedient servants of Rome. The Centurions and Optios here came of their own free will out of concern for my well-being."

Scribonius now stepped forward, having been selected by the others to be the spokesman.

"Triumvir, when we heard that our Primus Pilus was being unjustly charged with dereliction of duty, we came in a show of support, and to ensure that his rights as a Roman citizen are respected."

I do not know if it was conscious or not, but I thought Scribonius tapping his fingers on the hilt of his sword as he spoke was a nice touch. Lepidus looked to his minions, soliciting them for help. Surprisingly, none of those lions were willing to risk the wrath of a group of Rome's Centurions. Seeing no help from that quarter, he stood, holding onto the edge of the desk in support as I could clearly see him quivering in fear.

"Unjustly charged?" he squeaked. "I don't know where you heard such nonsense, but I assure you that it's not true. The charges against the Primus Pilus are well founded and very serious. Now, I appreciate your concern." His attempt at reasserting control was as comical as it was ineffective, as he pulled himself to his full height of a shade over five feet tall, while not relinquishing his grip on the desk so as not to collapse at our feet. "But I assure you that the situation is well in hand, and the Primus Pilus will be safe in custody."

"Custody?"

Scribonius affected a look of concerned puzzlement, then looked over his shoulder at the rest of the men. If it had not been so serious, with my life at stake, I probably would have enjoyed the performance more. Each of the men mirrored his gaze, albeit with varying degrees of success in making it look real. Scribonius turned back to Lepidus, and while his tone was quiet, I had never heard my normally mild-mannered friend sound so full of menace.

"I don't believe that's acceptable, Triumvir. The Primus Pilus is one of the most honored and respected men, not just in the 10th Legion, but in the entire Roman army. To see him led away in disgrace I'm afraid would rouse a great anger in the men, which I don't believe we," he indicated the rest of the Centurions, "could control. Triumvir, these are troubled times." Scribonius was now the voice of reason. "And it wouldn't do anyone any good to have a Legion on the rampage."

For the first time, I saw a glint of anger in Lepidus' eyes, not completely drowning out the fear, but it gave him enough courage over his tongue to speak up now.

"As you say, Secundus Pilus Prior Scribonius, that would indeed not only be tragic, it would be treasonous, and as much damage as one Legion might do, there are many, many more on the Campus

[83]

Martius alone that I know are loyal to Rome and would crush any such . . .misguided demonstration."

"I'm afraid that it would be more than one Legion." I was as unprepared as Lepidus seemed to be to hear a new voice.

Spinning around, I saw a small number of men wearing the same white crest of the Primus Pilus of a Legion as the one I wore, while at their head was Corbulo, who was the man who had spoken.

"Forgive me for intruding, Triumvir, Primus Pilus Pullus." He nodded in my direction. "But I felt it was my duty to come as soon as I heard what was taking place. I only heard part of what the Pilus Prior was saying, but I did hear your response that it would only be one Legion who would take any imprisonment of Primus Pilus Pullus extremely badly, but that's not the case. I have reason to believe that the 4th would follow the lead of the 10th."

Corbulo then stepped aside, giving a faint nod to the Primus Pilus closest to him, none other than my old acquaintance, Torquatus.

"My boys too," he said flatly, moving to the side as the Primus Pilus of the 12th Legion informed the Triumvir that his men too could be counted on to take my imprisonment as a slap in the face.

By now, even Lepidus could see that he was not going to be taking me into custody, so he finally threw his hands up in a gesture of surrender.

"I hear your concerns, gentlemen, and like you I have no desire for more violence." His shoulders slumped, and he closed his eyes as he spoke. "Very well, the Primus Pilus is free to go. However," he said, still grimly determined not to be denied. "I'm requiring two things in exchange. First, is the sworn oath of every Primus Pilus here that Primus Pilus Pullus will remain within the precincts of Rome. The second is that you allow a special tribunal to be held, and that you respect and abide by the decision of the tribunal as it pertains to this matter."

All eyes turned to me, waiting to see my reaction. I knew that at the very least, the Centurions of the 10th would do whatever I asked of them, but I was not about to ask any of them to take further risks with their lives and careers at this point, so I gave a slight nod. I saw Scribonius' brow furrow, opening his mouth to argue, but I cut him off with a shake of my head.

I looked at Corbulo, who shrugged but kept his eyes on me as he said loudly enough for all to hear, "We agree."

Although he had not asked them, Lepidus turned to Scribonius, who, clearly reluctant, agreed as well. With that, there was a release of tension akin to the torsion string of a ballista being loosed, and I was grimly pleased to see that Lepidus' tunic was ringed with sweat around the neck and under the arms. Finally, Lepidus cleared his throat as he tried to assume a control over the room that he had never had in the first place.

Motioning to the door, he said, "Gentlemen, if there is nothing else, I have other business to attend to." I turned to leave, and I heard him hiss, "You think you've won something. All you've won is a stay of execution."

I stopped, then turned to face him. Again, I was seized by an almost overwhelming urge to draw my Gallic blade to run him through. I started to speak, but for once, I governed my tongue. Instead, I looked him up and down the way I would a new *tiro*, making sure that the *numen* holding the invisible turd had a fresh, smelly one to put under my nose, then I turned to walk out. Unfortunately for me, Lepidus was right. All I had done was to buy myself time, but that had been my primary goal when I walked into Lepidus' office; to walk out without an escort. Now I had to get an audience with Octavian, as my whole career, indeed my very life rested on one throw of the dice. On the positive side, Lepidus had unwittingly helped me by restricting me not to just the Campus Martius, but to Rome. While Octavian had commandeered a residence on the Campus, I was better served going to his residence in Rome, and I knew that I had no time to waste. Once outside, I was surrounded by my Centurions, where I found Scribonius standing a bit apart. I did not know exactly what to say, so I held out my hand, which he took, a solemn look on his face.

"I hope you know what you're doing," was all he said.

"So do I."

Corbulo came up to offer his hand as well, which I took. Before I could say anything, he told me, "Just so we're clear, I didn't do this for you."

"I didn't think you did," I replied honestly.

"It's just that a jumped-up bastard like Lepidus doesn't have the right to touch any Centurion, no matter what he may think. If it hadn't been you, it would have been one of us."

I was not sure about that, but I was not going to argue the point. I thanked him again, as well as the other Primi Pili, then made my way back to my quarters. I had to send Diocles to secure an audience with Octavian and I had to do it quickly. I was risking everything on the belief that there was enough left of the wide-eyed boy who wanted to have dinner with Titus Pullus, that he would accept.

The perhaps two parts of a watch I spent waiting for Diocles to return were some of the longest of my life, and I was acutely aware that they could be some of the last of them as well. Never in all my imagining of how my life and career would go had I envisioned being so vulnerable and at risk without being anywhere near a battlefield. I was fighting for my life without drawing a sword, which for a man like me was both terrifying and confusing. I can only acknowledge now, in the safety of my old age and obviously having survived, that I have never been as scared before or since as I was during those days fighting Lepidus. As much of a worm and as empty of a uniform as he was, he was still more of an expert at this kind of warfare than I was, so I do not think it is a stretch to say that I was as overmatched against Lepidus in this arena as he would have been facing me with a sword in his hand. Now everything rested on Octavian, and again I opted to be alone as I waited for the sound of Diocles' footstep outside my door. When he finally appeared, it was all I could do to keep from leaping to my feet and running up, shaking him like a rag doll for taking so long, but one look at him stopped me cold. He was clearly exhausted, his face pinched and worn with worry, as I imagine much like mine looked.

"Well?" I demanded. My knees almost collapsed from the relief of tension when I saw him nod.

"He says he'll see you," he replied.

Nevertheless, I was wary of his expression, which was one of anything but relief.

"You don't look very happy that your master has a chance at saving his life," I said sourly, and I was a little mollified by his reaction as he put his hands up.

"No, master, it's not that at all. I'm more relieved than I can tell you. It's just that, I have to say that he seems . . . different," he finished in a guarded tone, and I could have sworn I saw his eyes dart around to the dark corners of the room. However, I was in no mood to hear his pessimism at this point. I waved my hand at him, dismissing his worries.

"Of course he's changed since you saw him last. It's been almost two years, and a lot has happened. All that matters is that he remembers me and agreed to see me."

"Oh, he remembers you very well," Diocles said immediately.

I should have been paying closer attention, but I was now hurrying to dress myself, and Diocles knew better than to try to talk to me when I was in such a state.

(I had never seen my master and friend as agitated as he was that evening, and as things turned out, I am happy that he did not question me further, because only the gods know how that might have changed things. My master has just relayed how frightened he was, and I was no less frightened, but not by Lepidus. If I had told him of my misgivings, who knows what might have happened? Octavian had certainly remembered him, but seemed decidedly cool at the mention of my master's name, and in fact, he seemed to have a scroll on his desk that pertained to my master at that very moment, because he referred to it at length while he asked me some questions about my master.)

Diocles had told me that Octavian was expecting me at the end of the second watch, which gave me barely enough time to make myself presentable before hurrying to his house without being drenched in sweat.

The house Octavian had chosen was large, yet not anywhere near the size of Pompey's old mansion, which Antonius still occupied. I approached it, ignoring the people passing by, and they gave me a wide berth anyway, because of my size and uniform, I suppose. My instructions were specific; I was to knock at the gate reserved for deliveries and servants, not the front. While I understood the need to do whatever I could to keep my visit from Lepidus' spies, it stung nonetheless. I had grown accustomed to the status of a Centurion, and a Primus Pilus. I would be lying if I said that I did not enjoy the trappings of my position, which usually included being welcomed at the main entrance of the upper classes' homes on those few occasions that I was invited. The delivery entrance was a large double gate, with a smaller door set into the wall next to it, so it was this on which I knocked. I was happy to see that it was opened immediately, by a nondescript-looking slave of an indeterminate age.

"I am Primus Pilus..." Before I could finish my sentence, the slave cut me off.

"I know who you are, Primus Pilus; you're expected. Follow me."

And with that, he turned, leaving me open-mouthed before I snapped out of it, hurrying to catch up with him, chagrined at the thought of the sight of me fumbling after a slave, thankful that none of the men were there to see it. I say Octavian's house was not large, yet it was large enough that I soon lost track of the twists and turns we made, the slave moving quickly towards wherever Octavian was located.

We finally arrived at a room whose doors were closed, and he turned to me, saying abruptly, "Wait here," before opening the door then entering himself.

I caught a quick glimpse, getting just a sense of Octavian seated behind a desk while surrounded by a number of people before the door closed. I stood in the hallway waiting, knowing that it would be a long time before I was called in, knowing how the game was played. That did not make it any easier to endure, but there was nothing I could do about it, so I contented myself with inspecting my uniform, making sure that everything was in place and not smudged. Perhaps the better part of a third of a watch passed before the door opened, then the slave who had escorted me beckoned me to enter.

"The Triumvir will see you now," he announced in a voice pitched loudly enough so that his master and everyone in the room could hear. Then, turning about to face into the room, he said in the same tone, "Centurion First Grade Titus Pullus, Primus Pilus of the 10th Legion," as he stepped aside to allow me to enter.

Taking a deep breath and squaring myself, I marched into the room, keeping my attention only on the slight figure sitting behind the desk at the far end of the room. His head was bowed, so all I could see was the mass of blonde curls as men stood about him holding parchments and scrolls, or quietly conferring with each other. It was reminiscent of his adoptive father, which I knew was exactly the effect he was working for, to impress on everyone that he was the embodiment of the great man. He had gone so far at this point to start calling himself Caesar Divi Filius, the son of a god, after the incident at the festival with the star rising to the heavens that the people had decided was Caesar's soul going to heaven. I was aware of the surreptitious glances of some of the men in the room, while one man in particular was studying me with no attempt to conceal his gaze like the others.

He was not as tall as I was, but he was still tall and well built, as muscular through the chest and arms as I was, which was unusual. He was a strikingly handsome man, and while he was dressed in a simple tunic, I could tell at a glance that this was a man born to the uniform. I stopped at the proper distance from the desk, saluting. I was expecting Octavian to play the same game as Lepidus and ignore me for a period of time, but he immediately stood, giving me a broad smile while moving from behind the desk to offer his hand, which I accepted, a little bemused if truth be known.

"Primus Pilus, it's wonderful to see you." He oozed warmth and charm, though I suppose that my reason for visiting colored my view of everything, because his demeanor struck a false note with me, despite returning his greeting with what I hoped was sufficient grace.

If he noticed my unease, he made no comment about it, though I realize now that he absolutely noticed; Octavian never missed anything, ever.

Turning to the well-built man, he motioned him over, exclaiming, "Agrippa, here's the man you've been waiting to meet all this time. Marcus Vipsanius Agrippa, meet Titus Pullus."

Agrippa approached, his own hand offered as well, his broad smile not seeming false in any way.

"Primus Pilus, I'm extremely honored to meet you. You're a legend in the army, and just from the looks of you, I can see why."

I could feel the heat rising from my neck at his words as I fumbled for the right thing to say to match his generosity.

"I've heard much of you as well, sir. I hope that one day we can serve in the field together."

"I would love that!" he exclaimed, looking so genuinely pleased at the prospect that it tugged at my heart a bit.

With these pleasantries aside, Octavian turned, calling to the rest of the men in the room.

"The Primus Pilus and I have some business to discuss. I would appreciate it if you all would give us some privacy for a few moments. I will send for you when we are through."

Everyone in the room was obviously accustomed to meetings of this nature because there was no hesitation or wasted motion as they moved to the door, some of them carrying their paperwork with them to continue working on. Agrippa had turned to leave as well, but Octavian stopped him.

"No, Agrippa, I would like you to stay."

Agrippa turned back, moving to a chair, then sitting down as Octavian moved back behind the desk, taking his own seat. I was unsure what to do, so I decided to follow my instinct and continue standing. It is a good thing that I did. As soon as the door closed, the smile and the warmth fled from Octavian's face, replaced with what I can only describe as something that reminded me of the winter seas between Gaul and Britannia, icy and unrelenting.

"Well, Pullus. It seems that you've gotten yourself into quite a predicament," Octavian began, his voice as cold as the rest of his demeanor.

Despite trying to prepare myself for this eventuality, Octavian's initial greeting had lulled me into believing that perhaps it would not be so bad. Now I was off-balance, which is exactly what Octavian was aiming for, and he did not give me a chance to respond.

"If my fellow Triumvir is to be believed, at the very least you're incompetent, and at the worst, you're complicit in the murder of Legionaries of Rome."

I was unsure if he was finished, so I said nothing.

Finally, he raised one eyebrow, asking sarcastically, "Has the great Titus Pullus been struck dumb? What is your response to these charges?"

Suddenly all the words I had carefully rehearsed in my mind fled at the very moment I needed them most, and all I could manage was a half-grunt, half-squawk.

"He's lying."

Octavian sat back, regarding me with that reptilian gaze as it finally fell into place why it had seemed familiar. When we had been waiting to fight Pharnaces, when I was with the 6th Legion, I had passed the part of a day watching a large lizard that seemed to be sunning itself on a rock, its eyes unmoving and unblinking, seemingly oblivious to the world around it. As I watched, a fly landed on the lizard, obviously thinking that the creature was dead and was offering itself up for a feast. The lizard did not flinch or move in any way, letting the fly wander up its body. Not even the blink of an eye betrayed that it was living, until the fly moved onto the head, then the nose of the lizard. Suddenly, with a movement so blindingly fast that my own eye could not track it, the lizard struck, its tongue sweeping out and up, snatching the fly, which disappeared down its gullet. The lizard never blinked, or moved anything other than its tongue as I watched it feed itself in this manner for more than a third of a watch. This is what I was reminded of with Octavian watching me before he finally spoke, the sarcasm still present.

"Well, you make a compelling argument, Primus Pilus, but I think I'm going to have to have a little more than that if you expect my help."

So then I told him the whole story, leaving nothing out, deciding that it was much more dangerous to lie to Octavian, even if it was by omission, than it was to tell everything, no matter how damaging it was to me or other people. He sat listening, sometimes glancing at Agrippa, who was sitting stone-faced and silent, communicating with him through a raised eyebrow, a shrug of a shoulder, or even a small smile as I talked. When I had finished, he said nothing for several moments, choosing instead to play with a stylus, tossing it end over end, catching it as he considered the problem. When he spoke, it was in a dispassionate tone, devoid of any inflection that might give me a hint of his true feelings.

"Lepidus is a fool," he began, "but he is also a Triumvir, like me. For me or Antonius to intervene in this matter requires the expenditure of political capital, something I do not expect you to understand, at least completely."

He stopped, as if gauging my reaction to what can only be described as an insult. I was determined not to reward his jab with anything other than the calculatedly blank stare that we gave officers when they were talking nonsense. Still, I could feel my fists clench as I realized that he was testing me, trying to find out my soft spots. Seeing no outward reaction, he gave a slight smile then continued.

"So if I am going to expend that capital, it only makes sense that I replace what I lose from somewhere. I don't suppose you have an idea where I'm going to find that capital, do you?"

In fact, I had a very good idea where it was coming from, but I decided that I would exact my own petty revenge for his earlier insult by playing the role that he ascribed to me, the stupid Legionary.

"No sir, I don't," I replied earnestly, and I was rewarded by a flash of irritation on his face.

"You, Pullus. I'm going to get paid back by you."

Now I was careful to keep my face blank, knowing that I was swimming in very, very dangerous waters. Men of my status are used as pieces in a game by the upper classes all the time, and our pieces are always the least valuable and most likely to be sacrificed.

However, we are expected to cooperate, doing what is expected of us without complaint or with any indication that we are anything but passive players, content with being sacrificed in some patrician's game. If we display any independence or resistance to accepting our fates, then it is an even earlier end to our string than if we had gone along, playing the part given to us. Octavian seemed to sense my inner turmoil, or maybe he understood how a man would have a natural resistance to having his fate determined for him, because he peered at me closely, watching me for some reaction that would indicate I rejected his plan. If I made the wrong move, if I gave him any indication that I was not willing to go along, or if he doubted my sincerity as I agreed, my life was just as surely ended as if I had never come to him and let Lepidus win.

"Not much of a choice, is it?" he asked softly.

"No, it's not," I blurted, but even though I winced at my tongue running off without my mind's permission again, he did not seem to take offense, in fact giving me a smile and a nod.

"But that's the choice facing you, Pullus," he said evenly. "Should you accept my assistance in this matter, you will be one of my creatures, as my enemies call them, though I can't imagine them saying anything like that to Agrippa's face, or yours, for that matter."

Agrippa gave a grim smile at the mention of his name as I consoled myself with the thought that I was being included with the likes of Agrippa.

I drew a deep breath, then said, "I accept, Caesar. Whatever you can do to help me will put me forever in your debt, and I'll be your man, as I was your father's."

Octavian nodded, clearly pleased, before his face turned grave again.

"While I can make this go away as far as you're concerned, Pullus, I'm afraid that at the end of it, the laws of Rome must be respected. Your Princeps Posterior Tetarfenus must be punished; he must die."

I drew a sharp breath as time seemed to stand still. I opened my mouth to protest, but nothing came out. Finally, I closed my eyes, simply nodding instead. With that gesture, I sacrificed one of my own men to save my life and career. With our business concluded, Octavian indicated that I should leave the room, asking me to tell the others to reenter.

"They're probably listening at the keyhole," Agrippa remarked, and they both laughed, but I did not share in the laughter.

I was about to open the door when Octavian called out to me. I turned and he was standing by his desk looking nothing like the dazzled young boy I remembered.

"One other thing, Pullus," he said as if he had forgotten to mention that chickpeas were being served for dinner. "I want you to keep our agreement to yourself, and that means from everyone, do you understand? Nobody must know, at least until I deem the time right to make it known."

I simply nodded, thinking bitterly that I had just become one of Octavian's agents that we all feared and loathed. I left his house, my stomach churning, trying to come to grips with all that had taken place. I had saved my life and my career, but I had betrayed a man who looked to me for protection and leadership. The idea that Tetarfenus was doomed no matter what I did never occurred to me, at least until someone else pointed it out to me. Although I look back now and realize that if I had died, he was still going to be alongside me, it does not make me feel any better. But even worse than that was the price I had to pay to save myself, because I had always prided myself on being above such seamy acts as selling my services. What I realize now is how much I had been shielded from how things were really done in Rome by virtue of my lowly status, and by Caesar himself. I had spent more time with the man than almost every other man in his army, at least those of us from the ranks, yet he had only talked of politics in the most general of terms, never talking specifically about doing the type of thing that Octavian had done with me. I know that I was naïve, about both Octavian and Caesar, since Octavian had sat at Caesar's knee soaking up the lessons from the great man. That did not make me feel any better as I was walking back to camp, my mind occupied with how I would tell Tetarfenus that his time on this earth was up.

By the time I arrived at my quarters, word of my trip to see Octavian had spread, so my office was crowded with the Pili Priores and the Centurions of the First Cohort. They were standing, most of them with what I took to be sincere looks of concern, though I noticed a couple of men who seemed more curious than anything, reminding me of the fact that there were men who would always be focused on how any event impacted their own fortunes before anything else. Scribonius looked concerned, which I knew was genuine, and I tried to reward him with a smile, but I found my lips could not make the necessary effort.

"Octavian will take care of it," I said loudly enough for everyone to hear, followed by a burst of air as men exhaled, before I was assaulted by slaps on the back and shoulders.

Only Scribonius knew me well enough to know that there was something more, and after thanking the men for showing their support, I dismissed all of them except for Scribonius, who I brought into my private quarters. I collapsed in a chair, and without asking, Diocles brought some wine, though I was suddenly struck with a craving for a kind of spirit that is popular among some of the Gauls, particularly the Britons, made of fermented honey. It tastes horrible, but it is incredibly potent, and more than anything at this moment, I wanted to make myself insensible. I took several gulps, emptying two cups before I felt able to speak. Then I told Scribonius and Diocles what had transpired, and what it would cost. After I finished, neither of them said anything for several moments.

Finally, Scribonius spoke.

"You understand that in all likelihood Tetarfenus was a dead man either way, don't you? Once Lepidus got involved, the die was cast as far as he was concerned. Now all that matters is that you're safe."

I gave a bitter laugh. "I doubt Tetarfenus would see it that way."

Scribonius shook his head sharply. "He had no business doing what he did, and you know it. We may understand why he did it, but when he decided to act on his own, without going through the proper channels, he threw the dice and they came up against him."

Diocles was no less adamant in his assessment. "It can be argued that Tetarfenus deserves his fate for endangering you and Nasica, though from everything I hear, Nasica knew what was happening and approved it."

I sat up; that was the first I had heard that Nasica had known, something he had vigorously denied when I had asked him about it. More importantly, it was something Tetarfenus had substantiated.

"How did you hear this?" I demanded.

Diocles looked at me calmly, accustomed to my bluster at this point and knowing that I would not take out my anger on him if he gave me an answer I did not want to hear.

"From Tetarfenus' body slave," he answered. "He said his master was drunk and talking to his brother one night. He told him that he and Nasica had discussed what to do about the murder of their men, and they came up with this plan. Except that Nasica supposedly swore to Tetarfenus that he would step forward and protect him if things got hot."

"They got hot all right," I said bitterly.

"To be fair to Nasica," Scribonius pointed out, "none of us thought that Lepidus would use this as his chance to get even."

That was true, but it did not change the fact that now Nasica was letting Tetarfenus twist in the breeze alone, so I was now confronted with a new problem to deal with at some point. First though, I had to tell Tetarfenus the bad news.

Before I sent for Tetarfenus, I had Diocles summon Nasica, as I thought about what to do with him. My first job was to determine what the truth was, yet I knew in my gut that what Diocles had recounted was the real story, and I wanted to see how Nasica reacted when I confronted him. However, even if he admitted that he told Tetarfenus that he would protect his subordinate, at that point there was not much I was willing to do about it. Enough lives had been lost; if I made Nasica's betrayal of Tetarfenus public and demanded a trial, it would only provide Lepidus with evidence that his charges against my weak leadership were true. I doubted that even in that event, he would be able to overcome Octavian, but it was not something I was willing to risk. When Nasica arrived, I did not bother with any of the formalities or niceties, so that when I did not give him leave to sit, he knew that I was in no mood to be trifled with. I think that contributed to his lack of resistance when I started pressing him about his role in the affair, starting out with what I had been told by Diocles, though I did not attribute where I had heard it. No sooner were the words out of my mouth than his shoulders slumped, his head dropping so that I could not see his face.

"It's true," he said in a hoarse whisper, and even I could not mistake the anguish in his tone. "I did tell him that, but then when Lepidus got involved, I got scared."

He refused to look at me as he said this. I found myself torn between compassion and revulsion for what he had done, knowing how much it cost a man who was a Centurion of Rome to make such an admission, while despising him for abandoning one of his men. Although he would not meet my gaze, I did not doubt the sincerity of his anguish, and for several moments, neither of us spoke. I was thinking about what I could do, even unofficially, to punish Nasica for his betrayal of Tetarfenus, but staring at him, I realized that he was punishing himself in ways that I could not match. Besides, we had already had enough trouble taking matters into our own hands.

I sighed, then said, "You're lucky, Nasica, since because of the circumstances I'm not willing to take any further action against you. But you're going to have to live with your betrayal of Tetarfenus for the rest of your days, however long that may be. I'm not going to strip you of your rank and position, though I have every right to, under both regulations and custom. There's nothing worse than betraying one of your men, and that's a stain on your name that will never wash off."

His head sunk even deeper, reacting to my words as if they were hammer blows. I suppose, in a sense, they were just that.

"Are you going to tell the other Centurions?" he asked dully.

And that was the second nub of the problem; despite giving me some personal satisfaction to leak word of what Nasica had done, it would destroy his effectiveness as the Pilus Prior of the Tenth Cohort, as well as endanger his life. While the latter prospect was not as unpleasant or as high a priority as the former, I was mindful of what was behind my decision in the first place, to end the bloodshed with Tetarfenus.

With that in mind, I replied, "No. I'm not going to tell anyone anything. But," I leaned forward so he could not avoid my gaze, "you're going with me to tell Tetarfenus what he must do. And you're going to have to endure whatever he has to say. I think that will be at least a partial punishment for what you've done."

His shoulders started shaking, I supposed at the thought of having to face Tetarfenus.

"And Nasica," I had one last detail to attend to, "there's something else you need to do, and you need to do it quickly and quietly."

He looked at me now, his expression wary, and with tears in his eyes.

"It concerns Tetarfenus' body slave. You need to sell him to someone outside the army. Immediately."

It took a moment for the meaning of what I had just said to register, then I saw his face redden, his lips thinning in anger.

Before he could say anything, I held up my hand.

"You will sell him, and he will be unmarked in any way," I said forcefully. "And I'm going to personally inspect him before the bill of sale is signed to make sure he's unharmed. Do you understand me?"

I imagine it would have been easier and in many ways neater to let Nasica do whatever he was going to do with the body slave, but not only had there been enough bloodshed, I wanted the existence of that slave niggling at the back of Nasica's mind for the rest of his days.

Suddenly inspired, I continued, "I'll witness the sale, so I know the identity of the new owner and where he lives. Just in case," I finished ominously.

Just as quickly as the blood came to his face, it drained away. I stood up, beckoning Nasica to follow me.

"We're going to fetch Tetarfenus now," I announced.

For a moment, I did not think he would obey. Finally, he moved to follow me, and I could clearly see his legs shaking, though I did not make any comment about it. I pushed past him and out the door.

Tetarfenus was in his quarters, but as I had feared, he was not alone. His Optio and the Sergeants of his Century were with him, so when I entered they all jumped to their feet to form a protective ring around him.

"Stand down, boys," I heard a voice say, then Tetarfenus pushed his way through them to face us.

When he saw Nasica, his lips thinned and he seemed about to speak before his mouth snapped shut, for which I silently thanked the gods.

"Decimus Princeps Posterior Tetarfenus, you need to come with us." I kept my voice flat and emotionless, yet maintained a tone that told men who had followed me for years that there would be no argument accepted at my order.

Again, the men around him tried to nudge him back, and while it was good to see they were showing such loyalty to their Centurion, I roared, "I am your Primus Pilus! Every one of you is under my command and my control and by the gods you will OBEY!"

I have been told that my anger is terrible to behold, and I unleashed every ounce of energy in my body in that command. I was grimly pleased at the sight of their blanched faces and the way their resistance melted like lard in a hot pan. Only Tetarfenus did not seem to be cowed, but I suppose that he understood the situation. When all hope is gone, there is not much of which to be afraid.

Stepping forward, he looked over his shoulder at his men, and despite his face being turned away, I could hear the smile in his voice as he said, "It's all right, boys. We all have to go sometime, and it's been a privilege and honor being your Centurion."

Then he surprised me, and I imagine everyone else when he turned to me.

"And I want everyone to know that I hold no hard feelings towards the Primus Pilus, for anything. He gave me a chance to be a Centurion, and I'll always be in his debt, no matter what happens. He's just doing what he has to do, and in his place, I imagine I would do the same."

He turned back to his men, shaking their hands one by one, before embracing each of them, whispering something meant for only their ears. Despite my resolve, I felt a lump form in my throat. Here was a leader of men, to his very last moment.

Once finished, he walked over to me, saying with only a slight tremor in his voice, "I'm ready, Primus Pilus. Let's get going."

Without waiting, he walked past me out the door to face his fate. Not lost on me, or anyone else in the room, was that Tetarfenus spoke not a word to or about Nasica, nor even acknowledged his existence.

His contempt for his former Pilus Prior could not have been made plainer, and whatever my personal feelings towards Nasica may have been, I did not envy his position with the men of the Tenth Cohort.

We returned to my quarters, where I had ordered Diocles to prepare my personal room. Spread on the floor was a large linen cloth that would serve as Tetarfenus' shroud, while I had cleared my personal shrine so that Tetarfenus could put his family gods on it to make his final prayers. As my last punishment of Nasica, I required him to act as witness. I also asked Corbulo to attend so that he could see that justice was done for his men, and to act as an impartial witness. For my own purposes, I had asked Scribonius to attend as well, which he agreed to do, albeit very grudgingly. We gave Tetarfenus time alone to say his words, while the rest of us stood in my outer office, talking quietly. Nasica stood in a corner by himself, which suited me fine, and we were talking softly enough that I could hear his sobs. Finally, the door opened and Tetarfenus' body slave, the man who had unwittingly created so many extra problems, came out to announce that his master was ready. We filed in, as I made sure that I screened Nasica from the slave, just in case Nasica's passions got the better of his reason, but all he did was glare at the man. Tetarfenus was standing in the center of the sheet. For the first time I could see fear on his face, his bare skin with a sheen of sweat covering it. He was trembling a bit, though otherwise was acting with great composure given the circumstances.

I offered him the use of my blade, but he declined, saying, "I want to use my own sword one last time, if that is all right."

"Of course," I agreed, and I do not know why, yet this was the most difficult point for me, as a flood of memories came rushing back.

"I remember when I first saw you," I whispered to him.

His eyes filled with tears, as did mine. "I remember. We were standing in formation, waiting for some jumped-up bastard from the 10th who liked to keep us waiting." He smiled at the memory, as did I.

Suddenly, he frowned, then his voice choked with emotion. "What are you going to tell Gaius?"

Gaius Tetarfenus was his brother, and had opted to end his enlistment to return to Hispania, where he took his grant of land and was now a farmer. Although he was technically still under the standard for a second enlistment, given that he had served in the 6th Legion prior to joining his brother in the second enlistment of the 10th, after a very boring first two years, he had decided that he would try his hand as a farmer. I was able to hide his transfer out in the paperwork, not begrudging his early departure, mainly because of his service to me in Egypt and out of respect to his brother, who I had promoted. Now he was a farmer somewhere.

"I'm going to tell him that you died fighting, with a blade in your hand and dead men at your feet."

"But in what battle? We're not fighting right now."

"Don't worry, I'll think of something," I assured him. "Trust me, he'll know that you're a good man who went down fighting. He'll never know it was by your own hand."

I stepped away, then said in a more formal tone. "Decimus Princeps Posterior Tetarfenus, are there any last words you wish to speak?"

He thought a moment, then turned to face Nasica. For a long moment, he just stared at his Pilus Prior before spitting on the floor, looking back at me, and shaking his head. Nothing could have been more eloquent than that gesture; not even Cicero or Caesar could have topped it.

Without any warning, he grabbed the hilt of his sword with both hands, plunging the blade deep into his abdomen, angling the blade upward with his thrust. His aim was true, his strike was hard, the blade obviously piercing his heart, because with little more than a grunt, he toppled over, dead before we could reach him. I knelt by his side, taking one still-warm hand in mine, then closed his eyes while putting a coin in his mouth to pay the ferryman, saying a brief prayer as I did so. It was in this manner that I thought this whole sorry affair was over and done with; I had made sure that Octavian's condition was met, while Corbulo could go to Lepidus to report that justice had been done, even if it was not in the exact manner that the Triumvir would have wanted. I was expecting some problems from Lepidus on that front, and trouble did come, just not from the quarter I expected.

"Did you plan on disobeying me the whole time, or was it something that just occurred to you after you left here? Was I not explicit enough?"

I was standing once again in front of Octavian, this time at his office on the Campus Martius, having responded to a curt summons from one of his creatures. He was visibly angry, and while he did not have the same kind of awful majesty of Caesar in a rage, there was something quite chilling in the coldness radiating from him. Where Caesar was fire, Octavian was ice, but there was no mistaking that the adopted son was just as dangerous, though right then I was more puzzled than afraid. I shook my head.

"I'm sorry, Triumvir, I'm afraid I don't understand. I didn't disobey any order you gave me."

"Oh really?" he said, his voice heavy with sarcasm, then he looked over at Agrippa, who this time was not alone on the couch.

Sitting next to him was a slightly pudgy young man about Agrippa's age, with the darker hair and complexion of a provincial, but who was even more richly dressed than either of the other two. There was a slightly feminine manner about him, perhaps in the delicate way that he crossed his legs, or fiddled with a string of beads in his hands, and I deduced that this was the other member of Octavian's inner council, Gaius Maecenas. He looked at me as if examining some particularly odious type of insect, while Agrippa wore his usual stony expression, but his eyes were as cold as Octavian's, and I turned back to face the young Caesar.

"Then perhaps you can explain this," he said as he pushed forward an urn, which I recognized immediately, then understood what this was all about.

"Those are the ashes of Quintus Tetarfenus," I said.

"Yes, that's exactly what they are. And why do I have this urn sitting on my desk now, before there was a trial and an execution?"

He sat back, then folded his arms, waiting for me to speak.

"Triumvir, as you made it clear, Princeps Posterior Tetarfenus had to die. He's dead, granted by his own hand, but that doesn't make him any less dead."

"That's not the point," he snapped, clearly nettled. "He needed to stand trial; he needed to be executed in the proper way, in front of witnesses. It was important that he be held accountable in an official manner."

Now I was getting angry, so I am afraid my tone was not as respectful as it should have been as I snapped back, "Which you didn't specify in any way.

You said that he had to die. The words 'trial' and 'execution' never left your mouth, at least to me."

There was a shocked silence as Octavian sat back, his face white with anger, his lips thin and bloodless.

My salvation came from an unexpected source, as I heard Agrippa speak.

"Triumvir, I'm sorry to say that the Primus Pilus is correct in what he says. You said that the man had to die, but you didn't go into detail about the manner in which it happened, although I have to say that it was obvious to me what you meant."

"You can hardly expect a man of the Primus Pilus' background to understand the necessities and nuances of politics," Maecenas said in a voice that underscored my initial impression of his femininity. While he spoke the truth, I certainly did not like it coming out of his mouth.

Octavian gave a snort, but his shoulders slumped as he waved a hand at me. "Fine," he said disgustedly. "It seems that you have unexpected allies, Pullus."

He glared over at the two men on the couch, yet I was interested to see neither of them blanch. In fact, Maecenas gave Octavian an impertinent grin, which forced a laugh from the young Triumvir.

Turning back to me, he waved to the door.

"Very well, Pullus. I accept that I may not have been as explicit as I should have been. In the future, if my orders seem vague, I'll expect you to ask me for further clarification in order to avoid any further confusion. Is that clear?"

In answer, I gave a salute, then Octavian dismissed me. I marched from the room, thinking about what he had said of a next time.

It was just a day or two after that I received another summons, this time from Lepidus. I did not mind receiving this summons, because I was confident in Octavian, knowing that he was infinitely more powerful than Lepidus. When I arrived, my faith was rewarded by the sight of his face, which looked as if he had just swallowed a turd. Without any pleasantries, he looked down at his ever-present scroll, blank as usual, as he cleared his throat.

"After further investigation, I have determined that your Princeps Posterior in fact acted alone and without your knowledge, and that there was no way that you could realistically foresee the events that took place with his Century. Therefore, given that your Princeps Posterior chose to end his own life, and because of the facts I have just described, this matter is closed and no further action will be taken."

He looked up at me. For a moment, the mask that was his face slipped, his mouth twisting in a bitter grimace. "You are free to go and continue your duties as Primus Pilus, and there will be no adverse entry into your record."

I did not move; somehow, I knew that he had something more to say, and he in fact did have one surprise in store.

"However, the men who participated in the killings of the men of the 4th must be punished. They will be given 30 lashes each with the scourge."

"No," I said instantly as his mouth dropped open in shock. "They were following orders of their Centurion, and he's dead. It's over. No more."

I did not wait for a response, just turned on my heel to walk out, not bothering with a salute. He did not say a word, while the men were never punished. The affair ended that day, though the knowledge that I was now one of Octavian's puppets, waiting for him to pull my strings, was never far from my mind.

Chapter 2- The Liberators

While the Triumvirs were busy settling affairs in Rome by proscribing seemingly all of Rome's upper classes, Brutus and Cassius had been busy in their own right. When Brutus first captured, then executed Gaius Antonius as governor of Macedonia, he ended up inheriting two Legions, which supposedly declared their loyalty for The Liberators. Then the Legion in Illyricum, under the command of Publius Vatinius, also went over to Brutus, ceding control of the province to Brutus as well. Cassius had gone on to Syria, where he had served previously as *de facto* governor, being the only man of his rank to escape the debacle at Carrhae when Crassus and his son, along with the majority of his army, perished, turning back up in Syria with quite a tale to tell. The seven Legions in Syria, along with the four still in Egypt, including my friend Cartufenus and the 28th all went over to Cassius. Suddenly, the two primary members of The Liberators each had a sizable army, although at that point they were still separated by a great distance.

On his own, Brutus knew that he could not hope to defeat the combined forces of Antonius and Octavian, so he began plans to march east, taking the overland route through Thrace and the Hellespont, heading for a linkage with Cassius. While Dolabella was busy torturing Trebonius, Cassius had wasted no time in getting to Syria, so that when Dolabella finally arrived with his two Legions, Cassius was too strong and firmly in control for Dolabella to do anything other than to seek refuge in Laodicea. Cassius immediately invested the city, and with ships he hired from Sidon and Tyre, affected a complete blockade from which there was no hope of escape. Dolabella knew that he could expect no mercy from one of The Liberators, so he committed suicide instead of allowing himself to fall into Cassius' hands. Cassius inherited Dolabella's two Legions, and now with a huge army to feed and maintain, began squeezing the cities of Asia for anything and everything of any value. Cassius began marching westward, while Brutus marched eastward, so when they met they would have a huge army that we had to defeat.

It was around this time that I received a piece of news from Scribonius, who appeared in my quarters with a grim expression. He was holding a small scroll of the type that we used to send home and received as mail, which he waved at me as he sat heavily across from me.

"No use beating about the bush with this. It's from Vibius."

I involuntarily stiffened at the mention of my former best friend's name before I made an effort to compose myself to affect an air of indifference.

"And?" I asked as casually as I could make my voice. "What's so important that you come running over here looking as if the world is coming to an end?"

"He's signed up again."

I sat back, all sorts of emotions flooding through me, but before I could say anything, Scribonius had more to tell me.

"He's not marching with us; he's marching with Brutus."

I suppose I should not have been surprised, given Vibius' feelings about Caesar and his belief that Caesar was the ruin of the Republic, rather than a man who recognized that the Republic was already dead and was trying to save Rome from itself, but I was nonetheless.

"Brutus?" I gasped. "Why on Gaia's earth would he be marching with Brutus?" Before Scribonius could answer, I grumbled, "Don't answer that. I know why."

"He says he was approached by a recruiting officer working for Brutus and that he was offered a Centurionate rank of the fifth grade."

I gave a short, bitter laugh. "Well, Vibius is finally a Centurion. He never wanted it when he was with us. Why now?"

"Money," Scribonius said flatly, waving the scroll again. "It seems that things didn't go well with his business, something about a fire and the drought that hurt the grape crop."

"Grapes?" I did not understand. "How does that hurt the tanning business?"

Scribonius gave me a look that I could not easily interpret, then shook his head.

"Vibius didn't go into the tanning business. He bought a tavern that he and Juno run, and apparently, it burned down, so they rebuilt it. Then, because of the drought last year, the cost of wine went sky-high and all his cash reserves had been eaten up rebuilding the tavern. So he needs the money, and Brutus is paying the same bonuses that Octavian did."

"He said all that in that letter?" I pointed to the scroll.

Now, Scribonius looked a little uneasy. "Not all of it," he admitted. "I knew that he had bought a tavern. I knew about the fire; that happened a few months ago. The rest of it he told me now."

"So you've been in contact with Vibius all this time?" I demanded, angry but not sure why.

Scribonius' chin lifted, his eyes narrowing, a sign that he was getting angry himself.

"He's my friend, Titus, maybe not as long as you were friends, but we shared a lot over the years."

My anger evaporated as I slumped back in my chair, knowing he was right.

"Why didn't you tell me all this before?"

"You never asked," he replied. "Besides, you never gave any indication that you cared to know what Vibius was doing with his life after . . . that day."

There was no need for him to elaborate on what day he was talking about, as I was suddenly transported back to the hot, dusty plain of Pharsalus, standing there facing my best friend with a sword in my hand, ready to strike him down for participating in the mutiny of the 10th Legion. The sight of his dust-covered face, the rivulets of sweat making streaks where the tanned leather of his flesh showed through, his eyes bright with anger and defiance was so vivid that I half-expected to see him standing there in front of me in my quarters on the Campus Martius.

"He asks about you all the time." Scribonius' voice snapped me out of my dream-like state, but I did not say anything, just looked at him.

"He and Juno have a child, a boy." I was not sure where Scribonius was going with this, but I had a sneaking suspicion, and he confirmed it by finishing, "They named him 'Titus.'"

Another memory flashed in front of my mind's eye, this time of another little boy, with a honey-smeared face and clutching a toy soldier that his father had given him, a boy I had named for my then-best friend Vibius, although we called him Vibi. For a moment, I thought my heart would literally burst with the pain of thinking of my old friend's namesake, dead now for longer than he had been alive, and I was glad that only Scribonius was present. I shook my head, trying to get the images out of my mind, trying to listen to what Scribonius was saying. He had moved on to some other topic, but my mind kept returning back to what he had said. Vibius had a son, and now he was marching for The Liberators, while at some point in the near future, we were going to be marching to face Brutus and Cassius. Despite knowing that the possibility of actually seeing him across from me at some battle in the future was remote, it still gnawed at me. That day at Pharsalus my anger was so great that I know I would have killed him, yet that had been long ago, so if we did face each other in battle, it would be completely different. There would be no flaring tempers, no passion of the moment. It would be killing because that was our job, and I did not know if I had it in me to kill him in cold blood. The idea that he could kill me never really occurred to me, for a variety of reasons, not all of them my own hubris. He had been out of the Legions for a few years, while I was still practicing at least a third of a watch a day, every day, in the same manner I had been doing for 18 years. I was about to turn 34 in a few months, and while I had lost a bit of flexibility in my upper body as a result of the wound I suffered at Munda, I was still as strong as I was in my youth. My endurance was good, although I did notice that it took me a bit longer to recover from particularly strenuous efforts than when I was younger. I just hoped that it would never come to a point where I would find out if I was right.

A couple of things delayed the Triumvirs from ordering us to march. One was that there were reports streaming in, most of them conflicting, about the location of Brutus and Cassius respectively. Part of the confusion stemmed from the fact that both of them were marching all over the hinterland of the Republic squeezing money from all the petty princes and client kings. Brutus was renowned for his greed and love of money, which apparently is not considered worthy of a patrician, although every one of them loves what money brings. I have noticed that patricians do not care about money as long as they have it.

The other reason, probably the most pressing, was that the Triumvirs, at least Antonius and Octavian, had decided that when we did finally pin Brutus and Cassius down, we would travel by sea, except the seas were controlled by Sextus Pompey, who at that point was friendlier to The Liberators than to the Triumvirs. It was a problem that had no immediate solution; while the two Triumvirs tried to solve it, we sat and did little but train on the posts, day in and day out. It was exceedingly difficult to keep men from growing slack when all they had to do was to whack at wooden posts with wooden swords, with an occasional mock battle thrown in. Early on, we tried pitting one Legion against another in exercises, except it soon became apparent that if we wanted to avoid men killing each other, we needed to confine the mock battles to men from the same Legion. Even so, as time passed, men became more and more frustrated at the lack of action, the exercises becoming more and more heated. We were still not allowed to march into the countryside, so we tried to keep the men fit by marching them around the Campus Martius, but the monotony of that wore on everyone, the Centurions included. While the 10th was technically a veteran Legion, the new men of this enlistment had still not been blooded, which gnawed at me more than anything, not knowing exactly how they would react when the time came and the fighting was real.

Meanwhile, the months marched by. On the other hand, we did not, so that it was not until Januarius of the next year that the Primi Pili were summoned to the villa on the Campus Martius, which served as the

Praetorium whenever Antonius was present. Antonius and Octavian had worked out some system that gave them the command of the army on alternating weeks, so their mutual hostility meant that they were rarely, if ever, in joint command, or even used the same building for their respective headquarters. It was quite complicated, trying to remember who was commanding the army at any given time, and I was just thankful that both men had dropped any pretense of including Lepidus, who was forced to content himself with his duties as Pontifex Maximus. When we were assembled, we were met by Antonius, who strode into the room with red-rimmed eyes and a surly disposition.

"He's hung over," whispered Corbulo, who I was standing next to as we stood to *intente*.

He certainly looked that way to me, but I had never paid much attention to the actions of Antonius, at least as far as they did not impact me, so I just shrugged.

"Just like half the men on any given day," I whispered back, but instead of a laugh, it elicited a grunt that I interpreted as disagreement of some type.

While Antonius busied himself snapping at some hapless Tribune attending him, I looked at Corbulo with a raised eyebrow.

Seeing me look at him, he looked a bit uncomfortable before he broke eye contact, looking away. He said defensively, "He's always drunk, carrying on like I don't know what. Did you hear about the time he tried to harness lions to a chariot?"

Of course, I had; not a Roman alive had not heard the tale by that point, but I did not see his point and I said so.

"It's just that he's one of the men running Rome right now. I would expect that he'd cut back on some of his binges. He's got a lot of responsibilities."

I could not help laughing. Nothing I had ever seen in the actions of Marcus Antonius led me to believe that he was capable of moderation in anything.

"That's asking a lot," I replied, but before the conversation could continue, Antonius finally called the meeting to order.

"I didn't ask you here to hear you chatter," he said sourly. "I've decided that we're going to move the army in preparation for finally putting those *cunni* Brutus and Cassius down to avenge the death of Caesar."

Now, this was about the most self-serving, cynical piece of talk I had heard, even coming from a man as self-serving and cynical as Antonius, who seemed oblivious to the sidelong glances we gave each other. It had been Antonius who instituted the policy of amnesty covering The Liberators, making public announcements that they were forgiven; now here he was acting as if he had always been about exacting retribution against them.

"I've also decided that we'll be moving by sea, and to that end we're going to begin transferring the army down to Brundisium. My Tribunes will be posting the schedule of movement by the end of the day. The first Legions need to be ready to march in ten days, and the entire army will be moved by the end of the month."

Instead of the usual buzzing of conversation, the silence was total, blanketing the room and was something that not even Antonius could ignore. Looking around at us, glaring at first one face then another, he finally let out a huge sigh, throwing his hands up in the air.

"What is it now? Somebody tell me."

There was a pause, then I heard a voice that I recognized as Torquatus' ask, "What about Sextus and his fleets?"

"That's for me to worry about," Antonius snapped. "Your job is to make your men ready to march. That is all."

With that, he turned then stalked out of the room, leaving a now-buzzing room behind him as we all began talking.

While I was thankful that we now had things to keep the men busy, it also meant that once again there were a thousand details to attend to, and as we were at least in theory marching to go into battle, that meant that everything had to be checked from the ground up. Although to that point we had never used any of our artillery for anything except training, the wood on some of the ballistae and scorpions was cracked and needed to be replaced, meaning that seasoned wood had to be found, which of course was high on the list of every other Legion who faced the same problem. There had been a bad drought throughout the countryside the year before, so that we had dug more deeply into the reserves of our food stores than we normally would have, and now that shortfall had to be made up somehow. We were one of the Legions marching the first day, requiring us to work the hardest, but the Centurions knew what they were about, so the work went as smoothly as could be expected. Right on schedule, we marched off the Campus Martius, heading down the Via Appia for Brundisium, the men in high spirits, and truth be known, so were the Centurions. We had been cooped up on the Campus for almost a year, and there is nothing quite like marching down the open road with your comrades. Even with the inevitable straggling and moaning, it was the happiest I had seen the men for some time. We did not march at quite the pace of a Caesar, but we covered more than 20 miles a day, and as we got fitter from the daily marching, the distance extended a little every day.

Once we arrived in Brundisium, I was happy to learn that the restrictions from marching about the countryside of Campania were not in place here, the Triumvirs obviously not as concerned for the citizens around Brundisium as they were around Campania. Whatever the reason, it allowed us to take the men out to continue their training, making sure the fitness they gained on the march down was not lost. Over a period of a couple of weeks, almost the rest of the army came down to Brundisium, whereupon we prepared for the second part of the operation: the transport of the army to Greece. Despite Antonius assuring us that there was nothing to worry about on the part of Sextus, from everything we were hearing we had plenty of cause for concern. Sextus was master of Sicily, and when Octavian sent one of his most trusted men, Salvidienus Rufus, to expel Sextus and capture his fleet, he was soundly defeated by Pompey's sole surviving son. That meant that Sextus' fleet was not tied down in any way, so with that in mind, I paid a hefty bribe to one of Antonius' Tribunes to ensure that we were not part of the advance wave going to Greece. I did not want untested men trapped onboard ships if Sextus' fleet showed up because it was nerve-wracking enough for veterans to be in that situation. We then spent the next few months waiting again as the Triumvirs squabbled about what to do about Sextus, along with just about everything else. As it turned out, I did not have to worry, since apparently Antonius paid a bribe of his own, this to Sextus, because his fleet was nowhere to be seen as the army finally made its crossing. We went in the third wave, just ahead of the last that carried supplies and the stragglers from the Legions that had already shipped over. This last wave was the only group that had any trouble, although it was from a fleet belonging to The Liberators and not Sextus, a couple of ships being lost. The advance guard had immediately started east along the Via Egnatia, while as soon as the rest of the army was gathered, we followed behind. The latest intelligence had Brutus and Cassius much further west, beyond the end of the Via Egnatia, though we did not know if they were marching towards us or were waiting for us.

On the march, I was disturbed by the mood of the men, who seemed much too subdued for my comfort. While I was aware that this march was different from everything we had done to date; we were, after all, marching to battle, at least that was the feeling among all of us, it was still unsettling to see the men in this state. Before, we marched from one place to another even though the prospect for a fight had been remote, yet this time there was a high probability that we would be standing in line, looking over our shields at men we were supposed to kill, and it was clear that this was very much on the men's minds.

Finally, one night I called the Pili Priores together to talk about what I was seeing.

"What's the problem with the men?" I demanded, looking from one face to another, who in turn were looking at each other, waiting for someone to speak.

Finally, Scribonius took it upon himself and answered, "They're worried," he replied, causing me to snort in derision.

"I know that," I shot back. "But why? We weren't like that back in Hispania against the Lusitani, and we had only been training for a couple of months when we fought our first battle."

"I think that's part of the problem," Scribonius countered, and I knew well enough to keep my mouth shut to let him talk. "They've had more than three years to sit and wonder what it's going to be like, and to hear the stories of the veterans about how horrible it will be, and how many friends they're going to lose. We didn't have much time to think about it before we were actually doing it."

"And they don't have Caesar," Nigidius added, and I saw everyone's head nodding at this.

I sighed, knowing that Scribonius had touched the nub of the problem, while Nigidius had spoken truly as well.

"So what do we do about it?" I asked, but this time, nobody had anything to say, no matter how much I prodded.

Finally, Scribonius shrugged, then said, "We can make offerings to Mars and Bellona that when the time comes, they'll do what they're supposed to."

With that encouraging word, I dismissed the Pili Priores, then sat and brooded the rest of the night.

The advance guard was commanded jointly by men named Norbanus and Saxa, and we received word that they had made contact with the forces of Brutus and Cassius at the far eastern end of the Via Egnatia, so in response they split their forces. Saxa occupied the high ground at the Pass of Sapaei, a few miles northeast of Neapolis, while Norbanus marched a few days eastward to occupy the Pass of Corpili. The Via Egnatia made its way through both of these passes, and both Norbanus and Saxa hoped to delay Brutus and Cassius, giving the rest of the army time to find favorable ground on which to fight. Included in their reports about the location of the enemy was the size of The Liberator army and in number alone, it was a daunting report. The dispatches detailed a force of 19 Legions and 13,000 cavalry, composed of Thessalian, Galatian, Thracian, and Illyrian contingents, along with a force of perhaps 4,000 missile troops. None of the Primi Pili wanted word of those numbers leaked to the men, but of course, our hopes were in vain.

The talking was even more subdued around the fires at night, as I found myself walking from one to the other, knowing that this was not the time to come down hard on the men. Instead, I tried to lighten the mood as much as possible, though I was not very successful. Less than a week after these reports came in, a dispatch rider on a lathered horse thundered into the marching camp for the evening, carrying word that The Liberators had managed to dislodge Norbanus. One of the assassins, Cimber, had loaded a Legion and some missile troops on the portion of The Liberator fleet that was shadowing the army along the coast, landing behind Norbanus and forcing him to vacate his position. He was now marching in retreat, heading towards Saxa, still intent on holding the other pass.

Octavian was not with us at that point; though he had shipped over to Greece, he had taken ill, something that happened to him quite a bit, so he was forced to stay behind in the main camp to recuperate. Antonius was in sole command, and when we reached Amphipolis, he ordered us to remain in place for a few days while the situation developed. His hope was that Brutus and Cassius would be stopped at the Sapaean Pass by Norbanus and Saxa, allowing us to circle around to fall on their flank or rear. It was a vain hope. Perhaps if Cassius had not been there, Brutus would have made that mistake, since he was not a military man in any sense of the word. Cassius, on the other hand, was too experienced and he was not going to get bogged down. However, by choosing to bypass the pass, he also gave Antonius an indication of where he was headed because he swung northwest, away from the coast and the protection and resupply of the fleet, which could only mean one thing. The Liberators were heading for Philippi, which was the major supply center of the region. Once their intentions became clear, Antonius wasted no time issuing orders. We were marching to Philippi.

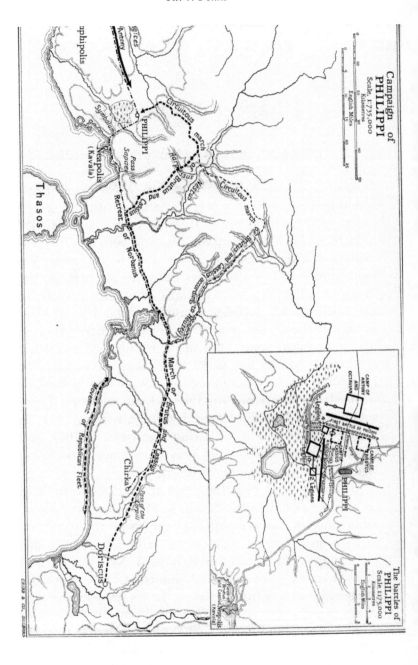

Chapter 3- Philippi

The Liberators beat us to Philippi by a matter of a couple of days, enough time for them to select the best ground on which to set up two camps, each one atop a hill that straddled the Via Egnatia. Brutus took the camp to the north, while Cassius took the southern, then they erected a rampart running between the two camps, blocking passage of the road to the west. We were forced to build our own camp to the east, on the low ground, with a large expanse of marshy ground to the south of us, running roughly parallel to the Via Egnatia, though the western end of the marsh ranged up closer to the road. Half the army worked while the other half stood in battle formation to watch The Liberators, making sure they did not try to attack while we built the camp, but we did not have to worry. There was a steady stream of men deserting, with all of them telling tales of the bickering between Brutus and Cassius, and how Brutus was constantly interfering with Cassius' command of the army.

I had learned over the years to take anything said by a deserter with a healthy dose of skepticism, as they all seemed to have essentially the same thing to say. Morale on the other side was horrible, the conditions were worse, the officers incompetent. No man wanted to be seen as a coward, and desertion, even from the other side, is a serious offense, so I suppose it makes sense that they would paint a grim picture. Still, from what I saw, it appeared that there was some truth in what the deserters were saying because after we had finished the camp, we arrayed for battle a day later, only to stand out in the hot sun. It was now September; we had wasted literally months either hanging about the Campus Martius, then in Brundisium, waiting for the two Triumvirs to agree on something. It was nice to see that we were not the only one with those kinds of problems, having two generals at each other's throats, constantly disagreeing about any and everything. The only event of any note was Antonius' decision to have the 10th positioned on the right, along with the 7th, and while I appreciated the vote of confidence, I cannot say that I did not have misgivings. After the first two days, when we would march out, then form up for battle only to stand there, it became apparent that The Liberators were in no hurry to engage us, instead hoping that we would run out of food, being so far from Dyrrhachium, where our principal supply base was located. Seeing and recognizing their inactivity for what it was, Antonius ordered the construction of a trench that cut through the marsh to the south of us, using it as cover to provide an avenue where we could approach the enemy undetected, at least that was the hope. As plans went, it was a good one, and from my viewpoint, it showed signs of Antonius' cunning and underhandedness, which in wartime is a valuable asset. In politics as well, perhaps, but despite my appreciation of the plan from a military standpoint, it did not make me any more of an admirer of Antonius. The work took almost ten days, and when it was almost finished, I was summoned to the *Praetorium*, where Antonius and Octavian waited, the latter man having arrived from Dyrrhachium on a litter.

This day he was still unable to stand, so he was reclining on a couch, his face even paler than normal. I admit I was a bit nervous when facing Octavian for the first time since our last meeting, worried that either he or I would inadvertently betray our secret agreement and alert Antonius. However, his face gave barely a flicker of recognition when I entered along with Torquatus and Corbulo, who I had met on the way. It soon became apparent that just the Primi Pili had been called to this meeting, though none of us knew exactly why. Once all 19 of us were present, Antonius wasted no time.

"I need a Legion's worth of good, salty men to launch an assault through the trench. I want veterans only, and I need each of you to recommend about four Centuries' worth per Legion."

His demand was greeted by silence, then he glared at each of us, looking from one face to the next, though none of us said anything, knowing better than to argue. Finally, one of the men asked the question that I know was rattling around in everyone's minds.

"Who's going to lead them? And who are the Centurions going to be? How are we going to organize the force?"

"What do I care about any of that drivel?" Antonius snapped. "Why don't you figure that out and earn your pay for once?"

"I disagree." This came from Octavian, whose voice, while weak, still carried clearly enough to be heard. "The Primus Pilus is right. This needs to be decided here and not left as some detail that might cause problems during the assault."

Antonius wheeled angrily on Octavian, who looked at him steadily, not flinching at all, despite Antonius walking over to deliberately tower over him on his litter.

"So says the boy general who's too weak to stand," Antonius sneered. "Of course, that means he's too sick to lead the men from the front. Again."

Octavian's face colored, two bright red spots appearing on his cheeks, his lips thinning in anger at the slur. This was a common theme with Antonius ever since his defeat at Mutina, when the two Consuls Hirtius and Pansa had fallen and left Octavian to receive the sole credit for defeating Antonius, despite the fact that Octavian had been ill again. To a man like Antonius, who was never ill, the only reason Octavian could have had for staying in camp was cowardice, so he never passed up a chance to rub it in Octavian's face. At that moment, the chance to do so in front of men like us was obviously too much to resist.

Despite his anger, Octavian's voice was cool as he replied, "Nevertheless, the leadership of this raid should be decided right now, by us."

I suddenly had a sneaking suspicion who Octavian had in mind. I studied his face intently, but he did not look in my direction, which only served to strengthen my suspicion.

"Fine," Antonius snapped, then began looking at each of us. He looked over to the Primus Pilus of the 7th, a squat piece of gristle by the name of Caecina, nodding at him.

"Caecina is the man for this job."

"I think not," Octavian interjected, causing Antonius to wheel on him, clearly enraged.

"And why not?" Antonius demanded. "Caecina is one of the best leaders in the army."

"You know why not," Octavian replied evenly, and so did everyone else in the room; Caecina was one of Antonius' men through and through.

"So I suppose you have someone better in mind," Antonius snorted.

"Indeed I do. I think Torquatus is a bit better suited for this mission. No disrespect to you Caecina," Octavian replied blandly, his face giving nothing away.

This took me a bit by surprise, but it should not have. Octavian was much more subtle than Antonius, and in many ways much more devious.

"I'm sure you do," Antonius shot back. "But I say 'no,' for the same reason you object to Caecina."

Torquatus, as Caecina belonged to Antonius, was owned wholly to Octavian. For several moments, neither man spoke, Antonius glaring at Octavian, while Octavian stared back with not a hint of nervousness. When it became clear that Octavian was not going to speak, Antonius whirled around to survey the group of us, until his eyes landed on me. He regarded me with narrowed eyes, then I saw the glimmer of a smile, which disappeared in the time it took to face Octavian.

He was turned away from me, but his voice oozed sincerity as he jerked his thumb over his shoulder at me.

"How about this big oaf? He's brave enough, and he's not a bad leader."

He looked over his shoulder at me, shooting me a malevolent smile.

"Even if he did let one of his Centurions run wild and cause Rome to lose some good men."

I kept my face a mask, but I think at that moment any chance there was of me choosing Antonius of my own free will, under any circumstances, was lost forever. I saw Octavian lean over a bit to look at me past Antonius, who was still looking back at me, so he missed the shadow of a smile that flitted across the younger Triumvir's face.

Octavian let out a sigh, then said indifferently, "I suppose Pullus will do."

With that settled, I was left with the task of selecting the other Centurions who would go on the raid with me. Each Primus Pilus gave me a list of candidates, along with a brief recitation of their qualities and accomplishments, then from them I selected the men who would each lead a Century of the most veteran men that we had. From the 10th, I selected Scribonius, Laetus from my Cohort, and Nasica; the last one I chose to give him the opportunity to redeem himself after the affair with Tetarfenus. I was going to leave Balbus in charge of both the Cohort and the Legion, having every confidence in his ability. The work on the trenches took another day before it reached the point from which we could launch an attack. Our objective was to build at least one redoubt, perhaps two depending on the terrain, athwart the enemy supply line back to Neapolis. Antonius believed that if we did that, The Liberators would have no choice but to abandon their strong position, or fight, which is really what both Antonius and Octavian wanted. The work on the trench was screened by a stand of reeds that stood above even my head, while the enemy had given no indication that they had seen the men working on the trench.

Shortly after the beginning of the third watch ten days after the work started, I led a force quietly out of the camp, all of the gear that tended to clink together and make noise wrapped in bits of cloth. Although we did not plan on being in place more than a day, Antonius certain that Cassius in particular would come out to fight, I ordered the men to take three days' rations, along with their entrenching tools. No tents, just a *sagum* for each man, in which were rolled the rations, tinderboxes, and other odds and ends deemed a necessity. I was always amused at what some men thought were crucial to bring along on operations such as this. Some men brought their household gods, others brought small blocks of wood that they were carving into figurines, but I could always count on someone bringing dice and other games along. The truth was that with a group as veteran as this, I did not care what they brought, as long as they did their jobs. I found myself wishing that these men were all in the 10th, because they reminded me of the 10th back in Gaul before we had been so whittled down by death and injury. Many of the men I knew, at least by sight from those days, and they all gave me a grin as they went padding by, their boots wrapped in cloth as well to further muffle the sound of our movement. I moved quickly to the head of the column, following the trench, peering into the darkness, looking for the dim figures of the scouting party that ranged ahead of us, but I could not see them. We moved quickly, despite the gloom, following the smell of the freshly turned earth of the trench as much as by sight, before I almost stumbled on the scouting party, who had stopped to crouch at the bottom of the trench. I could barely make out one of them kneeling up on the lip of the trench, at ground level, looking in the direction of the enemy camp. Through the thick reeds, I could only just see the reflected glow of the torches along the parapet of the camp, but there was no way to spot any movement. We would have to rely on the sound of the enemy crashing through the reeds to alert us. I asked the scouts why they had stopped, and one of them pointed.

"We've reached the end of the trench, Primus Pilus," the Optio in command of the party whispered. "What now?"

"Now, we dig."

During the construction of the entrenchment, Antonius had sent his engineering officers out to do a survey of the surrounding ground and they came back with two prospective points for us to build redoubts of sufficient size to protect my force, although they admitted that they had not actually been able to examine anything closely. From their vantage point, all they had really been able to see were two spots where the reeds stood taller than the rest, in a large enough area where they decided that it was not just a case of the reeds growing higher, but was, in fact, higher ground. Before I sent all of the men stumbling through the mud, I wanted to make sure that the engineers were indeed correct, so I sent a section out, putting a Centurion in charge of each, giving them the respective pace count and heading where they should find the high ground. They went moving off into the darkness, and no matter how quietly they moved, there was no hiding the splashing and the sucking sounds of feet being pulled out of mud. I was sure that they could be heard in the enemy camp, but no alarm was raised as we all sat crouched and waiting, my mind running through all the things that could go wrong. Although it seemed longer, it was not much more than a sixth part of a watch when the first group returned, the men caked in mud past their knees.

"There's ground there," the Centurion, whose name I forget, told me. "Though it's pretty charitable calling it 'high ground.'"

I bit back a curse, asking, "Is the ground solid enough for us to use?"

"Barely," he replied. "But it's the best around, and if we cut the reeds down and put them on the ground, it might help soak up some of the water and mud."

I turned to Scribonius, who I had named my second in command, patting him on the shoulder. "Well, we may as well get started."

Scribonius stood. Whispering a command to the men assigned to him, they crawled out of the trench.

"Wait," I commanded. He turned back to face me, his thin frame a blacker silhouette against the night sky. "Go across in small groups so you don't make as much noise."

"It'll take longer that way," Scribonius pointed out, and I bit back on my impatience.

"I know that, but if we can manage to at least get in place when we start work without being heard, I think it's worth the extra time."

He did not argue, but I could tell he was not convinced. Whispering the change in orders to his Centurions, he turned, then began moving across the marsh. By that time, the second party had returned, with slightly better news.

"The ground is pretty solid out there, and it's actually quite a bit higher than you would think," Nasica whispered, he being the one I sent on the second scout.

"Is it big enough?" I asked, and that was where the good news stopped.

"Not really," he replied. "If we stood shoulder to shoulder instead of our normal spacing, then it might be big enough."

I considered this, then decided. "Let's go," I said. "We'll at least get started on it. When the sun comes up, we might see something better where we can relocate to."

It was a faint hope, but truthfully, I was not expecting that we would have to hold the redoubt because I agreed with Antonius' assessment that our presence would cause Brutus and Cassius to either fight or withdraw. I relayed the same orders to my group of men that I gave to Scribonius, sending Nasica first. It took the better part of a third of a watch, and I do not know how we managed it, but it soon became clear that both parties had moved into position without alerting the enemy. That was about to end, however.

While it was possible to move the men into position without alerting the enemy, though I did not know how, there was no way to disguise the sound of a few thousand picks and shovels at work. No more than a few moments after we got started, I heard the *bucina* in the enemy camp sound the alarm.

"Ignore them," I told the men, some of whom made muttered comments, making me feel a bit chagrined, forgetting as I had that these men were veterans and not my youngsters in the 10th.

The work continued, and if it had not been dark, it could have been just a normal end of day routine on the march. My major concern was how to keep the two redoubts linked, so I decided to dig a short connecting trench back to the main one, which would serve as our axis of communication between the two redoubts. Sending a runner over to Scribonius' position, it turned out that he had already determined the same thing and was already building his own trench. I took a calculated risk by having all the men work, though none of them were allowed to be more than five paces away from their stacked weapons, while I made them work wearing their helmets, which was not popular. I was betting on the fact that there was no way that the enemy could approach us, despite being screened by the reeds, without being heard, even over the work we were doing. We had managed to move into position without being observed, but the enemy would not be worried about stealth if they came to push us out of the marsh. Because it was still dark, I also doubted that they would come charging out, since there was no way for them to tell exactly what was going on, a fact which I continually reminded the men of as they worked. By the time the sky was turning pink, we were almost finished digging the trench and creating the rampart, partially because all the men had worked. It was also because I had ordered that we go back to the old army standard width and depth and not use Caesar's dimensions, but as I did so, I offered up a silent apology to my old general. However, time was more important and I hoped he would forgive me.

The men were filthy, and as the light grew stronger, it was also easier to see how fatigued they were, but I could not call for a break. The news was not all positive; a third of a watch or so before this, a runner came from Scribonius, who reported that work on his redoubt was not going well. The ground was almost too soft to be firm enough for the parapet, while the trench was filling up with the groundwater. Scribonius reported that after a day of baking in the sun, the ground would probably dry out and be firm enough for our purposes, but that was only if the enemy did not try to dislodge us. There was not nearly enough room for the whole force in the redoubt we were constructing, so I was forced to tell him that we would just have to hope for the best, an answer I knew would not make him happy. Now that it was almost full light, I pulled some of the men from the work, having them form up in front of the partially finished rampart. With the reeds gone, and with the vantage of being perhaps ten feet higher than the surrounding marsh, I could see the upper portion of the enemy camp, barely making out the transverse crest and plumed headgear of some Centurions and Tribunes, all of whom were looking in our direction and pointing.

"Now we'll see what kind of general Cassius is," I said to nobody in particular, wishing that I had a better view of the lower part of the camp and the gate.

The camp nearer to us belonged to Cassius, and it was him who I worried about more of the two Liberators, so I spent the morning staring at his camp. Yet, the *bucina* never sounded, and troops never came boiling out to come after us. In some ways, this was more disturbing than if they had come to knock us off our perches, because it did not seem to make any sense. The road leading to Neapolis was now closer to us than it was to the enemy, so any supply convoy coming up the road could easily be fallen upon and destroyed before any sortie from the camp could reach us, while the position of Scribonius' redoubt meant that any force that did try to come and intercept us would expose their rear to roughly five Cohorts of hardened veterans. It was true that Cassius could easily overwhelm us by numbers if he chose, but there was a risk in that because he would have to reduce the number of men defending camp, making it vulnerable to an assault from our main force. Alternatively, Antonius could choose to fall onto the right flank of any force sent to attack us, rolling them up like a carpet. As I thought about it, I grudgingly had to admit that Antonius had dreamed up a maneuver worthy of Caesar, and I did not see how Cassius, or Brutus for that matter, could do anything other than what the Triumvirs wanted them to do. Perhaps that was why I was not a general.

The day passed uneventfully, with no overt movement by the enemy, other than to keep watch over our positions from their own parapet. After the first third of a watch or so, when there was considerable tension as we waited for some sort of move, it became quite boring, and I felt sufficiently secure enough in our position to allow the men to go down to half-alert status, giving them the opportunity to rest. At midday, I sent a runner to Scribonius to get a status report, while another runner was sent back to the main camp for instructions. It was becoming clear that there would be no overt action from Cassius, at least not immediately. We were told to remain in place, and I was glad that I had ordered the men to bring rations. Once the men were rested, they were put to work improving the position, while I sent for Scribonius to confer with him. He arrived a little less than a third of a watch later, informing me that the ground had firmed up somewhat, but was still a bit soft for his liking.

"We shouldn't be here more than another day," I said. "Cassius has to move one way or another before the next supply convoy arrives or he'll lose it, and that won't help morale any. So he's got to make his move tomorrow."

"Does he?" Scribonius asked, with that thoughtful frown I knew so well, as he stared over at the enemy camp as if he could divine what was in Cassius' mind.

"What else can he do?" I asked irritably, not liking the doubtful tone my friend was adopting.

"I don't know," Scribonius admitted, never taking his eyes from the enemy camp, then shaking his head. "But if there's one thing I've learned, men don't always do what we think they should."

He tore his eyes away from the camp, looked at me, then gave me a smile that I found hard to interpret. Was there a rebuke in there somewhere? I shrugged it off, as I had shrugged off his doubt. Talking a bit more about the situation, he soon returned to his own redoubt, leaving me to watch the sun sink lower in the sky. It became dark, with no more than the usual activity of daily routine in the enemy camp, making me comfortable enough to allow the men fires for cooking, though it was hard to find enough wood.

The night passed uneventfully, with the usual laughing and tales being swapped, the bones being thrown; all in all, a normal night. I had been a little worried that mixing men from so many different Legions, hardened veterans all, would lead to some sort of trouble, but I believe that the circumstances contributed to the men being on their best behavior, and while spirits were high, the men were getting along. It was not until the men bedded down and the redoubt grew quiet that I had the first indication that something was amiss.

I had just laid down, and in the quiet, I gradually became aware that there was something going on that was not part of the normal night sounds. I opened my mouth, since that always seems to help one hear better, but I could not really detect anything. Gradually tuning my senses to the environment around me, I realized that I was not hearing as much as I was feeling something, vibrating up through the ground into my body. As I concentrated every sense, slowly the vibration became a recognizable pattern, feeling like a series of scratches, in the manner of an animal digging in the ground, interspersed with thudding impacts. I sat straight up, seeing that other men were sitting up as well, looking about, then I got quickly to my feet, walking to the nearest sentry, who was alert but had not heard anything. As I stood next to him, straining my eyes in the darkness, it became clear that whatever or whoever was making the sound was too far off to be heard by ear; it was only when in contact with the dirt that it became apparent that something was going on. There was the sound of a challenge at the rear of the redoubt, and I ran towards the sound to find a panting runner from Scribonius being brought to find me.

"Pilus Prior Scribonius' compliments and he reports that there appears to be a large force that's up to something between his position and the main camp."

"Does he know what that something is, or do I have to guess?" I snapped, immediately regretting the harsh words since the runner was not to blame in any way.

The man shook his head, replying, "He says that he doesn't know for sure, but he suspects that the enemy is digging. He said that you'd ask, and that if he were forced to guess, he'd say that they're digging a counter-trench to cut us off from the camp."

My mind raced, realizing that he was undoubtedly correct, just like he had been right before when he expressed doubt that Cassius would do what Antonius, and I, thought he would do. He was digging his own trench to intersect ours, west of Scribonius' redoubt, but east of our camp. Instead of forcing Cassius to dance to the Triumvir's tune, he had chosen to pick his own song, and now we were going to be cut off.

The sun came up to the grim sight of the transverse trench of the enemy making its way towards our own entrenchment line. Now the tactical advantage was on the side of The Liberators; if I sent Scribonius out to try to disrupt the work of the enemy digging their trench, it would expose his rear. If I went to support Scribonius, the same would happen to my force. All we could do was watch as the enemy worked, marking their progress by the reeds being cut down as the trench was dug. They were moving slowly, so I supposed that they were using at least as many men to stand in formation in the event that Antonius launched his own sortie. Nevertheless, it was still a grim sight. About midday, I sent a runner back up the trench to ask Antonius for further instructions, expecting to be told to withdraw back to the camp, but two parts of a watch later the runner returned with a terse note telling me to remain in place. Nothing more was added to the note, no contingency or even words of encouragement. I cursed bitterly, throwing the note into the dirt, then thought better and retrieved it. I was learning that dealing with patricians was a treacherous business, and if things went badly, I did not want Antonius accusing me of disobeying orders, so I put the scrap in my bag.

The enemy did not finish the trench that day, only getting perhaps a quarter of the way, telling me that while Cassius may want this done, the men's hearts were not in it, a fact that I was sure to convey to every fire that night. The next morning saw the work resume, while I was running out of things for the men to do, having improved our positions as much as was possible with the materials we had on hand. I cursed myself for not thinking to have a scorpion broken down and brought with us, but there was no way that I could change things now. Slipping one man past the enemy patrols to carry messages was one thing, but a group of men burdened with carrying the scorpion and the ammunition would have been chopped up. I was comforted by the fact that the men were all veterans, and at this point while they were concerned, there were no signs of panic among them, for which I was thankful. I went to Scribonius' redoubt on the second day, hoping to get a better look at what we might be facing, but truthfully, there was not much to see, just dirt flying along with the occasional flash of a pick or shovel. We could see that my suspicions that there were at least as many men standing guard as working were confirmed, but that was about it. I told Scribonius of our orders, and he looked at me in astonishment.

"What do you suppose Antonius is up to, letting us stay out here without doing anything?"

"I don't know," I admitted. "If it were Caesar I would say that he had something up his sleeve and we were going to be fine, but Antonius is no Caesar."

"Well, I can't see him sacrificing a Legion's worth of his best men," Scribonius pointed out, which was something I had not thought about, making me feel a bit better.

"You're right. Not even Antonius would do something that stupid. So he must have something else in mind. I just hope we're around long enough to see what it is."

I looked around at the redoubt. The one advantage in the delay was that the ground had dried out quite a bit, so their parapet was now as solid as ours. The mood of Scribonius' men mirrored that of the men in my redoubt; like mine, ready for whatever came their way. Seeing that all was in order, I left Scribonius, promising that I would send word as soon as I had anything worth passing on. Night fell on the second day in our position, with the enemy now more than halfway to completion of their trench. The next day would see us run out of food, and if they worked a little harder, or at least longer, the trench might be done by the end of the next day. Then we would be out of food, and cut off.

While this was going on, the remainder of The Liberator army, namely the men in Brutus' camp, formed up every day for battle, as the men in our army at the main camp did the same. Just as it had been the case for several days, it was little more than a staring contest. However, the presence of an army that was standing ready to pounce meant that even after the trench was completed on the third day, Cassius was either unable or unwilling to use it to come after us. If he sent a force of a sufficient size down the trench to destroy us, it would weaken the force holding the camp, thereby making it vulnerable to being taken by Antonius. If Brutus shifted some of his forces, it would make his camp vulnerable in the same fashion. This was small comfort; no matter if Cassius came after us or not, we were now completely cut off from our own camp, and we were running out of food. On the second day, I had ordered the men to cut to half-rations, then on the third I cut that in half as well, but that bought us only a couple extra days. We were also cut off from all communications; the last two runners I sent asking permission to withdraw never returned, which I suppose was probably a good thing, for me anyway. We did have plenty of water, there being a stream running from east to west, which meant that it could not be cut off, while some of the men set snares to catch whatever stumbled into them, but that was nowhere near enough to feed a Legion of men. With all the bad things, there was one advantage that we had; the men themselves. All of them were veterans, but a large number of them had been in Gaul at the siege of Avaricum when we had almost starved, and we were working much harder then. Now the men could lounge about, and while I was usually of the belief that keeping the men busy at all times was the best way to avoid trouble, this was a time where I did not make the Centurions find things to do. We had to save as much energy as we could, because it was becoming clear that we were going to be here for some time. Once the initial concern and anxiety over the enemy's digging of the trench subsided and it appeared that things were going to go back to the mutual staring contest, the monotony that is so much a part of life in the army returned with a vengeance. In some ways, I was thankful that the men did not have the energy to fight each other when the inevitable squabbles arose. The days were getting shorter, the nights cooler, but we were not uncomfortable and thankfully it did not rain. It did get hot during the day, but with plenty of water, it was not much of a hardship, while the biggest challenge was staying alert, the men inevitably becoming weaker as the days dragged by. I was forced to shorten the watches each man stood because if I had not, I would have had to put a lot of men to death.

A week passed, our situation now dire, so I was forced out of desperation to ask for volunteers to try to sneak past the enemy, who had built their own redoubt at the junction of the trenches, in order to get word to Antonius of our plight. I summoned Scribonius to help me compose the message, knowing that just as my keeping of Antonius' order to stay in position could be used in my defense, anything I wrote could be used against me.

"Don't embellish, or try to emphasize how bad our situation is," Scribonius advised. "Just give the basic facts, as simply as you can put them. Remember Caesar's dispatches from Gaul?"

I did indeed. In fact, I had paid a hefty sum to purchase a copy of them, using Diocles of course, as another thing I had learned is how the upper classes take a dim view of men of my station concerning themselves with matters that demonstrated a level of literacy above our place. Nodding to Scribonius that I understood, I turned to the tablet, stylus in hand. I gave a brief summary of our strength, our supply situation, and the state of our equipment. I described our state of morale as high, but then I got to what I considered would be the most dangerous part of the message.

"I would just state the facts again," Scribonius said. "Tell him when we ran out of food, and let him draw his own conclusion. If you say anything about the men being weak, he might get angry for thinking that you're stating the obvious. You know how touchy he is."

Again, I did know precisely what Scribonius was saying, so I did exactly as he advised, making a simple statement that we had been out of food for more than four days, and that although we were subsisting on what fish and game we could snare, it was not enough to feed the whole force. Handing it to Scribonius when I was done, I watched him read it carefully.

He frowned for a moment, then he handed it back to me saying, "I just thought of something that you might add that will emphasize how much trouble we're in without appearing to rebuke him for leaving us out here."

I sat waiting as he composed his thoughts, then after he had finished speaking, I wrote down what he said word for word. In essence, I, or more accurately, Scribonius, said that I understood that circumstances outside Antonius' control had delayed him from implementing the second part of his plan, so my major concern was that with the men as weakened as they were, we would not be able to support him when he made his move in the manner that would give us the highest chance of success.

Scribonius read it, grunted then gave me a grin. "That should keep you from getting chopped, at least. If we don't starve first."

I had to scrounge four more tablets from the other Centurions, then painstakingly copy the message onto each one. By this time, I had my five volunteers, and I was going to send them out at intervals during the night. Each man knew that it was a likely bet that he would be caught by an enemy patrol, yet none of them wanted to let their comrades down. I promised each of them a bounty of 500 sesterces if they made it through, along with a recommendation for commendation, knowing the money would be a stronger enticement. As soon as it was dark, I sent the first man out, personally wishing him luck. He was a small man by the name of Asellio, I believe, and I could see his teeth, or what remained of them, gleaming in the darkness as he grinned at me.

"Don't worry, Primus Pilus. I've got some debts and I need that money. I'm your man."

With that, he disappeared into the gloom, moving down the trench to the west back towards the camp. It took about a tenth part of a watch to walk to the camp, if nobody were trying to kill you or you were just out for a stroll, so I figured that it would take him at least two parts of a watch to sneak past the enemy redoubt. He would not know the current watchword back at our camp, so he was in almost as much danger from our own men as he was from the enemy. However, that could not be avoided, and I was counting on each runner's ability to think on his feet to keep him from being turned into a porcupine. The last thing I put in my message was a request for a *cornu* call to be sounded as a signal to us that the message had gotten through. Even knowing it was too soon, I could not stop myself from straining my ears, listening for the notes that we used for message received. The *cornu* is the instrument that is used to send signals from one end of the army to another, it being a bigger, heavier, and louder instrument and I often wondered what possessed a man to volunteer to carry the thing around on his shoulder. For one thing, it was heavy, while being a *cornicen* did not carry the same status as a *signifer* or aquilifer. It also made you a target, especially from the missile troops, so all in all, it was not a position that I would have wanted.

The time seemed to drag by, and although there was no blast from the *cornu*, neither were there any shouts of alarm or the sound of a man screaming for help. Finally, I could delay no longer and, saying a silent prayer for Asellio, sent the second man out. I could not afford to wait as long for him as I did for Asellio, if I were to get all five men out while it was still dark and give them any hope for success. The night dragged on, then I stood facing the fifth and final man, who by now was as aware as all of us that apparently none of his comrades had made it through. The last man was one from my own Century, a veteran named Placus, who was not on his second but third enlistment. Placus was almost 50 years old, a gnarled knot of a man as brown as a year-old boot and twice as tough. Placus had been one of the veterans placed into the 10th in my *dilectus*, the kind of man who would never be more than an *immunes*, but who is the core of any Legion. Although we had run out of wood to burn days before, the moon was full, so I could see the grim set of his face, which he had blackened with charcoal, along with his arms and legs. He was not wearing his helmet or armor, instead strapping his sword across his back, the hilt sticking up just over his right shoulder. I did not say anything to Placus, for there was nothing I could say that he did not already know. Instead, I just offered him my hand, which he took, looking up at me, saying nothing as well, just giving me a nod before he was gone in the darkness.

Shortly before dawn, the *cornu* played the notes that told us that the message was received, and the men let out as loud a cheer as their weakened condition would permit. I was pleased, yet that had only been the beginning because now we had to wait and see what Antonius would do. While I outwardly shared Scribonius' belief that Antonius would not sacrifice some of his best men, inside I was not so sure. Antonius had shown another side to him after Caesar's death that none of us, at least those of us in the army with him in Gaul, had seen before, a cold grasping side that seemed to have no concern for how much blood was spilled on his behalf in pursuit of his aims. The easy familiarity and good humor that drew those men to him that day standing on the dock in Gaul had been nowhere in evidence in the times I was in his presence in the recent past, so I was not as sure as Scribonius that Antonius would do something to save us. As I pondered that happy thought, I heard the blast of the *cornu* again, sounding the exact same signal. Then a third call came, then a fourth, and finally a fifth. The men looked at me, but I could only shrug, because I had no idea what it meant. Finally, I sent for Scribonius again. When he appeared, I was struck by how haggard and drawn he looked, with dark circles under his eyes, which appeared to be sunken in.

"You look terrible," I told him, and he grunted.

"Have you looked at yourself lately?"

I asked him what he thought the five blasts of the *cornu* meant, but he had no idea either. The sun rose as we watched the respective armies starting their day.

"They're having breakfast now," Scribonius said wistfully.

"Shut up," I replied, my eyes fixed on our camp, looking for any sign that Antonius was planning to come to our rescue.

So far, it was looking like a normal day, where both armies would line up to stare at each other as we got hungrier and weaker. While our army was in one camp, the army was split into two commands, just as that of Brutus and Cassius, so when we formed up, it was in two wings, one under the command of Octavian and one under Antonius. Octavian's command was nominal, since he was still bedridden, but I watched as his half of the army marched out of the gates to form up on the left. A short time later, Antonius' half of the army followed, taking its place on the right, the usual shuffling and shoving as men arranged themselves for another day of standing about. Tearing my gaze away to look at my men, I saw that most of them were still lounging on their *sagum*, some of them engaged in a listless game of dice, others napping. Turning back to gaze westward, I felt anger growing inside me, convinced that Antonius was indeed going to do nothing to save us, forcing me to watch these men waste away in the name of doing their duty to Rome. I know there are many people who look at us Legionaries, pointing to us as part of the problem of those years, that we held too much power, that we were too greedy, and used the threat of our sword arms to make ourselves rich. Yet, as in any story, there is another side and I was looking at it. There was the side that spoke of the terrible misuse of men whose only crime was to choose to march for Rome, each of them individually being worthless until there were enough of them to be a force, and then only being used as pieces in some game to be used then tossed aside, or in this case, just left to rot. I decided then and there that no matter what the consequences, I was going to lead my men out of this place. If we were cut down, at least we would die fighting, not like a bunch of rats. Then, Antonius proved me wrong.

If there had been some prearranged signal, there was no way for me to know about it, and I certainly did not hear any *bucina* calls that would have given me a hint that Antonius had something planned. From where I stood, it was a matter of at one moment, Antonius and Octavian's wings were standing in place as they had so many days previously, then suddenly Antonius' whole wing leapt forward into the attack. They did not even march part of the way before launching their charge as was usual, but began running from the outset. I could see Antonius at the head of the army, astride his favorite horse, a gray that he boasted as the equal of Caesar's Toes, his *paludamentum* streaming behind him in a streak of scarlet, the black feathers on his helmet swept back so they were almost flat. A moment later, the actual sound of the charge reached our ears, and even as far away as we were, the roar of the men was still loud enough to drown out a thunderclap. As they went hurtling towards the enemy, their cohesion began to fall apart, the faster men opening up gaps in the ranks by outstripping their slower comrades. I watched, first in a state of relief that Antonius had decided to act to free us from our predicament, then it began to sour as I watched the attack unfold, seeing the beginning of a number of problems. After Antonius gave the order and the men began to run, it became clear to me that while his attack caught Cassius completely by surprise, still having a large number of his men engaged in improving fortifications, it obviously also caught the men of Octavian off guard as well. They were standing as immobile as the enemy was, watching the other half of the army engage Cassius and his men. Directly opposite Octavian was Brutus' troops, and as Antonius closed with Cassius, the first inkling that a disaster might be looming struck me. Without Octavian's men advancing to engage Brutus, Brutus was now free to launch his men down onto the left flank of what was rapidly becoming a disorganized mob. They were too far away for me to see, but I later learned that the 4th was given the left wing of Antonius' formation. Just when they were at the base of the hill that Cassius' men stood on and were beginning to run up it, and as suddenly as Antonius had launched his attack, the men of Brutus' left went charging down their own hill, the whole formation swinging like a huge gate pivoting on its axis to slam into the flank and rear of the 4th. The 4th's headlong charge up the hill immediately stopped, as they went from attacker to defender in the matter of a moment. Antonius was completely unaware of this, because as is the custom, he had stationed himself on the right wing, which was smashing into Cassius' left at roughly the same time. First, there was the sight of men dropping their tools in a panic as they scrambled for their weapons. Then, there was a cloud of dust, along with tools, helmets, shields, swords and pieces of men flying in the air that always marked the moment when two lines collided, it taking a moment for the sound to roll across to us. The right wing of Antonius was close enough that I could see the bull emblem of the 10th on the standard, and I strained my eyes watching as my men under Balbus went smashing into the enemy. Cassius' line held for a few moments, the shouting and clang of metal on metal continuing to reach us, but they were too disorganized from being caught when so many of them were working. After a moment, someone in Cassius' line took a step back.

Before I could draw more than one or two breaths, the whole enemy formation crumbled, with men in the rear abandoning their comrades and turning to flee. Although the men in the rear ranks can turn about safely, the men in the first two or three cannot. However, when panic sets in, all reason leaves a man's senses and his only thought, if it can be called that, is to flee. Consequently, despite it spelling their doom, the men in front did just that very thing, turning their backs to try to escape, only to be cut down with a quick thrust. The men of the 10th, along with the 7th, who were next to my Legion, crashed through the wall of brush that was set up as a screen for the trench as if it were not there, setting off in hot pursuit of those in the rear ranks who were running for their camp. I let out a shout of exultation, which was drowned out only because all of the men in the redoubt were doing the same thing. Like an oncoming tide, our men swept away the small pockets of resistance formed by men who rallied around a Centurion or signifier, trying to make a stand. I saw one figure, who was wearing the same *paludamentum* as Antonius was, doing the same thing with the aquilifer of one of his Legions next to him, his sword circling around his head in the signal we used to form a rally point. Some men did stop to turn about to face their attackers, but most ignored him, rushing past in their headlong flight. The dust was quickly obscuring our vision of what was going on, one of my last glimpses a little knot of men on the top of the hill, their shields turned out in an *orbis*. By this point, our men realized that the battle was won, at least from their perspective, so now the race was on to get into Cassius' camp to grab as much loot as possible. However, in the wider context of the whole field, the battle was not won; in fact, we were losing.

As successful as Antonius' attack was on the right, his blind rush at the enemy without any coordination with Octavian put the 4th and Corbulo in terrible jeopardy. The first of Brutus' Legions had swung down the hill onto the flank and rear of the 4th, who in their own right were now forced to order an *orbis*. If only one Legion had fallen onto the 4th, they probably would have been all right, but very quickly, first one then another of Brutus' Legions followed suit so the 4th was virtually surrounded, save for the 12th, next to the 4th, who soon became enveloped themselves. Still, if Octavian's wing had advanced off the hill, the 4th could have been saved, along with the tide of the battle turning overwhelmingly in our favor, but as I was to learn later, Octavian was not present. In fact, he was not even in the camp at all. The night before, Octavian was warned in a dream that if he stayed in camp he would be in grave danger, so heeding the warning, he left it, going into the marshy area to the south of our main camp. All I knew at the time was that Octavian's army, despite the obvious danger first to the left of Antonius, then to themselves, stood there doing nothing as more of Brutus' Legions came charging down the hill into the now yawning gap between our two wings. While a portion of their force concentrated on destroying the 4th, and the 12th with it, the rest of Brutus' men, taking advantage of being on the right flank of Octavian's men, wheeled to go charging into them. Naturally, once Brutus' men became involved, the dust cloud became so thick that we in the redoubts could see nothing, and for the first time in my career, I truly did not know what to do.

My prayers were seemingly answered when at the southern edge of what was now a huge dust cloud, I saw a dark shapeless form moving towards the rear of Antonius' right. Sensing more than seeing that it was a large group of men, the next question was whether they were friend or foe, because they could have either been reinforcing Antonius' right, who were now in Cassius' camp, or they could be about to fall onto their unsuspecting rear. Deciding that if they turned out to be friend we could always halt our assault, I told the *bucina*tor to sound the assembly, followed by the *cornu* call to alert Scribonius that we were moving. The men were already standing watching the action, so it took only a matter of a few moments before they were ready. Despite our weakened condition, I could see they were eager for a fight, though I was also realistic, knowing that what they really thirsted for was a shot at the enemy camp before their friends took all the choice bits. We went trotting up the trench back towards our camp to where the transverse trench was, picking up Scribonius and his men as we went. He trotted beside me as I gasped out what I wanted done, and once I was finished, he gave me a salute then went to his men. I planned on using the transverse trench to approach the last point where I had seen the group of men moving, hoping that they would prove to be friendly. If they in fact were not, we would at least be in time to prevent them from falling on the rear of our men. By the time we reached the transverse, all of the men, including myself, were gasping for breath and needed to stop for a moment, partly because of our weakened state but also because of the dust. I had not seen this much since Pharsalus, a direct result of having almost 40 Legions on both sides, along with 40,000 cavalry involved in battle. After a couple moments, we clambered out of the original trench, where once on level ground we could see that the enemy had been no more than 50 paces away from completing the transverse. Without wasting any more time, we went running into the dust cloud, choking and coughing as we moved into the fight, the sounds of battle even more disconcerting than normal because we had no visual references. The dust was so thick and pervasive that it seemed to warp our senses to the point where it was impossible to tell exactly what direction the sounds were coming from, so despite the urgency, I was forced to slow down to a walk as I peered into the choking fog. I could hear what sounded like a vicious fight going off to my left, but the last direction I had seen the group of men headed was off to my right, towards the rear of the 10th and 7th. I veered in that direction, counting on the Centurions to keep the men as closely formed up as was possible under the circumstances. I sensed more than actually saw the backs of the men I was following. Still, it was not until we were no more than 20 paces away that I was finally able to determine that they were indeed the enemy. Piecing it together later, what we had seen was the work party, more than five Cohorts strong that had been at the farthest edge of the transverse trench, working to finish that last 50 paces. I do not know how, but they had been completely missed by the oncoming 10th and I made a mental note to talk to Balbus to find out how it had happened.

First, though, I drew my Gallic blade, the metal making a singing sound as it left my scabbard, then I turned to make sure that there were men behind me and had not gotten lost in the dust before roaring, "Let's kill these bastards!"

Knowing that they were right behind me, we went charging into the unsuspecting enemy.

We slammed into what turned out to be the last cohesive remnants of Cassius' wing of The Liberator army, catching them totally by surprise. Just a moment before, they were about to fall onto the rear of our own troops, yet in a turn that only the gods can contrive, the tables turned on them as quickly as one could say "Mars." In less than a couple hundred normal heartbeats, we slaughtered a good number of these men, though many were able to escape in the dust.

Despite myself, I found that I was peering at every man of a certain height and build, looking first for the transverse crest of the Centurion, then into their face to see if it was one that I recognized from my childhood. I had resolved that I would not think about Vibius when it became clear we would be fighting The Liberators, but I could not stop myself, and it was with great relief that when I came across the bodies of the Centurions who were cut down, none of them were familiar to me.

Once we finished, I ordered the men to regroup, resting them for a moment while I tried to get my bearings, but it was almost impossible because of the dust. Adding to my confusion were the sounds that experience had taught me only come with the looting of a camp or sacking of a town; excited shouts and laughter of men, the sound of breaking amphorae, the shrieks of the slaves or freedmen who were unfortunate enough to be caught in the wrong place at the wrong time. The reason for the confusion was that there seemed to be two sources for those sounds, except that they were coming from opposite directions. I was fairly sure the sounds coming from our front were from the looting of Cassius' camp, but almost identical sounds were echoing from our left rear. Turning around in confusion, I called for Scribonius, who appeared out of the dust, coughing and spitting globs of mud onto the ground.

Pointing to our rear, I asked him, "What do you suppose that means?"

He cocked his head, and after listening, his face became grim and his tone even more so.

"It sounds like our camp is being overrun."

While he was only confirming what I suspected, I felt a shiver run up my spine at his words, hoping against hope that we were both wrong. For the second time in a day, I was completely at a loss about what to do. I was keenly aware that I had deserted my post without express orders to do so, though I did not see how I could have helped matters by staying put, except perhaps by being a bit removed from what was going on and being better able to see. Yet, while I was glad Antonius had apparently heeded my request for help, I still did not trust him a bit, knowing that if things ultimately went against us, he would figure out a way to blame me for what happened, saying that by leaving the redoubts I had ruined his whole master plan. The fact that I had seen Antonius and recognized his headlong rush into the enemy for what it was, just another impulsive act by a man who seemed to be ruled by his impulses, meant nothing.

I at last turned back to face towards where I was sure Cassius' camp was located, telling Scribonius, "We're going that way. I need to find Antonius and find out what's going on and see if he wants us to go back to the redoubts."

"If he does, maybe we can get something to eat," Scribonius said, nodding his head back in the direction of where our camp was. "If not from there, then maybe from Cassius."

With that decided, I ordered the men to form up, whereupon we marched to Cassius' camp. It is no exaggeration when I say that the gods were watching out for us, because if we had headed back to our camp, we would have been slaughtered.

What is now known as the First Battle of Philippi, out of the hundreds of battles large and small that I ever participated in, was perhaps one of the strangest because it was both a victory and defeat at the same time. Antonius' attack had been a brilliant success and complete failure. Successful for smashing Cassius' part of the army and sacking his camp, while ultimately driving the ablest of The Liberator generals to suicide, but a failure because in Antonius' impetuous rush, he isolated two of his most veteran Legions, the 4th and 12th, both them being virtually annihilated. My friend Corbulo somehow survived, despite being in the thick of the fight. Antonius had been at the head of his men, fighting with them, showing great personal bravery, marking him as a successful warrior. However, he failed as a general, although I suppose it is fair to say that he did come out ahead of Cassius in one regard, because he was still alive while Cassius was dead. We killed a great number of the enemy, yet Brutus' wing had inflicted almost twice as many on our forces, because they had taken matters into their own hands, ignoring Brutus, who from the accounts of some prisoners simply sat on his hill paralyzed by indecision. I believe that is when I somehow knew that Vibius was in Brutus' part of the army, because he was the sort that would take the initiative when there was no clear direction, and men like that tend to flock together. Brutus' men inflicted heavy casualties on Octavian's men as well, particularly the 3rd Gallic Legion, who lost almost half their number, dead and wounded.

My force arrived in Cassius' camp late, so the best loot was already gone, although every man of the 10th went staggering back to our camp loaded down. It was in this last act of the drama of First Philippi that once again the gods proved they liked to laugh at our expense. The dust from the fighting had still not settled, there still being minor skirmishes going on, by this point in the day mostly between cavalry, so when we went plodding back to camp carrying our new-found possessions, our counterparts in Brutus' force were doing the exact same thing, only headed in the opposite direction and they were carrying our possessions. The two forces apparently passed by each other on our return to our respective camps, completely unaware of the other. Only when we came within sight of our camp did it become apparent that what Scribonius and I had heard was no echo. There were howls of anger and dismay at the sight of the bodies of the two green Legions from Octavian's force that had been left behind to guard the camp. When we entered, we were met by an eerily familiar sight; our camp looked exactly as we had left Cassius' camp, in complete destruction. Our tents were either slashed to ribbons or burned, though only after being thoroughly looted. Along with the hundreds of dead men, there were at least as many if not more dead horses, mules and oxen, another mark of a veteran army because killing the livestock kills an army's mobility. Brutus' camp was untouched, except that it was now full to overflowing because the survivors of Cassius' wing had run there for shelter. On the other hand, we had nothing, at least in terms of shelter, not to mention our own personal possessions, so it was a dispirited army that began the task of burying the animals and burning the dead before trying to rebuild the camp. Fortunately, Brutus was either unwilling or unable to take advantage of our predicament, enabling us to spend the rest of that day and night trying to regain some semblance of order. I went to what was left of the *Praetorium* to report, walking right into the middle of yet another screaming match between Antonius and Octavian, who was again lying on a litter. I heard Antonius before I saw him, as a makeshift headquarters tent had been stitched together to offer the Triumvirs some semblance of privacy, but leather walls could not contain Antonius' roar under the best of circumstances.

"Where in Hades were you, boy? How could you let them get into our camp?"

I have to say that I thought it was a fair question and as much as I distrusted Antonius, I thought he had a legitimate cause for complaint. It was then that I heard Octavian explain about the dream he had, explaining why he had gone into the marsh.

"Juno's *cunnus*," Antonius roared after Octavian had spoken. "You expect me to believe that? You're a coward, you mama's boy, that's all."

"I...am...no....coward," I had never heard Octavian sound so angry, and I was now close enough that I could hear him wheezing in between each word. "Need I remind you, Antonius, that I am co-commander of this army, and I will not tolerate such insults," Octavian continued, after seeming to regain some of his breath, if not his composure.

I had reached the leather curtain that served as the door, deciding I would wait there until it seemed a better time to enter. Besides, I did not want to interrupt what was an interesting conversation.

"Or what?" The sneer in Antonius' voice was unmistakable. "What are you going to do, boy?"

"I will make you wish you had never been born."

There was something in Octavian's voice that seemed to stop even Antonius, because for several moments, he said nothing more. When Antonius did speak again, the anger had been replaced by what sounded like a bone-deep weariness.

"So what are you suggesting we do now?"

As usual, Octavian was ready with an answer.

"We need to either rebuild or relocate the camp, of course, but I think the men will survive sleeping outside for one night. I think that tomorrow we offer battle again."

I was surprised, because this sounded more like something Antonius would say.

The older Triumvir was evidently not in the frame of mind I thought he was, because he replied, "What? We just lost twice as many men as they did. The 4th basically no longer exists and almost all the Centurions of the 12th are dead. We're going to have to shift men into them, the 4th in particular because they're veteran. You have Legions that aren't much better."

"The Legions I lost were my worst, with the exception of the 3rd Gallica," Octavian replied.

I could not help noticing that if one were to go just by his tone, you would think he was talking about the number of chickpeas we had left instead of men who had died because of his mistakes.

Octavian continued, "What Brutus lost was some of his best men, and more importantly, he lost Cassius and Brutus is no Cassius. No, I think we might be able to end this if we can goad Brutus into giving battle tomorrow."

"Maybe," Antonius said doubtfully. "But I don't think we'll be able to goad him into doing anything, at least tomorrow."

"There's only one way to find out," Octavian replied patiently.

"Fine," Antonius grumbled, then there was a silence, so I took that opportunity to have one of the clerks enter to tell them I was outside.

"What's he doing here?" Antonius demanded.

The clerk stammered that he did not know, and Antonius growled in a loud voice, "Pullus. Get in here."

I entered, saluting both of them, thankful that the way they were positioned it was natural for me to salute Antonius first since he was standing directly opposite the tent flap. Antonius repeated his question, and I gave him as brief a report as I thought I could get away with.

I finished with, "I also want to thank you, sir."

Antonius looked at me blankly, but I saw Octavian's head shoot up, feeling his eyes on me.

"Thank me," Antonius said warily. "For what?"

"For taking heed of my report about our situation, sir. That IS why you launched the assault, isn't it, sir? Because we had been out of food for four days?"

He said nothing as he looked at me. In that instant, I saw that he had not done any such thing; that in fact, he had completely forgotten about us.

He jerked as if realizing that I had seen through him, as he said sharply, "Of course it is. As soon as I saw your report I knew that something had to be done, and that's why we made the assault."

I dared not look at Octavian, yet I could see the small smile playing at his lips, as I thought, I am glad you think it's funny, though I suppose it was in some ways.

Antonius frowned. "But why are you here now? Who's at the redoubts?"

"Er, nobody, sir," I admitted. "I was planning on going back as soon as we resupplied, but with the camp being in the shape it's in, I'm not sure that we can."

"Of course you can," Antonius snapped. "And you will. Right now."

"Sir, if we go back out now, we're going to be in the same predicament that we were in when you made your rescue," I argued, knowing that I was laying it on thick.

Despite that, I was speaking the truth and I could see Antonius knew it.

Then Octavian spoke up. Pullus, the redoubt that you built. Can it be enlarged?"

I thought about it, then had a question of my own. "How large?" I asked.

Antonius was looking at Octavian as well, his eyes narrowed, not so much in suspicion but in realization at what Octavian was driving at.

"You tell me," he countered.

I cursed the man for never giving a straight answer.

Finally I said, "In the redoubt that I was holding, maybe for five Legions, but not much more. Scribonius'." I shook my head. "The ground's too wet. If you got a whole Legion in there, it would be cramped. And too muddy to move."

"Where are you going with this?" Antonius demanded.

"We need to make a new camp," Octavian replied. "Rather than rebuilding here, how about we put some pressure on Brutus?"

"Sorry, sir," I still hated calling Octavian "sir," though I did it in front of Antonius mainly because it irritated the older man. "There's no way you're going to get the whole army, even after the losses we've suffered, into one camp out on that ground."

"Then we break them up into smaller camps, strung out from east to west, putting even more pressure on Brutus' supply line back to Neapolis."

"That will only work if we get someone back out there to hold that ground," Antonius countered.

Seeing a chance for redemption, I said, "If you can get me the food, I'll get out there as soon as we get it. I only have one request."

Antonius looked wary, as did Octavian, who was the one to ask, "What?"

"Now that the 10th has proven itself, I want to take my Legion out there."

Antonius scratched his chin, then shrugged.

"I don't see why not. Besides, we need those veterans to put in the 4th and 12th. All right." He signaled for a clerk. "I'll get you your supplies. You go get back on that ground, take those redoubts, and wait for the rest of the army."

While we were waiting for a week's worth of rations for a whole Legion to be scrounged up, the mystery of the five *cornu* signals was finally solved, much to my dismay. It turned out that all five men had made it back past the enemy, but since none of them knew the watchword for that night, the particular Centurion of the watch, an idiot of the first grade if not the rank, threw each of them into chains to wait for morning. The fact that five men, each with the same message and the same story approached our camp within thirds of a watch of each other did not alert the Centurion that something was afoot. Fortunately, the Centurion relieving him had a bit more in the brains department, so he released the men, all of whom went racing to the *cornu* player on watch, each determined to be the winner of my promised bounty, while the duty Centurion went to report to Antonius carrying five tablets bearing the same message. I do not know exactly what happened; I suspect that the five men worked it out and paid the *cornicen* to sound the signal for each of them, realizing that I would be forced to pay each of them if he did. So I was out 2,500 sesterces, which is a fair amount, even for a Primus Pilus.

The rations were delivered to us, then less than a third of a watch later, the 10th Legion marched out of the gates, heading back up the trench. Reaching the first redoubt, I ordered a stop, sending two Cohorts to destroy it, the decision made by the Triumvirs that since it was too small for our purposes, it should not be allowed to fall into enemy hands. Scribonius grumbled a bit at that, nobody liking to see the fruits of their labor go to waste, but it had to be done. The rest of the Legion continued on to the larger redoubt, while I sent a Cohort ahead to make sure that the enemy had not occupied it. Luckily, it was empty and exactly as we left it. We went immediately to work enlarging the redoubt, which we could not have done unobserved if Cassius' camp had still been occupied, but it remained wrecked and deserted, serving as a screen between what we were doing and prying eyes. The men were not happy at the idea of filling in the ditch on three sides, but it could not be helped since we had to make the redoubt much larger. The only part of the camp that could be used was the rampart closest to the trench that led back to the main camp, although it had to be extended to the east and west to accommodate the larger size of the new camp. We staked out the crest of the small hill as the site for the *Praetorium* while the men went to work. Drainage ditches were dug that emptied into the ditch surrounding the camp to dry out the ground so that when the rest of the army came it would not become a huge lake of churned mud. It took us two days to enlarge the camp, with another day for the ground to dry out enough before I felt confident in sending the message back to the main camp that we were ready for them. The day after the first fight, Antonius had actually done as Octavian had suggested, offering battle, but Brutus refused. In fact, Brutus refused to do much of anything, his camp overcrowded with his essentially intact forces along with the remnants of Cassius', not even bothering to enlarge his own camp to make room for the extra men. As Octavian had correctly predicted, Brutus was not a man of action, as the stream of deserters from his cause talked of endless thirds of a watch of speech-making by Brutus, talking of the Republic this, and high-flying ideals that, none of which his audience had any interest in whatsoever.

"I just couldn't bear to hear him rattle on any longer," one of the deserters told the men at the gate of the camp when he came to give himself up.

Four days after we marched back out, the first of the army came moving up the trench under the cover of darkness, reaching the trench leading to the camp to be met by men I posted there to lead them into the camp without any problems. As I stood by the Porta Decumana of what was now a regular camp, though we still did not have any tents, I began to become alarmed as the men marched past in numbers much larger than I had expected. I grabbed Torquatus when I saw him, asking him if he knew how many Legions were coming.

"Ten, I think," he answered.

"Ten?" I hissed, causing him to look at me with a raised eyebrow.

"I thought you'd be happy with that much company."

I waved my hand around the camp, which was pointless because it was dark.

"I told Octavian that this area was big enough for five Legions and that would be pushing it. We had to drain a lot of the marsh as it was, but we're not going to have enough room for ten Legions."

Torquatus peered around in the darkness, but all he did was shrug, then say, "Well, take it up with him. All I know is that there are ten Legions coming."

Once the last men arrived, the Centurions were kept busy trying to arrange them despite having about half the room that we were all accustomed to, so there were a number of squabbles that had to be broken up. Somehow, we got everyone settled down, though I had my own share of troubles because I forced the men to rearrange themselves to make room, causing a good amount of grumbling that was only quelled by the judicious use of the *vitus*.

The next morning, I headed to the main camp, but before I got very far I met essentially the rest of the army coming up the trench. The Triumvirs were shifting our positions completely, abandoning the ruins of the original camp. At the junction of Cassius' transverse trench and his old camp, Antonius placed four Legions in a redoubt. We had lost a total of three Legions in the first battle, after redistribution of some of the men, so the remaining two Legions marched out past what was now our main camp, building a third redoubt about four or five furlongs to the east. We were now essentially in a line running west from the junction of the transverse trench, north of the original trenchline, but neither Triumvir was much interested in how cramped conditions were in the larger camp, at least as long as they were given the proper amount of space. New tents were constructed for the *Praetorium* and for the Triumvirs, of course, and I will not lie, for all the Primi Pili as well. I did not complain at sleeping under a roof again, even if it was made of leather.

Once the army had moved into its new position, only then did Brutus make any kind of move, relocating his army back onto the site of Cassius' camp. Our supply situation was now dire, as on the day of the first battle a convoy of ships carrying supplies and reinforcements was captured. Fortunately, the men of Brutus' army were constantly agitating for him to give the command to array for battle, which he resisted for several more days. We were now close enough that we could hear the shouting of the men in Brutus' camp, calling for him to give the command to attack, usually being the loudest shortly after dawn, then continuing intermittently through the day. We were sending foraging parties as far afield as Thessaly, trying to find enough grain or anything else edible to sustain the army. They returned empty-handed, but then we got one break from the gods, from the brother of the man who had shown Brutus and Cassius the goat track that allowed them to bypass Norbanus, holding the pass. In an effort to redeem himself for not remembering its existence, the man led a foraging party into the lands of the Bessi, living along the river Strymon (Struma), and returning with enough food for a month. There were whispers among the men that the agitation that was taking place in Brutus' camp was due to the placement of agents working for Octavian, intent on forcing Brutus to battle with us.

During a meeting of the Primi Pili with Antonius and Octavian, I learned that this was indeed the case and, in fact, at least one of these agents was high enough that he could report on the state of Brutus' mind, that he was afraid of most of his own men because so many of them had marched for Caesar, while his adopted son was in our camp. Further, he was scared of Cassius' men because he did not think they had any faith in him. In short, Brutus was backed into a corner, from which the only way to extricate himself meant that he had to do the one thing he did not want to do, which either would see him victorious or dead. Still, he resisted for several more days, until a bit more than three weeks after the first battle, the *bucina* sounded the alarm that warned that the enemy was forming up. After running to the *Praetorium* hill with Diocles in tow to get a good look and assure myself that this was the day for battle, I sent him back to alert the Pili Priores while I went into the tent to receive orders. Antonius and Octavian were together, and for the first time I had seen, actually were in good spirits, treating each other jovially and with a great show of friendship.

"*Salve*, Pullus," Antonius called to me as I walked in. "Are you ready to wade in some traitors' guts today?"

"I'm ready to do my job, Triumvir," I replied, the image of Vibius leaping into my mind, while Antonius made a face at my lack of martial fervor.

"I hope you fight harder than you talk," he joked.

I stared at him for a moment without replying, happy to see that he broke eye contact first.

Turning away from me, he said, "You and the 10th will take the far left. The 7th will be next to you on the right."

Octavian had been silent this whole time, watching the exchange with quiet amusement, but he spoke now. "My men are going to be on the right this time, Pullus. They requested that honor to make up for losing the camp. This is not meant as any slight against you or your men, I assure you. It's just a chance for mine to redeem themselves."

It was to Octavian that I saluted first, happy to see Antonius' face turn red at my not-so-subtle insult, though he said nothing. I left the *Praetorium* to get my men ready for the coming battle.

It took almost a full watch to get the army formed up, while Brutus' army watched from Cassius' hill. The fact that they did not try to attack as we were moving into position was a fatal mistake, but it also showed how little Brutus wanted this battle. We could see him riding up and down the front of his army; as we learned later, his pre-battle speech was not the most stirring. He essentially told the men that he did not want this fight and that if they lost, it would be on the heads of the men and not him. I suppose that there have probably been worse pre-battle speeches given, but I never heard any other that qualified.

Once we were arrayed, it was time for Antonius and Octavian to parade in front of us, and I know that it irked Antonius a great deal when the men cheered more loudly for Octavian. Nevertheless, Antonius was not a novice at manipulating men himself, so immediately after Octavian had galloped the length of the army, Antonius returned to our front to announce that he had decided to give the men a bounty of 20,000 sesterces should we be victorious over Brutus. Octavian was still near our end of the army, so could I see his cheeks burn red with suppressed rage. However, he quickly recovered, aiming Caesar's smile at Antonius, though his eyes told a different story. I had been told of the bonus the day before, so I knew that it in fact was Octavian's idea. Now, Octavian could not say anything about it without appearing churlish, yet I had no doubt that Octavian would find a way to repay Antonius, in kind and with interest. The men roared their approval at the news, turning to pound the comrade next to them on the back, until I had to turn around to remind them that we were about to fight a battle, which shut them up. With the pre-battle rituals over, we settled in to wait, the custom being that the general who summoned his men to battle being the one who initiated action, except that Brutus' reluctance continued. The day progressed as we waited, then we finally sent for the camp slaves to bring food to eat while we waited for Brutus to get off his pimply ass and give the command to attack. Finally, at mid-afternoon, the enemy *cornu* sounded as both sides clambered to their feet, hefting their shields and javelins, making their final preparations to kill each other.

We did not end up using our javelins at all, the men dropping them in their rush to get at the enemy, who did the same. We had been waiting too long, while the first battle had not been a clear victory for either side, making the men on both sides anxious to prove who was better. The instant the signal was given, everyone let out a huge roar as I found myself struggling to stay ahead of the men, hurtling towards Brutus' men, who were moving just as quickly towards us. I picked out the Primus Pilus of the Legion opposing us, barely having time to register the standard of the 27th Legion next to him, he evidently spotting me heading for him at roughly the same time. Then we went smashing into each other, not bothering with any kind of fancy maneuvers. Once again, my size held me in good stead as the Primus Pilus, several inches shorter and perhaps 30 pounds lighter went caroming off me, his feet flying up in the air to land heavily on his back.

Before he could recover, I leaped astride him, pulling my blade back as I snarled, "What were you thinking?"

Then, before I could end him, there was a blur of movement to my left, which I started to turn to face, knowing that it was the aquilifer of the 27th coming to rescue his Primus Pilus, except my own aquilifer, a man named Tertullus, thrust the end of his standard out between the man's legs, causing him to stumble. Tertullus used the spike end of his standard, driving it deep into the gut of his counterpart, as I turned back to see the Primus Pilus scrambling to his feet. Before he could completely regain his footing, I was on top of him, yet I must say he did a good job of parrying my thrusts for a few moments before he overcommitted, leaving me an opening that allowed me to thrust under his arm and into his chest. He fell without a word, then

I turned to see that Tertullus had captured the 27th's eagle, passing it to a man next to him, who went whooping with it to the rear. In the first few heartbeats we had killed the Primus Pilus while capturing the standard of the Legion, but these were veterans, some of them Caesar's men, comrades who I had marched with in Gaul, so they were not so easily defeated. After the initial chaos of the charge, both sides quickly settled into the rhythm of the fight in the Roman manner, shield to shield, shoulder to shoulder. Whistles began blowing as the Centurions established the intervals each line would fight, men shoving each other off before heading back to the rear of each Century. We were aligned in the traditional acies triplex, on a front of three Centuries per Cohort, yet for some reason the Primus Pilus of the 27th had not aligned his men to correspond with our frontage. While they were in a triplex acies as well, they had been put in a front of two Centuries per Cohort, making them deeper, but this meant that we overlapped their line by a good distance. A runner sent from Nigidius, the Pilus Prior of the Fourth Cohort, alerted me to this fact and I sent the runner back with orders to wrap around the right flank of Brutus' forces. I called for my own runner, ordering the third line to move up and shift over to press the advantage as well. It did not take long for one of the Tribunes on Antonius' staff to come galloping up to find me, demanding to know why I had ordered up the third line without orders. I did not even bother saluting, pointing off to our left.

"Tribune, do you see that?" I demanded, and he did sit up in his saddle to peer off in the direction where I was pointing.

"They didn't extend their lines enough," he said quickly, then before I could say more, he finished.

"Carry on. I'll report back to Antonius and explain that you did the right thing."

"Thank you," I called after him as he galloped off, giving a wave of his hand as he went to find Antonius.

There are some good Tribunes in this army every once in a while, I thought, then turned back to the job at hand myself. The fighting was still at a fever pitch, men snarling and spitting at each other over their shields, bashing and thrusting, while I blew the whistle every few moments to give the men a break. About a sixth part of the watch into the fight, there was a roar from the far right of the line, and I looked over to see the entire left wing of Brutus' force collapsing, the men streaming up the hill back to their camp, with Octavian's men in hot pursuit. Men were being cut down from behind as they struggled up the slope. Very quickly, the hill was strewn with bodies, most of them belonging to Brutus. Once the support of their comrades to the left melted away, the center collapsed, most of the men suffering the same fate as the enemy left. Octavian's men went streaming into Brutus' camp, so before long, only the right wing of the enemy force was left on the field, but we had them surrounded. We were whittling them down, the outcome inevitable, but these men were going to go down fighting, it was clear. Some of the men from our center had now wrapped around the diminishing force of Brutus' right wing, so that we were now compressing them from all sides. They had formed an *orbis*, though their ranks were only three and in some places four deep, not enough to give men sufficient time to rest before they had to move back into the fight. I could see a couple dozen Centurions' crests bobbing about among the enemy, each of them working frantically to plug gaps in their line. There was no more wild shouting, from either side, men conserving as much energy as possible, the only sound now being the clanging of blade on blade or rim of shield, along with the dull thudding noise of shield boss smashing into flesh, punctuated by grunts and short, sharp screams as men fell.

"Kill these bastards," I kept roaring over and over, grabbing men to push them into gaps in the line.

Then, out of the corner of my eye, I caught a movement among the enemy, and to this day, I do not know why it arrested my attention. It was a Centurion who was moving quickly across our front to a trouble spot in his line. As I focused on him, I felt a sudden weakness in my knees, recognizing the bandy legs and muscular arms, arms that I had clasped and wrestled against since a day so long ago when I had pulled him from a bucket of *cac*.

Without thinking, I began moving parallel to our line, following Vibius as he ran to some trouble spot, seeing him step in over one of his men who had fallen, a blur of motion as he thrust his blade into the man who had knocked his down. Immediately, he moved again, this time in response to a shout for help from another of his men. I continued following him behind our own lines, shoving men out of the way to keep pace with him. We were still pressing against the pocket, which was growing smaller every moment, then after Vibius had dispatched another of our men, I saw him turn to look about, surveying the situation. He still had not seen me, or at least I did not think so, but I could tell he now saw the hopelessness of his situation. Then, obviously making a decision, he turned and, spotting a point in our lines where there was less depth, he grabbed a number of his men, making straight for it. Where he headed was on the far side of where I was standing, so it was not defended by my men, yet I was so focused on Vibius that again I pushed my way through the crowd of men to make my way to him.

As I moved past the Second Cohort, I heard Scribonius yell, "Where are you going?"

I pointed at Vibius, hearing Scribonius utter a string of oaths, finishing with, "Titus, don't!"

But I was oblivious to everything except the need to reach Vibius. Making my way through the mass of men and closing the distance, I saw that Vibius was leading a substantial number of men to press the thin spot in our line hard, and looked close to breaking out. I began running, knocking men down in my haste to get to Vibius before he could escape, intent on stopping him. Somewhere, as I was running, I had made the decision that I was going to finish what I had been unable to at Pharsalus; I was going to kill Vibius.

Reaching what was now a breach in our lines, it was just as the first of the men with Vibius began to start running for their lives, leaping over the fallen men who they had cut down to open the gap. They did not look back, knowing that this was really the only way to escape, not wasting any time to see if there was someone hot on their heels. They ran off to the north, apparently heading for Brutus' old camp. Vibius was staying put, pushing men through the gap like a good Centurion, his back slightly towards me as I approached. Some of his men saw me running towards them, calling a warning to Vibius, who turned around, his blade up and ready in the first position, legs shoulder-width apart and slightly bent. Seeing him face to face brought me up short, and when our eyes met, it was as if a knife were plunged into my vitals. His eyes widened as he recognized me, but he had the presence of mind to snap an order over his shoulder, telling the rest of the men to keep moving to make good their escape. He turned back to face me, his face unreadable, though he did not drop his guard in any way. As quickly as it had come, my resolve to finish him here and now disappeared. It was as if the strength drained from my arm, and I dropped the point of my sword. Time seemed to stop, the sounds of the fighting going on all around us drowned out by the sound of my own breathing as Vibius and I looked into each other's eyes, neither of us seeming to know what to say.

Finally, I jerked my head in the direction of his fleeing men, then said quietly, "Go."

He turned and started to head after his men, then he stopped to look back.

"Tell Juno I said 'hello,'" I called, surprising both of us, and he laughed.

"I will," he replied, then turned serious. "May the gods keep you safe, Titus. You're still my oldest and best friend."

And with that, he turned away to run off. That was the last time I ever saw Vibius Domitius, my oldest friend. I heard a cough behind me, and turned to see Scribonius standing there, panting for breath.

"You did the right thing, Titus," Scribonius told me, putting a hand on my shoulder. "You would never have been able to live with yourself if you had killed him."

"I know," I said, then turned to give him a tired smile. "Let's finish this so we can get some rest."

The Second Battle of Philippi, unlike the First Battle, was a complete success for the army of the Triumvirs, with The Liberator army effectively ceasing to exist after that day. That is not to say that most of the men marching for Brutus were killed, though a substantial number were, but many of them scattered to the four winds, never to be heard from again as far as being an army. Most of those men returned to their homes to pick the plow back up, although some of them made their way east to become mercenaries for the Parthians. A substantial number volunteered to serve in the army of the Triumvirs, the offer being accepted by both Octavian and Antonius. Vibius was not one of these men. Brutus had watched the disaster unfolding and when he saw that his cause was lost, made haste to escape, prevailing upon one of his freedmen by the name of Lucilius to don his armor and cape to pass himself off as his master. As Octavian's men, led by Agrippa, were tearing down the front wall of the camp, Brutus and a small party escaped by the back gate, heading up into the Sapaean Pass, where Brutus quoted some Homer, then killed himself. With his death, the Triumvirs were now the undisputed masters of Rome and most of the known world.

However, that did not mean that the strife was ended, because things were still unsettled between Octavian and Antonius. One might think that their shared victory might have led to a little amity between them, at least for a short period of time, but almost immediately the squabbling began again. This time it was over the disposition of Brutus' body, which was found by a cavalry patrol, who brought it to Antonius, the Triumvir planning on a full military funeral with all honors. However, Octavian would have none of it, so there was another blazing argument between the two. By the time the proverbial dust had settled, neither of them were happy, which is a sign that a true compromise was reached, though I imagine Brutus would not have seen it that way. Antonius got the body to burn, while Octavian got the head to defile. Personally, I was with Octavian on this, not believing that Brutus deserved anything but to be carrion for the dogs. The other piece of good news was that our food problem was solved for some time to come, as The Liberator camps was stuffed with supplies of all sorts. Brutus' head was sent to Rome in advance of the army, but the ship carrying it sank in a storm, so Octavian never got the chance to put it up on a spike on the Rostra of the Forum. While most of the rest of the assassins of Caesar either chose to fall on their swords or were killed, a few had escaped, some of them going to join Sextus Pompey, while others went to seek their fortune in the east, along with the men who hired themselves out as mercenaries. Antonius had announced that he would be going to Parthia, to fulfill Caesar's dying wish to subdue what was considered as one of the last great threats to Rome. I was summoned to the *Praetorium* to be informed that the 10th would be going with Antonius to Parthia.

"You've been to that part of the world, as I recall," Antonius said.

I confirmed that I had, with the 6th, and he replied, "Which is one of the reasons that I want the 10th, because you have experience in that part of the world."

I tried to point out that while I had faced the Parthians, the 10th had not, but Antonius waved a dismissive hand.

"Same difference," he declared. "You and the 10th are going."

I recognized that there was no point in arguing, so I saluted, then went to tell the men that we would be heading east. I was not happy about being assigned to Marcus Antonius, but I did not feel any real conflict at that point, knowing that I had no choice in the matter.

R.W. Peake

Chapter 4- Ventidius' Men

Before we would land to march into Parthia, Antonius had to raise money, a lot of money. Taking a ship from Greece and heading east, we made a number of stops, none of which outdid his entrance into Ephesus, where he announced that he was Dionysus incarnate, and as a god demanded recompense worthy of his status. The howls of the citizens could be heard over the walls and in our camp, where we were waiting in case there was trouble. I could certainly understand their feelings. It had only been the year before when Brutus and Cassius had come parading through here demanding ten years' tribute, which Antonius demanded be matched. Finally, he relented somewhat, accepting a total of nine years', but giving the citizens two years to pay. We traveled overland from Ephesus, marching through Asia Minor, Syria, and Palestine, with Antonius demanding tribute from those provinces that had sided with The Liberators, no matter how unwillingly. He rewarded the Lycians and Rhodians, for they had resisted The Liberators, namely Cassius, at great cost to themselves. He gave Cappadocia to a man named Archelaus, whose mother Glaphyra Antonius lusted after, at the expense of the late king's son Ariarathes, who seemingly had a more legitimate claim to the throne. From there we went to Cilicia, where he tied up the last of his business by summoning a puppet monarch who had supposedly agreed to supply Antonius with money, ships, and troops. When I heard who it was, I resolved to do everything I could to be present when the two met, knowing that Antonius was about to meet his match in Cleopatra. I was right, but not necessarily in the way that I thought.

[180]

She arrived in all the pomp and panoply befitting the queen of a kingdom much more ancient than our republic, even when it was run by kings, wearing the same outfit I had seen when I was in Alexandria and a guest at her banquet. She came up the river Cydnus (Berdan) on her massive barge, reclining on her couch in plain sight, while being attended by young girls dressed as Graces and Nymphs, the little boys adorned as Cupids. I must admit that I felt a bit smug, letting it be known that I had personally been on that barge. We were standing on the bank, watching the approach of the massive vessel, and Scribonius shot me a look that I like to think was a mixture of respect and curiosity.

"Really?" he demanded. "When was this?"

I told him about the trip up the Nile, and Caesar's holiday, most of it spent in the arms of Cleopatra.

He shot me a grin.

"One thing I'll say for Caesar. The old boy knew how to live."

I could only agree, then without warning, I felt a twinge of grief as I thought of the man who had given me so much. Fortunately, Scribonius did not notice, his attention drawn back to the barge, which was now mooring at the dock. Cleopatra rose from the couch, as once more I tried to figure out how such a small woman could move at all with the enormous contraption on her head, let alone make it seem so easy. The dock was lined with onlookers, most of whom were cheering her, yet she gave no sign that she heard them, such a display not being seemly for a monarch, I suppose. However, she did survey the crowd, her head turning slowly, which I was sure was due to the height and weight of her great hat. When she came to where Scribonius and I were standing, I saw her stop for a moment. Even if she had given a sign of recognition, her face was so heavily made up that I doubt that I could have seen it, though I still found my hand about to raise to give a wave. Thankfully, I stopped from making a complete fool of myself, pulling my hand down. Still, I was sure that she had seen me, and recognized me. It did not take long to discover that I was right.

Only a few thirds of a watch later, I received a summons, brought to me by one of those creatures that were such a part of the palace scene in Alexandria, requesting me to attend to the queen in her quarters that evening before dinner. I am afraid I wore poor Diocles out making my uniform and decorations presentable, while I was as nervous as a virgin bride on her wedding night. I followed my escort to the residence that Cleopatra had commandeered, he taking a roundabout way that avoided going through the forum, a precaution for which I was thankful, with good reason as it turned out. I was announced, and I was both flattered and more than a little disconcerted to see that there were no other guests present. The queen was reclining on a couch, wearing another of her diaphanous gowns, this one a deep and rich blue chased with golden thread, her hair plaited in the manner that I had seen her wear for Caesar, the back tied with a ribbon at the nape of her neck. The eunuch that I supposed was in charge of such things announced me. She rose to her feet, favoring me with her most dazzling smile, and once again I was reminded that despite her plainness, there was something absolutely captivating and alluring about her.

"Primus Pilus Pullus, how wonderful to see you again." She offered me her hand, which I remembered I was supposed to kiss and not shake. As I bent down, I could feel the heat rising to my face.

"I had quite forgotten how large a man you are," Cleopatra said.

Although it was true that I towered over her, she was one of the smallest women I had ever met, yet I was still more flattered than I probably should have been.

"It's wonderful to see you again, Highness. You're as lovely as ever." I congratulated myself for sounding as if I said such things all the time, my reward the sound of her laughter as she playfully slapped me on my arm.

"Spoken like a true courtier, Primus Pilus. If I didn't know better, I would say that you've been spending time in some other queen's palace. Should I be jealous?"

She assumed a sly expression, giving me a wink. Despite not thinking it possible, I felt a second rush of heat and I knew that my face was even redder. I stammered that this was not the case at all, as Cleopatra laughed even harder at my obvious discomfort. She turned to wave to one of her slaves, who moved to a door at the other end of the chamber I had been escorted into, opening it so I could see that it was a dining room, the table set for two.

"I was hoping that you would join me for dinner, Primus Pilus." Cleopatra spoke as if it was a request, but I was no fool. I had seen her temper and had no wish to bear the brunt of it, so in answer I offered her my arm, wondering what she had in mind.

"Tell me about Antonius." Cleopatra stared at me over the rim of her cup after we were seated. There it is, I thought, the reason revealed, and I would be lying if I said I was not somewhat disappointed. I considered the question, wondering how far to go.

"He's no Caesar," I said carefully, to which she gave a snort.

"I know that, Pullus," she replied with more than a trace of impatience. "But tell me why you think he summoned me here, and what he's after."

"To squeeze you for every last sesterce, chickpea, kernel of wheat, and ingots of iron he can get from you," I replied.

I was happy to see that my answer had pleased her.

"Now you're telling the truth, and truth, no matter how ugly it may be, is what I need right now, Pullus. His creature Quintus Dellius has been whispering honeyed words into my ear about how much regard Antonius has for me, but then I am summoned here like a vassal!"

She was clearly angry now, making me extremely uncomfortable.

"Highness, you realize you're putting me in an extremely awkward position," I said, causing her to lean back, her expression unreadable, but I had to continue. "Antonius is my general, and he's a Roman. You are queen, that's true, but you're foreign and I'm a loyal Roman. If word were to get out that we met, it could be very bad for me."

"Pullus, why do you think you're my only guest tonight? I gave Quintus Dellius, who has been my shadow, a task this evening to carry a message to Antonius announcing my arrival, just before you arrived. I also requested that Dellius wait for Antonius' answer, so I do not expect him back this evening, but even if he were to return, we would be warned in more than enough time for you to return to camp unobserved."

I considered this, then slowly nodded my head.

"Very well," I said. "I'll answer your questions to the best of my ability, for the sake of Caesar's memory and your son."

I was not prepared for the glint of tears in her eyes at the mention of her old lover and my general. For several moments, we sat there, sharing our own silent memories of the man who had such an impact on our lives. Finally, I decided to ask a question that had been rattling around in my head since I received her invitation.

"Why me?" I asked suddenly. "Surely there are higher-ranking men in the army whose acquaintance you made while you lived in Rome that know Antonius far better than I do."

She considered the question, staring into her wine cup. When she finally answered, she spoke slowly, clearly choosing her words carefully.

"For several reasons, not all of which I'm willing to divulge to you, Pullus. First, because I don't trust any of Rome's upper classes any farther than I can throw them, and you see how small I am."

I laughed politely at her jest.

"Secondly, even if I did trust them, they would tell me what they thought I wanted to hear, and I know that a large number of them despise me. Cicero was the worst of the lot." Her mouth twisted into a bitter smile as she spoke his name. "But he wasn't the only one. Finally," now she looked directly into my eyes, her tone almost challenging, "because I trust you, though I don't exactly understand why I do, although I'm sure that much of it has to do with Caesar. You know that he thought very highly of you, don't you?"

"I know that he respected my fighting ability," I answered.

I was surprised when she shook her head.

"No," she said. "It wasn't just that. He said that despite your lack of education, you're extremely bright, and of all things that Caesar respected most, it was a powerful mind. He said that he expected to make you a Senator at some point in the future, after all his reforms went through and you had elevated yourself to the equestrian class. That was something of a test, you see, to watch and see if you had the ambition and ability to do that yourself. Caesar told me that if you did that, he would find a way to make you a Senator in the future."

I sat there, stunned and completely speechless. I have often wondered whether Cleopatra was telling me the truth, or if she was just doing exactly what she had accused the upper-class Romans of doing; telling me what she thought I wanted to hear.

Returning to the subject at hand, Cleopatra asked me, "What kind of general is Antonius?"

"He's not Caesar's bootlace," I said quickly, and then wincing at myself for speaking too quickly, I hurried to expand on that. "Oh, he's brave enough, I think to a fault," I continued. "But he's much too impulsive, and he tends to rush headlong into a situation when he would be better off taking his time and surveying the situation and the ground."

She considered this for a moment, then asked, "But the men love him, don't they?"

"Some do," I admitted. "Although that number has shrunk considerably since he served with us in Gaul. This...situation with Octavian has exposed a side to him that I don't think has endeared him to any of us. He can be extremely vindictive, and yet in almost the same breath he can do something extremely generous, though in truth I haven't seen much of that lately. But it makes him unpredictable, and if there's one thing a

Legionary wants more than anything in his commander, besides competence, it's predictability."

"You mentioned Octavian," Cleopatra's tone was casual, but it sounded forced to me. A suspicion began blooming in me that perhaps he was her real reason for this dinner. "Tell me about him."

This was a subject I was not willing to discuss, and I said as politely as I could that Octavian was off-limits. She clearly did not like it, but seeing that I was not budging, she was gracious enough about it, returning to Antonius. We talked of Antonius for another third of a watch, in between bites of food, which were brought in by relays of slaves. Finally, the talk turned to more pleasant things, like the trip up the Nile and the work she had done in rebuilding Alexandria in the seven years since we were there and almost destroyed the city. The talk then turned to her son, Caesarion. For me, this was the most difficult part of the dinner. Her love and pride in her son was plain to see, which made me think of Vibi and Gisela.

I suppose that something must have showed in my face, because Cleopatra said, clearly offended despite the lightness in her tone, "Is there something wrong, Pullus? I suppose hearing the prattling of a proud mother must be quite tedious."

I do not know what prompted me to speak thus, but I imagine part of it was that I saw that she was not just offended; she was hurt. I shook my head.

"It's not that at all, Highness. It's just that hearing you speak of your son reminded me of mine."

"You have a family?" she asked, clearly surprised.

"Had," I said through the lump in my throat.

For a moment, she did not appear to understand, then her eyes softened and she reached across the table to put her hand on mine.

"I am sorry, Pullus. I didn't mean to bring up a painful memory."

Again, I shook my head. "It's quite all right, Highness. You had no way of knowing."

She seemed to hesitate for a heartbeat, then asked, "How were they taken from you?"

Then I told her the whole story, of the furious ride to Brundisium with Diocles, and the moment of realization that the gods had taken my family from me. I talked of Gisela and her beauty, of Vibi and his ferocious temper that was so much like his mother's, and his sturdy body and size that was so much like me. I talked of the daughter I had barely known; I talked with Cleopatra in a way that I had never done with anyone before or since about my loss and the almost unbearable pain that it had caused. When I was finished, I looked up and was surprised to see tears streaming down her face, which she made no attempt to hide, and I will admit that I fell a little in love with Cleopatra that night.

"I couldn't bear to lose Caesarion," she whispered, then suddenly a tremor passed through her whole body as the very idea made her shudder with fear.

"I don't think that there's anything worse than outliving your children," I replied.

We sat there for several moments, each of us lost in our own thoughts.

Then, it was time to leave, and as I was thanking her for a wonderful evening, I made my big mistake, one that has haunted me through the years. I had turned to leave when she called out to me. I turned to see standing before me no queen, no temptress; nothing but a concerned mother, wringing her hands, clearly tormented by the turn our conversation had taken.

"Pullus, do you think Caesarion has anything to worry about from Octavian?"

I should not have answered, but when I looked in her face, I saw the ghost of another mother who loved her child very much, a woman with flaming red hair. It felt like my heart was being squeezed by the hand of some god, and I could not leave her standing there looking this way.

Shaking my head, I assured her, "No, Highness. He's just a boy, and he poses no threat to Octavian whatsoever. He may be many things, but he's no murderer of children."

She looked obviously relieved, and when I left I felt good about myself, happy that I had eased her fears. Despite how things turned out between us, many nights my sleep has been disturbed by the sight of her face, smiling in relief and happiness at my lie.

I was present when Cleopatra made her appearance before Antonius in Tarsus, catching him by surprise, the Triumvir clearly not anticipating a woman, even a queen, to take the initiative. He was clearly expecting to see her in his own good time, but Cleopatra was not one to wait for anyone. Antonius was hearing cases from a number of litigants in the forum, and I suppose, because of my size, I had been delegated to stand slightly behind Antonius in full uniform, carrying my *vitus*, with strict instructions to look as imposing and nasty as possible. As Antonius was listening, with barely concealed impatience, to a complaint from some merchant, there was a stir at the back of the crowd, accompanied by a rolling murmur as the crowd parted. Looking over the heads of the people, I could see a little brown man, the same one who brought me to see Cleopatra the night before, garbed in the pleated linen vestment worn by members of the Egyptian court, gently pushing people aside.

Following him was another of her creatures, a eunuch named Philo, who announced in a loud but surprisingly deep voice, "All hail Pharaoh, Lord of the Two Ladies Upper and Lower Egypt, Mistress of Sedge and Bee, Child of Amun-Ra, Isis and Ptah!"

He stamped a golden staff on the floor three times, then stepped aside to allow Cleopatra entry, which she did while being carried on an enormous gold litter adorned with peacock feathers and borne by eight huge Nubians, all of them bedecked in gold and peacock feathers in the same manner as the litter. The Nubians set the litter down smoothly, then without waiting for assistance, Cleopatra alighted from it, wearing her traditional royal garb, minus the huge headdress, choosing a simple diadem instead. I was not sure, but I supposed that was to emphasize her Macedonian heritage and to make her seem a bit less foreign to the Roman contingent.

Still, I could see the other Romans present who had never seen Cleopatra or anything Egyptian gaping at her strangeness, yet she was seemingly oblivious as she said in her clear, carrying voice, "Marcus Antonius, you summoned me and I am here."

All eyes turned to Antonius, whose face was a mask, yet his tone was courteous as he replied, "Your Highness, I am sorry to say that your name is not on the list to be seen today, and my schedule is full. You must see my secretary, but I promise that your name will be first on my list to be seen in the morning."

There was a sudden stillness in the air, and I could see two spots of color rise on Cleopatra's cheeks. Meanwhile, the crowd, who had removed themselves to the edges of the forum in order to give her the deference and respect due to a monarch, seemed as shocked as she was. She was not so easily outmaneuvered though; recovering quickly, she favored Antonius with a brilliant smile.

"Of course, Imperator," I had to suppress a smile at her use of the term, knowing that Antonius would preen at being hailed as such. "I will send Philo to see your secretary. In the meantime, I was wondering if you would care to join me for dinner aboard my barge this evening, say, just after sunset?"

Antonius had been outflanked, at least in the eyes of the crowd and he knew it, though I could see he was puzzling out exactly how it had happened. I knew enough about people of the East to understand that they placed much more emphasis on the rights and prerogatives of kingship than we Romans did, according monarchs a deference that we found repugnant. Antonius had come across to them as a boorish oaf whose heavy-handed attempt to establish his dominance looked like little more than bullying. Cleopatra was appearing as the magnanimous one, forbearing Antonius' rudeness with grace and aplomb, and I found myself applauding her performance. Silently, of course.

Antonius gave a curt nod, saying, "I have no other plans. I will be there."

"Wonderful." Cleopatra smiled, then turned back to her litter. Before alighting, she turned back as if something had just occurred to her. "If you wish, please feel free to invite Quintus Dellius, Lucius Poplicola, and say, fifty of your friends?"

As she said this, I saw her look over Antonius' shoulder, our eyes locking for a moment. My heart began beating wildly as she seemed about to say something more. Please don't invite me Cleopatra, I kept thinking over and over. Finally, the moment passed as she closed her mouth, then slid back into the litter. I was thanking the gods that she had not included me in her invitation when Antonius turned to look at me, suspicion written all over his face. Cleopatra's litter exited the forum, with Philo taking up the rear of the small procession, before Antonius turned back to the litigant, who was standing helplessly throughout the exchange between Triumvir and queen.

Once the business with all the cases was finished, Antonius ordered me to dismiss the people. I stepped forward, waving my *vitus*, shooing people out of the forum. A couple people were a bit reluctant, so I gave them a good shove to get them going. Once the forum was deserted, I turned to leave, but Antonius called out to me, telling me to attend to him. His face was cold, his tone matching it when he jerked his chin in the general direction of where Cleopatra had gone.

"What was that all about?"

"What was what about?" I asked, determining that answering too quickly would only arouse Antonius' suspicions, so accustomed was he to men in my position acting stupid in front of their superiors.

"You know exactly what," he snapped. "That cozy little look she gave you? She was about to say something to you; I saw it."

I furrowed my brow, the picture of confusion. "I'm not sure what you're referring to, sir. I wasn't watching her; I was watching the crowd to make sure that there wasn't any trouble." I paused as if thinking about it, then said, "But if she were looking at me, I'm sure it's because she recognized me. Remember, I was with Caesar in Alexandria with the 6th."

Either Antonius had forgotten or had not been aware of this, because his demeanor changed immediately, but his tone was still doubtful.

"That makes sense, I suppose," he said slowly, rubbing his chin. He looked at me sharply then asked, "So you've been around her a lot, then? You know something about her?"

I shook my head. "I wasn't around her that much," I replied, lying through my teeth. "I only know what I saw, which was pretty much what you just saw. Acting like a queen, putting on airs. Typical royalty, I suppose."

He grunted, and I could tell that I had satisfied his suspicions, because his mind was clearly elsewhere. I waited for several moments, but he was clearly lost in thought.

Finally, I cleared my throat, then asked, "Will that be all, sir?"

"What? Oh, yes."

He waved a hand, dismissing me, and I walked out of the forum, trying to ignore my tunic soaked completely through with sweat.

Thus began what has quickly passed into legend as one of the great tempestuous love affairs of all time. From that first party on her barge there began a series of revels, alternating between her barge and his palace, to which I was invited on one occasion, towards the end of the time before Cleopatra returned to Egypt. I still thank the gods that it was not one of those accursed costume parties that the upper classes seem to love, because I do not even want to think what kind of frippery Antonius would have made me wear, probably nothing more than a loincloth, if that. I do not know if they had become lovers by this point, but if not, it was not for a lack of trying on the part of Antonius, who was panting after Cleopatra like a man who had been chained as a galley slave and had not seen a woman in years. Even during my one relatively short exposure to their particular song, it was clear that Cleopatra was playing Antonius like a harp and frankly, it was a little disgusting to see one of the most powerful men on the planet behave so shamefully over a woman, though I could somewhat understand in her case. The rumor was that Cleopatra had demanded that if Antonius wanted her favors he had to prove himself worthy by killing Arsinoe, the sister that caused so many problems along with her tutor Ganymede seven years before. I dismissed it as rumor; until, that is, after Cleopatra's return to Egypt, Antonius went to Ephesus, where Arsinoe was living as a priestess in the temple to Artemis, had her dragged out, then run through with a sword. From Ephesus, Antonius went on to Antioch, Tyre and Sidon, doing his job as governor of the East in the same manner as he had at Tarsus, hearing cases and dispensing justice. It was about this time that two things happened, both of which would have enormous ramifications to further events, rippling outward through time like a stone thrown into water makes waves that reach farther and farther.

Nobody had ever accused Lucius Antonius, the Triumvir's brother, of being the brains of the Antonius family. While Marcus was no Caesar, when compared to his younger brother he was an absolute Colossus of intellect. So perhaps it was not surprising that Lucius, along with Marcus' wife Fulvia, took it upon themselves to start a war in Italia. Lucius was Consul for the year, which I suppose helped to nudge him in the direction of declaring war. Fulvia contributed to the cause by convincing Munatius Plancus, who had managed to that point to stay neutral, into donating the services of the veterans he was charged with settling around Beneventum, about two Legions' worth of men. Lucius, using his status as Consul, recruited two fresh Legions of his own down in the boot of the peninsula, then began marching north towards Rome. To make matters even more confusing and difficult for Octavian, Fulvia also convinced that idiot Tiberius Claudius Nero, who had served briefly with Caesar and the two Cohorts of the 6th in Alexandria before being dismissed by Caesar, into raising a slave revolt in Campania. I should say, that was what he was charged with doing, but as usual he bungled the job so badly that not one slave rose up.

Octavian was caught out, because he had no official status other than being Triumvir, meaning he could not afford to engage Lucius, choosing instead to try beating Lucius' army to cities and towns containing supplies in an attempt to starve him out. The third Triumvir, my old enemy Lepidus, marched two Legions to Rome, where he supposedly made speeches about how he would wade in Lucius' guts should the Triumvir's brother dare to show his face. In reality, Lepidus immediately disappeared when the standards of Lucius' army were in view from the Capitoline Hill, taking his two Legions with him. Surrounding Italia on all sides were men loyal to Antonius, each of them with a substantial army of their own; Pollio was in Cisalpine Gaul with seven Legions, Quintus Calenus was in Transalpine Gaul with eleven, and Ventidius the mule driver was in Liguria with another seven. All Marcus Antonius had to do was send word to each or all of these men, and they would have been more than happy to crush Octavian, yet he sent no such word. Further compounding Octavian's woes was the presence of Sextus and his fleets, squeezing off the mainland from Sicily, Sardinia and Africa, thereby starving the peninsula to death. Lucius marched, now with six Legions, to the city of Perusia. He was obviously counting on Antonius' generals in the provinces to come to his aid, because he basically penned himself up in the city, then settled down to wait for Octavian to come, expecting that the young Triumvir would be trapped between his own force and that of whichever general came to his rescue.

By this time, Marcus Antonius had moved on to Athens, where from all accounts he was living up to his reputation for debauchery. I imagine that he was never sober enough to bother answering the procession of letters from every one of his lieutenants asking for direction. As a result, they did nothing, allowing Octavian, or more accurately Agrippa to surround Perusia then invest it, cutting off not only its food but its water supply. This was the situation as winter set in during the year of the Consulship of Lucius Antonius and Publius Servilius Vatia Isauricus. It was atthis time of utmost crisis that Marcus Antonius decided that it was time for a holiday in Alexandria with Cleopatra.

The part of the army with Antonius was left behind in Ephesus, where we moved into winter camp, with Saxa left in command. Meanwhile Antonius sailed to Alexandria from Athens, after a brief stop in Ephesus. He held a meeting of Primi Pili, and I was shocked at his appearance; his face puffy from night after night of excess, his eyes dull and his breath rank, but his voice was strong and he was his usual blustering self. His orders were the usual useless drivel. Keep the men fit and ready to fight, announcing that he planned on leaving for Parthia the next spring. Corbulo was standing next to me and we exchanged a glance at this news, Corbulo raising his eyebrows in doubt, a feeling I shared. It just seemed that there was too much going on in Italia for Antonius to feel secure enough to summon the bulk of the army to join the expedition. I refused to believe that even Antonius would be so reckless as to march on the Parthians with a fraction of his army. Word had reached us just how bad things were in Italia, the gossips in the upper classes telling tales of how Antonius' wife Fulvia had apparently lost her mind, taking up residence in the camp of Plancus, walking about with a sword strapped to her hip, giving orders while, if the most outlandish tale was to be believed, issuing the daily watchword like she was the general and not Plancus. As one can imagine, this was the main topic of conversation in our winter huts, the men grinning at each other as they speculated on what was really taking place in the *Praetorium* between Fulvia and Plancus. It did not take long after Antonius arrived in Alexandria that word reached us that he had finally achieved his conquest of Cleopatra, more or less picking up where he had left off in Tarsus a few months before. The parties and revels were so licentious and bawdy that the subject of them quickly replaced all the conjecture about a possible illicit affair between Fulvia and Plancus. Apparently it did not take long for Cleopatra to fall into the spirit of what was going on, as together they formed the Society of Inimitable Livers, he as the new Dionysus and she as Aphrodite. I will not detail all of the legendary excess of this "society," but while it did not sit particularly well with the army, it did give us a topic of conversation to while away the long winter nights. Men of all ranks tried to come up with the most bizarre and wasteful acts imaginable, claiming that they had it on good authority that these were not figments of their imaginations, but had actually happened. The more outrageous the act, the easier it was for the men to believe, and as I sat and listened in the Centurions' mess, I must admit that I was just as likely to believe as anyone. Through Diocles' slave network I was hearing what was supposedly actually taking place, and the things I heard through Diocles were barely different than the imaginings of my comrades. This was the manner in which most of the winter passed, along with the normal drudgery and routine of army life in winter camp. Scribonius, Balbus and I spent many thirds of a watch together, discussing the political situation, reminiscing about times past, and letting the dice fly, as we waited for spring.

The year of the Consulship of Gnaeus Domitius Calvinus and my old general, Gaius Asinius Pollio, started eventfully, with two events on opposite sides of our world. Perusia fell, and with it Lucius Antonius and Fulvia's attempt to destroy Octavian, an attempt that would have succeeded had Marcus Antonius simply given the orders to his other generals to come to the aid of his brother and wife. While Lucius was allowed to keep his head and his freedom, as were the men of the army, all of them receiving pardons from Octavian, the citizens of the city were not so lucky, Octavian ordering the execution of many of its leaders, as well as allowing his own troops to sack the city. This act did not sit well with the Italians, Octavian's reputation suffering accordingly, but he clearly did not care. In the East, the king of the Parthians, Orodes, sent one of his sons Pacorus, along with another famous general's son, none other than Quintus Labienus, at the head of an army into Syria. The news of a Parthian invasion bestirred Antonius from his idyll in Alexandria, prompting him to travel overland to Antioch, and it was in Antioch that he got word of the fall of Perusia. Only then did he seem to recognize that no matter how alarming the situation in Syria was, Italia was more important. He rode hard to Ephesus, not staying long enough for any kind of meeting with us, taking ship to Athens. We were left with no clear instructions, because Saxa had gone to Antioch to monitor events in Syria, so the Primi Pili had a meeting on our own, deciding to step up the training schedule to make the men as ready as we could in the event that the Parthians continued their advance or we were ordered to stop them.

The men grumbled, but their hearts were not in it, being just as bored as the Centurions, knowing that sweating more now meant bleeding less later, so they fell to the increased training with a will. By the time Antonius arrived in Athens, Fulvia had already arrived there. If there had not been enough to talk about before, Antonius' treatment of Fulvia was soon the fodder of mealtime conversations, as he took his rage at the reverse at Perusia out on her, not that I can blame him much. Women, especially noble Roman women, are not supposed to be giving commands to armies, in fact have no business in an army camp, unless they want to be thought of as a camp follower. Still, Antonius threw Fulvia out in the street. Depending on which version you heard, he either beat her so badly that she never recovered and died, or that she killed herself. Either way, it was a bad end for a woman who had been married to some of the most famous men of the Republic. While all this was going on, the Parthians were consolidating their gains, the absence of Antonius making the petty princes of the region feel it more politic to throw their lot in with Pacorus and Quintus Labienus. Saxa was captured and executed; at least that was what we heard. With these developments, Antonius sent word that we were to leave Ephesus to sail to Apollonia, with orders to wait for the situation in Italia to stabilize before Antonius could turn his attention to the Parthian problem. It took the better part of two weeks to get the men ready to move, then find adequate shipping, so that by the time we left, the Parthians were less than three days' march away. We had no illusions about any ability to stop the Parthian army, our scouts reporting that we were outnumbered more than ten to one, so nobody complained about a sea voyage under the circumstances.

We ended up sitting in Apollonia for the next two years, as first one problem, and then another kept popping up that involved either Antonius, Octavian, or the both of them together. Their relationship was as tempestuous as any love affair, seeming that on almost a daily basis, there were stories of blazing arguments and threats of war, followed by pacts of amity that lasted only as long as the next fight. Sextus Pompey was a constant thorn in the side of Octavian, and it turned out that Antonius and Sextus had formed their own secret agreement to work against Octavian. There were betrayals at all levels; the most sensational and shocking was that of Salvidienus Rufus, who made a secret deal with Antonius. Antonius revealed this to Octavian in a fit of temper during one of their arguments, resulting in the execution of Rufus for treason at the order of Octavian. Finally, the two of them made yet another solemn pact, this time meeting at Brundisium, for which the pact became known, where Antonius solemnly vowed to stop helping Sextus and sided with Octavian to defeat the last Pompey, among other things. Despite the pact, Antonius did not feel secure enough to leave the vicinity of Italia, and therefore divided his time between Athens and the peninsula, while the Parthians, in the person of Quintus Labienus and Pacorus, consolidated the gains they made in the East.

Labienus, in particular, was making quite a name for himself in his own right, following in his father's bloody footsteps while adding a few wrinkles of his own. Once the Pact of Brundisium was finalized, only then did Antonius turn his attention back to the East, but instead of choosing to lead the army himself, he put Publius Ventidius, Caesar's old quartermaster, in charge. He was in his sixties by this time, but in good health. Despite the fact that he was Antonius' man through and through, he was widely respected. He was best known for what had happened to him as a child in Asculum, which had been taken and sacked during the Italian War, when he was forced to walk under the yoke by none other than Pompey Magnus' father, Pompeius Strabo. Strabo flogged, then beheaded every Asculan male between 15 and 70, sending the remaining women and children out into the cold of winter, where several thousand more died. Ventidius survived by his wits, living off what he could steal, until a mule breeder took pity on him and gave him a job. The mule breeder was a wealthy man in his own right, having a daughter who fancied the young Ventidius. They ended up married, with Ventidius inheriting everything when the old man died. Ventidius started by selling mules to Caesar, then using his position, sought an audience with him, somehow convincing Caesar to give Ventidius a position as a Legate of one of the Legions. This was in the later stages of the Gallic campaign, yet Ventidius distinguished himself nonetheless. Now, Antonius was entrusting him with an army of eleven Legions, plus whatever cavalry he could scrape together. His orders were to sail to Ephesus and expel Quintus Labienus from Anatolia, but to go no farther. Antonius still meant to grab the lion's share of the glory; all he wanted Ventidius to do was to gain a toehold from which Antonius could operate.

Part of the army was in Brundisium, while the rest of us were in Apollonia. From somewhere Antonius provided a fleet of 500 ships, which sounds like a lot, but when you're loading more than 60,000 men, 6,000 mules, along with more than 500 artillery pieces, it makes for extremely cramped conditions. Ventidius alleviated the problem somewhat by having the men row the ships instead of slaves, which the men did not care for one bit, but for which the Centurions were thankful, since it helped keep the men in shape and too tired at the end of their shift for any mischief. Despite assurances from Ventidius, we were all very concerned about Sextus showing up with his fleet of triremes in the Ionian Sea. However, the horizon remained clear of any sign of him for the whole voyage.

We arrived in Ephesus, where we were immediately dispersed into a number of camps, while another four Legions stationed in Africa joined us, bringing the strength up to 15 Legions. Calls went out to Galatia for drafts of cavalry, which we considered to be perhaps the most important arm of the entire army, given that we were going to be facing the dreaded horse archers of Parthia, the same force that cut down Crassus and the bulk of his men at Carrhae. We needed men who could drive the archers away when called on, in addition to men who could actually bring down these Parthians who fought in such a cowardly fashion. To that end, Ventidius also sent out calls for more slingers to augment the 500 who had sailed with us. Normally, a rock thrown from a sling would not be nearly potent enough to bring down a horse, but Ventidius also ordered the casting of thousands of lead missiles of a slightly larger size than normal. After testing it out on a mule that had gone lame, we felt much better about our chances of not only keeping the horse archers at bay, but actually being able to defeat them. Not everything was going our way, however; Antonius had sent Plancus, Fulvia's favorite general, to govern Pergamum, which was located some distance to the north of the territory conquered by Labienus. An agent working for Labienus convinced Plancus that Ephesus had already fallen, even as we were landing and setting up camp, so in a panic, Plancus scurried away from Pergamum, heading to Chios while sending word to Antonius that all was lost, thereby giving Labienus Pergamum without a fight. It was now early spring in the year of the Consulships of Lucius Cornelius Balbus and Publius Canidius Crassus, as Ventidius called a meeting to announce that he planned on marching against Labienus at the beginning of May. Almost daily, more Galatians were riding in, so that before we marched our cavalry arm numbered ten thousand. In the last week of April, we were called to the *Praetorium*, where we were told by Ventidius, with his Legate Silo standing next to him, that we were going to be marching on the Kalends of May.

"We'll be marching by the most direct route to the Cilician Gates. That's the only place where Labienus can move into country where he can employ his horse archers. I'm going to cut him off."

Ventidius pointed to a large map pinned to the wall, his finger tracing a line cutting through the middle of Asia Minor.

"I'll be going ahead with the cavalry force to take and hold the pass, then wait for the Legions to catch up." He turned to look at us sternly. "I expect 30 miles a day. You have 500 miles to cover, and I want the

Legions in place in 20 days from the day you march out of your respective camps. Is that understood?" We all nodded, knowing that what he was asking was hard, but not impossible. We were dismissed to make our preparations. It never occurred to any of us that we would be facing anything other than the same force that had defeated Crassus, further proof that erroneous assumptions in war are worth ten Legions to the other side.

The first erroneous assumption we made was that Labienus and Pacorus were still together, which meant that we would have to defeat the combined forces of the Parthians. Only a few days into the march, we learned that Labienus and Pacorus were not together; Labienus was commanding a force of mostly infantry that he had trained in the Roman manner. According to the scouts, they marched as Romans, wore Roman-style equipment, and they were organized in Legions. As soon as Labienus' own scouts spotted the forces of Ventidius, it did not take him long to realize what Ventidius was trying to do. Labienus immediately abandoned his baggage train, which Ventidius and his force came upon a day later, finding several thousand talents' worth of gold and silver that Labienus had looted from every town and temple that he came across. Labienus also sent word back to Pacorus, who was on the other side of the Cilician Gates and Taurus Mountains, calling on him to come to the aid of Labienus with his own force. I suppose I must give credit to Labienus, because despite commanding a force composed of mostly infantry, he still managed to beat Ventidius to the Cilician Gates by a matter of two or three days, where he built a camp blocking the pass from the side that we were approaching. We arrived with Silo three days later, beating the Parthian relief column, which had to climb up from the coast at Tarsus, a much more difficult approach. Ventidius put us immediately to work. Space was at a premium, both in making camp and in deploying the Legions when it was time for battle, so in an effort to alleviate the problem Ventidius sent five of the Legions north to Mazaga, where they were ordered to be ready to march should they be needed. He picked a spot on a hill that actually was higher than Labienus' camp and had a slightly flat top, putting us to work clearing it. There were tradeoffs with this position; while it gave us an advantage of plunging downhill in an attack, its position also gave Labienus an open route to escape back to Tarsus. We spent the next few days working on and improving the camp, which in hindsight was probably a mistake. We should have gone ahead and tried to crush Labienus while he was waiting for Pacorus, but Ventidius was completely confident in his slingers and their missiles and what they would do to the horse archers, especially given the terrain. So, when Balbus came pounding up to me, despite being the commander of the guard, which meant that he was deserting his post, I knew that it was important.

"A scout just rode in," he gasped, hands on his knees. "The Parthians have been spotted."

"And?" I asked, sensing that there was more to this than just the announcement of something we had been expecting.

"Not a horse archer among them." He was getting his breath back, but now it was my turn to fight for breath, suddenly knowing what he was about to tell me.

"Cataphracts?" I hissed, to which he simply nodded his head.

I know I have said it many times before, yet it bears repeating. There are no secrets in the army, so it did not take long for this news to flash through the camp, seemingly in less time than it took for the sound of one *bucina* call to travel from one end to the other. To Ventidius' credit, he wasted no time in trying to stop the news from being spread and infecting the army, choosing instead to meet it head-on by calling a meeting of all 600 Centurions. With such a large group, trying to maintain secrecy of any sort was pointless, so he did not even bother posting provosts around the edges of the forum while he talked to us.

"We were all caught by surprise," he said without any attempt to soften the blow. "And I take full responsibility for this, but the jug is broken and can't be mended now. We need to do whatever we can to negate the advantage of the cataphracts. Obviously, our slingers are useless against their armor, and neither can we afford to try and meet them in our standard formation. But that doesn't mean that they're unbeatable," he said fiercely, looking into our faces as if daring any man to contradict him.

"In fact," he continued, "if we can get them to do what we want, this may turn out to be one of the easiest victories you'll ever be part of."

I shot a sidelong glance at Scribonius, taking comfort that he looked as doubtful as I felt about this claim, but we continued to listen.

"First, we need to entice them into trying to attack us up here, charging up this hill. There are a couple of major weaknesses with the cataphract, and that's their stamina and their lateral mobility. Those poor beasts are so burdened down with armor that if they have to charge more than a furlong at a gallop, they're next to useless when they get there. Make them charge uphill, and it's even worse for them."

When explained that way, it did not seem nearly as outlandish that we could win a victory, but there was still a problem, and it did not take long for one of the other Primi Pili to raise his hand.

"General, how are we supposed to get them to charge like we need them to?" asked Caecina, Primus Pilus of the 7th.

"The men who are atop those huge lumbering beasts are all Parthian noblemen," Ventidius replied. "Jumped-up bastards who think their *cac* doesn't stink. You know, just like we Roman nobles."

There was hearty laughter at that, helped by the fact that it was true.

"All you and your men need to do is prick that pride of theirs a few times. Talk about their mothers, talk about their wives and what you're going to do to them after we whip these cocksuckers. Use your imagination," he said with a smile, then turned serious. "But it's absolutely crucial that you succeed in making them lose their heads as a group. Actually, you only need to get to a few of them; once a few of them start up the hill baying for our blood, the rest will follow."

One of the marks of a good general is making his men believe, and by the time Ventidius had outlined the complete plan, we all walked out of the forum as believers in what we needed to do to achieve victory.

The next morning saw our men arrayed in front of our camp, facing down the hill towards where the Parthians had begun forming up. They had arrived at dusk the day before, not even bothering to make a proper camp, counting on Labienus to protect them from a sortie from our side. It took the Parthians the better part of the morning to prepare themselves as we watched what had to have been quite an ordeal getting the armor on the horses, each horse requiring at least two men to lift the blanket of armor plates onto the beast. The cataphract horse wears what is essentially a coat that covers his head all the way down to just below the knees, with little iron plates sewn into the blanket, each plate about two inches square, with less than a finger width of space between each one. The only spot uncovered by armor is where the saddle and rider sit; even the horses' heads are covered with a hood. The riders are armored in a similar manner, while each man carries a ten-foot lance with a barbed iron tip, and wear helmets with cheekguards so broad that they almost completely obscure the face. They certainly did not seem to be in a hurry, but I suppose that moving with undue haste only serves to tire the horses out. Still, it was almost midday before the enemy horsemen were formed up, moving slowly past the camp of Labienus, his men doing much the same thing we were, lining the walls of their camp to watch their allies slaughter us, or so they hoped. Just on our side of Labienus' camp, the Parthians drew to a halt to dress their lines, and I have to say that they were formidable looking, sitting so closely together that one could not see any space between horses and riders. I could just imagine how devastating it would be for such a densely packed formation weighing that much to come slamming into our lines, so I offered up a prayer that Ventidius' plan worked. Once the Parthians settled down, it became clear that they had no intention of making the first move, sitting there and daring us to come charging down the hill at them.

"You know what to do," I heard Ventidius bellow as immediately some of the men with the loudest voices began yelling at the Parthians.

"I still owe your mother a sesterce for the fuck last night!"

"Your father's a pig!"

"After we kill you, I'm going to fuck your wife and your daughter!"

That was just starting out; as the men got into the spirit of things, the inventiveness of the taunts grew in leaps and bounds. At first, it seemed as if we were having no effect, but then someone found one of the prisoners from Labienus' force who spoke Parthian. After some persuasion, he translated the insults we had been using into Parthian. The effect was immediate and dramatic; even with the atrocious mispronunciation we were obviously understandable to the Parthians, as suddenly there was a ripple of movement along the lines, with men turning to each other while gesturing to us. The tension of the men was communicated to their horses, many of them beginning to dance nervously about, the movement of the metal plates creating a shimmering effect from the sun. The beasts started tossing their heads, as if they too could understand what was being said about their riders, their families, and loved ones, and they were taking offense as much as the men sitting astride them. Then, one man suddenly spurred his horse forward, brandishing his lance at us while shouting something back.

"Your mothers are whores," he shouted at us in heavily accented Latin, but instead of making anyone angry, it just caused hoots of derisive laughter.

"Tell me something I don't know," someone called out. "But at least she's worth it, unlike yours."

"My mother is dead, you Roman bastard," the man roared.

"Well, at least that explains why she smelled so bad and just lay there," our man shot back, eliciting an enraged howl from the Parthian.

The men behind him called out to him, whereupon he turned back to say something to his friends, who let out a roar. Suddenly, without the sound of horns or any other obvious command, that first small group of Parthians charged, quickly followed by the rest of them.

"Here they come, boys," Ventidius called out. "You know what to do."

Despite appearances, only a small fraction of the army was in the formation facing the Parthians. The rest of us were gathered in the camp on either side, where a number of men were standing with ropes whose other end was tied to a section of rampart stakes, each stake loosened from the dirt. On a blast from the *bucina*, the men yanked the ropes, pulling the stakes out of the way, then we went boiling out over the rampart and into the ditch where bundles of sticks and other debris had been thrown to fill it up to a level that was not visible to the Parthians, yet allowed us to cross the ditch quickly without having to pull ourselves up and out of it. The Parthians did not see us immediately; between the angle of our approach and the fact that their helmets seriously hindered their peripheral vision, we were able to close to less than a hundred paces on each side before we were noticed, first by just the Parthians on the fringes of their formation. Even after they spotted us, the momentum created by the mass of horseflesh each man was astride was such that they could do little more than watch helplessly as we darted in among them, ducking underneath their mounts while stabbing upward into the horses' bellies with our short, killing swords. For this was the second part of Ventidius' plan, to ignore the men and kill their horses, knowing that there was one chink in their armor, one place where there were no plates to block the thrusts of our swords. After all, who would be brave enough or stupid enough to essentially throw themselves under the pounding hooves of these massive killing machines? But that is exactly what we did, descending on both flanks of the Parthians who had already begun to slow as their mounts started laboring from being whipped into a full gallop up a hill that was dotted with stumps of trees, making it even more dangerous for them. The air was rent with the screams of horses in agony, still one of my least favorite sounds, and I was thankful that because of my size, I was not expected to participate in what was rapidly turning into a one-sided slaughter. Instead, I concentrated on finishing the men thrown from their mounts as my men disemboweled the poor beasts; at least those Parthians who managed to jump free and were not crushed under their collapsing horses. The surprise was total, and the ground was soon heaped with the bodies of men and horses as the air filled with the stench of offal from our men savaging the Parthian mounts. There was the familiar buzzing sound of our slingers, who were concentrated on the wall with the orders to aim their missiles into the center of the mass of Parthians, the idea being that even if the lead shot was not potent enough to puncture their heavy armor, at the very least it would give them something to worry about as we pressed in from either side. However, it became clear very quickly that the missiles were much more effective than we imagined, punching through the armor plating, then becoming deformed from the impact, turning into jagged pieces of death that tore into flesh, causing horrible wounds. The screams of the men and horses targeted by the slingers added to the din, becoming so loud that none of the Centurions could be heard when they shouted orders. Fortunately, the men, once they knew what needed to be done, required little direction as they weaved in and out between the thrashing hooves and the ineffectual downward stabs of the Parthian lances, our men thrusting upwards over and over. It was incredibly messy; few of the men were quick enough to leap out of the way of the falling guts of the horses, so before much time at all had gone by, every one of them was covered black with blood and other matter. I tried to be careful where I stepped, as I moved among the still-steaming carcasses of horse and man, looking for survivors to finish but quickly giving up. Before long, I was as filthy as the men from mid-thigh down. This was not a battle, it was a slaughter, one that took less than a sixth part of a watch to complete. The Parthians in the rear ranks, once they saw what was happening, tried to wheel about to gallop down the hill, but the combination of tree stumps and the bodies of their comrades made them easy targets for our more nimble men to run down. These Parthians were pulled from their saddles from behind, our men leaping astride the back of the horse, then grabbing the rider around the neck, stabbing with their swords. I noticed that men were no longer trying to kill the horses, and I have to believe that they were as tired of killing defenseless animals as I was seeing it. A few Parthians managed to escape, streaming down the hill, the tails of their horses flying as their riders whipped and spurred them mercilessly, intent on nothing more than staying alive a few moments longer. Labienus, seeing what was happening from his camp, seemed to be the only man to keep his head, sending perhaps two Cohorts' worth of men out to form a line in front of their camp, the men opening their ranks to let the fleeing Parthians through, then closing back up to wait for us.

Those two Cohorts enabled Quintus Labienus to escape with the rest of his force, except for the two

Cohorts left behind, who paid for their effort with the lives of every last one of them as, with the advantage of our uphill momentum, we slammed into them at full speed. These men had been trained to fight in the Roman manner, but they were not Roman, so it did not take long for the first of them in the rear ranks to take that step backwards, sealing the fate of the entire force. However, they did manage to buy Labienus enough time to lead his army into the heavily forested flanks of the mountain slope that led down southwards to Tarsus, forcing our Galatian cavalry to abandon trying to run them down, since sending horsemen into the woods after infantry is essentially the same as ordering the entire force to fall on their own swords.

I stood watching as the rearguard of Labienus' force made the cover of the trees, the Galatians pulling up short, waving their weapons while shouting curses at the backs of the retreating enemy. I was panting for breath, my legs shaking from the all-out exertion of the last third of a watch, and this was another moment that I still acutely remember to this day as one where I realized that I was getting old. I had just turned 38 years old a few weeks before, and there was a healthy amount of gray in my beard, though it had yet to show up in my hair. As I tried to catch my breath, I turned to look up the hill, the sight so striking that I let out an exclamation that caused the men around me to turn and look at me with some concern. Balbus came trotting up, asking me what was wrong. Not wanting to speak and betray that I was still out of breath, I merely nodded my head up the slope. He turned, then let out a low whistle.

"I don't think I have ever seen anything like that before," he said.

I did not reply, but neither had I. The slope all the way up almost to the edge of the ditch of our camp was completely covered with bodies of men and horses. They were in heaps, packed so tightly that only if I looked very carefully could I see a few patches of open ground. Sticking up at odd intervals were stumps of some of the trees we had cut down to construct the camp, except every one of them was covered in blood, or worse. There were ripples of movement as men walked among the bodies, alternately looking for signs of life, which they would end with a quick thrust of the sword, then bending over to search the bodies of the dead Parthians for loot. As I watched, I noticed that men were going to the horses that still lived first, reinforcing my suspicion that they were as sickened by the slaughter of the animals as I was. My wind finally returned, so I began directing the men in cleaning up our part of the field, ordering them to drag the bodies of Labienus' dead into the ditch of his camp, then walked up the hill to find Ventidius to receive further orders. I had to wade through the gore to get there, while I stopped a few times to put a horse out of its misery, but I did not bother with any Parthians, partially because I knew that the rankers would take care of them, and also because I wanted them to suffer.

The decision was made to abandon our camp to set off in pursuit of Labienus, leaving the bodies to the elements and the animals. Our losses were incredibly light; a few men had been slow moving among the horses and suffered a crushed skull, but other than those deaths, there were mainly bumps and bruises. The 10th lost four men in the fight with Labienus, with another half-dozen wounded, only one serious, and he died within a day. The next morning, we set out in pursuit, moving quickly down the slope of the mountains north of Tarsus. When we arrived there, the place was in a shambles from the previous two years' of occupation by the Parthians, so Ventidius was forced to call a halt and take command.

In Tarsus, we learned that Pacorus had not been with his Parthians when we slaughtered them, and according to some reports, still commanded a considerable force. Ventidius ordered Silo to press on with cavalry, instructing him to block Labienus' retreat to hold him in place while we marched to meet him. We were in Tarsus for more than a week before Ventidius considered the situation stable enough for him to leave. A day into our march, the traveling much easier because we were moving along the coast on a good Roman road, Silo sent word that he had pinned Labienus down by taking the pass known as the Syrian Gates, the only way into Syria from that direction.

We came upon Labienus, along with about a thousand cataphracts left over from the slaughter at the Cilician Gates, trapped between Silo's cavalry up in the pass and our own force. We did not even bother making camp, grounding our gear while leaving a Legion to guard our baggage train, moving into battle array with only a short break to catch our breath. For reasons I did not understand, Labienus chose to come out from behind the rampart of the camp he had built, facing us, while the cataphracts faced their rear, looking up the slope of the pass at Silo and the Galatians. Perhaps he was just tired of being chased and decided to risk all on one throw of the dice, but if so it was a terrible choice to make because he was heavily outnumbered. His men did put up a ferocious struggle, fighting with the courage of warriors who knew that their fate was sealed and were determined to take as many of us with them as they could. However, being trained by a Roman and being a Roman are not the same thing; it takes a lifetime to be a

Legionary worthy of the name. While we were engaged, the Parthian cavalry made a last desperate attempt to break through Silo's blockade, but the heavily armored horses of the Parthians had the same problem as at the Cilician Gates in making the charge uphill. Normally, one of those cataphracts was more than a match for two, or even three of the Galatians, but not ten of them, as Silo and his men swarmed around each Parthian like so many dogs around a bear, waiting to dart in at the right moment. At least I assume that was what was happening, since we were busy in our own right. We pressed in and around Labienus' men as their numbers dwindled, cutting them down without letup, with the battle over in less than a full watch.

Sometime in the confusion, Labienus escaped with a few of his bodyguard. Men began trying to surrender, and while we had been ordered to take prisoners that would march in Ventidius' triumph, it took some time to get the men to obey. Although our losses were heavier than at the Cilician Gates, they were still laughingly light, although my Princeps Posterior Celadus had a serious wound to his thigh that consigned him to the wagons for a bit, while the Hastatus Prior in Trebellius' Fifth Cohort was killed by a sword thrust through the mouth. We spent the next two days in place resting and taking care of the dead and wounded before pressing on through the Syrian Gates and on to Damascus. At Damascus, we learned Pacorus had retreated up into Mesopotamia and indeed had not been present at the last battle. That meant Labienus and Pacorus were still on the loose and posed a threat, but since it was late in the season Ventidius made the decision to settle the army into winter camp a month earlier than normal, splitting us between Antioch and Damascus, with Silo in command in Damascus. We were assigned to camp outside Damascus, and when the announcement was made that we would be staying put, I was certain that the cheers could be heard all the way back to Rome. Damascus is a legend throughout the army for being the fleshpot of the East, where any vice can be indulged as long as a man has enough coin to pay for it. Despite the men's eagerness to test this belief to the fullest, I was equally determined to avoid a repeat of the episode with Tetarfenus, so I held a meeting with the Centurions, informing them that the men were to be held under a tight rein during our time in Damascus. I was pleasantly surprised that there was no argument, even from those men who I could normally expect some sort of bickering about my decision. I suppose that Tetarfenus was on their minds as well.

This is not to say that the men did not indulge themselves; it would have made matters far worse if we had tried to keep them in camp the whole winter without any outlet. However, we only allowed small groups out on the town on any given night, while the Centurions were always present, along with provosts to ensure that if there was any trouble, it was quickly snuffed out. Still, there will always be incidents and as the men learned the hard way, while the whores of Damascus were as pliable and licentious as advertised, the men of Damascus were much more protective over their daughters, sisters, and wives than other places we had been. It was not uncommon to see a man running for his life, carrying his clothes, and shouting the daily watchword at the top of his lungs as he sped barefoot for the main gate, with at least one, but usually more men waving the curved daggers that are the favored weapon in these parts hot on his heels, clearly intent on parting our man from his most prized possession. If it was a man from my Legion, I would be forced to face the angry father, brother, or in some cases, husband, who would be waving his arms about, yelling and carrying on, making it clear how much he had been damaged by the horrible deed one of my men had done to their innocent woman. I could not help noticing that the level of outrage and indignation would dramatically drop whenever I produced my purse, and in this, the men of Damascus were little different from the men of Gaul, Greece, or Egypt. Fortunately, none of my men got caught before they made it to the safety of the camp, but there were a couple of unfortunates from other Legions who were gelded and had to be discharged from the army. I heard that in every case, the men chose to fall on their sword rather than live with the shame of what had happened to them, though I do not know if that is true.

In some ways, it was fortunate that Pacorus chose to invade again because it was getting expensive for me to stay in Damascus. We learned of his plans from a greasy little toad named Herod, who at the time was just one of several contenders for the throne of Judaea, though of course now he is king of that country and has been for some time. He will probably live forever, given the amount of luck he has. His information was accurate, for all that, as he informed us that Pacorus was crossing the Euphrates at the ford at Samosata before heading in the direction of Antioch.

Not wanting to face Pacorus with a divided army, Ventidius sent immediate orders to Silo to march from Damascus with all haste, giving us no time to get the men prepared for hard marching. We set out from Damascus just two days after receiving the order, the first day putting in almost 30 miles, and it was one of the hardest marches I, or anyone for that matter, had ever done. Fortunately, it was still early in the year, just past the new year of the Consulship of Appius Claudius Pulcher and Gaius Norbanus Flaccus, so that it was not especially hot during the day, though it did get cool at night. However, Silo ordered us to dig ditches and ramparts only, while not pitching tents so that we could get back on the march more quickly. We rolled up in our *sagum* instead, the nights punctuated by the groans and moans of suffering men who had been living the high life back in Damascus but were paying for it now. Truthfully, I was exhausted and hurt just as much as the men were, despite my daily exercises. As much as I hated to admit it, my age was beginning to catch up with me more every day. However, I had to set an example, meaning that as always I was first up, Diocles waking me a third of a watch before the *bucina* sounded, meaning I would be in roaring form, walking about kicking men who were a little slow getting to their feet to begin the march. We did not even tear down the rampart and fill in the ditch; we just pulled up our stakes then got back on the march, the men stumbling and cursing at their sore legs and back. Despite this, we covered more than 30 miles the second day, though we had more stragglers than the previous day, some of the men not arriving in camp until after dark. Normally men who fell out were put on some sort of punishment detail, but under the circumstances, I did not see much point in working men harder who were unable to keep up, at least until some point in the future when we were more settled. About the fourth day of the march, a dispatch rider came thundering down the road towards us. Just a few moments after reporting to Silo, he called the Primi Pili to inform them that we would not be heading directly to Antioch. Pacorus was apparently in no hurry, moving no more than ten to twelve miles a day as he let his horses fatten up on the new grass. As a result, it gave us the opportunity to pick the ground, which Ventidius had already done, choosing the slopes of a small mountain called Gindarus.

We arrived at Mount Gindarus two days later, where Ventidius' portion of the army was already in place, making camp at the top of the mountain, really little more than a hill with a gentle slope facing the road that led to Antioch. It would be up this road that Pacorus' army would be traveling; at least that was the belief. I just hoped that he would not be arriving immediately, as the men desperately needed rest before facing the Parthians. However, we were in camp little more than a third of a watch when scouts came to report that Pacorus had made camp just about seven miles away, and would be marching by the next day. I immediately called a meeting of the Centurions, telling them the news. I could see the concern written on every face as they shot sidelong glances at each other, waiting for someone to speak up.

Deciding not to wait for one of them to find the courage, I said, "While it would be better if we had at least a day to recuperate, Mars has decided otherwise. Each of you needs to spend time with your men and make sure they know what's expected of them. I know they're tired; Pluto's cock, I know YOU'RE all tired because I surely am."

They gave a polite laugh.

"But we have to stop the Parthians when they come, and we've done it twice before, so I know we'll do it again. If we end this here and now, it will make our invasion of Parthia easier by killing more of them tomorrow. Make sure that the men understand that."

The Centurions saluted, then left to their respective Centuries, while I went to my own to try to prepare the men for the coming trial.

As the scouts had predicted, the Parthians appeared on the horizon a little before mid-morning the next day. Clearly not expecting any trouble, they rode in a long column, with no outriders on the flanks and only a small advance guard. They moved much more slowly than would have been expected for a mounted column; when they finally got close enough to make out individuals, we could see that the reason the horsemen were moving so leisurely was in order to give their horses time to graze. Because it was early in the year, it was clear that they felt that their horses still needed to be fattened up. Only when they were no more than a mile away did their advance guard pull up short, peering in our direction. It took them a long time before they finally seemed to understand what they were seeing, before two of them finally yanked their horses about to gallop back to the main column, which was about a mile farther back. I was standing on the rampart along with the other officers, with the men formed up, ready to march out of the camp then move into formation, and Ventidius wasted no time in giving the order. We moved quickly and smoothly, using the front along with both side gates in a maneuver that is rehearsed over and over during our winter training. The 10th took up its position on the right, except that I made a slight change in our normal array by moving the higher Cohorts to the front, while putting the Second, Third, and Fourth in the rear line, which did not sit well with any of the men. Nevertheless, my mind was made up that I needed to give the more junior Cohorts some seasoning against the Parthian cataphracts, knowing that we would be facing them again when Antonius finally decided to invade. As the enemy moved into their own position, we saw that unlike the last two times, Pacorus' force was not entirely composed of cataphracts; out of the 8,000 men, it looked as if about 3,000 of them were horse archers. The moment Ventidius saw this, he ordered the slingers, stationed behind the center wing, out in front of us. Spreading out in open order, Ventidius sent a detail of some of the auxiliaries with us to drag bags of the lead missiles made for just such an occasion to place at the foot of each slinger. Normally, the range of the Parthian bow is superior to a sling, but because we were uphill, that advantage was negated almost to the point where the respective ranges were equal.

The Parthians only discovered this the hard way, when they began galloping up to loose hails of arrows. In order for their own missiles to reach their real targets of the Legionaries, they had to draw within range of the slingers, whereupon the whizzing sound of the lead missiles flying downhill was quickly drowned out by the screams of men and horses as the lead shot hit muscle and bone, flattening out and turning jagged from the force of the impact. The first volley of the horse archers was their last real one, and although some of the arrows struck their targets, most of them landed harmlessly in the ground, none hitting a Legionary. The horse archers wheeled about, galloping out of range of the slings, not bothering with their own famed Parthian shot, knowing that it would be useless.

We stood watching as the leader, obviously Pacorus, received the report of the commander of the archers, then we saw him point up the hill at us, clearly commanding the man to try again. It was a credit either to his bravery or stupidity, or perhaps his fear of

Pacorus, but he obeyed. Despite the fact that his men followed him readily enough, even from where we stood it was plain to see that their hearts were not in it. This time, they tried to present a more difficult target by weaving their horses back and forth in short spurts, never heading in one direction for the same length of time as the last. At first, it worked, so they were able to draw closer without being savaged, at least as quickly as in their first attack, but our slingers had an almost endless supply of ammunition. I considered that this was another example of the justice of the gods, since it was well known by then that at Carrhae, the Parthian general who led the forces that attacked Crassus used trains of camels carrying wicker baskets full of arrows to follow the archers as they harassed Crassus and his men for days, whittling them down one by one until there was no army left; just individuals or small groups of men who managed to slip through the Parthian net. Of course, the reward for this general's ingenuity was to be killed by Pacorus' father, who reportedly was jealous of the man's success. Apparently, this lesson was lost on Pacorus, because this force of archers had no camels following them. Even if they had been present, it would not have mattered; our slingers would have slaughtered the camels along with the archers.

A few arrows managed to land in the ranks of the Legions, but they did not come in a shower that blackened the sky, so it was relatively easy for men to pick the missiles off with their shields before they did any real damage. The second attack ended as the first. When the Parthians finally turned to flee back down the hill, we knew there would not be a third attack from the archers, there being perhaps only 500 men still left mounted and able to fight. Pacorus did not even try to order them back, turning instead to a man who raised a purple flag with an embroidered symbol on it. Although it was impossible to make out what the symbol was, it was obvious that it was meant for the cataphracts, because the instant the banner was raised, they began to move. They aligned themselves roughly in the same three wings as we did; they nevertheless did not have the depth of reserve that we did, and Pacorus ordered them into a single massed line only four ranks deep. He was clearly planning on using the mass of horseflesh and armor to punch through our line, counting on the shock of the impact to break us, sending us streaming back into our second, then third line. If it worked, we would be slaughtered because our cohesion would be shattered, and then it would be a cavalrymen's dream, running down and skewering fleeing men with their long lances. Our Galatians were on each wing, yet given our success against the cataphracts with the Legions alone, Ventidius had given strict orders that they were there as a reserve, only to pursue once the cataphracts were routed. We watched as the cataphracts jammed themselves closer and closer together, so that their legs were touching each other.

I heard someone behind me say with affected boredom, "Won't these bastards ever learn?"

Some men chuckled, as another man called out, "You better hope they don't, Gallus. I've seen you run, and you'll be the first with a Parthian lance up your ass."

This provoked a roar of laughter, but as much as I wanted to join in, I could not.

"That's enough," I snapped over my shoulder. "And, Gallus, you're on report. You can thank your big-mouthed friend for using your name."

I heard a muffled curse, while I was glad that my back was turned so the men could not see me smile.

As at the Syrian Gates, the Parthians seemed to have no respect or regard for Roman infantry, once again pounding up the slope, lathering and tiring out their heavily laden horses. The one difference this time was that instead of immediately ordering the slingers out of harm's way, Ventidius ordered one more volley fired before they turned to scamper through the ranks in enough time for us to re-form after they passed through. I will say that I was shocked to see how devastating those lead missiles were, even against men and horses so heavily armored. The damage of the volley was magnified by how closely packed the Parthians were, so that when one horse went down, at the very least the beast behind it went tumbling as well. Even when it was just the rider who fell, his body was enough of an obstacle for a horse to stumble, so before they were halfway up the hill, there were gaping holes in their ranks. Their charge was so headlong that they did not take the time to close up, giving us gaps to shoot into and use the exact same tactic as at the Syrian Gates. When they were no more than 50 paces away, the front ranks of our army leapt forward with a roar; the smaller men darted into the spaces, quickly thrusting up with their swords, while men close to my size reached out to drag men off their gutted mounts, ending them with a thrust into their face or throats. Before a few moments had passed, I had personally slain a half-dozen men. Out of those, only one bothered to drop his lance to draw his sword, realizing the longer weapon was useless. However, the Parthian's sword is a typical cavalrymen's blade, longer than ours, which is fine when you are on horseback stabbing down, but when you are on your feet face to face with a Legionary, it is almost as useless as the lance. The Parthian took a wild swing with his blade, clearly trying to behead me. Knocking it aside with my own, before he could recover, I stepped inside the arc of his sword, bringing mine up under his ribcage, deep into his chest. His jaw dropped in surprise as he looked down at where my Gallic blade had punched through his armor plate, which had been no protection as it went in, except that now I had to wrench it out. Holding him up with one hand, I pulled the blade back and forth trying to extract it. He had made no loud sound to that point, but now he began shrieking in horrible agony, not helping my concentration and I am afraid it prolonged his suffering before the blade finally came free with a wet, sucking sound. Through all of this, he remained alive, his eyes fixed on mine, his body convulsing as his hands clutched at me while he tried to form words. I could not understand what he was saying, but I knew what he wanted. Giving him a grim nod, I drew my blade across his throat, watching as his eyes dimmed, his hands letting go of my belt. All around me were similar scenes of death as both man and beast met their end on the slope of the hill. Our men were roaring with bloodlust, the Parthians shouting or screaming in desperation or agony, while above it all was the sound of the horses as they flailed about, trying to escape from this horrible place. I saw one horse streaking away, trailing both its rider and its own guts behind it, oblivious to anything other than the need to escape to find a quiet place to die. Surveying the scene, I blew the whistle for the next line of men to enter the battle, and they went bounding past the men of the first rank, intent on killing the rear ranks of the Parthians, who were now trying to turn their mounts about to get back down the hill. Some of them managed, while most were caught from behind, our men having the double advantage of running downhill, as well as chasing down mounts already blown from being galloped up the slope. The slaughter continued down the hill, but as I looked in that direction, I saw that a fair number of the enemy had managed to escape. They were forming up around a small knoll, on the top of which sat Pacorus and his bodyguard. The initial fury of the battle had subsided, men now going about their business with efficiency and detachment, grimly working in teams as the last of the Parthians stranded on the slope either tried to escape or decided to go down fighting.

I looked back up to where Ventidius had positioned himself, then saw that he had put the Galatians into motion, both wings swinging wide as they headed down the slope to get behind Pacorus' position in order to cut him off from any chance of escape. I believe that if the Parthian had moved right then, he might have gotten away, though only if the rest of his men had sacrificed themselves. Even so, it would have been a chancy business, as no cataphract was going to be able to outrun a Galatian for more than a mile at the most before the Parthian horse foundered. Perhaps that is why he chose to stay in place, recognizing it as futile. Whatever his reason, he and the remainder of his men only watched as the Galatians swung around behind him, then once we finished off the last resistance on the hill, the *cornu* sounded the recall, whereupon we formed back up. I had my own *cornicen* give the signal for the last rank, where the Second, Third and Fourth was, to move forward to take the first position, the men of those Cohorts grinning from ear to ear, happy not only to be in on the fighting but for the chance to kill a Parthian prince. More importantly, they knew that the men of his bodyguard and most likely the remainder of his forces were the highest-ranking nobility left on the field, making them the wealthiest, and nothing cheers a Legionary more than the idea of killing a rich man. The other Cohorts were naturally a bit put out, but I assured them that they had their pickings of our part of the field on the slope, cheering them a great deal. We waited for the Parthians to charge us, yet they seemed content to wait for us to come to them, thereby sacrificing the only advantage they had to try to inflict as much damage as possible. In the moments while we waited, before Ventidius gave us the order to move forward in preparation for the final charge, someone began banging their sword against the rim of their shield, which was quickly picked up by the rest of the army. No cheering, no yelling insults, just the steady, rhythmic sound of metal on metal, the message to the Parthians that their doom was approaching, and I suddenly remembered a similar moment more than 20 years before against the Helvetii, and I recall wondering if the Parthians knew just how inevitable their defeat was.

Pacorus was killed, but by a man from a Legion other than the 10th, a source of great embarrassment to the men, though I assured them that they had no reason to feel that way. I had been involved in enough moments like this to know that it was essentially a throw of the dice, with as much chance behind it as skill. Still, it was a bitter draught to drink for all of us, particularly since we had to hear about it in camp that night. The remaining Parthians went down fighting. In fact, most of them chose to dismount in order try to fight on foot, but again their weapons and training are just not suited for such an endeavor, so we slaughtered the lot of them with little effort and even less loss. The only bad news was that despite orders to the contrary, the men had not taken any prisoners; their blood was up, and being honest, I do not think any of the Centurions tried all that hard to stop them. The result was all the Primi Pili being called in front of Ventidius, who chewed on us as thoroughly as a dog does a rat. I, as well as my comrades, was just thankful that the amount of loot, in the form of precious gems and ingots of gold and silver, were such that it was impossible for Ventidius to stay angry. Once it was all tallied, it was in excess of 10,000 talents worth of loot, a good day's work by any standard. Of course, the men, along with their Centurions, managed to do quite well for themselves off the bodies of the dead nobility of Parthia, though it was nowhere near what Ventidius had plundered. Further good news reached us just a few days later with the news that Quintus Labienus was captured in Cyprus and executed. All in all, it had been a good piece of work, for which Ventidius was largely responsible, our regard for this crusty old mule trader going up immeasurably. Unfortunately for him, like the general who engineered the defeat of Crassus, sometimes there is such a thing as being too successful.

There was one momentous event that came out of the Pact of Brundisium that I should mention, and that was the way in which Octavian and Antonius sealed the agreement. As I have recounted, the two Triumvirs had made solemn vows, agreements, pacts, and treaties almost too numerous to mention, some of them lasting only a few days. Because of this, I believe they both realized that they needed to do something noteworthy to show the Republic that this pact was different from all the others. To that end, they arranged a marriage. This is a very common event with the upper classes, who almost never marry for love, yet I think everyone was surprised when it was announced that Antonius would marry Octavian's sister, Octavia. I assume, gentle reader, that most people who take the time to read this account will know how well loved and highly regarded Octavia's sister is. For those of you who do not, where her brother is respected out of equal parts love and fear, I have never once heard anyone, of any class, utter a harsh word about Octavia. She is the model of Roman womanhood; while her betrothal to Antonius was understood, and she was lauded for her loyalty to her family and Rome, things did not go so well for Octavian. Antonius' lechery, debauchery, and licentiousness were the stuff of legend, so it was like pairing a lion and lamb together. Most people blamed Octavian and his ambition for subjecting such a beloved woman as Octavia to the supposed depredations of Antonius. However, perhaps Octavian knew his sister and Antonius better than people give him credit for, because by most accounts they were extremely happy, at least early on. The evidence is the children produced from this union, although Octavia was not the only flower to bear fruit from Antonius. By this point, the world knew of the twins Cleopatra had borne Antonius from his winter sojourn in Alexandria, although he had not been back to Egypt since. At the time, most people believed that the affair between Antonius and Cleopatra had run its course, that despite the way things appeared on the surface, the union between Antonius and Octavia was destined to be a happy and fruitful one. It was certainly the latter, except that given the way things turned out, I cannot say that it was happy. All of this is background to explain why Antonius still seemed in no hurry to come take command of the army to begin his expedition to Parthia.

Antonius was still in Athens with Octavia, apparently enjoying domestic life too much to be bothered with any military endeavors. This did not mean, however, that he was willing to let any of his subordinates receive what he considered too much credit for doing what he himself was too lazy to do. When word reached him that Ventidius was successful, indeed a bit too successful to suit him, only then did he rouse himself to come to the East to take command of the army. Word came that Antonius was extremely angry at Ventidius, and was coming to publicly relieve him of command of the army, in front of us no less. The shock, dismay and outright anger in the army was widespread and at all levels, while there were even rumblings among the men of mutinying, then throwing their support behind Ventidius. However, it was the old general himself who flatly refused to countenance such talk.

"Boys, I appreciate the sentiment, but we've had enough warring between Romans," he explained to a largely silent audience of the Centurions.

His face was even more lined than usual, looking every one of his sixty-plus years, but his tone was firm. "I'm in the army, just like each of you, and as I'm ordering you to stand down and obey me, so will I obey." He paused to survey our faces, and I was close enough to see the ghost of a smile cross his lips. "But that doesn't mean that while we're waiting for Antonius we can't continue our work here. In fact, I was thinking of marching up to Samosata to give King Antiochus a good thrashing for letting Pacorus cross over in his lands without making any attempt to hinder him. What do you boys think of that?"

We cheered this idea loudly, happy with the thought of not sitting idly waiting for Antonius as we had for the last two years. Personally, I was also pleased at the stick in the eye to Antonius. Setting out almost immediately after that meeting, it was about a month after the battle, having had such negligible losses that there were only two or three wagons full of seriously wounded, who were left behind to recuperate or die. We took a more direct route to Samosata than Pacorus had, for a number of reasons. Some of them were military, but mainly our route was for political purposes suiting Ventidius. By avoiding the roads leading to the city, which is the capital of Commagene, a small section of land in the province of Syria, Ventidius could plausibly claim that the dispatch rider carrying Antonius' order to halt and wait for him never found him. In reality, it had arrived while we were still in camp on the slopes of Gindarus. The rider carrying the message was immediately detained and held in close confinement, though he was treated well. Meanwhile, we began making our way to Commagene.

As was his habit, Diocles had cultivated relationships with some of the key slaves in the household and staff of Ventidius, so it was through Diocles that I learned of the contents of the message from Antonius. Although I did not see the message myself, to this day I have no reason to doubt its authenticity or accuracy. The tone of the message is what convinced me that it was genuine, Antonius' anger clearly communicating itself to Ventidius. The Triumvir even went so far as to question whether Ventidius had aspirations of his own concerning Antonius' position. The more exposure I had to Antonius, the less and less I liked him, which in itself was not that important, except that I had also lost so much respect for the man that at times I would lay awake at night, worrying about what would happen when I came face to face with him again, it always being difficult for me to disguise my thoughts. Most of the time I did not care if I did or not, yet there were times when not only my career but my very life rested on my ability to maintain an expression and attitude that did not betray my true feelings. Antonius was one of those men with whom it was extremely important to do so, particularly as his struggle with Octavian became more and more bitter. But Ventidius, for a number of reasons of his own, would not and could not answer Antonius in any manner whatsoever, at least not until matters had progressed to a certain point. That point came only after we had arrived at Samosata in Commagene, which was far from the collection of miserable huts with a wooden wall that we had believed it to be, although Ventidius had known better. Its wall was made of stone, a black type of stone that most of us had never seen before. While I had seen such a wall when I was with the 6th, I never had to lay siege to it.

Despite the black stone wall, Ventidius was unimpressed, or at least appeared so, taking the Primi Pili and his staff on a circuit around the city, surveying for weak points while his engineering officers made the necessary sketches to lay out the plans for besieging the city. The garrison watched us from the walls but made no attempt to harass us with artillery or missile fire, seemingly content to just watch. They probably are feeling very secure behind their black walls, I thought to myself, wondering how many other cities had made the same mistake. I recalled the siege of the Aduatuci town in Gaul where the defenders had openly laughed at us because of our diminutive size, mocking us as a race of midgets while they lounged against the battlements watching us work in silence. If Antiochus' people were laughing, they would be stopping soon enough, though as we made our circuit I was forced to concede that this would be no easy or quick assault.

Only after we settled in, building a total of two camps, one on either side of the river, then began digging our mines, the walls too high for a siege tower even with a terrace, did Ventidius acknowledge Antonius' message demanding that he halt.

Ventidius' reply, which I thought was brilliant, acknowledged Antonius' order, then essentially asked him, "I've surrounded Samosata and it will be falling shortly. Do you want me to give it back?"

We did not stop working to wait for the reply, as Ventidius was confident he knew what the answer would be. There is nothing quite as demoralizing or dangerous to future operations as calling off a siege, for whatever reason. It not only is a tremendous blow to the morale of the besieging army, and a corresponding rise for the defenders, but militarily it gives the defenders an extremely useful idea about weaknesses that the attacker found. The walls and defenses of a city look completely different depending on the perspective of who is examining them. While both sides are looking for weaknesses, the viewpoint is so different that it generally is only after a siege begins that the men charged with holding the city become aware of where their true problem areas lay. Almost within the third of a watch that an army lifts a siege, you can rest assured that a swarm of laborers will be hard at work shoring up or completely rebuilding the trouble spots. Antonius, as I have said many times, was not Caesar's bootlace, yet he was competent enough to know that lifting the siege, especially for no other reason than to appease his ego, was tactically and strategically senseless. This time the dispatch rider from Antonius had no trouble finding the army, bringing a reply that was exactly what was expected, a terse order to continue with the siege, along with the news that Antonius had been delayed because of yet another meeting with Octavian. While Antonius did not go into any detail in his message, Ventidius was like any other Roman nobleman; he had his own network of friends, kin, and informants that kept him apprised on the bits and pieces that Antonius would not provide.

Octavian's war with Sextus continued, and it was not going well for the young Triumvir. Sextus' grip on the grain supply of the city had tightened even further, and he was squeezing, aided by yet another poor harvest. Octavian was in desperate need of cash, but even if he had any, with the prices Sextus was charging for wheat he would not have had enough to feed the people. Naturally, the lower classes were not happy, and when they are rumbling, nobody living in the nice villas up on the hills sleeps well. All of this meant little to us, except of course for those of us with families in Rome, but the 10th, even in its second enlistment were mostly men from Hispania, so the situation there, while not very good, was not nearly as dire as in Rome and Italia. Back home, people were going hungry, but nobody was starving. As far as the men of the army were concerned, we still ate well. Scribonius, Cyclops, Balbus and I spent many a watch discussing the fairness of it all.

"Do you think it's right that we have full bellies every night, not just from bread but bacon, chickpeas, and lentils?" Scribonius asked of us one night, ironically as were finishing our meal in my private quarters.

Cyclops just shrugged the question off while Balbus gave a grunt, and I shot a look at his scarred face, but he was just grinning.

"I've already heard this," he said. "It's your turn now."

In fact, I was surprised, because I had never really thought about it prior to that moment. Yet in fairness, things had reportedly never been this bad before, at least in living memory. I chewed on my bread as I considered, then suddenly, what had been a particularly tasty loaf lost much of its flavor. Diocles was hovering quietly in the corner, so rather than provide the answer, I turned to him to ask him what he thought.

"I didn't ask Diocles," I could see Scribonius was not going to be put off by my tricks, and I recognized a particularly intense look on his face. As I thought about it, I realized that he had been somewhat withdrawn as of late, yet I had paid it no attention.

That is how it is, I suppose; things and people around you change, moved by the currents of their own lives and problems, except that you are so involved in what you are doing, you miss it until it is shoved in your face. Putting the bread down, I spoke slowly, knowing that this was not a time where a joke would do.

"No, Scribonius, I don't suppose it is fair. In fact, now that you mention it, it's most decidedly unfair. So what would you do about it?"

It was clear he had been thinking of this a great deal, so it was a bit of a surprise when he could only shrug.

"I don't know," he said honestly. "Other than make all the upper classes stop playing these political games that cause people to starve to death."

"You might as well try to tie a knot in a column of smoke," Cyclops interjected. "They suck politics down with their mother's milk. It's as much in their blood as fighting is in a German's."

Scribonius' long, thin face was shadowed, his gaze inward, and I saw a great sadness in his eyes as he stared into the flame of the lamp sitting on the table. The guttering fire moved pockets of darkness about his features, filling the crevices in his face, particularly the long and deep lines that framed his mouth almost like two knife wounds. The thought crowded into my mind that Scribonius was older than I was, meaning he had to be in his early forties. Sitting in a comfortable chair, or reclining on a couch, reading these words by lamplight, or while enjoying the fresh air in one's garden or triclinium, it may sound laughable to think of a man in his early forties as ancient, but in the Roman Legions, it is. War is, and always has been, a young man's pursuit. Because of its very nature, Mars rewards very few of his adherents with the gift of longevity. Perhaps a fifth of the army was above the age of 35, and of that fifth, less than a quarter above the age of forty. Most of those men, quite naturally, were in the Centurionate. However, there were a fair number of men, like Vellusius, who were rankers, yet for all of us of a similar age, it was a lonely life, with just a few companions left, in most cases men who had been our closest comrades for our entire time in the army. Vellusius could at least mingle with the younger men of his own rank, but for Centurions, we could only fraternize with each other, while we older Centurions tended to associate only with men closer to our own age, for the same reasons as men in the ranks. We simply did not have as much in common with the younger men as we did with men our own age, except for the inveterate drinkers, gamblers, and whoremongers who had somehow managed to survive. Simply put, what interested men in their twenties was not the same as men in their forties. All we had, really, was each other's company. I do not know if Scribonius' and my thoughts were running along the same lines, but he looked over, giving me a smile tinged with so much sadness that I believe they were.

Finally, he shrugged, then repeated, "I don't know. Sometimes I just wonder what all this is for."

We sat in silence for several moments, then I turned to Diocles.

"All right, Diocles. What do you think? Is it fair or not?"

To my surprise, he answered immediately because I was sure he would either try to evade the question, or say he needed time to think about it.

"Fairness, justice, whatever you want to call it, doesn't exist. Those are just words we use to make us feel better. There is no fair; there just is. The gods make their decisions, and we turn on their wheel. And that's all there is to it."

"Spoken like a slave," Balbus sneered.

I opened my mouth to say something to Balbus about speaking to Diocles in such a manner because I had long since stopped regarding him as property, but before I could, Diocles replied.

"That I may be, master." Diocles emphasized the word in such a way that it sounded like an insult, and I could see Balbus' face darken. "But if you think that you're anything other than I, just with a different name, then you're blind."

That made Balbus truly angry, and he started to rise from his chair. Before he could fully stand, I put a hand on his arm, giving him a level look that left no mistake, so he immediately sat down, although it took him a moment before he could speak calmly.

"I'm very much the master of my own destiny," Balbus said tightly.

As soon as he said it, I saw the look of triumph in Diocles' eyes, causing me to sigh loudly enough that all eyes turned towards me.

"Now, Balbus," I said with a grin, "it's your turn."

We spent the rest of the night listening to Diocles as he, acting as teacher while we four hardened Centurions played the role of pupils, politely but methodically proved to Balbus, and to Scribonius, Cyclops, and me, that control of any sort is an illusion. Although I had been subjected to this lecture some time before, already accepting it as truth, and I suspected Scribonius had arrived at the same conclusion on his own, I doubted that Cyclops had given it much thought at all. This was not because of a lack of intelligence, but because he did not care all that much.

"So you make all the decisions regarding your life?" Diocles began, directing his question to Balbus.

Balbus was like me in many respects; he had little formal education, but he had a quick mind, though I knew he did not enjoy reading the way I did. I saw him smirk as he was sure he saw the trap that Diocles was laying for him, while I suppressed my own smile.

"Of course not," Balbus shot back, to which Diocles made a great show of surprise, though I knew he was not shocked in the least.

Scribonius and Cyclops sat silently, Scribonius watching the interplay with just a slight lift of his eyebrows and a look that struck me as if he were reliving something from his past as he watched.

"The army, through my chain of my command, my Primus Pilus for example," Balbus made a mock salute in my direction, "dictate what will happen to me on a day to day basis. But," he said triumphantly, "it's a choice I made to give them that authority the day I enlisted in the Legions."

Diocles pursed his lips, his brow furrowed as he thought this through.

"I understand, I think. So, these people, the Primus Pilus sitting here, are the men who control your life, but strictly because you choose to let them?"

Balbus nodded, but there was the flit of a shadow across his brow, and I mentally congratulated him because he did not seem altogether surprised by Diocles' next question.

"But isn't the Primus Pilus in the same position as you are in regards to surrendering control of his actions to others? Aren't his actions determined by others? As are theirs?"

Balbus clearly did not like where this was going, yet he nodded his head, saying grudgingly, "Yes, I suppose that when you put it like that, it's like . . ." He struggled for the right example.

"It's like the ripples in a pond when you throw a rock," Scribonius interjected. Balbus gave him a grunt of thanks.

"Yes, like that."

Diocles rubbed his chin as he stared at the floor. I remember thinking, stop overacting, you clever little bastard, but Balbus did not know he was doing so.

"So would it be fair to say that at the very least, we don't have quite as much control over our actions, and thereby our immediate future, as it would appear, at least in the example we are discussing?"

Balbus' eyes narrowed suspiciously, sure that there was some trick in the question, but after carefully considering it, he slowly nodded his head.

"Yes, I suppose that's fair to say."

"But you're at least the captain of your physical being then, yes? You can make your body do what you want it to do, when you want to do it?"

In truth, it was not fair, and I could not help but wince when Balbus took the bait. Just as a fox knows exactly what the squirrel will do, Diocles knew his prey, confident in the knowledge that of all the things that a Legionary is proud of, it is his physical prowess that is dearest to his heart. He further knew that a first-grade Centurion would have more of that pride than most.

Balbus was no exception, his tone brooking no argument when he responded with a flat, "Absolutely. I can endure anything that I choose to endure."

"Then, would you care to make a wager on that?" Diocles asked.

It was at this point that I intervened, because it is just bad business to let a Centurion owe money to a slave, as I already knew how the wager would come out, having lost it myself.

"No money," I said firmly, ignoring both of their protests.

"An amphora of Falernian then," Diocles suggested, and I found this acceptable.

I looked over at Scribonius, asking, "Care to wager, Scribonius?"

"Only if I can take Diocles," he responded, and we both burst out laughing at Balbus' complaint that neither of us would back him.

However, when he turned to Cyclops, my one-eyed friend merely shook his head, irritating Balbus further.

"You better pay him, Balbus," I could not help goading him a bit more, and I was happy to see that I was getting to him.

"Fine," he almost shouted. "I'll take whatever challenge you care to give me you miserable little . . . Greek," he spat out the last as if it were the worst thing he could think of.

In answer, Diocles stood up, excusing himself for a moment before coming back with a peacock feather. I remember wondering why he had something like that lying around, then realized there were some things I did not want to know. Balbus looked puzzled, as did Scribonius and Cyclops. I must admit I felt a bit smug knowing what was about to take place.

Diocles pulled his chair until it was directly across from Balbus', then he waved the feather in Balbus' face. I had chosen that moment to take a sip of wine, almost choking on it as I saw a look flit across Balbus' face, a mixture of horror and acute embarrassment as his mind ran through all the possible uses for that feather. I am sure that Diocles' Greek heritage was foremost in Balbus' mind, because every Roman has been raised on stories of Greek depravity. Diocles was clearly enjoying himself immensely; it is not often that a slave, especially one as physically diminutive as Diocles, can hold a physical specimen like Balbus in a torment of suspense and not a little fear.

The feather was waving about, then suddenly Diocles turned to Cyclops, his tone completely serious as he asked, "Master Cyclops, I've always been a huge admirer of Alexander. What do you think about him?"

There was no need for Diocles to expand on the identity of the man he was speaking of; there is only one Alexander. While there is much about him that we Romans admire, there is another side to his personality that many of us found distinctly uncomfortable to discuss, yet to Cyclops' eternal credit he was just as smooth as a river stone, not cracking a smile at all.

Pretending to consider the question, he responded, "Truthfully, there's much about him to admire; he had many fine qualities, both as a general and as a man. What do you admire about him most, Diocles?"

I had decided to stop sipping from my cup because of the danger that I would spew mouthfuls over my companions, as it was hard not to spoil what was turning out to be one of the most entertaining evenings we had experienced in some time, so in order to hide my face, I began inspecting my fingernails.

"Loyalty," Diocles answered Cyclops' own question instantly. "His loyalty to his friends. Particularly to Hephaestion."

He turned back to Balbus as he said Alexander's lover's name. Seeing the look on Balbus' face, I could contain myself no longer and began roaring with laughter, pointing at Balbus as I gasped for breath. Both Cyclops and Scribonius were doubled over, and then Diocles began to giggle, still waving the feather in Balbus' face, his features now turning a bright red. For a moment, I saw his eyes narrow in anger, but then the absurdity of the moment evidently struck him, and he began laughing as well, congratulating Diocles on catching him out. After we had regained our collective breath, Balbus began to stand, but Diocles turned instantly sober, motioning at him to sit back down.

"Oh no, Master Balbus. That was a jest on my part, but we're not through. We still have a wager, and I'm thirsty."

Balbus looked to me, but I shook my head, then pointed him back down.

"You started this; you're going to see it through," I told him.

With a resigned sigh, Balbus sat, then folded his arms, looking at Diocles.

"All right, what do you want me to do?"

Diocles extended the feather so that the tip was just below Balbus' nose, replying, "I'm going to tickle your nose with this feather."

"But all that will do is make me sneeze . . ." Balbus gave a triumphant grin. "Oh, so you want to try and make me sneeze."

He looked at me, rolling his eyes heavenwards, but Diocles' next words brought his full attention back on the little man.

"Oh no, master. I do want you to sneeze."

Balbus frowned in confusion. Now, even Scribonius looked mystified, while Cyclops was leaning forward, intent on the action.

"With your eyes open," Diocles finished. "I'm going to make you sneeze and I want you to keep your eyes open."

As I had learned the hard way, it is physically impossible for a person to sneeze while keeping their eyes open, though I will give Balbus credit for trying. He made 12 attempts before giving up, his nose red and running an almost continuous stream of snot that he kept mopping up with his neckerchief. Once he finally waved his hands in surrender, Diocles laid the feather down, waiting for Balbus to regain his composure, while Scribonius and I exchanged smiles over the rim of our cups.

"It would appear, Master Balbus, that there are some things that one can't control in their own body."

"One thing," Balbus shot back, obviously stung by the thought of losing; whether it was what he lost or to whom he lost, I cannot say. "That's a cheap dinner trick."

"Then would you care to make another wager?" Diocles asked, and to his credit, Balbus was instantly cautious.

Thinking for a moment, he gave a tired grin, then said, "No, I wouldn't. You're playing with loaded dice." He was silent for a moment, then without looking Diocles in the eye, he continued, "All right, I'll accept that there are things that we can't control, both outside our physical body and within ourselves."

"That's true, and thank you for your concession, Master Balbus. But I would go further and say that we control nothing, that we're all at the whim of the gods and they're the true masters of our fate and in our actions, big and small."

Balbus had given in, but he was not willing to go that far, making one last stand.

"But if I chose, I could draw my sword and end my life right now, and it would be my decision."

"Would it?"

We all turned in surprise, for it was Scribonius who spoke, his head cocked to one side as he gazed at Balbus.

"Of course it would." Balbus frowned. "Even if the three of you stopped me, you couldn't watch me every minute, so I could do it when I was alone. If a man chooses to die, then nothing can stop him."

"I think Cato would disagree," Scribonius countered. "There's no doubt that he had every intention of killing himself the first time, but he didn't die. So, he couldn't control that act, could he?"

"But he ended up dead, which is what he wanted," Balbus argued.

"Not before other events took place, though. And those events were clearly the will of the gods, or Cato would have died immediately."

Now I was surprised, because I had never heard Scribonius talk in such a way, and to that point I had not thought of him as a religious man. Balbus frowned as he thought this through, then finally he heaved a great sigh.

"Fine," he grumbled. "You win."

Looking over at Diocles as he said it was as much of an apology and admission of defeat as Balbus was willing to make to a slave, but Diocles nodded gravely, saying nothing.

"So why do you ask so many damn questions?" Cyclops asked suddenly, and I opened my mouth to answer for Diocles, mainly because I wanted to show off what I knew, but I was beaten to it.

"It's the method Socrates used for teaching his pupils," Scribonius replied, causing me to gape at him in a combination of surprise and irritation.

"How by Cerberus' balls do you know that?" I demanded, but he refused to give a straightforward reply, saying only that he must have picked the knowledge up somewhere.

The mystery of Scribonius' past still lingered, as for perhaps the thousandth time I resolved that one day I would ask him, when the time was right.

It was now full winter, but a siege is the only endeavor of war not governed by the seasons, so our work continued, though very slowly. With walls too strong and high to climb, our only option was to undermine them, except that was proving extremely difficult because once we dug more than a half-dozen feet down, we hit limestone rock. Despite being soft for rock, it still requires quite a bit of work. The advantage to tunneling through limestone is that it does not require as much shoring up as dirt, which takes a fair amount of wood, which is scarce in this part of the world. However, it also requires a special set of skills to know exactly how to do it, and men with that knowledge were proving harder to find than the wood. Also, only a relatively small number of men can work on a mine at any given time because of the small space. While the work of dragging baskets of rock can be done by anyone, the work had to be shared equally among the army, meaning there were large chunks of time where the men were idle. Being a siege, this meant that we were in a war camp, with much more restrictive regulations, so even if the men had more freedom there was nowhere to go except for the shantytown of the camp followers, where the faces of the whores and wineshop owners were the same day after day. It was similar to the time the army spent restricted to the Campus Martius, except that the number and variety of whores in Rome is almost infinitely greater, although the period of confinement in Rome was much longer, or at least so we hoped. Under these circumstances, it did not take long for the men to grow bored and tempers short, so the punishment detail got its share of bodies and then some.

Word came from Antonius that he would not be arriving as quickly as originally planned, putting Ventidius in a bit of a cleft stick. In his message to Antonius, while he had not stated it explicitly, he had certainly implied that Samosata was as good as taken, yet that was not the case at all. The word in the *Praetorium* was that Ventidius had hoped to time the siege so that it would be ready for assault shortly after Antonius arrived, as a way of getting back into Antonius' good graces by letting him take the credit for taking the city. Now that we had no idea when he was coming, certainly not until mid-spring at the earliest, Ventidius would be forced to conduct the siege and assault on his own. To further complicate matters Antiochus had, just a few days before, sent an emissary offering a thousand talents if we would lift the siege. Knowing that Antonius was always interested in money, Ventidius relayed the message, asking for instructions from the Triumvir, but we had not heard from him. Everything considered, it was a miserable time, compounded by the equally miserable country we were in. For the life of me, I could not see why anyone wanted to live in such a barren, desolate place.

It was not a desert like I had seen in Egypt, just endless rolling brown hills with nothing but scrub vegetation that only the goats, which they had in abundance, would eat. Only along the Euphrates, in a strip of perhaps a half mile on either side was there anything that could be called green, yet it was nothing like the lush Nile Delta, or even further upriver. The wind always blew, carrying with it a fine layer of dust that settled on everything, which at least kept the men busy cleaning their gear constantly, but not busy enough. It was so bad that men actually looked forward to working in the mines, of which there were four, while the Centurions did not even have that to look forward to. All the while, those big black walls stared down at us, the warriors of Samosata perched atop, waiting for an opportunity to strike one of us down when he got careless. It was under these circumstances that the 10th had an event occur that had never happened since I had been the Primus Pilus, the desertion of two men.

It is no secret that many men who seek a life in the army do so because they are too dull to do much else. Usually, those men who are the most stupid either never make it through their probationary period, or are killed in the first two or three battles. Nonetheless, sometimes, through a combination of luck and the help of sympathetic comrades, a few of the stupid ones actually survive for quite some time. Then, a combination of events will occur where for whatever reason, these dullards are forced to think and act for themselves, usually with a bad result at the end of it. Such was the case with these two men, whose names I will not divulge for I have no wish to shame their families. I do not know whether it was blind luck or, as Diocles would insist, the will of the gods that these men, two of the slowest in not only their Cohort but the whole Legion, managed to be paired up as close comrades, keepers of each other's wills, each charged with watching the other's back at all times. Usually, a slow man will end up with a smarter sort who does the thinking for both of them, yet somehow these two had managed to survive together for the close to ten years that this enlistment of the 10th had been marching. The crushing boredom and harsh discipline of a war camp had finally gotten to them, so they made the decision together to desert. The men were in the Tenth Cohort, and a very nervous Pilus Prior Nasica came, along with the Hastatus Posterior, a man named Fulvius, to report the men missing. As he made his report, I was almost convinced that it was some sort of joke cooked up by Scribonius, or maybe even Corbulo, but after looking at the two of them and seeing Nasica's knees literally shaking, I knew that it was no laughing matter. I was seated at my desk, doing what I always seemed to be doing, filling out some interminable request for chickpeas or something similar, and I set the tablet aside to give them my full attention. Diocles was hovering off in the corner, pretending not to be listening, but this was such surprising and unexpected news that he soon dropped all pretense, avidly listening as Nasica told me what he knew.

"Primus Pilus, I regret to report that we have two men who have deserted. We've conducted a thorough search of not only our Cohort area of the camp but the Legion area as well and they're nowhere to be found."

"Did you check the hospital?" I asked, and I was pleased to see Nasica nodded. At least he was being thorough, I thought.

"Yes, and they're not there."

At that point, I was more perplexed than angry. I waved in the direction of the door to my tent, indicating the vast expanse of nothing on the other side of the rampart.

"They deserted to where? Where could they go?"

I was then struck by the obvious question, one that I had forgotten to ask, and inquired as to the identity of the two men. Nasica turned to Fulvius, who cleared his throat, then gave the names of the men, names that I knew.

"Those two?" I gasped. "How by Pluto's cock did the two of them come up with that idea?"

While a Primus Pilus does not know every man of his Legion well, he is familiar with most, even if it is only through the reports of their respective Centurions, but these two were well known to me because their stupidity was something of a legend in the 10th. They were men of the last Century of the last Cohort, as over the years an informal system had developed where the least competent men were assigned to the higher number Cohorts. This extended to Centurions as well as men, at least in other Legions. I did not agree with this practice, so I had tried at least to change it in my assignment of the Centurions, though I am afraid that most of them did not agree with my idea. It had become so ingrained as an accepted practice that men changed hands, moving up or down the Centuries and Cohorts according to their ability. The result was that we had the worst Legionaries in the last Century, and of the last Century, these two were the end of the chain. I do not wish to be harsh to men now long dead, and being fair, it was not because they did not try. In fact, they both tried very, very hard to be the best Legionaries they could be, which was why they had made it as long as they did. By all accounts, when it came to fighting, they were competent Legionaries; unfortunately, we do not spend that much of our time actually in combat, while in every other area they were sorely lacking.

Fulvius could only shrug at the question, Nasica not much more.

"I really couldn't say, Primus Pilus. All we know is that they're gone."

"Well, they can't have gone far." Then I was struck by another thought as I looked at both men sharply. "How long have they been gone?"

I was relieved to hear that they were present for the evening roll call, but they went missing at morning formation. I sighed, telling Diocles to summon the provosts while I thought about making an immediate report to Silo, who had the duty, then decided to wait until I knew more. I could not imagine that it would be that hard to find them, and in that at least I was right. Less than a third of a watch elapsed before Diocles informed me that the provosts requested entrance, and they had two prisoners in custody. Telling Diocles to keep the men outside, I had him send in the provost. Normally, provosts are about as sour and humorless a bunch as can be found in the army, theirs a thankless and unpopular job, but the duty provost came in clearly fighting the urge to laugh, although he rendered a proper salute before making his report.

"We found them in the shantytown, Primus Pilus. They came willingly; didn't put up a fight of any sort."

"Where did you find them?" I asked.

Apparently, this was too much for the man's composure because a snicker escaped from him, irritating me.

"I'm glad you think it's funny that these two men are dead for all intents and purposes," I snapped, and that did wipe the smile from his face.

"Sorry, Primus Pilus," he said, then hesitated. "You're right, of course. It's just that we found them under rather . . . unusual circumstances."

I was not sure I wanted to hear it, but I also knew that if it was as unusual as it appeared to be from the way the provost was talking, it was going to be common knowledge around the camp before nightfall, so I decided I might as well be the first to know.

I indicated he should continue, and he said, "We found them hiding."

He stopped for a moment, puzzling me.

"What's so unusual about that? If I deserted, especially out here in the middle of nowhere, I'd try and hide too."

"They weren't just hiding, they had disguised themselves."

I suddenly had a stomachache, and though I did not want to, I asked, "Disguised as what?"

"As, er, workers at Venus' Grotto."

I sat for several heartbeats, trying to digest what I had just heard. Venus' Grotto was the rather fanciful and far-fetched name of one sadly dilapidated shack where some of the camp whores plied their trade.

"Are you saying what I think you're saying?" I asked this slowly, my mind still struggling with what I had heard. "That these two tried to disguise themselves as women? And whores at that?"

The provost could only nod; I suspect he was worried that if he tried to speak he would burst out laughing. Suddenly, a horrifying, sickening thought flashed into my mind, and it was at that moment I also realized that Diocles had disappeared and not returned.

"By the gods, they're not standing out there right now, dressed as women, are they?" I gasped, but while the provost did not answer, the look on his face gave me the answer. "Then get them in here," I roared. "Or get them out of sight. Are you out of your mind?"

I am afraid I was ranting by this point. At least the provost suddenly did not seem so amused.

It probably will not surprise anyone who reads this when I say that two men of the 10th being brought in chains through the camp, while still dressed in the gaudy finery of camp whores, was an event that we did not hear the end of for the rest of the time I was in the army. Even Diocles, who was normally as quick-thinking on his feet as anyone I knew, had been standing as if growing roots, staring at the sight of the two quaking men, who not surprisingly by this point had gathered quite a crowd. They were dragged into my presence and such was my state of shock and dismay that I was not even angry, actually more curious than anything.

"What were you two thinking?" I asked. The look they exchanged gave me all the answer I needed. It was as if each was saying to their comrade, "I thought this was your idea."

"Well?" I roared at them when neither answered.

Then finally, one of them, the taller, thinner of the two, spoke, his voice audibly shaking. "I don't know, Primus Pilus. We just wanted to go home."

"You wanted to go home? How? You're in the middle of a war, on the border of Syria and Mesopotamia. How were you planning on getting home from here?"

The tall Legionary opened his mouth, then shut it. Finally, he just shook his head, replying miserably, "We hadn't gotten that far yet. First, we just wanted to leave this place."

As I questioned them, it became clear that their idea of escape extended only as far as the shantytown, whereupon both of them had convinced themselves that the answer would reveal itself, somehow finding a way to cross the province of Syria to get to the coast, then hire passage back to Hispania. With every answer to the questions I posed, I felt worse and worse that their punishment was essentially already decided. These were two profoundly simple men for whom, from their viewpoint, life in the army had become unbearably dull, so they decided that they would rather do something else. I did learn that their use of women's clothes was a case of panic when they were alerted that a search for them was taking place, but I also discovered that their decision to hide in Venus' Grotto was not an accident. It turned out that one of them had a woman who worked there, and in fact, if they were to be believed, she had encouraged the two of them, promising to help them in exchange for their agreement to take her with them. As their tale tumbled from the tall Legionary, I wondered how bad the prospects had to be for a woman who would throw the dice to rest her fate on their shoulders. At the same time, I knew that she would have to be arrested as well, though I doubted she would be executed, just beaten severely, no doubt after she was raped by the punishment detail. No, it was a sad and sorry business all the way around.

The worst came when I stood to signal the provosts, and the tall man asked, "Primus Pilus, sir, I know Sextus and me have to be flogged and all, but after that, we'll be able to go back to the Century, won't we?"

Looking into his eyes, I could see that he truly did not understand that his days on earth were numbered in thirds of a watch, that he honestly thought that this was a minor offense that he and his comrade would have to endure. I glanced over to his comrade, who had said not a word, instantly reading that he in fact did understand, that he knew he was about to die, but evidently did not want to say anything to destroy his friend's last hope. I was about to tell the man the harsh truth, then his comrade gave me a silent, pleading look.

"We'll have to see about that, Gregarius," I said. "You go with the provosts now and I'll see what I can do."

The man's gratefulness was pathetic to witness, while his comrade was no less so, except it was for an entirely different reason and I will always remember the look he gave me as he was led off. He knew what awaited them, but his major concern was still for his friend.

During my questioning, I had sent Diocles to stores to get the men some proper clothes before they were led to the small cell that is kept in the stables nearest the *Praetorium* where men awaiting punishment are held. Since the men were found quickly, there had been no need to alert Silo, but their being dragged through camp in women's dress could not be hidden behind the tent flap, as we liked to say, besides the fact that any executions had to be approved by Ventidius. I was writing the report that I would be carrying to the general when Nasica requested permission to see me. Sure that I knew what he wanted, I was tempted to deny him permission, but instead decided to see him. My suspicions were confirmed when I saw that he had both Fulvius and Fulvius' Optio with him, all three of them dressed in their best parade ground uniform, with their respective decorations gleaming brightly. The three of them saluted, which I returned, then sat back, waiting for what was coming.

"Primus Pilus, we've come to formally make a plea for mercy for the two men in custody." Nasica spoke their names.

I remained silent, which I guess he was not expecting, because he suddenly looked unsure of himself, so he turned to Fulvius, who cleared his throat.

"Primus Pilus, I know these men have done a terrible thing," he began, but I waved him to silence, suddenly unwilling to put all of us through what I knew would be a waste of time.

"Gentlemen, I'll cut to the heart of it, and not waste all of our time." I looked down at my report as I spoke, which I was sure would give these men an idea of what I was going to say, it being very unlike me to not look men in the eye as I talked to them. "I know why you're here, and they should appreciate your willingness to speak up for them, especially given their crime." I was fiddling about with my stylus, which was also unlike me. Finally, I blurted out, "But there will be no clemency. These men will be executed."

"But, sir, you haven't even listened to what we have to say," Nasica protested, seeming to me to be more upset at being denied the chance to talk than the actual decision, something that I thought rather odd.

"I understand that, Nasica, but would you rather I wasted your time?" I responded, looking him in the eye now.

His face flushed and he began to speak, then his mouth snapped shut as he shook his head.

"Can I at least ask why you won't consider it, sir?"

While it was a reasonable question, it was surprising because of who asked it, even Nasica and Fulvius looking surprised as we all looked at Fulvius' Optio, a short, tightly muscled man with flaming red hair that gave him his cognomen, Rufus. In situations like this, it is an unwritten rule that the most junior ranking man, especially an Optio, is expected to be as mute as the furniture. Despite turning bright red when I turned to inspect him, he returned my gaze without flinching, but without any defiance. He was simply asking a question, and I made a mental note to keep an eye on Rufus as a man who might be worthy of promotion.

"For two reasons," I lied. "First, we're in a war camp, and the regulations are extremely clear. These men are not *tiros*, they've been under the standard more than ten years." I held up my hand, cutting off the protest I knew was coming. "I realize that neither of these men are particularly bright, but nothing in army regulations makes allowances for the intelligence of Legionaries, only for their obedience."

This did not make them happy, but neither could they argue the point as I pressed on, just wanting to get this whole mess over with.

"The second reason is because of the shame they've brought on the 10th Legion. For that, they must be punished."

"But men have deserted from the 10th before," Nasica protested, and I felt anger rising, which must have shown in my face, because he hurriedly added, "Granted, it's been a long time."

"Since before I was Primus Pilus," I pointed out, probably unnecessarily, yet it was a huge point of pride with me.

Sitting there, I appreciated that it would not be unreasonable for the men to assume that this was the basis of my second reason.

"But that's not why they must be executed. When I say they've embarrassed the 10th, it's not as much because of their desertion, but by the way they did it."

All three men's expressions changed as understanding hit each of them, in different ways, but it was Fulvius who spoke, his voice tight with anger, though I did not know if it was aimed at me.

"Because those idiots tried to dress up as whores," he muttered, then he turned to Rufus, the two exchanging a look that told me that there was still more to what was going on than I knew, but I did not want to know.

"Exactly right," I snapped, my own anger taking hold of me at the thought of the ridicule and derision that men of all ranks in the 10th would have to endure. "Do you have any idea what it's going to be like for all of us for the next few weeks, or at least until something more interesting happens? By the gods, they were dragged through the middle of the camp," I was truly angry now, all three men blanching a little as I stood up, smashing the table with my fist.

The combination of my size and the fact that I rarely displayed a physical side to my anger served to make all three of the men uncomfortable. Even Diocles, sitting unobtrusively in the corner, looked nervous.

"The best thing that could happen is that the city falls, because that's about the only thing that will take the rest of the army's minds off the sight of those two stupid bastards dressed up like whores." I took a breath to calm myself before sitting back down. "That's why these two will die. The other Legions may laugh at us, but they'll do it behind their hands after these two are executed."

Seeing that I was not going to change my mind, the three officers saluted, then left the office, leaving me to sit and brood about the exchange that had just taken place. I say I lied to Nasica, Fulvius and Rufio, but it was a lie of omission more than an outright falsehood. The strongest reason I had for wanting the men to be executed was rooted in my unwillingness to approach Ventidius essentially to ask a favor of him. I respected Ventidius, and I suppose I liked him well enough, yet bitter experience had taught me that it was not wise to owe any member of the upper class anything. Most importantly, and always in the back of my mind was my pledge to Octavian. Knowing that Ventidius was steadfastly loyal to Antonius, I could envision a situation where Antonius, through Ventidius, made some demand that was in direct conflict with what Octavian was requiring of me, and down that path was nothing but disaster. I was at a point in life where my career was sufficiently established that it was not the burning passion that possessed me every moment of the day, but the last few years had taught me that when dealing with the patrician class, damage to my career was the least of my concerns. I was a piece in a game where the stakes were life and death. If Octavian were to believe I betrayed him, no matter the reason, I would die. It would not be done in a public way; that was not Octavian's style; my rank and status meaning that it would be carefully arranged, with nothing left to chance. Nonetheless, I would be as dead as any of my fallen comrades. This was behind my refusal to ask Ventidius to intervene, and with my report finished, I could not postpone meeting with him any longer.

"Are these the two who paraded through camp dressed as whores?"

Ventidius eyed me over the wax tablet of my report. Despite preparing myself for this, I felt my face redden.

"Yes, sir." There was no point in evading what he already knew, and he blew a snort that sounded suspiciously like a laugh.

"Other than the fact that they're supremely stupid, do they have any other redeeming qualities?" he asked.

I hesitated, which he did not miss, and he set the tablet down to pierce me with a gaze from under his bushy eyebrows. Like many men as they grow older, his eyebrow hair had seemingly gained while the hair on his head lost, with a few stray black ones sprouting in all directions from the otherwise uniform gray. I had always noticed that when he talked, the eyebrows moved in seeming harmony with the tone of his voice; the more excited he became, though, the more his eyebrows moved as if they had a mind of their own.

I watched his eyebrows as I replied, "They're the slowest men in the Legion, but they're brave enough, and they're good in battle."

"Too bad there's more to the Legions than that," Ventidius mumbled as he looked down at my report, but I knew that he was not reading it; he was thinking.

For several moments, neither of us spoke, and I knew that he was waiting for me to make a plea for the two men. Yet I said nothing, watching his eyebrows moving up and down as he alternately glared at me, then viewed me with open puzzlement.

Finally, he threw down the stylus he was holding, bursting out in exasperation, "Pluto's balls, Pullus, don't you have anything else to say?"

Giving him the professionally blank stare of the ranker addressing an officer, I responded, "No, sir. There's really nothing else to say."

"Pullus, if you ask, I would be willing to consider granting these men clemency. I know that we're in war camp, and the . . . er . . . method of their desertion was such to cause you and the 10th some embarrassment." I could see he was fighting a smile as he said this. "But given their limitations and the fact that somehow they've managed to survive ten years in the Legions, that tells me that they must have been doing something correctly."

As he peered at me, I could see that he really wanted me to ask him for clemency, and the thought suddenly struck me that this was a trap, that he was in fact trying to put me in a position where I was in his debt. I had always thought of Ventidius as an honorable man, but I was taking no chances.

"Sir, I recommend that the sentence be carried out as you see fit. I'm not asking for any special consideration to be made for either of them."

Ventidius' expression hardened, then he gave me a look that held no warmth, or respect.

"Very well," he said through clenched teeth.

Taking his stylus, he signed the report, then added his own addendum. Snapping it shut, he handed it to me.

"You have your execution, Primus Pilus. Carry it out on your own. I will not officiate."

I had half-expected the men to be sullen, as they usually were for an execution of one or more of their own, but they had been laughed at enough over the last days since the deserters' capture that their mood was anything but downcast or resentful. They were not acting like they were going to a festival either, instead just watched silently with hard expressions as the two men were marched out in front of the assembly, no pity showing on any face. I will say that the two condemned men did not need help getting to the punishment square, though I believe that was due more to their bewilderment and disbelief that they were actually going to be executed. Both of them wore pitifully hopeful expressions, looking at me as if expecting that at the last moment I would step forward and call a halt to the proceedings. But I did nothing;

the sentence was carried out, both men beheaded at the same time so that one did not have to watch the other die. Their heads made a sodden thudding sound as they hit the ground, followed by their bodies, which had been on their knees, collapsing into the dirt in a pool of blood. The Legion was silent, but I could feel a ripple of emotion pass through the assembly as the two condemned men died, the men stone-faced as they were marched back to their area, leaving the bodies of their two former comrades behind. I was proven right about one thing; any laughter at the 10th was done behind our backs after the executions, though the incident would resurface from time to time for the rest of my time with the Legion.

Meanwhile, the business of the siege continued, as we made slow but steady progress with the mines. One blessing from the gods was that because of the bedrock, the enemy had to wait to dig counter-mines until we were almost under the walls, since trying to tunnel through the rock was so difficult. It meant that their period of opportunity to stop our efforts was substantially reduced, but it did make the fighting underground that took place all the more fierce and bitter, as the enemy knew that they were running out of time. Antonius had still not arrived, but Ventidius made the decision to commit to taking the city in the most efficient and speedy manner possible, once Antonius had sent word that he would be delayed. I have no doubt that Antonius' attitude towards Ventidius and his actions played a part in our general's decision, for which I do not blame him. As far as Ventidius and I were concerned, he remained angry with me for the rest of the time we served together, though he never said anything to me. In fact, he did not treat me any differently than before, being a true professional in every sense of the word.

The weeks dragged by, with progress measured in feet; still Antonius did not come. Finally, our mines were close enough to the enemy walls that they deemed it advisable to start the counter-mines. It was high summer now, and though it was exceedingly dry country, Samosata was near enough to the river that despite not having access to the Euphrates itself, there was sufficient water in the ground that they were able to dig wells within the city, much like we had done during the siege of Alexandria. Their food supply, while not sufficient to last through the winter and into the next spring, would last until the end of the year, and none of us wanted to be here for almost a year.

During the third watch one night, the *bucina* sounded the alarm in the vicinity of one of the mines, in our camp, but in another Legion's area. I still had the men roused in case we were needed. Work was going on in the mines through the watches, men laboring in shifts to close the last remaining distance to get under the city walls. Knowing that we were now near enough to expect counter-mines, Ventidius had ordered two Centuries to be ready at all times, sitting next to the mine entrance in the event there was an attack, and it would be these men who were given the order to go down under the ground to repel the enemy attack. First they had to go into a half-crouch, carrying their swords but no shields since there was no room, then hurry as quickly as possible to the end of the mine, the way only dimly lit by a guttering oil lamp every 20 or 30 feet. I had never been in a mine; my size was a true blessing from the gods in this case, as I have no stomach for enclosed places, but Vibius had described the scene to me when he was one of the men to go down into the mines in Gaul. While the tunnels were not very high, they had to be wide enough for men to work and pass each other as they carried their baskets of dirt or rock out, so that there was just enough room for two men to crouch side by side, but not much more. Of course, once the mines reached the spot under the walls, they had to be widened enough so that when the wall collapsed a section of men could enter the breach. This mine was just 50 feet away from that point when the enemy counter-mine had broken into our own shaft. Tunneling a counter-mine is a very tricky business, since of course the other side is not telling you exactly where the mine is. Although you can hear the men picking at the rock and digging quite clearly, from what Vibius told me it is almost impossible to tell exactly what direction and how far away the noise is. So a counter-mine is rarely a straight tunnel dug directly to a spot that intersects the original mine, and in fact, several shafts can branch off the main counter-mine as the search continues. Once the mine is located, the enemy must work quickly to hack out a space large enough for several men, at least ten and more ideally twenty to gather, who then wait as the men doing the work then try to knock down the remaining partition to create a hole large enough for more than one man to charge through. If the entrance into the mine from the counter-mine is not large enough for more than one man, it is relatively easy for our men to cut down the enemy as they appear one at a time. Obviously, the enemy was successful in this endeavor, because quickly enough the *bucina* gave the signal for the second Century.

Balbus and I were standing there as the men yawned and scratched, grumbling about their sleep being interrupted, while the two of us peered in the direction of the fighting, idly speculating about what was happening. Balbus was like me, happy that we were not involved and that he was also too large to go down into the mines. A third of a watch passed before the *bucina* sounded the all-clear, the signal that we could send the men back to bed, and I thought about going to the *Praetorium* to find out what had happened then decided that it would wait.

The next morning during our briefing, we learned that the fighting the night before was extremely bitter, and the enemy, despite being repelled, had inflicted heavy losses on both of the Centuries.

"If this is what we can expect when we assault the city, it's going to be a bloody business," Ventidius said grimly. "But in regards to this mine, they actually did us a bit of a favor. In their attempts to locate our own mine, they actually dug out a cavity that our engineers calculate to be directly under their walls, and is already almost half the size that we need to bring it down. That means that this mine could be completed by tonight."

That was good news indeed. None of us expected that all of the mines that we started would actually be finished; usually the odds are about three in four that a mine will actually either be intercepted and destroyed by the enemy or there will be some sort of collapse on its own. In the case of Samosata, because of the rock we were tunneling through, none of the mines had collapsed, though one had run into a formation of rock that was made of the same material as the wall, proving to be impossible to get through, leaving three, still a larger number than we expected.

"Because of this, I've decided to abandon work on one of the mines, to concentrate all of our efforts on the remaining ones. Naturally, I've chosen the one on the north side of the river."

We were on the south side, where both the successful first mine and the one that was to be abandoned were located, so it was an easy decision to focus all the work on a mine on the northern side. This way, when we attacked the enemy would have to defend the two sides farthest from each other, making it hard if not impossible to support each other.

"The engineers believe that the second mine could be ready by first light. I've instructed them to make it ready before that. Of course, we'll have to make offerings to the gods that when we fire the mines, the wood burns quickly and does its work, so that the breaches occur at about the same time," Ventidius spoke confidently, as if whatever offering he planned on making was sure to be accepted.

Even so, I saw many of the Centurions exchange glances and heard them muttering to the man standing next to them. A simultaneous collapse of both mines was far from a certainly; in fact, it is also a reason why we prefer just one breach, because trying to coordinate more than one almost never works when it is attempted. The last piece of a mining operation is in many ways the most difficult. Once the cavity is created under the wall, it is stuffed with wood and any other readily flammable material, doused with oil then set alight. I do not know exactly why it does so, but the flames weaken both dirt and rock, causing them to give way from under the wall and the foundation, forcing that whole part of the wall to collapse under its own weight. The problem lies in predicting how long that will take; I had seen it affect a breach in less than a full watch, but I had also seen it take more than a day. Regardless of how long it took, we had to be ready to charge into the breach as soon as the dust from it settled, making the waiting nerve-wracking to say the least. Now, trying to plan an assault where the breaches would occur at roughly the same time would take more than just a sacrifice to the gods, it would take their intervention.

That is exactly what happened. Oh, I do not know if the gods actually intervened, nor do I know exactly what Ventidius sacrificed, though the rumor was that he had found a white bull, the most expensive and propitious of sacrifices. I think it was more a case of the gods favoring Ventidius himself, given his run of success. Whatever the case, both breaches happened within a third of a watch of each other, which in fact turned out to be a blessing itself, because it lulled the enemy into believing that there would be only one breach. The general commanding the enemy troops sent all of his men, save for a small force keeping an eye on the other camp, to plug the first hole in his black wall. The opening of the two breaches was far from perfect, however; while they occurred as close to simultaneously as it is probably possible to get, it took the better part of two watches for the fires to do their job, so that we had to conduct the initial assault well past first light, in fact in broad daylight. Also, since the enemy thought that the first breach was the only one, the fighting was fierce and bloody for the first men in, though the killing lasted little more than a third of a watch. As might be expected, given the happy accident of the cavity unwittingly created under the wall by the enemy, the southern breach in our camp was the first one opened. In yet another sign that I was getting older, when I was informed by Ventidius that it would not be the 10th, but the 7th and Caecina into the breach, I made only a half-hearted protest. I believe that his decision was a residual of Ventidius' anger with me, yet when compared to the type of thing that Lepidus tried to do to me, I give thanks to the gods that Ventidius was a better man than Lepidus. This did not mean that we saw no fighting; we were the second Legion into the breach, and were charged with driving into the city center where the palace of Antiochus was located and surrounding it. We were also given strict instructions that we were not to assault the palace itself; that would be Ventidius' honor, if Antiochus chose not to surrender. Our job was to surround the palace and seal it off, but Ventidius was very specific about not setting foot in the palace proper. The wall had come crashing down with a huge roar, a column composed of smoke from the underground fire mixed with black dust from the crumbled wall rising several hundred feet into the air, covering all of us in a fine coat of black rock and ash, making us spit globs of mud onto the ground so that we could breathe.

The dust was barely settled when Caecina gave the order for his men to charge, and with a roar of their own, they went pounding up the rubble pile. Clambering up a heap of crushed rock that had just moments before been a wall, while keeping some semblance of cohesion, is as close to impossible as it is to get, but in this case, speed is more important than being properly aligned in our normal fighting formation. The key is to take advantage of the shock and confusion of the enemy. Despite divining what is happening from the smoke escaping out of the holes that are bored into the ground for ventilation, it is impossible for either side to know exactly when the wall will come crashing down. Once it does, the attacker has a very brief period of time before a well-trained defender begins to collect themselves and prepare for the coming attack. Caecina knew this, and like any good Primus Pilus, went sprinting up the rubble pile, jumping from one large piece of wall to another, yelling at his men, cursing them for being slow and letting an old man beat them to the top. Many of his men, most if not all of them intent on being the first into the breach themselves, so that if they survived they would win their own corona muralis, were hot on his heels. A couple of men, taking awful risks, leaped ahead of him, disappearing into the roiling wall of dust that was just beginning to settle. For several moments the only thing that could be heard were the shouts of our own men, then the first clanging sound of metal on metal carried back to us, followed by a short scream, quickly followed by others as men saw the end of their time on earth come. The rest of the First Cohort of the 7th reached the top, then went hurtling down into whatever enemy had gathered their wits to form up in the first clear space on the other side of the wall. The entire First Cohort and part of the Second had made it over before the last Centuries of the Second came stumbling to a halt, some of them unable to stop and running into the backs of the men in front of them. The enemy resistance had clearly stiffened, so that for the next several moments matters remained the same, as the rest of the 7th stood, one Century lined behind another, each man either leaning to the side or standing on tiptoes, trying to see what has happening. The battle was at full pitch now, the air filled with the sounds of men fighting, killing, and dying, the musical notes of blade ringing on blade, or sometimes the cracking sound that told us someone's weapon had failed them, breaking on impact with either another sword or something else. The duller thud of a blade or something hitting a shield, which does not have the same ringing tone but for some reason carries farther, was as common. Punctuating it all were the shrill whistle blasts as each Centurion called for his front line to move back to allow the next line to step forward in relief. This was a good sign that at least the 7th had managed to establish a wide enough front where they could fall back on our training, and after perhaps a sixth part of a watch, they managed to push into the city enough so that the rest of the 7th, save for the last Cohort was now inside the walls. I gave the command to move into position, watching as the Tenth Cohort of the 7th made their own climb up the rubble then into the city. Again, things came to a standstill as the Tenth stood at the top of the breach, looking down at the fighting that we still could not see. The dust had subsided somewhat, though it was still as if a black fog were passing through, and when I glanced back at the men, I could have been commanding a Legion of Nubians, so covered were their bodies in the black dust. It was quite a striking sight when I saw men smile, their teeth flashing white, matching the two white orbs in their faces, and I was suddenly struck by a shiver as the thought that they could almost be an army of demons or monsters of some sort came to my mind. I turned back to the front, not wanting to think about that, just in time to see the Tenth Cohort disappear.

I raised my arm, calling to the men in my loudest voice, "There's women and gold in this city, boys, and it's ours for the taking. Let's go get it!"

The roaring approval was almost a force pushing me up the pile and into the city as the 10th rushed towards its reward. Just as we crested the pile, my mind was absorbed in the scene before me. It was at that instant that I saw the same cloud of dust roil into the air on the far side of the city as the northern breach finally gave way.

The fight for the city did not take much longer, once the defenders were assailed from both sides, and while there was a brief resistance from one of the more enterprising commanders of the Commagene force trying to stop us from reaching the palace, they were swept aside with just a few losses. Reaching the center of the city, where Antiochus' palace was located overlooking a huge square that held the market and a number of temples, we quickly surrounded it. Facing us were the remnants of whatever warriors could be scraped up, but while they remained in a formation of sorts, we could see men looking over their shoulders at the sounds of the rest of the city falling. It did not take long for men to start slipping away, presumably to go protect their families, as soon as their officer's backs were turned, something that I did not begrudge in the slightest in the event that we were ordered to assault the palace. Not long after we had secured the area Ventidius and his staff arrived, the clatter of the hooves of their horses preceding them as they rode into the square. Saluting our general, I gave him my report, his only reply a grunt as his eyes never left the palace itself. It was on the border of being rude, but he had been so brusque and short with me after the executions that I was not surprised. Turning to one of his Tribunes, he handed the man a tablet.

"You know what to do," Ventidius told the younger man.

Saluting Ventidius, the Tribune took the javelin offered to him, on which had been affixed a white cloth, then went trotting toward the assembled Commagene.

"Now we'll see how badly this bastard wants to save his city," Ventidius said, although I do not know who he was talking to.

It did not take long for Antiochus to reply, acceding to every demand made by Ventidius, for which I was thankful. Their sudden and complete capitulation meant that the Legion was released from standing in the square and could head towards a section of the city designated as ours for the taking without too much time being lost, while Ventidius detailed one of the other Legions to handle the prisoners. We hurried down streets that were rapidly filling up with Legionaries staggering about, some from the loot they were carrying, others from the women slung over their shoulders, and still others who had found the wine supply. Reaching the part of the city marked with the number of our Legion, there was a provost waiting to show me the boundaries. I was happy to see that most of our section seemed to be in a relatively prosperous part of the city, home to merchants and landowners, I assumed. Not home to the nobility, but frankly better than I expected given how Ventidius had been acting towards me. Again, he was a better man than I gave him credit for. While the overall boundary was determined, it was up to me to assign individual blocks and streets to each Cohort, a chore that I detested because nobody ever was happy with their assignment, a sign that I took to mean that I was fair. Being Primus Pilus meant that not only did I get the first choice for my Century and my Cohort, but the whole Legion, yet I was careful not to abuse this and, in fact, I probably did not take as much as I could have, mainly because I had already become extremely wealthy between my time in Gaul and all the bounties paid to us during the civil wars. I did not gamble much, for a Roman anyway, nor did I drink or whore much. What expenses I did incur that were not reimbursable, like the money I had laid out for the enlistment of more *immunes* and for which Pollio had been good to his word in reimbursing me, were extremely low otherwise, so I did not need much.

However, I also knew if I took nothing then it would be viewed as a sign of weakness by the other Centurions, so I always took something.

The morning after the capture of Samosata saw men holding their heads, throwing up, or poking through their hoard of loot, just a normal day in camp, but this was not to last long. Shortly before midday, there was a sound of a *bucina* from the guard Cohort that alerted us that a party was approaching the gates of our southern camp, where Ventidius was flying his red pennant and his personal emblem in honor of his victory. It did not take long for one of Diocles' slave friends to come running up to breathlessly announce that the Triumvir Marcus Antonius was approaching.

The Centurions of the Cohort were in my tent having a meeting, and I believe it was Asellio who said, "Oooooh, he is *not* going to be happy to see that the city has fallen."

"That's too bad," Laetus said curtly, poking his finger in the direction of the gate where presumably Antonius was entering. "He should have gotten his muscled ass here sooner and not been lying about Athens and Brundisium all these months, getting his wife pregnant."

"I'm sure he had pressing business." I felt that I had to make some sort of effort at defending Antonius, though my heart was not in it, and the others knew it.

"You did your duty, Primus Pilus," Balbus said with a grin. "Now tell us how you really feel."

"That he should have gotten his muscled ass here sooner."

This provoked a laugh, which was cut short by the sight of the runner from the *Praetorium*.

"General Ventidius requires the presence of all Primi Pili to the *Praetorium* immediately," he announced.

I sent him back with word that I was coming immediately, then looked at my comrades, who were clearly enjoying the thought of my ordeal.

I sighed as all I could think to say was, "This should be interesting."

The other Primi Pili and I were kept sitting in the outer office, but while the walls of a *Praetorium* tent are surprisingly resistant to sound, when men are yelling, they are not enough of a barrier, particularly when it is Marcus Antonius doing the yelling. The Triumvir was bellowing at Ventidius, but much to our surprise, Ventidius was giving as good as he got. Essentially, the gist of the disagreement was what we had all surmised; Antonius was not in the least bit happy that Ventidius had been so successful, accusing him of trying to steal all the credit for victory against the Parthians. Ventidius responded just as heatedly that he was merely doing what Antonius had ordered him to do, and that while he had no desire to make Antonius look bad, he could hardly be blamed for trying to do the job he was given to the best of his ability. Antonius apparently had no rejoinder for this, instead changing the subject to the thousand talents promised by Antiochus, whereupon Ventidius reminded him that he had been ordered to refuse the thousand talents by Antonius himself, which Antonius denied doing. There was a period of silence, I assume because Ventidius was shuffling through his papers, then with a shout of triumph he obviously shoved the order in Antonius' face, practically daring Antonius to deny the authenticity of the written order. There was a mumbled exchange, then the shouting started anew when Antonius said that written orders were all well and good, but he was still sending Ventidius home for disobeying orders. Corbulo and I exchanged looks that conveyed our shock, while it apparently rendered Ventidius speechless as well. Finally, after several heartbeats, he began speaking again, not shouting, but the intensity in his voice was clear to all of us, though we could not make out what he was saying.

"He can't be serious," I whispered to Corbulo, who was sitting next to me, with Balbinus of the 12th on the other side of me.

"Who knows with him?" Corbulo grumbled. "I used to have a lot of respect for the man, but these last few years, he's changed."

"Or his true nature is finally showing itself," Balbinus interjected, surprising me a great deal.

He had always been an Antonian man from the very beginning, something I could understand to a point because Antonius had commanded the 12th for periods of time when we were in Gaul. My face evidently showed my surprise because he shrugged defensively.

"What? I'm not blind. I see it too. But I saw signs of it as far back as Gaul, though they were few and far between."

"It didn't keep you from hanging on to his *paludamentum*," Corbulo snorted, but Balbinus did not seem to take offense, just shrugging.

"I had to pick somebody in this mess, and he seemed like the best bet."

I shot Corbulo a sidelong glance, seeing that he had not missed it either. Balbinus had used the past tense when describing Antonius' chances, and I suddenly wanted to be somewhere else. Was Balbinus one of Octavian's men, I wondered? Was he going to record our conversation to send back to him, my mind racing as I tried to think of all the things I had said in Balbinus' presence that I might have to explain. Corbulo looked uncomfortable as well, but while we were friendly, I was not about to broach such a sensitive topic with him. Sitting there, I was hit with the realization that for all intents and purposes, I was Octavian's man; the fact that he had not yet called in his debt did not make me one of his creatures any less, and my stomach churned at the thought. All I wanted to do was command my Legion, fight who we were told to fight and live to a ripe old age, but the times were such that it was a practical impossibility to do anything of the sort. However, there was nothing I could do at that moment so I turned my attention back to the confrontation between Antonius and Ventidius. I could hear that Antonius was speaking now, though he was not yelling, making it impossible to hear what was being said.

"So do you think it was really Antonius who had us come here?" Corbulo whispered.

I considered the question for moment, then nodded. "Yes. I think he's planning on relieving Ventidius in front of all of us."

Corbulo nodded his own agreement, adding, "I think you're right. What a pathetic thing to do. I like Ventidius."

"So do I."

That brought a chuckle from Balbinus, who said, "Well, he doesn't seem to like you very much."

I was about to make an angry retort, then thought better of it. I did not know if Balbinus would be busily writing away that evening, yet I was not willing to take any chances, so I just laughed it off. Finally, the flap that served as a door to the general's inner office was pulled aside then both men stepped out, and I heard more than one man's sharp intake of breath at the sight of the Triumvir.

The months away from the army had not been kind to Antonius. Though he was still trim, he was not the physical specimen he had been not even a year before. I am not ashamed to say that Antonius had the only physique of which I was jealous. Despite the fact that he was nowhere near my height, nor as large through the chest and arms as I was, his muscles were so well defined that he looked as if he was carved of marble by Phidias himself. He certainly made the women swoon, though I believe as much of that was due to his status as his looks, but try as I might, I could never seem to exercise enough to make my own body look like his. His face was even puffier than the last time I had seen him, but I believe it was the sight of his hair that caused the reaction, his mass of curls now liberally spiced with gray. Antonius was growing old before our very eyes, striking me particularly hard because he was not much older than I was. His eyes were red-rimmed, which could have been from hard travel, but I suspected that it was from other causes. Still, his gaze was sharp, while his mouth was turned down in an expression with which I had become all too familiar. Ventidius looked surprised to see us, confirming our suspicions, whereupon he looked at Antonius with undisguised anger, but I sensed that all had not gone the way Antonius had planned.

"I'm glad that you're here," he said without any other greeting. "I've traveled a great distance because I was concerned with the way things were going. But I'm happy to see that the reports I received were erroneous." In fact, he looked anything but happy, as he continued. "Now that I've seen for myself that I had nothing to worry about, I'm sending Ventidius home immediately . . . to celebrate his triumph." He finished his statement through gritted teeth, his mood clearly not helped by our spontaneous cheer. "Yes, yes," he said irritably once the noise died down. "It's well deserved and all that, which is why I've decided that Rome should see her victorious general as soon as possible. Ventidius will leave immediately, and I will take command. Between us we'll decide who will be going with him, but I warn you, your work here is far from over and you are needed. I can't guarantee that we'll be able to release any of the Legions in this army to march in the triumph, though Ventidius and I are going to discuss this as soon as I have refreshed myself. That is all."

And with that, he stalked out, his aides in tow, all of them mirroring the expression of their commander. Once he and his bunch were gone, we walked to Ventidius to offer our congratulations. He offered us a tired smile, making me wonder what had taken place that made Antonius change his tune.

I was not surprised in the least when Ventidius informed me that the 10th would not be going to Rome with him, but I knew the men would be disappointed. Marching in a triumph is the pinnacle of a Legionary's career in terms of honors, though the prospect of being allowed to stay drunk for days on end without spending a sesterce of one's own money is probably a bigger enticement. The one consolation was that none of the Legions would be going; Ventidius would have to make do with some of the Legions stationed in Italia that belonged to Octavian. This was just another slap at Ventidius by Antonius, who was doing what he could to minimize Ventidius' accomplishments. He knew that men who had been there would speak glowingly of Ventidius' accomplishments since it would allow them to bask in the reflected glow, making their own contribution more heroic, which Antonius certainly did not want. He also did not want Ventidius lingering about, but the old general knew Antonius too well, insisting on staying until the spoils that had been collected and were designated to be part of the triumphal parade were catalogued, packed up and ready to go. As it would turn out, the triumph of Ventidius would be the only one celebrated for victory over the Parthians, but at the time I imagine that Antonius thought that there was less harm in letting Ventidius celebrate his triumph because his own plans would bring about a triumph that would dwarf anything ever seen before, even Caesar's. Antonius was nothing if not ambitious and he had very big dreams. For perhaps a week, Antonius was all business, holding meetings several times a day with Ventidius' staff and all of the Centurions, picking their brains about facing the Parthians, as he gave every indication that we would be invading Parthia as soon as the weather broke. Ventidius departed with much sadness on the part of the men, and despite our soured relationship, I was sorry to see him go as well.

Antonius ordered us to break camp, leave Samosata, and march back to Damascus, where he intended to spend some time handling matters pertaining to the governing of the province before putting us in winter quarters. None of us were sorry to leave that bleak place, while the men were looking forward to some time in Damascus. Arriving in Damascus, we moved into our old camp, making the necessary repairs and sweeping out the sand that seems to get in every crack and crevice. It felt as if we had hardly settled in when the Primi Pili were summoned to the governor's residence where Antonius was staying.

"I have pressing business that must be attended to," he told us, and while his tone was brusque, I noticed he refused to look any of us in the eye, preferring to gaze at his signet ring on his finger. "In Italia. I'll be leaving immediately and I don't know when I'll be back. Plan on being ready to march in the spring. I'll continue planning with my staff while I'm in Italia."

I stifled a groan, as did the others I suspect, thinking that I had heard this from the man before, but knowing that there was nothing that could be done about it. The next morning he left for the coast. We did not see him again for almost two years.

That period in Damascus waiting for Antonius was one of excruciating boredom, lightened only by our periodic forays out into the region when the locals acted up, which at least did happen with some frequency. The governor left behind by Antonius, a man named Sosius, loaned out the 10th and the 3rd Gallica to that toad Herod, who marched us into Judaea to Jerusalem, intent on expelling Antiochus, not the Antiochus of Samosata, who was currently sitting on the throne of Judaea. Antiochus, trying to avoid being pinned down, scurried out of Jerusalem with his army, but we brought him to ground outside the city of Jericho. It was not much of a battle and this Antiochus was captured and promptly executed by Herod, giving him the throne of Judaea. I could not keep track of the different tribes and who each was quarreling with, since they all seemed the same to me in their customs, manner of dress and tongue. The people of that region are the most fractious I have ever come across, always arguing with each other and with us about anything and everything, whether it is over the price of a cup or a point of law. They seemed to enjoy being unhappy and only content when they made us feel the same way. Many men picked up relationships where they had left them when we marched off; others did not, which did not sit well with the spurned lover, particularly if they took up with someone else.

During that first winter, I received a letter from my sister Valeria, concerning her son Gaius, who I had last seen ten years before. As I read the part where she brought up Gaius, I tried to calculate how old he would be, supposing him to be perhaps 13, so I was very surprised when she informed me that he was planning on joining the Legions. . . . at the next *dilectus*, which meant he had to be at least seventeen. I sat with the scroll in my hand, staring off into space as I absorbed what I had just read. Where had the time gone, I wondered? The last I had seen him, he had been like a puppy tumbling about my heels, full of questions about the army, something I had put down to normal boy's curiosity, yet now Valeria was telling me in no uncertain terms that I was to blame for this development. She maintained that since I had visited all those years ago, Gaius had never shown any interest in his father's farm, instead talking incessantly of the army. Since it was my fault, she said, it was up to me to fix things by making sure that Gaius did nothing so foolish as to join the army. Like most civilians, my sister had no idea about how the army really worked, assuming that since I was relatively high in the ranks, all I had to do was speak to the right people. How I was to do that in Damascus I was not sure, but what I was sure about was that she would not care about such details. I wrote a letter to a man I knew in Rome who was in charge of selecting men for recruiting parties, a plum assignment that men paid a lot of money to procure, partly for the easy duty but mainly because of the opportunity to squeeze new recruits for a variety of "fees". My goal was to find out who was assigned to manage the *dilectus* in the part of Hispania where Valeria and her husband lived, though I did not really know what I would do when I found out.

In Italia, Antonius and Octavian continued their struggle for supremacy, but because of their agreement, it was a clandestine war as they openly cooperated with each other in Octavian's struggle against Sextus. In the past, Antonius had been lukewarm in his support of Octavian's quest to stop Sextus' stranglehold on the people of Rome, but finally Octavian found the one lever that worked on Antonius every time by offering to equally share in the proceeds of Sextus' treasury. For the last several years, Sextus had been extorting Rome for every *modius* of wheat that he, through his fleet, had stolen from Sicily, Sardinia, and Africa, charging more than double the going rate, thereby bankrupting Rome in the process and making him the wealthiest man in the world. Meeting for what seemed like the hundredth time, this time at Tarentum, the two Triumvirs renewed the Triumvirate for another five years, with Antonius promising up a large part of his fleet, mostly the warships, for Octavian to use in his war against Sextus. Of course, it was not as simple as I describe it. The two were in Tarentum for more than a month wrangling over all the details, so that there was no way that Antonius could make it back to Syria because of the winds. Instead, he went to Rome, while Octavian, and more importantly, Agrippa prepared to defeat Sextus. It was a mo*numen*tal undertaking, and will surely go down in history as not just a great military feat, but one of the greatest accomplishments of engineering in Roman history. Agrippa did nothing less than create an inland sea, linking the lake named Avernus with the Lucrine by a canal, the Lucrine being separated from the sea by a strip of land so narrow that barely more than two wagons could pass each other.

The Avernus was well inland, sheltered from view from the sea where Sextus' ships prowled, surrounded by high, forested hills, which supplied the raw materials for a new fleet. It was a massive undertaking, taking more than a year before the fleet was completed, but Agrippa was not content with just building a fleet, he had to learn how to command at sea, having never done it before. Therefore, using the lake, he trained his men and ships relentlessly. Meanwhile, Antonius decided to use his time to help himself, and more importantly the rest of the army in Syria, by recruiting more Legions, which he was allowed to do by the terms of the pact made at Brundisium some time before.

In my own little world, I received a letter from Rome containing the names of the men who were now working for Antonius to find recruits to fill the Legions. I did not know any of them, though I was familiar with the names of a couple of them, but certainly not to the extent that I felt comfortable sending them a letter asking them to refuse to enlist my nephew. Blocking the enrollment of an otherwise eligible man into the Legions is a serious offense, though like everything in Rome that meant only that it would be expensive to accomplish. Nonetheless, approaching a virtual stranger to ask him to take that risk was not something I was willing to do for a variety of reasons. I suppose that at the heart of it I was angry with my sister for implying that while a career in the Legions was good enough for me, her only brother and surrogate first son, it was not for her son by blood, so I did not try all that hard to stop it.

During this time, I took a woman, the first semi-permanent liaison I had since Gisela died, and though I was fond of Miriam, I did not love her the same way as I did Gisela, at least at first. I met her while browsing in the market for some new reading material; such was my boredom that a job that I had previously left to Diocles I now pursued with a passion. What was a chore before, doing it only because my job had required it, had now become my primary leisure pursuit, and I think that in many ways Scribonius had much to do with it. He had not only been literate when we were *tiros*, he had always read for enjoyment, spending much of his fortune on books, many of which he lent me as my love of reading increased. In truth, I felt the need to read as much as I could because I was tired of Scribonius thrashing me when we would spend the evenings debating all manner of things. While my tastes still ran towards reading histories and military treatises, I was forced to expand my horizons in order to give Scribonius a battle during our conversations.

The day I spotted Miriam, I was looking for some texts on geography that Scribonius had mentioned reading some time before that discussed the terrain that we would be marching through. She was shopping in the stall next to the one where I was browsing, and at first glance, she was not much to look at when compared to the women of Gaul. Where Gisela had been coppery fire, with curves in the places where a man expected them, Miriam was dusky and slim, her face dominated by a nose that bespoke her Semitic heritage. Still, there was a flash in her eyes as I saw her looking sidelong at the huge Roman that must have reminded me of my wife, for she was the first woman who I ever turned to examine in anything other than an appraising manner as someone suitable for a night of rented passion. She was not wearing a veil, though her hair was hidden by a scarf, a sign that she was no longer a maiden but was unmarried and belonged to no man, which intrigued me as I wondered what her story was. Our eyes met briefly, then as quickly she looked away, turning her attention back to the pile of dates that she was standing in front of as she picked up a few. She began haggling with the merchant, while I turned my attention back to my own business, though I kept glancing over to see what she was doing. Then I got absorbed in examining one scroll in particular, which I ended up selecting, along with two others, and when I turned around, she was gone. I paid the man who ran the stall, a bearded older Jew who exuded a quiet dignity that not even the presence of a Centurion of Rome could shake, before turning to survey the crowded market. Heading to the left would take me back to camp, and it was a temptation because I was eager to start reading one book in particular, but before I did, I took one last look off to the right, telling myself that I had nothing special in mind. Spotting her moving through the crowd, her drab brown dress and robe could not hide the litheness of her movements.

On an impulse, I turned right instead, as I continued lying to myself by thinking that perhaps there was another bookseller that I had not seen yet. I walked without any real haste, knowing that my long legs would cover twice the distance as hers with every step. Keeping my eye on her retreating back, I pretended to look at the various wares for sale along the dusty street, ignoring the pleas and cries of the merchants who knew that a Centurion of Rome had money to buy anything they had to sell. When she would stop to examine something, I would suddenly become interested in whatever some crone or old man was thrusting at me. I had reached the part of the market where the sellers of potions and cures was located. In front of one stall in particular, I noticed that the old woman was leering at me, though I did not think anything of it until she spoke.

"Ah, Centurion."

Her Latin was heavily accented but understandable, while I just grunted in response, which she apparently took as a sign that I was interested in what she was offering, because she let out a coarse chuckle, then said, "Having problem with your *vitus*, neh?"

I looked at her curiously, whereupon she made a gesture with her hand as it hung down in front of her that needed no translation.

"It's gone soft, neh? Do not worry; I have just the thing for you. It will make it as if it is made of iron."

She turned to begin rummaging through the little vials sitting on her table, but before she found what she was looking for, I had beaten a hasty retreat, feeling the fire in my face as I worried that somehow this woman I was following would see me and misunderstand why I was talking to the old woman. I looked around, but she had disappeared. Cursing, I quickened my pace as I neared an intersection, trying to determine in which direction she had gone. I suppose at this point I probably should have just turned around and gone back to camp, but something kept me going. Instead, I chose to turn to the right, which I could see led away from the market into a residential area. The street I turned onto was less crowded, but I could not spot her so I walked farther up the street to where it made a slight bend, telling myself that I would turn and go back to camp if I did not see her by that point.

"Why are you following me, Roman?"

Almost jumping out of my skin, I whirled around as my hand unconsciously went to my sword, which is probably not the best way to make a good impression when meeting a woman, yet she seemed more amused than scared. She was standing in a doorway, her brown clothing blending into the darkened recess and door, and she stared up at me, one hand holding the cloth bag that carried her purchases, the other on her hip. As I said, she looked as different from Gisela as a woman could, but there was something in her posture, and the almost defiant expression on her face, showing no fear at all that wrenched at my heart in a way that I was not expecting.

"I wasn't," I stammered. "I was just looking for a bookseller that I heard was around here somewhere."

I lifted my own bag of scrolls as proof before realizing how stupid that was.

"It looks as if you already found this bookseller," she replied, lifting her chin and I could see the corner of her lip twitching.

I was struck by how full her mouth was, wondering what it would be like to kiss it.

That sudden thought shook me as much as the woman standing there, so all I managed was a shake of my head, along with a mumbled, "No, there was supposed to be another one somewhere, but I can't find it."

"I live just up the street." She was very calm in stark contrast to my agitation. "And I can tell you that there are no booksellers up this way. They are all in the market."

"Oh, er, thank you, then. I suppose someone told me wrong," was all I could think to say.

For a moment, we stood there, neither speaking as she continued her frank examination of me, while I tried to think of something else to say.

Suddenly inspired, I blurted out, "This looks like a dangerous area, not safe for a single woman. Maybe I should escort you home to make sure you arrive safely. It's part of our job to make sure that the city is safe for its citizens," I added helpfully, trying to make it sound as if I was just doing my duty.

She laughed at that, but it was not a cruel laugh and she shook her head.

"Roman, I have lived here most of my life. I know this area better than you ever could. I assure you I am in no danger from anyone here."

"Very well." I tried to keep my voice level, yet her laughter had stung, striking me once again in her similarity to Gisela and her ability to cut me with her laughter and a few words. I turned to leave, just catching a look flashing across her face and she called out for me to wait.

"I am sorry, I did not mean to offend you, Roman," she said softly, looking up at me.

As I looked in her eyes, I noticed that there were small flecks of gold in the brown, and I tried to remember where I had seen that characteristic before, then it came to me. Cleopatra had eyes like this.

"That's all right," I replied, and I was being honest. "I understand why you might not want to be seen with a Roman. I apologize for being so forward."

"Oh, it's not that," she said a little too quickly, the transparency of the lie suddenly causing us both to laugh.

With that, I offered her my arm, saying in a joking tone, "Wouldn't you like to start some tongues wagging? I'm sure there are some old women on your street that need something to gossip about."

I did not think she would take my arm, but after perhaps a heartbeat, she gave a shy smile, then put her small hand on it, and we began walking towards her home.

"Do you read a lot?" she asked me after we had introduced ourselves, and I learned her name was Miriam, with a last name that my Roman tongue could not get around, though I tried a couple of times, making her giggle at my efforts.

I nodded in answer to her question, then realizing she was expecting more than just a simple yes or no, I explained how I had gotten started reading just for my duties, but how I had come to love it.

"What do you love about it?"

I considered this, for nobody had ever asked me the question before.

"I suppose that I love the idea of learning new things. It's exciting in a way."

She nodded at that.

"My father used to say that a thief can rob you of your fortune, a murderer can take your life, but no man can take your knowledge, whether they are a king or . . ." She suddenly stopped, looking embarrassed.

"Or," I asked, but she was clearly reluctant. "I won't be angry, I promise."

"Or Caesar," she finished, causing me to throw my head back and roar with laughter.

She looked bemused, but after seeing that I was truly not angry, she smiled, clearly pleased that she had made me laugh.

"Your father is a wise man," I told her when I caught my breath.

"Yes, he was," she said quietly, and there was just a glimmer of sadness flashing across her face.

"He died?" I asked, knowing that there would be no other reason for her to use the past tense, something that Gisela would have never let go by without a remark about my grasp of the obvious.

However, as I was to learn, Miriam was kinder than Gisela, though at least as intelligent.

She nodded. "Two years ago, of a bloody flux."

"I'm sorry, I didn't mean to bring up a painful memory," I said, wincing at how awkward I was sounding, but she did not seem to notice.

"So whose house do you live in now?" I asked as casually as I could, but she shot me a look from under her lashes, her expression both coy and amused.

"Is this your way of asking if I am married?" she asked me.

"Not at all," I protested, lying through my teeth. "I know that if you were married you wouldn't be walking with me right now because your husband would never let you out of his sight."

As mawkish as it may have sounded, I could see that she was flattered.

"I live with my sister and her husband."

We walked in silence then, ignoring the stares that inevitably came my way, something that I had long grown accustomed to, though it seemed to make Miriam uncomfortable. I could see her studying me out of the corner of my eye, but I decided to wait for her to continue the conversation. Finally, she seemed to make a decision.

"I was married. My husband was killed."

I started to say that I was sorry, then shut my mouth, both because I was not sorry, but also because I sensed that there was something more to it. Instead, I stopped walking to look down at her, watching as she chewed her lip, clearly struggling with something.

"He was a soldier like you, but not an officer. He was just a regular soldier. He joined to provide for me. We had only been married a few months."

I nodded, encouraging her to continue. She refused to look at me, gazing down the street as people walked by going about their business, oblivious to what was taking place between a huge Roman Centurion and a drably dressed slim woman. She took a deep breath, then blurted out what she had been struggling to say.

"He was with Quintus Labienus. That's who he was fighting for when he was killed."

As we finished our walk to her home, she filled in the story, which had obviously gotten my attention. Things had been very bad during the two years the Parthians occupied Syria, Miriam explained. There was no work as the local economy had come almost to a standstill. Then Quintus Labienus started recruiting, offering a cash bounty for men who would join his army and Miriam's husband, who had been a stonecutter, jumped at the chance. It was a familiar story; a man desperate to provide for his new wife would not be thinking about the long-term consequences of his actions. I wondered if it ever occurred to him that even if Labienus were victorious, he would likely never have seen Miriam again for more than a few days at a time, for however long he remained alive. Men like Miriam's husband are nothing but fodder for the swords of men like me, their lives on the battlefield generally measured in moments once the fighting starts, and I could not help wondering if I had anything to do with his death. Miriam did not know the circumstances of how he died, only learning about it from one of his friends who stopped long enough to tell her as he was fleeing after Labienus' defeat. That was the other aspect of what Miriam's husband had done that would have haunted him for the rest of his days, for if he had managed to survive the fighting, the instant Labienus had gone down in defeat, he would be running from Rome. In all likelihood, he would have been forced to go to Parthia, where he would undoubtedly have found himself with a wicker shield and a spear, standing once again as little more than glorified stalks of wheat waiting to be cut down. In short, the moment Miriam's man made his decision his fate was determined by the gods, and it was not a happy one. I believe that men are born to the profession of arms or they are not; stonecutters, laborers and tradesmen are the chaff to be cut down by the swords of men like me. I never said anything of the sort to Miriam, not wanting to disrespect the memory of her husband, who she clearly had loved a great deal. I did not begrudge her that love, as I did not expect her to hold my love for Gisela against me, and in truth after that day, we never talked about our respective romantic pasts very often. When we reached her sister's home, a two-room apartment on the second floor of a three-story tenement made of stone, she invited me in for a cup of wine, which I accepted.

"Wait here for a moment while I go tell my sister that we're having company," she said, running up the stairs to enter the apartment before I could even respond.

As I stood waiting, I kept asking myself what I thought I was doing, but I did not leave. A few moments passed without her reappearing as I began to wonder if she had changed her mind and had just decided that not coming out to tell me was the best way to handle things. Then I caught the sound of raised voices, and despite being unable to tell what was said, it was clear that they were arguing. I was beginning to think that this was a very bad idea so I was turning to leave when the door opened as Miriam came out on the landing with a bright smile, beckoning me to come up. I ascended the stairs, then stopped at the doorway, looking down at her.

"Are you sure it's all right?" I asked. "I don't want to cause you any trouble with your sister."

"It's not any trouble at all," she insisted. "I just surprised her, that's all. Please, come in."

She motioned me in and I stepped inside, ducking my head to avoid the low ceiling. The main room was cramped, with a table in the middle of the room and benches on either side, a blackened fireplace against one wall with a large copper pot hanging over a smoldering flame. Standing over the pot with her back to us was a woman, dressed almost identically to Miriam, who only turned when Miriam called her name, clearly reluctant to face me. She looked much like Miriam, except there was a hardness about her eyes and mouth, as if she had experienced a lifetime of bitterness and disappointment, making her smile anything but warm. She gave me the ritual greeting of her people, welcoming me into her home, spitting the words out as if they left a bad taste in her mouth, which I pretended was offered graciously. Miriam's sister pointed to the table, indicating that I should sit, which I did, unclipping my sword to lay it on the bench next to me in an automatic gesture that clearly startled both women and made them uncomfortable. A look passed between the two, and there was no mistaking the pain on Miriam's face. I realized that she must have had the same thought as I, that maybe this very sword had ended her husband's life. Shaking her head but not speaking, her sister brought a jug and two cups, setting them on the table while giving me a forced smile, then went to get a bowl filled with olives, placing it on the table between us. She turned to

Miriam, saying something in her tongue, which I did not understand, whereupon Miriam turned to me, translating for her sister.

"You are welcome in our house, Titus Pullus, and we apologize for the quality of the wine and refreshments, but we are not wealthy people."

"I'm sure it's much better than I'm used to in camp," I replied, then turned to give Miriam's sister what I hoped was my most winning smile. "Thank your sister and ask her to accept my apology for my imposing on her like this."

Miriam translated, her sister giving a grunt and nodding before she turned back to her cooking. I took a sip of the wine, which almost gagged me because it was in fact not even close to the quality of what I was accustomed to in camp, yet I smiled, making a sound that I hoped indicated how delicious it was. Evidently my face betrayed me, because Miriam burst out laughing, causing her sister to turn around in curiosity.

"Not quite what you're used to?"

Seeing that there was no point in lying, I laughed back. "Not in camp. Maybe when we've been marching for a month or two."

Miriam's sister said something, causing them both to laugh.

"She says that you Romans are spoiled."

"We are used to living well when we can," I conceded, smiling to show that I had taken no offense. "But we can endure much hardship when we have to."

"Is that why you have conquered most of the world?"

There was no mistaking the tinge of bitterness in Miriam's voice, but I chose to ignore it, taking the question seriously.

"That's part of it. I think that it's a combination of things really. We're better organized, better trained, and better equipped than most of our enemies. That was certainly the case in Gaul. The Gauls are very brave individually, and they fight like demons, yet we never lost to them."

"What about Gergovia?" she asked quickly. I could not hide my surprise, and she laughed. "We may be on the other side of the world, but that does not mean we do not hear things, especially when Rome loses."

"That was a setback, not a defeat," I snapped, speaking more sharply than I intended, her face coloring as she immediately dropped her eyes, looking in her lap.

"I'm sorry, Titus Pullus, I did not mean to offend you," she murmured.

I could see her sister glaring at me out of the corner of my eye, and I felt horrible. I awkwardly reached out to pat her on the hand.

"No, I'm the one who should apologize. I shouldn't have spoken so harshly." I took a deep breath. "Especially when what you say is true. We were defeated at Gergovia. I should know, I was there and I saw what happened. All I'll say in our defense is that Caesar, with the help of the 10th, made sure that it wasn't a decisive defeat."

"So you said that was only part of it," Miriam said as I took a sip from my cup, still trying to keep from gagging. "What else?"

"We've been fighting a long time, against a lot of different enemies. We have more experience than most armies we face." I thought of something else. "And we learn from our mistakes, and we'll adopt things that work that our enemies use." I pointed to my sword as an example. "Like this short sword. It was used by the Lusitani in Hispania, which is where I'm from," I said proudly. "But for fighting the way we fight, there's no better weapon in the world, which is why we adopted it."

"What have you learned from the Parthians?" she asked, picking at a loaf of dark flat bread that her sister had set on the table next to the bowl of olives.

"That cataphracts can't beat us," I said instantly. "And that slingers will beat their horse archers off before they can do any real damage."

"Why do strong countries like to take advantage of weak ones?" Miriam asked sadly, gazing down at the table.

For a moment, I was not sure that she was expecting an answer. Then she looked up at me, and I saw a glimmer of tears in her eyes as I fumbled for an answer that would not make her more upset.

Finally, I said the only thing I could think of.

"Because they can, and because that's man's nature, to take what he can. Besides," I tried to find some sort of bright spot, "who would you rather be ruled by, Parthia or Rome?"

"I would rather that we were ruled by neither, that we would be allowed to decide what is best for ourselves," she answered, looking at me steadily as she spoke.

"That isn't likely to happen," I said as gently as I could, but I wanted to make sure that there was no doubt that what I was saying was true. "And at least with Rome you're allowed to worship your own gods, in your own way and run your lives and businesses the way you see fit, for the most part. All we expect is that you pay taxes and not try to kill each other all the time."

She laughed.

"We've been killing each other since long before Rome arrived and I suspect we will continue long after Rome is gone."

"Rome will never be gone." I was adamant about this, and I still am.

Rome will live forever, as long as there is light in the world, since it is Rome that provides that light. It has been deemed by the gods that it should be so.

"Perhaps," she said, but there was no mistaking the doubt in her voice. I let it pass.

We talked a bit more, then Miriam's sister said something. Miriam stood up.

"I am sorry, Titus Pullus, but my sister is right. Her husband will be home soon, and she thinks it would be best if you were gone. He has no love for Romans, and seeing one in his house could cause trouble."

I was about to make a retort that there was no trouble some laborer could start that I could not finish, but I realized that it would be rude and would ruin whatever chances I had of seeing Miriam again, so I agreed and got up to leave. Thanking her sister, I walked with Miriam outside and down into the street. Standing there, I saw that it was getting dark, yet I did not want to leave, and she seemed reluctant to see me go as well.

"When can I see you again?" I blurted out, causing her to blush, but she was quick to answer.

"I will be in the market tomorrow. I help out my brother-in-law a few days a week. He is a butcher and I handle the sales while he does the work."

This was not what I had in mind. However, while there were similarities between Gisela and Miriam, there were some major differences, mainly in their respective customs. Gallic women have much more freedom than the women in this part of the world, which extends to their interaction with men who are not related to them, and I had no wish to get Miriam in trouble. The fact that she was a widow and had no surviving male relative gave her a bit more liberty than her counterparts, but she still had to be more circumspect. Thus began what I suppose was a courtship over the next month as I found myself visiting the market on an almost daily basis, duties permitting. Fortunately for my romantic life, our garrison duties were very light, helped by the fact that the men were sufficiently experienced that they did not require as much supervision, which the Centurions took care of in any case. My Optio Mallius was a Centurion in everything but name, since the duties of the Primus Pilus in running the Legion means that he is in charge much of the time. Miriam's sister Naomi began to warm to me a bit, signaled by an invitation to dinner, which I accepted on the condition that I supplied the wine, which had become something of a standing joke between the three of us. I will say that it was a bit tense at first, as I met Hashem, Naomi's husband, still wearing his bloody apron from his day of slaughtering animals. Nonetheless, he was polite enough, and before long, we had found common ground discussing the games that had recently taken place. Hashem was a huge fan of the gladiatorial games, and through Miriam, I told him of some of the contests I had seen while in Rome featuring some of the famous gladiators like Lucan the Thracian and Felix, who had won his freedom by not only surviving but winning the required number of bouts. In reality, these were good, simple people, in most ways like the people I had grown up with and could not wait to get away from because I found them boring when I was young. Now I found that I enjoyed spending time with them, and I believe they felt the same about my company, once they got past the fact that I was one of their conquerors. They enjoyed some of my scandalous stories of the Roman upper classes, although I cleaned them up a bit, and I had them roaring with laughter as I talked about the antics of some of the Legionaries I had known over the years. One memorable night, Hashem and I drank more than we should have. Despite the language barrier, we had a great time, slapping each other on the back in appreciation of some witty thing the other said, then ending up thrashing around on the floor wrestling while the two women sat rolling their eyes at each other and at us. I cannot say that this was entirely spontaneous on my part; I had determined that the best tactic to win Miriam was to win her family first and it was one of my more successful ploys, for when the time was right, I invited Miriam to dine alone with me in camp and neither Hashem or Naomi put up much of an argument. I like to believe that both of them were pleased to see Miriam so happy, because she clearly was, laughing more and more with each meeting. When she would see me coming in the market, if I were meeting her there, her face would light up, causing my heart to skip a beat. While her only display of affection was squeezing my hand, I could tell that she was truly happy to see me. Meanwhile, I found that I was smiling more than was normal for me.

So much so in fact that more than once I caught Scribonius, Balbus, Cyclops, and a number of the other Centurions eying me with either suspicion or open curiosity. The night she came with me back to camp was a night that the 10th had the guard duty, so I made sure that Cyclops was the duty Centurion. When I told him why, he gave a smile of genuine pleasure, promising me that the men would be on their absolute best behavior. I knew all too well how men will leer at the women that Centurions brought into camp, as we are the only rankers officially allowed to have female guests in winter camp, whereas the lower ranks had to go outside the ramparts for their assignations. Miriam was clearly nervous, chattering more than was usual for her, clutching to my arm tightly, but she showed no sign of wanting to turn back. Once we entered camp, walking past the stone-faced Legionaries on post who gave me their best parade-ground salute, I could see that she was impressed. In fact, there seemed to be more of my men out in the Legion streets than normal, every one of them stopping to come to *intente*, whipping out a salute and a crisp greeting. I could not help noticing that they were all turned out in their best uniforms, and I reminded myself to have a talk with Cyclops.

"You are very important, aren't you?" she asked me.

"Well, I am the highest-ranking Legionary in the 10th Legion," was all I would say about it, though I was secretly very pleased that she had noticed.

"Did you have your men do this to impress me?" she teased and I felt my face go hot.

"No," I protested. "I didn't have anything to do with this."

"Then one of your Centurion friends then," she guessed, as my silence confirmed it. "They must think very highly of you to make your men get all dressed up," she said.

I was about to point out that Legionaries did not "dress up," but bit my tongue.

"Well, they certainly are afraid of me," I said lightly, but she shook her head.

"This wasn't done out of fear, Titus Pullus." She always insisted on using both my names, even when we were alone.

I said no more about it, as we had arrived at my quarters, where Diocles had been alerted by a runner and was standing outside in a fresh white tunic. Making the introductions, I believe that this was the first time that I was careful not to refer to Diocles as my slave, remembering how Gisela had felt about the subject, though Diocles showed no surprise. Ushering us through the door, Diocles led us through the front office into my private quarters, while I tried not to show my shock at the transformation of my space. In it, Diocles had placed a dining couch, with a low table in front of it on which were bowls of olives, onions, and a number of delicacies that had to have been hard to find.

Recovering, I gestured to the couch, saying, "I thought we would eat in the manner of the Roman upper classes, on a couch."

Miriam looked puzzled as she tried to determine how it worked, making me laugh.

"We eat lying on our stomachs," I told her.

She shot me a suspicious glance, sure that I was fooling her.

"It's true," I insisted as I had Diocles lead her to the place of honor, where he gently guided her into the proper position.

Once she got comfortable, I joined her, making sure that I was a respectful distance away and we were not touching, for which she gave me a grateful smile. We began the meal, and before long her nervousness disappeared as she experienced new tastes, finding she liked them for the most part. I had made sure that Diocles spared no expense in this dinner, so I had not eaten this well in some time. As we ate, I told her of the banquet with Cleopatra, which she listened to with wide-eyed wonder as I described the golden plates, how the peacocks were cooked before having their feathers reattached. She laughed at my experience with crocodile eggs and the sight of the tails hanging from men's mouths as they slurped them up. Before much time had passed, she wriggled closer to me as I fed her bits of fowl smeared with garum with my fingers, laughing as she wrinkled her nose at the smell and taste.

"We love garum," I told her. "We put it on everything, for breakfast and dinner."

"No wonder you Romans bathe so much," she laughed. "That stuff must come out of your skin."

I had never connected the two habits, and I shook my head, saying as much. All in all, it was a wonderful and memorable dinner, much more enjoyable because of the company, and of course for what happened later. That night, Miriam became my woman in the most important way, at least to a man. She was not as passionately fiery as Gisela; it was more of a smoldering type of sensuality, yet it matched her personality, for she was naturally more reserved and circumspect than my wife had been. In some ways, Miriam and I were a better match, both in bed and in other ways than Gisela and I, but I never seriously considered making our union more permanent in those early days. If she did, she never spoke of it. More than anything, we were comfortable together, and I was thankful that while she could be mulishly stubborn I never had to worry about flying crockery. We were careful to avoid the complication of children, for a number of reasons that we never discussed, but I am sure we both understood. Still, there was one time she was forced to use sylphium, which was very unpleasant for her. Perhaps a month after we became lovers she came to live with me, whereupon she and Diocles very quickly formed a secret alliance to curb what they considered to be some of my more annoying habits. Perhaps the most interesting, and somewhat mystifying, aspect of Miriam's entrance into my life was the effect that she had on my Centurions, who behaved as if she were a younger sister that needed protection. There was none of the lewd commentary that would normally be expected and while some of that I knew was due to her status as my woman, there was just something about Miriam and her air of quiet dignity that did not stir men to voice their coarser opinions. In fact, I was subjected to a lecture from Scribonius after Miriam and I had an argument in front of him one evening at dinner.

"You know, you were excessively harsh with Miriam," he told me the next day when we were out on the training field doing our daily sword work. "She's a wonderful girl and you should realize that."

I stopped what I was doing, not sure how to respond.

"What, are you her father now?"

"No, but I have eyes and ears, and I was there," he shot back. "And you didn't have to yell at her."

"I didn't yell, exactly," I knew how weak this sounded as it came out of my mouth.

While I do not remember what the argument was about, I do remember how it must have looked to Scribonius as I towered over Miriam, shaking my finger at her and while not bellowing, certainly speaking loudly.

Scribonius snorted.

"She doesn't know that," he pointed out. "She's never seen you leading the Legion."

"But I was right," I protested, as he let out another snort.

"Has it really been that long since you've had a woman to know that it doesn't matter if you're right? Besides," he added, a grin on his face. "You weren't right; you were wrong."

I sighed, then grumbled, "Fine."

I bought Miriam a bracelet by way of apology, which smoothed things over nicely.

The year of Agrippa's Consulship passed uneventfully for those of us waiting in Syria. The same cannot be said for Italia and the campaign to eliminate Sextus Pompey. The plan was ambitious; a three-pronged assault, with one arm consisting of the fleet built from scratch by Agrippa on the Avernus, another led by Octavian using the ships that Antonius lent him, with the final thrust coming from the worm Lepidus, who was skulking about Africa with an army of 16 Legions and about 5,000 Numidian cavalry. Somehow, despite his ineptitude, Lepidus managed to land 12 of those Legions on the southern coast of Sicily, taking Lilybaeum on the western tip of the island. Meanwhile, Agrippa and Octavian were moving their fleets into position when a huge storm struck and despite attempts to take shelter, both fleets suffered massive damage that would take more than a month to repair. The storm hit in the beginning of Julius, making it late summer before another attempt could be launched, which was dangerously close to the point where the prevailing winds changed direction and would actually be working against the Triumvirs and not for them. A prudent commander probably would have decided to postpone the offensive until the next year, but Octavian was under enormous pressure from all levels of the Roman world. While the fleet was being repaired, he went rushing around to the various veterans' settlements assuring them that all was well. Maecenas was doing the same in Rome with the upper classes, and I have no doubt that for every positive thing that was being spoken by Octavian and Maecenas, Antonius was busy spewing whatever he could think of to drag his young colleague down. The problem was that Antonius seemed unable to focus his hatred on the things that Octavian was actually doing, concentrating instead on his personal life. No manner of filth was too low for Antonius' agents, everything from Octavian's love of gambling to his supposed love of being buggered, which may have lowered the masses' estimation of Octavian as a man, but from what I saw and heard, did nothing to damage his reputation as the best chance to bring Rome back on her feet. After observing both men, I have reached the conclusion that for Antonius a man's character was his true measure and how he should be judged; Octavian did not give a rotten fig for what people thought of him personally, as long as they recognized his competence in public affairs. As licentious as Antony was in many ways, he was conservative in ways that Octavian was not, although there were no lengths that Octavian would not go to in order to create stability and bring peace to Rome.

Once the fleet was repaired, Octavian tried again, shifting his tactics somewhat to try to defeat Sextus through the overwhelming superiority of land forces and pin Sextus in his main port of Messana by cutting off the rest of the island. Using their fleets, Agrippa and Octavian would blockade the port to trap Sextus in the city with a combination of Lepidus' Legions and Legions that Octavian would land on the eastern coast of Sicily. To do this, he would have to cross the narrow strait between Scolacium and Tauromenium where his slow transports would have no chance against the warships of Sextus' fleet. The only way to neutralize Sextus' fleet was with Agrippa, who was ordered to try drawing Sextus' fleet into a battle off the northern coast of Sicily, which would allow Octavian to slip past to land at Tauromenium. To support this operation,

Lepidus was ordered to bring up the other four Legions from Africa, but Sextus intercepted that fleet with a small force he had patrolling the sea between Sicily and Africa, two Legions being drowned before ever setting foot on dry land. The other two managed to land, but were in complete disarray. Octavian was scouting in his own vessel and saw that most of Sextus' fleet was now on the north side of Sicily, so he gave the order for Agrippa to engage the enemy. The senior Consul did, and there followed a battle in which Agrippa took the upper hand, but was far from being decisive, so Sextus was able to withdraw with most of his fleet in good order. More importantly, Sextus divined what the Triumvir and his chief admiral were about, so keeping part of his fleet in place to fool Agrippa he sailed with the bulk of it to Messana, where he would lay in wait for what he had determined to be the main thrust of the attack. Meanwhile, Octavian received word that Agrippa was completely successful instead of partially, so instead of crossing at night, which would have been the prudent thing to do, he ordered his fleet composed of both troop transports and warships, to cross in broad daylight. This, of course, was what Sextus was waiting for.

Proving that some of Pompey Magnus' blood ran through him, Sextus did not do what might have been expected by attacking the fleet while it was still at sea, which would have allowed many of the Triumvir's troops to escape in the confusion. Instead, he waited to let Octavian reach Tauromenium and begin unloading his army before striking with a combination of his navy and land forces. It could have been a complete and total victory; while Octavian's army was landing and starting on their camp, from the north came Sextus' cavalry by land, along with his fleet from the same direction by sea. From the south was Sextus' Legions, yet for some reason the commander of Sextus' Legions did nothing, while only his cavalry harried Octavian's forces. Neither did Sextus' fleet, which also held back and did not engage Octavian's ships forced to be at anchor as the army made camp, instead letting them discharge their cargo before making way back out to deeper water. Sextus could have crushed Octavian's army and trapped him on shore, but instead Octavian took the opportunity to escape in a Liburnian and join the fleet, while his army, despite the constant harassment from Sextus' cavalry was able to build a fortified camp by working through the night. With his army now safe for the moment, Octavian's greatest danger came from Sextus himself, who finally sailed out with his fleet to engage the Triumvir, inflicting heavy damage, only being stopped by nightfall.

Octavian was left afloat amid the wreckage of a number of his ships, cut off from Sicily, so he made for the mainland with Sextus in hot pursuit. He made it ashore, but he was forced to hide from shore parties sent to hunt him down and kill him. Octavian survived by spending the night in a cave in the hills with only one of his slaves with him. The next day he was walking along the coast road when he spotted the sails of some ships and, thinking that they were part of his fleet, ran down to the shore to signal them, only to discover that they were in fact Sextus' ships, forcing the young Triumvir to run for his life again. Somehow, he made his way back to his camp with the help of strangers who sheltered and guided him there, where after a day or two of rest he recovered, then prepared to start again.

While Octavian and Agrippa were planning their next move, the stranded army on Sicily, led by Cornificius, was facing a situation where they were surrounded by Sextus' army without any resupply from the sea. Realizing that staying put would not solve his problem, Cornificius burned the boats beached near his camp, then began marching in the direction of the northern coast, crossing the flank of the volcano Mount Etna. The whole way he was harassed by Sextus' cavalry, which on the third day was joined by Sextus himself, who brought the infantry. Cornificius suffered losses in dribs and drabs, and while at first men refused to leave their comrades behind, after a time the burden of carrying the wounded slowed them down too much, so they were left behind to be butchered by Sextus' men. Still, Cornificius managed to lead his ever-shrinking army to a spot on the northern coast to wait for some form of aid from either Agrippa or Octavian. That succor came from Agrippa, who had followed up his own victory over Sextus by landing on the northern coast with the troops assigned to him, taking the towns of Tyndarus and Mylae. Almost as quickly as he had it, Sextus lost the advantage, when Octavian finally brought the rest of his own army over to Sicily, and now commanded 23 Legions, 5,000 cavalry and 20,000 auxiliaries. Sextus was forced to retreat to the only major port and city under his command, Messana in the northeastern tip of the island. Penned up there as Octavian consolidated his hold on the island, Sextus' options were reduced to only one, to launch an all-out attack with his navy to try breaking the blockade to extract his fleet and army, and in early September, that is what he attempted. The Battle of Naulochus was fought in plain view of the respective land forces of both sides, who instead of fighting each other, chose to watch the naval battle from the shore. When I was told of this, I did not understand it, until a day a few years later when I found myself doing the same thing. What I realize now is that everyone on both sides knew that the naval battle was the one that would decide the outcome of not just this engagement, but the whole war, so what was the point of risking your life when it ultimately did not matter whether or not your part of the battle was won?

Consequently, they stood on the shore watching, each side cheering for their rowing comrades as the battle raged back and forth. The fighting lasted most of the day, until finally Agrippa and his fleet gained the upper hand, breaking the enemy formation to start a rout. Much like a battle on land, the real slaughter only begins when one side's cohesion is lost by the inevitable step backwards, taken by first one man then another until the formation breaks into pieces. In the case of the naval engagement, it's a ship instead of a man, but the principle is the same. There is strength in the unity of a compact formation, but the moment one captain allows his vessel to lag behind the others, or even worse gives the orders to reverse oars and pull out of the line, he dooms his comrades. Seeing what was happening on the water caused much confusion and consternation among Sextus' ranks, while Octavian's forces raised their voices in salute to Agrippa's victory. Sextus, seeing that all was lost on the sea, ordered his own ship back to Messana, assuring the victory of Octavian. This was when the real slaughter began as captains either tried to make a break for it on the open sea, or rowed their ships onto the beach, where they and their crews were cut down by the troops waiting on shore. The commander of Sextus' cavalry immediately went over to Octavian, as did at least one Legion, yet somehow Sextus managed to slip away in the night aboard his fastest ship with nothing but as much money as he could carry and his young daughter. It would be expected that Octavian would have ordered his entire fleet to hunt Sextus down, but it was at this moment that Lepidus chose to demonstrate once and for all that he was Rome's biggest fool.

Lepidus had been stewing in Africa for the last few years, no doubt convincing himself that he was just as worthy a candidate to be First Man as either Octavian or Antonius were. However, until he came to Sicily, he had no opportunity to try and show it. Puffed up by his success in taking Lilybaeum, he ignored the fact that the Legions of Sextus that he defeated there were the dregs of the Roman army, consisting almost entirely of deserters and men considered unfit for service in the true Legions, along with escaped slaves. Lepidus began making plans for his own campaign to take over first the island of Sicily, then the rest of the Roman world. He did have a large army, with about a third composed of veteran Legions, mostly the boys of the Thirties, as we referred to the Legions numbered Thirty and higher. The most senior Legion in Lepidus' army was none other than the star-crossed 14th, which had been wiped out under the command of Sabinus back in Gaul now almost 20 years before. The veterans of the second enlistment of this Legion were scheduled for discharge, but had been enticed by Lepidus to remain under the standard with the same kind of promises of huge bounties that had worked so well for Octavian. The rest of his force was composed of Legions recruited from the Romans of Africa and were green as grass, but he had a lot of them, as well as those Numidians who gave us so many problems almost ten years before.

Despite his ineptitude, Lepidus managed his part of the Sicilian campaign competently enough, which I put down to the fact that he had some capable, experienced Legates and senior Centurions. My opinion may be biased yet it is also supported by the evidence of Lepidus' actions, when he marched into a blocking position in time for the Battle of Naulochus. His army was part of the force gathered on the shore and managed to be the first to get to the gates of Messana, where the defenders threw open the gates to him and surrendered, whereupon he immediately showed his profound stupidity. Somehow, Lepidus got the idea into his head to convince these men to swear allegiance to him, temporarily swelling his army to a size of more than 20 Legions, though he either refused or was too stupid to recognize how practically worthless in battle most of that army was. With these reinforcements, such as they were, he managed to convince himself that he was now in the stronger position. None of this would have happened if Octavian had been present at that moment, but he was not. His absence was again the subject of much talk and speculation, particularly on the part of Antonius and his agents.

Similarly as at Philippi, Octavian had been struck by one of his bouts of illness the night before the battle, at least that was the story put out by Octavian's agents. Naturally, Antonius did not see it that way, in fact paying to have a series of verses written that his agents recited at every inn and around the Legion fires that mocked and ridiculed Octavian, calling him a coward. I will make no comment about this matter, since I was not there and I have lived this long and have no desire to end my days by some accident, but it is not treason to say that Octavian's absence no doubt emboldened Lepidus to take the actions that he did. For a period of a few watches, Lepidus was ruler of Sicily and was thereby the strongest man in Rome. Nevertheless, when word reached Octavian of his colleague's actions, he made a miraculous recovery, and what he did next makes the accusation of personal cowardice ring hollow in any fair man's ears. Agrippa was still at sea, so Octavian, with only a few of his companions and dressed in plain tunic and cloak, came to Lepidus' camp, asking permission to enter, which was granted by an undoubtedly confused commander of the guard. I can only imagine the dilemma of seeing one of the Triumvirs approaching the camp of another who has for all intents and purposes declared war. I am sure that the calculation of the relative worth and abilities of each entered into the commander's thinking, because the gate was opened and Octavian allowed entry. Octavian then began walking among the men, calling to them to honor the agreement made between the Triumvirs to cooperate, but more than anything just showing them that he was unafraid, which always has a powerful effect among fighting men. It did not hurt that I am sure that the veterans among the army saw the vision of Caesar walking among them, so much so that many of them saluted him as their true commander. However, there are always toadies and lickspittles so that when Lepidus, hearing the uproar, ran from his tent to see what Octavian was doing, he ordered some of these scum to hurl their javelins at the other Triumvir, which they did. Some of Octavian's companions were struck down, two of them being killed, while one javelin reportedly struck Octavian before miraculously bouncing off his chest, which many of the men put down to divine intervention. Personally, I suspect it had more to do with what Octavian was wearing under his tunic. Whatever the case, Octavian was unhurt, but forced to flee. Despite it appearing to be a defeat, in reality his actions and courage in daring to appear in the enemy camp, along with Lepidus' own cowardly actions in ordering men to do what he should have done on his own by facing Octavian with sword in hand, turned out to be a victory for Octavian as men began talking among themselves.

It did not take long for sentiment to turn against Lepidus, the atmosphere becoming so hostile that Lepidus, fearing for his own skin, made his own journey to Octavian's camp, where he threw himself down at Octavian's feet, begging to be saved from his own men. Octavian had every right to execute Lepidus on the spot for ordering his own attempted murder, but one thing that Octavian had gleaned from his walk through the camp of Lepidus was the men's desire for the fighting between Romans to end. We were all tired of the prospect of facing other Romans and though if we were ordered to do so we would do our duty, it held no appeal to us. So, instead of doing what I am sure he wanted to do, Octavian brought Lepidus to his feet, doing no more than sending him back to the mainland as a private citizen, with a suggestion to Lepidus that it was best for him to retire from public life. Despite having every reason to do so, Octavian did not even strip Lepidus of his title as Pontifex Maximus, though he was never allowed within the sacred precincts of Rome. He spent the rest of his days in Circeii, where he died not too long ago, making the world a little better place. With the removal of Lepidus, there were only two players on the stage, Octavian now undisputed master of Rome, Italia, and Africa. While this drama in the West was being played out, Marcus Antonius was leading us into disaster, death, and ruin in the wastes of Parthia.

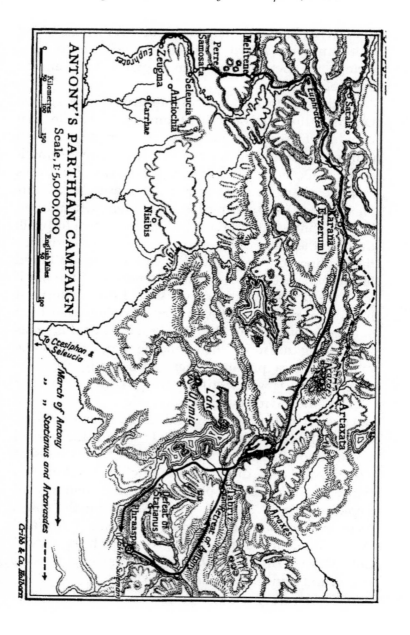

Chapter 5- Parthia

Antonius finally arrived in the East for the third, and what would turn out to be the final time, it being his destiny never to see Rome again. He came just after the beginning of the same year as the Battle of Naulochus, which at the time of his arrival was still several months in the future, bringing with him levies of fresh troops and a huge surprise for me. Antonius installed himself at Antioch, giving immediate orders for our part of the army in Damascus to relocate there, in preparation for the invasion, which appeared finally to be moving forward. The news that we would be leaving Damascus was not the kind of thing that could stay secret for long, even for the time it took me to walk from the camp to the market where Miriam was working that day. I approached the stall, where she was standing at the front of it as if she were waiting for me. Drawing closer, I could see that she was trembling, obviously struggling to keep her composure. Hashem was standing in the stall, holding the knife he used to slice off hunks of meat, his face clearly showing a desire to use it to slice something off of me.

Not seeing any point in denying or avoiding the subject, I said, "I suppose you've heard."

She did not say anything, just nodded her head, looking up at me with eyes full of unshed tears, and I felt horrible.

"Miriam," I said gently, "you knew this day was going to come, that I would have to leave. I've never hidden that from you, have I?"

"No," she said sadly, dropping her head so I could not see her face, which somehow made it worse. "You have always been honest that you would be leaving. It does not make it any easier, though."

"No, it doesn't," as I realized with some surprise that I actually meant it and was not just saying what she wanted to hear.

I would genuinely miss Miriam, and I was not ready to lose her from my life.

"Why don't you come with me?" I asked suddenly.

She lifted her head sharply to look me in the eyes. I saw happiness there, but only for a moment, then her head dropped again and she shook her head.

"I cannot, Titus Pullus," she said softly. "If I left with you, it would only postpone the end of . . . us," she finished. "But you would still leave, and every day we are together, I love you more."

That was the first time she had ever said she loved me, and despite not knowing what to say, I could see that she was right.

"Besides," she went on, "if I were to leave with you, I could never come back to my people. Naomi and Hashem would never accept me back in their home."

This made absolutely no sense to me, and I said as much.

"They're all right with you living with me as long as it's here in Damascus, but if you go with me to Antioch, it's somehow different?"

"If I were to leave with you, then return by myself, it would mean that you never had any intention of marrying me. The only reason that Naomi and Hashem, and the rest of my family have tolerated what has gone on between us is that they expect that you will marry me. That, and they liked seeing that I was happy."

"You mean they've been expecting me to marry you?"

I was incredulous, and I suppose my tone was what prompted Hashem to make a step forward, holding his knife by his side, but in plain sight. Miriam gave him a look then a quick shake of her head, saying something to him that got him to step back towards the back of the stall, though he still glowered at me.

"But you know I can't be married; it's not allowed," I told her. "I told you that from the very beginning. Didn't you tell them that?"

Now she looked completely miserable as she shook her head in answer.

"Why not? Why didn't you tell them when we first started seeing each other?"

"Because if I did, they never would have allowed me to see you again," she replied quietly, completely dousing the embers of anger that had started to glow inside me.

"They're going to know now," I said softly, to which she only nodded.

"Yes, and they will not be happy, Hashem in particular." She gave a sad smile. "I think he rather liked the idea of having a Roman Centurion as a brother-in-law, no matter what he says about not liking Romans."

A sudden thought crossed my mind, a horrifying image of what I had seen happen to a young girl who was involved with one of my men, done to her by her own family.

"Will Hashem do something to hurt you?" I demanded, but she shook her head, firmly and with no doubt.

"No, he will just yell. Hashem would never do anything to physically harm me."

"How can you be so sure?"

"Because I am not related to him by blood, for one thing. For another, I was not a maiden when we met. I was a widow, and the rules are not the same."

That did not make me feel much better, and I said as much, but she was adamant that she was in no danger. The way things were left between us at that moment was that she would stay with me for the remaining time before we left for Antioch, then would return to the home of Hashem and Naomi, which made none of us happy.

We broke camp a few days later and made the journey to Antioch, where Antonius had brought the reinforcements, and where the rest of the army was already making preparations to begin the invasion, and it was after we settled in that I got a second surprise. One of the Legions that came over with Antonius was the new draft of the 14th, raised in Cisalpine Gaul in anticipation of the 14th under Lepidus being disbanded, though as it turned out later, had not been done. Therefore, when Diocles told me that there was a Gregarius from Antonius' 14th Legion requesting to see me, I assumed that he was a runner sent on some errand by their Primus Pilus, who I had not yet met. I was scratching away on some report, so I did not bother looking up, instead just giving a grunt that from experience Diocles knew meant I was giving permission for entrance into my office. I could tell that the Gregarius entered by the shadow he cast on my tablet, yet I did not bother looking up or acknowledging that I knew he was there, because that is just not what a Primus Pilus does in these situations. Continuing tallying up figures, the Gregarius then made the worst mistake a man in his position could make; he cleared his throat in a clear signal that he was standing there, thereby ensuring him another several moments of standing at *intente*. I remember thinking irritably that I would have to have a talk with the Primus Pilus of the 14th to give this impertinent youngster a few whacks of the *vitus* to remind him of his place.

"Uncle Titus?"

At first, I did not think I had heard correctly. I certainly did not recognize the voice, my stylus freezing in position above the tablet as I slowly looked up, while my mind tried to absorb the scope of those two words. Standing before me was a young man in the uniform of a Gregarius in Rome's Legions, devoid of any decorations and still showing signs of its newness. Yet what caught my breath in my throat was his face. Looking back at me was a face from my childhood, except while familiar, at the same time it was different; the chin firmer, jaw a bit squarer, not to mention both covered with a fine stubble that Valeria never had. Otherwise, the eyes staring back at me, the mass of curly hair, though much shorter, even the nose belonged to my oldest and dearest sister. Such a storm of conflicting emotions washed over me, I dropped my stylus, sitting back in my chair as my mouth tried to find the words.

Finally, I could only think to say, "Gaius? Is it really you?"

When he smiled at me, any lingering doubt vanished, as one thought lanced through my mind; Valeria was going to kill me. I suppose this showed on my face because his smile became more uncertain, and he shifted his weight from one foot to another. When I saw that I remembered this from my visit as a habit of his when he was a young boy, in trouble for some mischief, rocking back and forth as his mother scolded him. Shaking the thought from my head, I stood, walking out from behind my desk, not exactly sure what to do, since it would not be seemly for a Primus Pilus to hug and kiss a young Gregarius. Thinking that I was in my own office and only Diocles was even in the tent, I in fact embraced him, kissing him on both cheeks before holding him at arm's length to examine him more closely. I noticed with approval that while he was not as tall or as broad as I was, he had a muscular physique, and when I commented on it, he blushed to the roots of his hair.

"I remember you saying that it was important to be strong if you wanted to succeed in the Legions, so I began exercising every day when I turned twelve."

I do not know why, but I felt absurdly pleased at this, though I covered it up by saying gruffly, "Well, as long as you know that you'll never be as strong as me. How about your sword work?"

He did his shuffle again as he looked at the hard-packed dirt floor, mumbling, "Not so good. I try hard, but I just can't seem to pick it up like the others." Looking up into my eyes then, his jaw clenched as he said, "But I'll work harder than anyone else to make sure that I'm better than anyone in my Legion."

"That's half the battle right there," I said encouragingly, wondering just how bad he was. "Have you asked for extra help from your Century weapons instructor?"

He grimaced. "Yes. He says I'm hopeless."

Gaius heaved a sigh and I could see how troubled he was, his brow creasing as he doubtless was recalling the smacks of the rudis he had received, at least if his instructor was any good. Realizing that we were still standing there, I stepped away, pointing to a stool while I sat back down in my chair as my mind turned to more unofficial matters.

"So, Gaius, I can't imagine that your mother is very happy with you."

Despite the subject, he gave a weak chuckle, replying, "Only slightly less than with you."

"She told you she wrote me?"

I was surprised, though I do not know why, and he nodded.

R.W. Peake

"Oh yes, she was so sure that you'd stop me just because of who you are," he said with a combination of pride and embarrassment. "You're the most famous man to come from Astigi, Uncle Titus, and probably in that part of Hispania. Everyone knows who you are and what you've done. Mama was sure that all you had to do was write a letter and the recruiting officers would treat me as if I had the plague."

Now he was looking distinctly uncomfortable as his feet shuffled back and forth, despite being seated.

When he continued, he looked apprehensive, but his tone was defiant.

"That's why I went to Cisalpine Gaul, where I knew that there was a *dilectus* for the 14th going on."

I frowned, proud of the boy's determination, but there was something troublesome about his story.

"But you have to have your father or someone who's known you all your life to swear that you're a Roman citizen. Did your father go with you?"

I could not imagine that Gaius' father, Porcinus, that placid gentle farmer, would risk the wrath of my sister, who in her mind was just protecting her only son. Gaius confirmed my suspicions, shaking his head, but said nothing, obviously reluctant to say any more.

"Then who provided their testimony?" I asked.

He looked at the ground, shrugging before mumbling something about a friend. I gave a grim nod, not needing him to provide any details, knowing what had happened. As I have mentioned, men claw and scratch to get assigned to a recruiting party because of the many and varied opportunities to squeeze money out of the men joining the Legions, first when they are prospective recruits, then afterward, when they are raw probatios still under their command, before they are officially enrolled in a Legion. One of the most common methods is when a

[321]

young man like Gaius shows up, apparently of age and being a citizen, but unable to prove it. Then a "family member" or "lifelong family friend" would be produced who would sign the required document and make the oath, all for a fat fee.

"How much did it cost you?" I asked, enjoying seeing his eyes widen in surprise.

Watching his face as he was clearly calculating whether or not to try and lie, he finally gave a shrug and named the sum. Despite myself, I let out a gasp.

"Where by Pluto's thorny cock would you get that kind of money?"

His face flushed, though I do not know whether it was the language or the question, but his tone was steady.

"I got it from you, Uncle Titus."

At first, I thought he was lying to me. I began to get angry, before I realized that he was right, or at least that what he was saying was possible. I had used Caesar's bankers to handle the money I received for my service in Gaul, and I remembered authorizing them to send a large sum of money to Valeria, with specific instructions that a portion of it be given to Gaius, to be spent as he wished. Obviously, Valeria had respected my wishes, and inwardly I winced at one more piece of ammunition that Valeria would no doubt use as proof that I had failed her.

"Well," I tried to say it lightly, "you've dropped my fat in the fire, young nephew."

His face fell, clearly upset that he had disappointed me in some way, and he replied miserably, "I'm sorry, Uncle. I didn't mean to get you in trouble with Mama. It's just been my dream since I was eight years old to be in the Legions like you. I know I'll never be as good a Legionary as you, but I want to be one of the best and I'm sorry if that causes problems for you, but I'm 18 and I won't go back no matter what anyone says or tries to do to me."

He had risen from his seat, his face suffused with the kind of fire and determination that only the very young are gifted with by the gods. I could not help smiling as I held my hands out in surrender.

"Pax, young Porcinus, pax. I can see that you're determined, and as I said, that's half the battle right there. We'll figure out how to deal with the problem of your mother, but let's both give an offering of thanks that she's on the other side of the world right now."

Turning serious, I motioned him to sit back down, and he sat on the edge of the stool. I must say that it was good for my spirit to see someone as passionate as I had been about the Legions.

"The first thing we need to do is to get you transferred to the 10th where I can properly supervise you."

As I had expected, his face lit up at the prospect of being in the same Legion as his Uncle Titus, but what I said next was like a bucket of cold water in his face.

"I promise you one thing; that before I'm through with you, you'll wish you had never walked in this tent and looked me up. When we're outside of this tent, you're not my nephew; you're a Gregarius, and a green one at that, being brought under unusual circumstances into a veteran Legion. The men in the Century and Cohort I place you in are going to resent you because there are no secrets and they'll know you're my nephew, and they're going to make your life miserable. You'll wish you had never been born, and that's before you work with me, because I'm going to train you myself, and when I'm done you'll wish your father had never been born either. Do you understand me?"

I will say that he was a quick study, as he jumped to his feet to come to *intente*, giving me a perfect salute.

"Yes, Primus Pilus," he said crisply. "I understand perfectly."

I stood as well, indicating that the audience was over, then we both moved to the flap leading to the outer office.

There was still one thing puzzling me, however, and I asked Gaius, "You said that I'm famous in Astigi?"

"Not just Astigi. Through the whole district," he said proudly.

"But how?" I asked. "It's not like I wrote home bragging about the things I've done, and I've only gone home a couple of times in the last twenty-odd years. It just seems odd, is all."

"Vibius," he said, looking a little worried as he mentioned the name of my oldest friend. "Whenever people stop at his inn, he tells everyone of the things that you did, all the men you killed, and how you saved his life those times. He says that you're the bravest man he ever met, and the best Legionary in the army."

How does one respond to that, I wondered? So I said nothing, sending Gaius on his way before heading to the *Praetorium* to start the business of transferring Gaius Porcinus into the 10th Legion.

Transfers of the nature that I was executing were a bit unusual, but hardly unique in those days, and my status as Primus Pilus ensured that it would happen without any undue trouble. I paid a visit to the Primus Pilus of the 14th as a courtesy, explaining the situation, but he had a green Legion that was still in need of training and could not worry about one lowly Gregarius, though naturally he expected a payment for the administrative trouble. This is customary, and the price was fair so I paid it willingly. The next question was where to place him. While the natural spot was in my Century, for a youngster as green as Gaius was, going into his first campaign, with the Parthians in the bargain, putting him in the First Century of the First Cohort, even in one of the last sections, would be akin to a death sentence. However, I was not willing to put him so far out of the action that I could not keep an eye on him. Besides, I had higher aspirations for young Gaius above being in the Tenth Cohort. Really, I decided there was only one real choice, so I summoned Scribonius. When he arrived, he instantly knew there was something afoot; we had been friends much too long to be able to fool the other.

"What's on your mind, Titus?" he asked as soon as he sat down.

"You remember my dilemma with my sister and my nephew?"

He frowned as he thought about it, then nodded and laughed.

"Oh yes. She told you that if her baby boy enlisted she would do to you what so many others have tried to do and skin you alive."

"Close enough," I grumbled. "Well, guess who showed up in my tent yesterday?"

His eyes widened in surprise, then he began laughing harder. I must say his amusement at my predicament did not help my mood.

"I'm glad you think it's so funny," I snapped. "Because I'm putting him in your Cohort."

That stopped him laughing. He even began frowning when I finished, "And in your Century."

"No," he protested. "You can't put a green man in a senior Century just before we start on campaign."

"I can, and I just did," I shot back, still nettled at his laughter.

Realizing that I needed Scribonius to do more than just obey orders, but to fully accept the role I was telling him to fill, I softened my tone.

"Scribonius, I need you, and you know I can't put him in my Century, or even my Cohort. But there's nobody else out of all the Centurions I trust more than you."

"What about Cyclops?" he countered, and in truth, I had not thought of this, despite how obvious it seemed. I considered it; Cyclops was now the Pilus Prior of the Eighth Cohort, which would be as high as he rose, both because he wished it to be so and because he was now in his fifties, and was one of the oldest men in the Legion. He was able to march as well as any of us, yet I could see that he was tired at the end of the day, so that asking him to take on the responsibility of spending his spare time training a new youngster would tap into his reserves, perhaps too deeply. Reluctantly, I shook my head, explaining my reasons. Equally unwillingly, he nodded that he understood, heaving a sigh. For a moment, nothing was said.

Finally, with a shake of his head, he agreed. "Fine, I'll do it. I just hope that this works out."

"It will," I said with confidence. "Because if it doesn't, Valeria won't have to kill me. I'll do it myself."

Almost as soon as Antonius arrived in Antioch, he sent his newest toady, a patrician named Fonteius, who replaced Quintus Dellius in that role when he switched sides to Octavian, to see Cleopatra, demanding her presence. While he waited on the queen of Egypt, he took care of other matters on the political front, making appointments and confirming a series of kingships of client kingdoms, filling them with men he trusted to keep their respective territories peaceful and stable while we marched on the Parthians. He confirmed Herod's throne in Judaea, put Amyntas on the throne of Galatia, Polemon over Pontus, and Archelaus-Sissines was given Cappadocia to run. Naturally, each of these petty kings was expected to provide their share of troop levies to march as auxiliaries in our army. The Parthians were similarly busy, however, when their king Orodes, father of Pacorus, could not summon the energy to rule any longer after the death of his favorite son. Orodes abdicated his throne, passing it to his eldest son Phraates, who promptly repaid the gift by murdering his father, other brothers, and anyone he deemed to be a threat to his own reign. His bloody-mindedness prompted the defection of several Parthian nobles, including one Monaeses, next in line to the throne of the surviving nobles, over to our side. Antonius welcomed him and as a show of good faith, gave this Monaeses character three towns in Syria to rule as a client of Antonius. Phraates, through his emissaries, claimed that it was all a misunderstanding, that he had murdered everyone he was planning on and that Monaeses had nothing to worry about, sending lavish gifts and promises to entice Monaeses back to his court. Monaeses went to Antonius, asking Antonius what he should do, unwittingly presenting Antonius with an opportunity to lure Phraates into believing that peace with Rome was possible. Antonius replied that Monaeses was free to go back to Phraates if he desired, with Antonius' good wishes, on the sole condition that he carried a message to Phraates that all Antonius desired to ensure peace between Rome and Parthia was the restoration of the Legion standards that were lost by Crassus at Carrhae. In this act, Antonius showed his cunning, because he had no intention of calling off the invasion.

However, if he could convince Phraates that peace was possible at a time when the Parthian was more concerned with consolidating his own power, this gave us an advantage. In fact, this brief interlude at Antioch showed Marcus Antonius at his very best, as he prepared both militarily and politically to embark on the greatest invasion in the history of Rome. Then, Cleopatra arrived.

She brought young Caesarion with her this time, arriving in state, coming overland and not on the huge barge like the last time, but with the same pomp and ceremony. They both wore the regalia of the thrones of Upper and Lower Egypt, the streets of the city packed with people gawking at this sight. As dramatic as their entrance was, the meeting between Cleopatra and Antonius was decidedly anti-climactic when compared to the last time, but I suppose having children together will do that to a couple. It did not take long, however, for the queen of Egypt to strike. Before she was in the city for more than a week, a pronouncement came from Antonius granting Cleopatra Phoenicia, Coele-Syria, the island of Cyprus, part of Nabataea, and the mountainous region of Judaea that produced balsam oil, which did not sit well with Herod at all. In fact, I happened to be at Antonius' headquarters when he came waddling in, his face matching the purple in his robe. Back when Quintus Dellius was part of Antonius' staff, he and Herod had been thick as thieves, but while I viewed Fonteius as nothing more than a different version of Dellius, to his credit he was clearly not of the same mind as Dellius when it came to Herod. I was amused to see him peremptorily order Herod to take a seat in the outer office while he went to ask Antonius if the Triumvir would see the fat toad. I had been bringing my daily report and really had no reason to linger, but I could not leave until I saw what happened, so I stopped to talk to Ahenobarbus, a supremely disagreeable man in many ways, yet one who was a true military man, despite his patrician status. I could see that he was doing the same thing as I, waiting to see what would happen, so I am sure he had no idea what we were talking about either. After a moment, the door opened and Fonteius emerged, but before he could shut it, I caught a glimpse of Cleopatra, reclining on a couch in a simple linen shift, looking very pleased with herself, with Antonius similarly dressed sitting next to her and reading a scroll. She had not aged much in the more than five years since we had last seen each other, at least as far as I could see, still having the same birdlike thinness as always. Her hair was pulled back in braids in the style that she preferred, and as she was watching Fonteius leave, our eyes met briefly so I bowed to her. I saw her eyes show recognition and I was absurdly pleased when she nodded her head in return. Regally, of course, just the merest nod of recognition that a queen makes to a subject, but Ahenobarbus did not miss the exchange, his interest in our conversation clearly increasing as he looked at me sharply. Before he could say anything though, Fonteius told Herod that the Triumvir Marcus Antonius was indisposed, engaged in several pressing issues pertaining to matters of state and could not be disturbed at this moment. Of course, Herod had the same view as we had and knew that this was a bald lie, so he did not take the rebuff well.

"This is because of that . . . that woman, isn't it?" he demanded of nobody in particular, I supposed, given that none of the men in the outer room were likely to say anything.

"I assure you that this was Marcus Antonius' decision alone, and it is not that he won't see you at all, he simply cannot at this time," Fonteius said smoothly, but Herod cut him off with an impatient gesture.

"That's not what I am talking about and you know it," he snapped.

I marveled that his face seemed to be turning a darker purple with every beat of his fat heart, and I began to wonder if I might actually get to see him explode.

"I am referring to his decision to cede the balsam production of Judaea, my kingdom," he emphasized, "to that . . . woman."

I was sure that nobody present, with perhaps the exception of me, thought much of Cleopatra, but neither was anybody willing to utter a slur against her, not even when he was a king himself. By this point in time, there was no doubt in any Roman man's mind that Cleopatra held Antonius completely in her grasp, that grasp being around the most sensitive part of a man's body, so any insult to her, Antonius would view as an insult to himself.

"I do not presume to know what the Triumvir based his decision on, but I can assure you that it was done in the best long-term interests of Rome, and not one of her vassals."

Oh, Fonteius was smooth, I will give him that. Still, that was a huge insult to refer to a king, even if it was of a client kingdom, as a vassal, and for a moment I thought I was going to get my wish in seeing Herod splatter himself all over the walls. His mouth opened then shut several times like a fish pulled out of water, but no sound came out. Finally, he came to his feet, not without some effort because of his girth, and stormed out, as much as a waddling man can.

"Well, that was interesting," grunted Ahenobarbus and for an instant, I thought he had forgotten what he had seen as I turned to leave.

"But what was more interesting was that little exchange between you and her." He said this more loudly than he needed to, since I had only moved a couple of paces away. Nonetheless, it had the desired effect as I turned to face him, walking back so that we could talk quietly. Ahenobarbus was an ugly man, in about every possible way, completely bald and I towered over him, but he was still an officer who outranked me, so I kept my tone respectful, not using my size to intimidate him as I sometimes did.

"She obviously remembers me from Alexandria," I said truthfully. His face clouded as he tried to make sense of what I said, while I went on to explain.

"Ah, that's right. That business of the siege when Caesar dallied there. I don't see the appeal in her, frankly." He shook his head, frowning. "But she must have something to trap a man like Caesar into giving her a child."

"And Antonius," I added helpfully, relieved that he seemed to accept what I had offered at face value. He gave a sour laugh.

"It doesn't take much to trap Antonius. Just the right equipment between the legs. Although I will say that I've never seen him like this before," he added, making it clear that he did not approve.

As we prepared for the invasion, I spent every available moment with Gaius, my appreciation of what his Century weapons instructor had to endure rising dramatically with every session. It was not that Gaius was particularly bad working with sword and shield; it was more a case where the things that came naturally to me did not come as easily to him, partly because of our respective size, but also because I believe that the gods just endow some men with more ability and talent in certain areas than others. Gaius was just not as gifted. However, he was willing to work, and no matter what he had been forced to endure during the day, he would be at my tent after dinner to take his extra lessons. And I was as hard on him as on any *tiro* that I trained, probably more so because of who he was and the circumstances we both found ourselves facing. There were moments that he could barely stand, and it would not take much to knock him down with my shield when we were working on his offense, but he would always climb to his feet to try again. Gradually, he improved, until I was confident that he could at least survive the first several moments of his first engagement, though I was dubious about anything more than that. Scribonius worked with him as well, and I have to say that I was somewhat chagrined to see that he seemed to respond better to Scribonius' instruction than to mine.

"You're working under a couple of handicaps," Scribonius explained one evening when I asked him why this was. "First, you're his uncle and you care about him, probably more than you realize, and he picks up on that and it makes the both of you tense."

I considered this, then nodded my understanding, seeing the truth in what he said.

"The second problem is that you're just unnaturally gifted at this, Titus. What comes so easily to you doesn't with most other people, and you get impatient when others can't do what comes so easily to you."

While I did not particularly like hearing this, it was not the first time. In fact, his words echoed something Vibius had complained about many years before. I thought I had learned to compensate for this attribute, but apparently, I had not, at least as much as I thought.

In every other respect, Gaius was the perfect Legionary, and despite the men's initial ambivalence to having a youngster suddenly thrust into their midst, the combination of his cheerfulness and his willingness to do more than his share gradually won the men over, until he not only was accepted, he became something of a mascot for not just his Century, but the whole Second Cohort. I wrote to Valeria, assuring her that Gaius was safe and was at the very least under my care and guidance, though I did not expect that to soothe her all that much.

As we learned, despite what Ahenobarbus thought, Antonius was not the lovesick fool that his fellow patrician believed him to be. For ceding the territories to Cleopatra that she had asked for, in return Antonius extracted a payment of several thousand talents to help pay for the Parthian expedition. This came at a cost; in return for such a heavy investment, Cleopatra insisted on not only accompanying the army when it marched, but being present at strategy meetings. Not confining herself to the higher command, she insisted on inflicting her presence with the Primi Pili as well. As can be imagined, this did not sit well with any Roman, at any level, though I cannot say that I was all that surprised when I walked in to see her sitting in a chair next to, but slightly behind, Antonius. I had walked to the meeting with Corbulo, who grunted in disbelief at the sight of the Egyptian queen sitting there, acting as if it were the most natural thing in the world for a woman to be in a council of war.

"What by Cerberus' balls is she doing here?" he muttered.

"She's paying for this expedition," I answered, remembering back to our time in Alexandria. Cleopatra had insisted on being present then as well, but whenever she tried to voice her opinion, Caesar had gently but firmly put her in her place, so that after a time she had ceased showing up. Now I was curious to see whether Antonius would do the same to an older and more assertive Cleopatra.

"So? She's a woman. She doesn't have any business in a war council. I don't care if she is a queen," Corbulo grumbled as we took our seats near the back.

There were ten Primi Pili, along with the commanders of the auxiliary forces and members of Antonius' staff, so there were perhaps 50 men all together, along with Cleopatra. It was clear to see that Corbulo's reaction was not unique; the grumbling and whispered comments only subsiding when Antonius called the meeting to order, refusing to acknowledge the undercurrent in the room while acting as if having a woman in a meeting of this nature were the most natural thing in the world. Antonius began the meeting by outlining the basic plan, starting with our planned date of departure for the initial staging area at Zeugma, which would be accomplished in phases, segments of the army making the march from Antioch over a period of a few weeks. From Zeugma, we would follow the Euphrates back to Samosata, which was still recovering from our siege and assault, then turn north, instead of into Mesopotamia, which was what Crassus did. It was somewhere about this point that Cleopatra spoke. While I do not remember what she objected to, or what point she raised, I do remember the reaction. There was an audible gasp from several of the men, most notably from Ahenobarbus and Marcus Titius, who was serving as the army quartermaster. All eyes turned to Antonius, waiting for him to rebuke Cleopatra and put her in her place. However, he did no such thing, in fact answering her instead in a tone that made it clear to everyone that he considered her input equally as valuable as anyone else's in the meeting. This was too much for Ahenobarbus, for one, who leaped to his feet, clearly furious.

"See here, Antonius. You might choose to treat your lover as if she's Bellona incarnate, but that doesn't mean that we have to sit and listen to it."

Before Antonius said a word, Cleopatra sat forward, staring directly into Ahenobarbus' eyes, not blinking.

"In fact you do, Gnaeus Domitius Ahenobarbus, because not only am I funding this whole adventure, but I am no stranger to military matters. I can boast of having none other than Gaius Julius Caesar as my tutor. Can you say the same? No, I think not."

She sat back, her eyes piercing Ahenobarbus, who looked instead at Antonius, the Triumvir just shrugging and saying nothing, which was eloquent itself as to his intentions. Seeing no help coming from Antonius, Ahenobarbus turned to his fellow officers, but suddenly all of them found something exceptionally interesting about the floor. Finally, in desperation, he looked towards the back rows where the Centurions were seated, except none of us were inclined to stick our collective necks out to risk both Antonius and Cleopatra's wrath. I had my own reasons for not supporting Ahenobarbus, but none that I was willing to share with Corbulo, or anyone for that matter. The truth is that I at that time I admired Cleopatra a great deal, and perhaps was a little in love with her, though the gods know that feeling would change. No matter what people think of her now these years later, I remember a woman who was willing to listen to a common soldier's tale of loss and woe and for that, I will be forever grateful, no matter what happened between us later. So when the others remarked about the effrontery and cheek of the woman after we left that meeting, I kept silent, only mumbling something when I was prompted. One thing that I learned with the help of Diocles' network of slaves was that Cleopatra was dead set against the Parthian expedition, in fact was urging Antonius to turn his attention to Rome and send his army against Octavian. Although I was not surprised to hear this, it was unsettling nonetheless, but fortunately, at that point, her hold over Antonius was not nearly as strong as men like Ahenobarbus believed because he steadfastly refused. He also somehow convinced her to accompany us only as far as Zeugma, which was the true jumping off point of the invasion anyway. Despite this setback, she insisted on doing so dressed in what I suppose was a queen's version of armor, which did not endear her to the men as I am sure she thought it would. The truth is that we were all relieved when she left our company at Zeugma, traveling back to Egypt to continue plotting and planning, leaving Antonius to at last do what he had been planning for so many years and invade Parthia.

The first disappointment we faced when the leading contingent of the army arrived at Zeugma was the presence of Parthian garrisons on the other side of the river. Antonius had hoped that our overtures of peace, sending Monaeses back to Phraates along with the request of the return of the Legion standards lost by Crassus would lull the Parthians into believing that we had no intention of invading. While Phraates had agreed to this, he obviously had not been fooled. Over the next few weeks, the army converged at Zeugma, the Legions coming from Antioch, along with the cavalry, while the native auxiliaries marched from their respective countries to the south. We were informed that there would be other forces joining us as we marched as well, swelling our numbers to well over 100,000 men.

The army that assembled at Zeugma was the most massive in the history of Rome, at least for one side. I imagine that there were more Romans in total at Philippi, but there we were divided into two armies opposing each other. There were eleven Legions in total; the 10th of course, the 5th, the 7th, the 12th, 14th, 17th, 18th, the Deiotaran Legion, and the 3rd Gallica as it is called now, among other, newer Legions raised in Asia and Africa. Accompanying us were 10,000 cavalry from Gaul, Hispania and Galatia, along with three Cohorts of special troops that were Antonius' personal bodyguard, called the Brundisium Cohorts because that is where Antonius recruited them several years before. This bunch was close to useless for anything other than looking fierce and breaking the heads of civilians that Antonius wanted to terrorize. Polemon of Pontus was bringing 30,000 infantry of dubious quality, along with Herod sending 5,000 Jews, who I knew could fight from my time in Egypt, though I had serious doubts about their commander, one of Herod's courtiers. There were about 20,000 more men from the client kingdoms, a mix of infantry, cavalry and missile troops that were just more mouths to feed as far as we were concerned, with the possible exception of the missile troops, mainly the slingers. Finally, there were the Armenians of King Artavasdes, who had been a steadfast ally of the Parthians until the rise of Phraates. I suspect due in no small part to the success of Ventidius, they had thrown in with Rome, and were going to act as our guide on the expedition. In fact, it was Artavasdes who convinced Antonius to take a northern approach through Media, following the Euphrates to Samosata then turning north for a distance before striking east. Artavasdes was supplying 7,000 infantry, but more important was their cavalry, 6,000 men more or less evenly divided between horse archers and cataphracts. As a long-time ally of Parthia, the Armenians were trained to fight in the same manner as the Parthians, so they would be useful not only in matching the enemy on the field, but in telling Antonius and the officers the best way to fight them.

Naturally, an army of this size required a massive baggage train to support it. Still, even for such a large force the train was excessive, with more than 300 wagons and 11,000 mules. A disproportionately large number of these wagons were used to haul the personal baggage of Antonius and the potentates accompanying us, some of whom also insisted on bringing their concubines, who in turn had their own baggage with them. The most important part of the baggage train, aside from our food of course, were the wagons carrying the siege equipment, because where we were headed was devoid of natural materials needed to build such tools. The most interesting piece of the baggage train was a massive battering ram over 80 feet long that required twelve oxen to pull, the largest such I have ever seen and was undoubtedly inspired by what Antonius had seen at the walls of Samosata, for only a ram of this size could have done any damage to those walls. I must say that it at least appeared as if Antonius and his staff had thought of everything, so it was a confident army that he was leading.

The disadvantage of going on a campaign where the commander tries to prepare for every eventuality and carry everything that might be needed is that it means that progress is ponderously slow, since the army can only move as fast as the slowest wagon. Not surprisingly, the slowest piece was the ram, but it was also the most important so we plodded along, stopping twice an interval instead of the usual one time. Even following a good road, before we actually started crossing rough country, we were happy if we made twelve miles in a day, and it would only get worse when we turned off the road. We camped one night under the ramparts of Samosata, where the Commagene king had patched the sections of the walls that had been undermined, using the pieces of the original as material. He could not have done anything other than this, yet we all understood that if the moment ever came to attack this city again, we knew exactly where we would focus our efforts.

Leaving Samosata, we turned north to head up a valley between two ranges of hills, away from the Euphrates. Because it was still late May the grazing for the livestock was good, the terrain not too rough. We reached Melitene about a week after leaving Samosata, where we had a rest day, more for the livestock than the men, who had not been pushed to this point. Young Gaius was holding up well on the march, but I had to remind him when he would come to visit that we had not really started the hard part at that point. To press this point home, we used the rest day to work on his defense with just a sword and no shield, and I was happy to see that he was gradually improving. That evening, I thanked Scribonius for staying on top of his tutelage. He looked surprised, then a little embarrassed.

"Truthfully, I haven't been working with him, and I haven't been checking to see if Poplicola has either," he said, Poplicola being his weapons instructor.

"Well, someone has, because he's gotten better since the last time we worked together in Antioch."

My friend shrugged. "Maybe he's been working on his own. Or more likely, his section leader and his tentmates are helping him."

"I'm happy either way. He still has a long way to go, though."

I could not help worrying about him, thinking of Valeria and how awful it would be if she lost her only son, knowing that pain. Scribonius looked at me, his face unreadable.

All he said was, "I don't believe you have as much to worry about as you think with young Porcinus."

I trusted his judgment, but I hoped he was right and not just telling me what I wanted to hear.

We picked back up with the Euphrates north of Melitene, following it north to the point where it turns east just south of Satala. It was about this time that I heard the first mumblings of worry about our progress, along with concern about how late it was getting, now mid-June when we reached the great bend of the Euphrates. Whereas Crassus' plan of attack had been to cross at Zeugma then take the most direct route to the Parthian capital, both the presence of a garrison there and Artavasdes had convinced Antonius to take the long route through Armenia and into Media, swinging well north before turning east, essentially approaching the Median capital of Phraaspa from the back door. As a plan of campaign, this was sound strategy, but the one thing Antonius had not properly calculated was how slow the baggage train would move. To his credit, it was Scribonius who first voiced his concerns.

"We shouldn't have spent so much time at Zeugma," was how he started the conversation, but he shrugged as if it was not weighing heavily on his mind. "But I suppose Antonius had to appease Cleopatra, so it probably couldn't have been avoided."

It was true that we spent an extra three weeks at Zeugma, even after the army gathered. At the time the whispers among the men, and the louder voices of the officers was that it was only because Antonius could not bear to be parted from Cleopatra, wanting to spend as much time with her as he could. This was also about as much criticism of a superior Scribonius would utter; he never said anything that blatantly questioned or criticized the generals, which was smart of him, except that we had known each other too long, and I recognized that if it bothered Scribonius to the point that he actually said something, it had to be weighing heavily on my friend.

"We're being slowed by the baggage train more than he planned," was my reply, but truthfully, I was not as worried as Scribonius at that point.

As events later showed, I should have been.

We plodded along, now heading east. It was during the march one day when we had the vanguard and crested a low hill that it was brought home to me just how massive an undertaking this was. While the men marched by, singing their songs or bantering back and forth, I paused, ostensibly to watch them as they marched by, but really to catch my breath, which I was doing with more frequency than in the past, and I looked back along the column. I had seen more than my share of such sights, yet what lay before me made me gasp. As far as the eye could see, stretching even over the horizon was a ribbon of black movement, rippling as if it were a giant serpent moving along the ground, except this serpent was composed of a mass of men and horses. Out on the flanks on either side were squadrons of cavalry, along with units of the native infantry, watching for any sign of the enemy, or more likely for a small village or hut that they could plunder. From my vantage point, I saw the command group just behind the last Cohort of my Legion, identifiable by

Antonius' standard, dispatch riders galloping up and down the column carrying messages of one sort or another. Following was some more of the cavalry, walking their horses to save them in case they were needed, then behind came the rest of the Legions, for no matter what order we march in, the Legions always march ahead of the auxiliaries, which I suppose led to some hard feelings on the part of the native troops, though none of us cared. Row upon row of men, each with their *furca* over one shoulder with the pack attached, from which their wicker basket hung, their long-handled tools lashed to the staff of the *furca* along with their spare javelin. Strapped to each man's back was their shield in its leather cover; attached to the shield were their helmets, though every man was wearing their armor from the moment we crossed into Armenia on the orders of Antonius. In their free hand was the other javelin, which was used as a staff to help over rough terrain, also being available for its primary purpose in the case of an ambush. Century after Century, Cohorts, and Legions stretched back as far as I could see. I could barely make out where our men ended and the auxiliaries began, distinguishable only by the more indistinct shape they made when compared to our precise spacing and intervals between each group. Legion eagles, Cohort, and Century standards all bobbing with each step of their bearers added to the spectacle, while hanging just above it all was the veil of dust that followed us everywhere except when we were slogging through mud. From tip to tail, the column was 15 miles long, and with the flanking guard of both cavalry and auxiliary infantry spread on either side, was almost three miles wide.

I did not envy the Legion marching drag, because they would be scraping the muck and filth left behind by thousands of animals when they finally did make it into camp in the middle of the night, then could look forward to perhaps a watch's worth of sleep before setting out again. I also dreaded when it would be our turn, but as bad as spending the day in the rear of such a massive column is, the next day is invariably the worst. Although a Legion never goes from rearguard to vanguard the next day, they still have to be roused at first light to strike their tents, then pack everything up. Only then are they allowed to lie back down in their Legion area of the camp, using their pack for a pillow, rolling up in their cloak if the weather required to get a precious third of a watch or two of sleep before being roused to take their place in the column. In a march like this, the auxiliaries actually had it the easiest of all, since their spot in the column never varied as they were never expected to march drag, nor were they ever allowed to work on building the camp. Of course, neither were they allowed to shelter inside the camp; only in the event of an attack would they be let in, meaning they had to set their own up a short distance from ours. The fires at night stretched as far as one could see from any spot within our walls, which also served to guide the end of the column into camp. The Legion mules carrying our tents, stakes and grain marched with each Legion, while the wagons carrying the heavy supplies, artillery, the officers' luxury items, and the like would come rumbling in late each night. The only blessing for the men and animals of the baggage train was that their spot in the column was always the same, so they knew the exact time each day when they needed to be ready to move out, thereby giving the animals and men a sufficient amount of rest. Furlong by furlong, mile by mile, this massive host plodded through increasingly barren land, while it became more and more difficult to find enough wood to have a fire for every tent in such a large army. Before we had gone much farther, the cavalry was roaming over vast tracts of countryside, dragging whatever scraggly piece of brush they could find back to camp, along with every scrap of food they could lay their hands on.

Before a month had passed, we were forced to reduce the number of fires down to one for every two sections of men, even then the fire only used to cook, the unburned sticks being dragged out of the fire after the meal was prepared, in order to be used the next morning. None of the Centurions spoke of it openly, but I know we were all thinking about what would happen when it got colder.

In mid-June, we reached a mean collection of huts that is now the settlement of Calcidava (Erzerum), meaning that we were not yet halfway to Phraaspa, which is not even Parthia proper, but Media Atropatene. Now the quicker and more experienced of the rankers were beginning to have quiet conversations about the fire. We were joined at that point by the bulk of the Armenian army of infantry and mixed force of horse archers and cataphracts, whereupon Antonius decided that it was a good idea to have a review of the entire army, in full inspection uniforms. This meant that plumes had to be dug out of packs, leathers had to be varnished, and decorations polished; all of these items being stored in the single wagon designated for each Legion devoted to that purpose. While the men worked to make themselves ready, repairs were made to the wagons, some of which had evidently begun to start breaking down as the bouncing and rattling over the increasingly rough terrain began to take its toll. The march to Calcidava had also been over a gentle uphill grade, so the air was noticeably thinner, giving the air a bite at night, in stark contrast to the blinding sun that beat down on us during the day. The only constant between night and day was the wind, always keening in our ears, continually throwing up a fine veil of dusty sand that clung to everything, making the men's task of readying for inspection that much harder. The review itself was a farce, consisting of Antonius, Artavasdes, Polemon, and a gaggle of other officers, both Roman and foreign trotting by on their horses, barely casting a glance in our direction as they talked among themselves.

Every few moments, Antonius would come to a halt, sliding off his public horse, who was named Clemency as a not-so-subtle criticism of his late patron's policy, to walk among the men; making a joke, pretending to inspect a man's leathers, or asking to test the edge of his sword before slapping him on the back while making some light remark before climbing back on Clemency, resuming his conversation where he had left off. This was in marked contrast to the Antonius of a few years before, shortly after Caesar's death, when he and Octavian first started contending with each other, where Antonius could barely be bothered to meet with delegations of his own troops. While I wanted to think that Antonius had learned his lesson, as I watched him I believe that he just was doing what he needed to do, because he needed his army as he never had before, here in the wilds of Armenia. Simply put, it was the wildest country that I had ever seen, with the possible exception of those vast tracts of forest on the other side of the Rhenus, which this country reminded me of in some ways. In appearance, they could not have been more different; where the sun could barely be seen even when there was not a cloud in the sky in the Germania forests, in Armenia it was always present, the rays seeming to bounce off the ground, hitting a man from every angle. There was wood and game in abundance in Germania, while we would go days only getting a glimpse of the backs of antelope or wild goats, but they both had a wildness about them, along with a sense that a man could be swallowed up and never be missed.

We were at Calcidava for three days before the review, then ended up staying another week. Almost immediately after we began the march again, things began to go wrong. Although the going was rough before, now the land was crisscrossed with small gullies and holes, the road nothing but a dirt track that had obviously never seen a wagon wheel, so that wagons that had just been overhauled and repaired began breaking down. Wheels would shatter when a careless driver would miss seeing a hole, or in extreme cases would topple over, requiring dozens of men armed with ropes, shovels, and tackle to set them back upright. Our progress slowed even more, so we were doing less than ten miles a day, while on some days we covered only seven or eight. By the middle of Julius, we had made less than 50 miles from Calcidava, after two weeks of marching. The prospect of even worse terrain ahead of us on the route we were taking prompted Antonius to make a choice that sealed the fate of thousands of men and doomed his grand campaign to failure.

"I've decided that we're going to leave the baggage train behind," Antonius announced to an assembly of the Primi Pili and Pili Priores and our auxiliary counterparts.

Antonius had clearly discussed this with the client kings and princes, along with his own staff, because they were all sitting behind him stone-faced, none of them with the same look of surprise that were on our faces. Our reaction must have struck home with Antonius, because he raised a hand.

"Actually, I'm not leaving it behind as much as I'm letting them take a longer route that's less arduous for the wagons and livestock. Artavasdes has provided a guide who knows the region well, and I'm assigning a Legion and the equivalent number of auxiliaries, along with 2,000 cavalry to guard it. I have appointed Oppius Statianus as the overall commander and the Legate of the Roman Legion, and King Polemon," he indicated the broad-chested man with the oiled ringlets and beard sitting to his left, "will command the Pontic contingent and cavalry."

Oppius Statianus was sitting just behind Antonius to his right, and had nodded his head at the mention of his name, but he looked anything but happy at being given an independent command. I wondered what the scene in the *Praetorium* had looked and sounded like as I made a note to have Diocles poke around.

"Where are we going now?"

I did not see who asked, but I recognized the voice as another of the Primi Pili, sounding as unhappy as Statianus looked.

"We're still going to Phraaspa," Antonius said, tight-lipped, though his tone was calm enough. "Artavasdes has assured me that not only is it the capital of Media, it's where the other Artavasdes keeps his fortune locked up, and more importantly, it's likely to draw Phraates out to come to the aid of one of his allies."

He turned to the Armenian, who nodded in confirmation, then Antonius turned back to address what was on everyone's mind.

"If we can make Phraates come to us, we don't have to keep marching deeper into Parthia and can still end this campaign this season. I don't want to spend the winter here any more than any of you do."

"Who are you sending with the baggage train?" If I remember correctly, Corbulo asked this question.

"I'm sending the boys of the new enlistment of the 35th." He nodded towards their Primus Pilus, a tall, rangy man with a reputation of being one of those whose rise through the ranks was due more to his cultivation of his patron than any fighting ability, though I did not know the man personally.

Unlike everyone else involved with this venture, he was the only one who looked pleased at the thought of striking out with a plodding line of wagons, oxen and slaves, and I suppose he viewed this as a chance to make his mark with an independent command. He certainly did that, but I doubt it was in the way he had hoped.

Leaving the baggage train behind, we took only our own mules with us, which we loaded down with as much extra food as they could carry, along with the wagons designated for use by the *medici*, and of course, those wagons that carried items that Antonius deemed he could not live without. One consequence of leaving the baggage behind was that we would now be forced to live off the land, something we had not done much to that point because we were traveling through Artavasdes' Armenian kingdom. Once we crossed into Media, we were given permission to pillage or scrounge for food and anything else of value, so to that end, every day a Cohort from each Legion was sent out, along with a contingent of cavalry, their orders being to bring back whatever we could carry back to supplement our rations. Naturally, men brought back more than just food; sometimes in the form of two-legged captives, almost always female, but we could not keep captives as they would slow us down and required food, so once the men were done with them, they were disposed of. It did not take long for those Medians who did not have their towns and farms raided to flee into the hills, taking everything with them in the way of stored grain and their livestock, leaving empty buildings and barns, with barely a kernel of grain left behind.

Now that the baggage train was making their own way, we certainly were able to make better time, but we were now surrounded by huge mountains, all covered in snow despite being high summer. The largest was a mountain called Ararat, only those of us left who were in Gaul and in the high Alps seeing anything so high and massive. The air was even thinner than in the Alps, and although we were passing through the barren valley at the foot of the mountain, higher up on its flanks we could see some sort of animals bounding about the crags, making us wonder what manner of creature could survive so high in the sky.

Artavasdes had assured Antonius that taking Phraaspa would not be a problem for us. The way he made it sound, it was little more than a bunch of mud-baked hovels whose only defensive feature was being set atop a hill. Approaching from the north, we crested a ridge leading down into a valley a few miles across, in the middle of which rose a flat-topped hill. The hill itself rose at least a hundred feet above the valley floor, while the walls of Phraaspa rose another 50 feet, easily. The sight of this hill-fort city was so formidable that without any order given, the vanguard came crashing to a halt once the men spied what they were facing and would be expected to take. Word came rippling back through the ranks, leaping from Legion to Legion, and as usually happens, the prospect of what we were up against became more and more daunting the further back in the column the word was passed. The buzzing became a roar as men talked to each other, adding their own coloring to what they had just heard, until the Centurions were forced to use the *vitus* on a few of them to shut them up, and that was in the more experienced Legions, so I can barely imagine how widespread that panic was in the youngsters.

We were near the rear of the column, meaning that it was some time before we crested the ridge and were able to lay eyes on Phraaspa. When I saw it, I realized that for the first and perhaps only time, the men ahead of us had not exaggerated about the challenge. I forced myself to keep from coming to a standstill, knowing that men feed off the reaction of their Centurions, so I looked at the city across the valley with studied indifference as I kept walking. To our surprise, as we marched down into the valley, no Median force came down to meet us, or tried to harass us in any way, so we were allowed to settle in, then build a camp. As we worked, our cavalry escorted Antonius and the command group on a circuit around the city to survey the ground and to come up with an initial plan of assault. The auxiliary infantry moved farther up the valley, where there were some outlying villages, but they returned empty-handed, reporting that they were deserted.

It was our turn to pull guard duty, giving me time to do my own, albeit limited examination of Phraaspa, as I called Balbus over to talk over our impressions. Although Phraaspa was no Samosata as far as the strength or height of its walls, what made this a tough nut to crack were the steeply sloping sides of the hill on which the city perched. The hill was roughly oval in shape, but I noticed there were a couple of folds in the flank of the hill where the slope was a bit more gradual which, if filled in with a ramp, seemed to provide the best opportunity for an assault. Pointing these out to Balbus, he just grunted, a sure sign that he was not as optimistic as I was.

"Well?" I demanded, nettled a bit by his lukewarm response. "Do you have a better idea?"

"No," he admitted. "It's not that so much. I think you're right that those provide the best approach, at least from this side. That's not what I'm worried about."

"What is it then?"

He turned to look at me and said seriously, "Let me ask you a question. How long do you think that's going to take?"

I saw immediately what he was driving at; a project of that size would take at least two months to complete, and that was only if the enemy never sallied out or did anything to disrupt our work that succeeded.

"Well," I thought for a moment. "The other alternative is to wait for the baggage train. The walls aren't that thick; they're just high on the hill. Our artillery could knock them down fairly easily. But," I pointed out, "we still have to build a ramp regardless to get up there in a position to go through the wall if we knock a hole in it.'

"Either way, we're here for a good long stay," Balbus pursed his lips, clearly not liking the prospect. "And we aren't even in Parthia yet."

I reminded him of Antonius' hope that investing Phraaspa would force Phraates to come to us so that we could defeat the Parthian king and his army. He shot me a sidelong glance, then seemingly turned his attention back to the city in front of us, but I was not fooled. Balbus had something on his mind, so I told him he needed to speak.

"If Phraates does what Antonius wants," he said quietly, "he's going to bring his entire army, and it will be composed almost entirely of mounted archers and cataphracts."

He jerked his head in the direction of where the auxiliaries were milling about, making their version of a camp, nothing more than a haphazard collection of tents and shelters set up in no discernible pattern or organization.

"We have a huge army," he continued, "but how good are they, really? Those Armenians, just as an example. Antonius calls them cataphracts, but we've seen the Parthian version. How do these Armenians compare? Have you seen how much smaller their horses are? And that means that neither horse nor man is as heavily armored as the Parthians."

"But we defeated the Parthians before. We'll do it again," I argued.

"We defeated 5,000 of them," he responded. "But if Phraates comes, he'll be bringing every man in his army. Can we defeat ten times as many? And don't forget, Antonius didn't bring any more slingers than we had with Ventidius."

In fact, I had forgotten that, suddenly recalling Antonius' disdain when one of the Centurions had brought it up, the Triumvir completely dismissing the idea that the slingers were crucial in keeping the archers at bay while allowing us to face the cataphracts without worrying about being pierced with arrows.

"So what are you saying? We should march back to Armenia?"

"No," he conceded. "I'm not saying that we should retreat now." He gave a sigh, then shook his head. "I don't know what I'm saying, really. Except that I have a bad feeling about all of this."

Now I was worried, wondering what I was missing, because I had never seen Balbus act like this before, and I trusted his judgment implicitly. I decided to poll the rest of the Centurions to find out if they were as pessimistic as Balbus was, wondering what I would do if they were.

When Antonius returned to the main camp, he promptly gave orders for two more camps to be constructed, with the Legions divided between them. One camp was located on the far side of the valley, in a position that effectively blocked the other entrance into it, thereby preventing any force, whether it was the Medians who left with Artavasdes the Median, the Parthians with Phraates, or both from surprising us. The auxiliaries were also distributed in a ring of their own camps around the valley so they could mutually support each other and the Legion camps in the event of an attack. The third camp was located equidistant from the other two, so that each was protected if one camp was attacked. As we worked, we saw a few men on the ramparts watching, but scouts reported that they had picked up the trail of the Median army and, judging by the amount of tracks, they were sure that the bulk of the army had left with Artavasdes the Median. However, they had clearly left several days before and our scouting parties could not pin down their exact location. What was worrying was that they said the Medians appeared to be headed back to the west, in the general direction of our baggage train. Without the train with us, we did not have any of the heavy siege equipment, particularly the onagers, a piece that was an addition to our normal complement of artillery, along with both the large and the other battering rams. This meant that the next day we began to dig, using only our hand tools, creating entrenchments to cut the city off. Then we carried the spoil in our wicker baskets from the entrenchments to the point that the engineers had deemed the best spot to begin building the ramp up to the base of the wall, the plan being to build a terrace on which the huge battering ram would be placed. After a close examination, it was clear that tearing down the wall would not be the hard part; it was building the ramp with a slope gradual enough so that the ram could be pushed and pulled into place by a combination of men and animals that would require most of the work. At the same time, we had to worry about the defenders of the city firing down at us when we got to a point close enough to the walls to be in range. We had no idea when the baggage train would arrive, but besides the equipment, we would need the food and other supplies, so the men counted the days, of course wagering with each other about its exact arrival.

The work was backbreaking, tedious, and slow; we did not have any of the heavy draft animals to help, or the heavy wagons, which would have been emptied of their contents to carry large loads of dirt. On a dozen of the wagons, there were large logs slated to be used for just such an eventuality as the foundation of the ramp, yet without those logs, or wood of any size for that matter, the engineers were forced to change the design. Instead, the men were ordered to cut slabs of rock that would be used as a foundation and the first challenge was finding rock that was soft enough that we could cut squares of it with just the tools we had. Consequently, it was just a matter of a few days before those tools that we usually used to cut turf began breaking. Normally, repairing these tools is not a big job, the metalworking *immunes* being highly skilled in forging new pieces in a matter of a day. However, the ingots of iron that they needed to fabricate the new tool heads were also on the wagons, along with the ash poles to replace the broken shafts, which were as abundant as the ruined tool heads, the pile of discards growing every day, with the broken shafts ending up as firewood. The second problem was getting the cut blocks back to the construction site from the makeshift quarry, which was located about three miles away at the base of the ridge to the south. The only draft animals we had were our pack mules, and while they were accustomed to carrying a tent, stakes and food on their backs, they were not trained, nor were they suited for dragging large stones across rough ground, so that they began going lame. While this solved part of our supply problem, no Roman likes eating mule meat, meaning morale took another hit, both because of the diet, but also because they knew that losing mules this early in the campaign was not propitious and did not help our prospects for victory.

A week passed, then another, and another, still with no word of the baggage train. Now there was no attempt by the men to hide their concern, the conversations at night glum, focused on only one topic. The cavalry was spending almost all of its time foraging for whatever scrub wood and food they could carry back, though after the first week they had stopped coming back with anything to eat. The most disconcerting part was the behavior of the Median garrison left behind in Phraaspa, as they made no attempt to disrupt our work, not even engaging in the usual insults, instead just leaning on the ramparts to watch us dig, drag, and sweat in total silence. I suppose the fact that the men were not engaged in their usual grumbling banter gave them no reason to taunt us, so that the only constant sounds were of thousands of shovels and picks striking the rocky soil, over which was the keening sound of the wind that never, ever stopped. This was the atmosphere in which we worked, and which Antonius chose to ignore, assuring us every time we trudged to the *Praetorium* for our morning briefing that word about the baggage train would be arriving any day, if not any moment. Then, at the beginning of September, after more than five weeks with no word, his prediction came true, as we learned where the baggage train was, or more accurately, where the remains of it and the men guarding it were laying out in the barren wastes.

Suspiciously, at least to some of us, it was the guide and the companions who had accompanied him that came staggering up to the walls of the westernmost camp, which happened to be the one we occupied, shortly before sunset, after we had retired from our labors for the day. Corbulo's men had the watch, and once they ascertained the men's identities, they brought them to the *Praetorium*. It was a matter of moments later that the word of their arrival went streaking through the camp. Diocles had been delivering some reports, and came running into my tent as Cyclops, Scribonius, Balbus and I were consuming our meager meal; I had ordered three-quarters rations in anticipation of the order coming from Antonius at some point in the near future.

"By the gods, Diocles, don't you know not to come rushing in here?" I said irritably, but one look at his face told me something important, and bad, had happened.

"I apologize, master," he panted. "But I thought you'd want to hear this."

Diocles was never one to get excited over trivial causes, and we all knew it, so I motioned at him to continue.

"The guide of the baggage train has just arrived in camp, with the men who were part of his party," he said once he caught his breath.

This raised a shout from Cyclops, while even Scribonius was smiling, but I was paying attention to Diocles' expression. Not liking what I saw, I held my hand up to cut the other two off.

"What is it?" I asked.

"I don't know exactly, but I do know that it's not good. They walked in, and they looked as if they were closer to death than life. They were immediately shown in to see Antonius, and that's all I know."

The three of us looked at each other, then I stood and without bothering to put on my armor, I grabbed my *vitus*, telling the others I would be back as soon as I could. Exiting the tent, I immediately saw men running about, finding friends, talking in grim tones, waving their arms in the general direction of where we thought the baggage train would be coming from. I walked down the Legion street, where it became clear that the men were close to panic, so reversing myself, I went to the tent next to mine where my Optio Mallius and the *cornicen* Valerius shared a tent, walking in unannounced. They looked up guiltily, but I did not waste any time reprimanding them for doing what everyone else was doing, simply telling Valerius to sound the call for all Pili Priores to come to my tent immediately. They began streaming in just moments later, their expressions all almost identical, so I wasted no time once they were all present.

"While I don't know exactly what has happened, I know that it's probably bad, and so do the men. I can tell by your expressions that you do too, but I need each of you to go back to your Cohorts, brief your Centurions, and get a handle on the men. We can't have a panic right now, not while we're in the middle of a siege and we don't know exactly what's going on. I'm going to the *Praetorium* immediately, and as soon as I know, I'll come back and brief you."

Not waiting for any questions, I strode out of my tent, then walked quickly, fighting the urge to run, knowing that the sight of a Primus Pilus sprinting for the *Praetorium* wearing just his tunic would do exactly what I was trying to avoid. A few streets away, I saw Corbulo just as he turned onto the street I was on, and I called to him. He stopped to wait for me, one look at his face telling me all I needed to know, but perhaps I still held out some absurd hope because I asked him what he knew.

He looked around quickly as we walked, then seeing nobody within earshot, he told me quietly, "The baggage train has been destroyed. Every wagon, every man."

Even when you're expecting it, when news this catastrophic reaches your ears, it is a shock, so I came to a halt, and I could feel my mouth hanging open.

"What?" I gasped. "How?"

"I don't know the details yet; that's why I'm headed over to the *Praetorium*. Come on. Don't stand there. We need to find out what's going on."

Somehow, I forced my legs to begin working again as my mind raced, trying to digest this and what it meant. There was a large group of men of all ranks clustered around the entrance to the *Praetorium*, yet the men of the Brundisium Cohorts who were supposed to guard the tent and everyone inside it were making no attempt to disperse the mob. In fact, they looked more scared than the rest of the men, and I felt a surge of anger. These men got better rations, pulled none of the regular duties of the Legions, but here they were not even doing their job.

"What by Cerberus' balls do you think you're doing with your thumbs up your asses?" I snarled at the men.

One of them, an Optio, turned and opened his mouth to argue. Before he could say anything, I was standing on top of him, poking him with my *vitus*.

"Optio, I know you and your men think your *cac* doesn't stink because the general recruited you as his bodyguard, but you better do your duty and disperse these men. We don't need a panic here at the *Praetorium* and the more you let them hang about and let their imaginations run wild, the worse it's going to be."

The Optio's face flushed at my assault, but to his credit, I could see that he got the message and he nodded. "Yes, Primus Pilus. I understand."

He turned, snapping an order at his men, who began shoving the men away, while Corbulo and I entered.

"I hope that's enough," he whispered to me. "But that's going on all over camp."

"We have to do something." I shrugged as we stopped to survey the scene, which can only be described as chaos.

Clerks were running about carrying scraps of paper or wax tablets, evidently trying to determine the exact scope of the loss, comparing notes with each other, and conversing in shocked whispers. Centurions were standing in clusters, trying to make sense of what they had just heard, while the officers were doing much the same. Antonius was sitting on a clerk's desk, his head in his hands, surrounded by Titius, Fonteius, Ahenobarbus, and Publius Canidius Crassus, who was known as Canidius and, next to Ahenobarbus, was the most experienced military man in the army, at least in the upper ranks. Canidius was whispering urgently to

Antonius, but he did not seem to be listening. The foreign princes were huddled in their own group, arguing in the Eastern manner, making extravagant gestures, clutching and twisting their oily beards, and just in general acting like a bunch of frightened women. Sitting on stools in a far corner was a small group of men, their clothes little better than rags, their faces lined with exhaustion, with a couple of them sporting bandages that were filthy and bloodstained. These were obviously the guides, and if they had been part of the treachery, they were certainly putting on a good show of being victims instead. I was about to walk over to talk to them myself, but I overheard two of the other Primi Pili talking, and what they were saying stopped me in my tracks.

"I just heard from one of the clerks that the Mardians are saying that Artavasdes the Median and Phraates have joined forces and are heading for us."

The other man swore, as the first Primus Pilus continued. "Those Mardians over there swear that Phraates and Artavasdes have an army as large as ours, composed almost entirely of cataphracts and horse archers."

I looked over at Antonius, waiting for him to rouse himself to address us, but he still sat there, looking dully at the floor as first Ahenobarbus, then Canidius whispered urgently in his ear, one on each side. Finally, he waved his hands at them in the same way a man tries to wave off a swarm of gnats, as he stood up to begin pacing. The noise in the room steadily increased as more men showed up, their agitation growing as first one version of events, then another swirled around the *Praetorium*, each one direr than the other, until I heard someone swear that the Parthian horde was a third of a watch's march away.

"Enough!"

As many faults as Marcus Antonius had, a bad set of lungs was not one of them, and because I was standing just a few feet away, I got the full effect of his verbal blast, making my ears ring. Turning, I saw him standing there, eyes blazing in rage as he surveyed the men around him, most of whom had the good sense to not only stop talking, but look a little shamefaced. Glaring at any man in his line of vision, Antonius said nothing for several moments, then as quickly as it came, the rage obviously left him, his shoulders suddenly slumping.

"I suppose this is my fault, letting you carry on like a bunch of women." He took a deep breath, closing his eyes before continuing. "But you need to hear what's happened, as painful as it may be."

He then proceeded to tell us what had befallen the baggage train.

According to the Mardian guides, the combined host of Media and Parthia waited until the baggage train was passing through a narrow defile before launching a simultaneous attack from front, rear, and sides of the column, surrounding it completely. The Mardians said that while the fighting was fierce, it did not last long, because the 35th broke and ran, which is suicide when facing mounted troops. Statianus was killed trying to rally the Legion, Polemon was taken prisoner, while the auxiliary troops were butchered. The wagons were looted, with everything the enemy could not carry away burned to the ground. The Mardians insisted that because of their position at the head of the column, they managed to cut their way out of danger, then rode their horses to death trying to get to Antonius and the army to warn them. They said that they spent the previous four or five days on foot, making it probable that the Parthians were close behind. The only consolation was that the numbers I had heard bandied about were, at least according to the Mardians, grossly exaggerated. They insisted that Phraates had perhaps 30,000 men, while Artavasdes the Median had about the same number. That was small comfort because, if true, while they did not have a powerful enough army to defeat us in open battle, what they could do was starve us to death. In fact, later that day, three of the half-dozen foraging parties sent out did not return, never to be seen again, and that was just the beginning. As alarming as that was, there was one more piece of news that was even worse. The Mardians insisted that they saw the Parthian prince Monaeses leading one of the columns of Parthian cataphracts, the same Monaeses on whom Antonius had lavished rewards and honors. If it was indeed Monaeses, he undoubtedly had passed information to Phraates that helped the Parthian cause. We had been in front of the walls of Phraaspa now for 70 days; it was the beginning of September, and all of our work was predicated on the idea of using heavy siege equipment that no longer existed.

As soon as we learned the true scope of the disaster, we were dismissed to go to our respective Legions with orders to do what we could to avoid a panic, as Antonius realized that not saying anything would just make things worse, though I was hard-pressed to see how things could be much worse. I made my way back to my tent, then had the Pili Priores summoned first, getting fully dressed while I waited. Once they arrived, I told them exactly what we were facing, watching as each of them struggled to make sense of what they had just heard.

"I've decided I'm going to address the Legion myself, rather than have each of you tell your Cohort. What I want you to do now is go summon your

Centurions and tell them first, then have them tell their Optios and *signiferi*. We'll assemble the Legion in a sixth of a watch, so get moving."

When I marched to the forum where the men were formed up, I used one of my old tricks, coming up behind them silently to stand there, just listening to the whispering for a few moments to gauge their mood, and while I was not surprised, it was disturbing nonetheless. The men were not in a state of panic, but they were close, as they openly speculated about what we would be doing. Unfortunately, I had nothing to share at that moment because Antonius had not announced his decision. Not that there was much to decide, at least as far as the other Primi Pili and I were concerned. We could not take Phraaspa without completely changing our approach, which meant starting over, and without any heavy equipment, the only way we could take the city was to starve them out, which would take months. After listening a few moments, I pushed through the rear ranks of my Cohort, stopping the chattering instantly. Taking my place at the head of the Legion, I told the men what had happened, in most cases confirming what they had already heard. I also assured them that our general had matters in hand and would be issuing orders based on the changed situation very shortly. Honestly, that was more of a hope on my part than anything else. Once finished, I dismissed the men to attend to their evening meal, it now being past dark, but very few men ate anything that night, me included.

As I said, we all expected Antonius to announce his decision either that night or the next morning, but we were not called to the *Praetorium* that morning, nor the rest of that day. The only order that came was to stop the siegework and keep the men in their Legion area, where they sat outside their tents listlessly playing at dice or tables, the only topic of conversation being our predicament. The day passed uneventfully enough, but as night fell, only four of the foraging parties returned, the other six obviously suffering the same fate as the first groups that had disappeared. Luckily for the Legions, once we had begun the siegework, the foraging was done exclusively by the auxiliaries, so the losses did not come from our ranks.

Still, no word came from Antonius and the next morning the situation deteriorated even further when there was a commotion coming from the camp of the Armenians, whereupon I was summoned by Titus Voconius, Luscinus' Princeps Prior, whose Century had the duty on the rampart of the camp. I hurried over, knowing that Voconius was not the type to be alarmed over nothing. When I mounted the rampart, without saying a word, he pointed across the valley floor. Following his finger, I saw immediately what had disturbed him. Riding out of their camp were the Armenians, and it was instantly clear that they were leaving, because they had their pack animals in tow. Letting out a string of curses, I turned and ran to the *Praetorium*, intent on finding out what was happening. As soon as I entered, I saw Ahenobarbus, who was engaged in an intense discussion with Fonteius, so I headed directly to the two officers and saluted. Ahenobarbus gave me a sour look, but it became clear that it was not aimed at me, that his anger was with Artavasdes.

"I suppose you're here to find out what's happening. Well, I'll tell you. That faithless, gutless bastard Artavasdes is pulling up stakes and leaving."

Although this just confirmed what I had seen, it was still devastating news. My first and most immediate concern was what it would do to the morale of the men, afraid that this would tip the balance and finally send the men into a full-blown panic.

"What does Antonius say about it?" I asked.

Ahenobarbus snorted in derision while Fonteius gave him a sharp look at the obvious disrespect, but the other man was oblivious.

"The same thing he said about the baggage train. Nothing. He just sits and mopes about as if ignoring the problem will make it go away."

"Ahenobarbus," Fonteius hissed.

This did catch Ahenobarbus' attention, and he turned to look at Fonteius, who gave an almost imperceptible jerk of his head in my direction. The older man had the grace, or sense, to at least look embarrassed for speaking of our superior in such a manner in front of a ranker, yet said nothing to try to cover up his gaffe. Fonteius looked up at me, his eyes boring into mine, and while he spoke quietly, it was with a throbbing intensity.

"I hope you know better than to repeat what the General just said, Pullus. Things are bad enough and we don't need the men any more needlessly worried by the mistaken belief that our commander isn't fully in control of the situation."

I knew he was right. Still, I had to bite back a retort that what would help the men more than anything that I did or did not say was our commander getting off his ass and giving the order we all knew had to come. Nevertheless, I assured him that I was not going to be repeating anything I had just heard, pointing out that it would make my own job even more difficult than it already was. I was about to leave, then decided that I had to at least try to find out when that order would be forthcoming.

"Do you have any idea when Antonius is going to give the order to pack up and march out of here?"

"The Triumvir hasn't made the decision that that is what we're going to do," Fonteius replied stiffly, and I gaped at him in open astonishment.

Ahenobarbus just looked away, obviously not wanting to be involved in this conversation any longer.

"Are you serious?" I was incredulous, refusing to believe that Fonteius was indeed sincere. "Is Antonius truly considering keeping us here through the winter, with only the food we have with us, which I'm sure I don't have to tell you is only going to last us another week, two at most if we go down to half rations? Without any way to take the city, other than to try and starve them out, which is going to take the gods know how long, but a lot longer than a couple more weeks?"

"You forget that with the departure of the Armenians, that's 13,000 less mouths to feed," Fonteius said, his face flushed with his rising anger.

"And those are also the troops best suited to fight the Parthians on their own terms," I shot back. "So while I appreciate the fact that it gives us another couple of days of short rations, it also takes away our best chance of beating the Parthians, should they decide to attack us."

"I can assure you, Primus Pilus, that the Triumvir is well aware of every aspect of the situation." Fonteius was shouting now and out of the corner of my eye I could see heads turning to watch.

As angry as I was, neither did I want this exchange to become a spectacle.

"I have no doubt that he does," I said in a voice that I hoped was as calm as I could make it. "I would just like to have an idea of when he plans on letting the army know what his assessment of the situation is, and what he intends on doing about it."

With that, I turned to stalk away.

There is a saying that even the blind can see clearly when looking back, and in hindsight, I think that what Antonius was waiting for was some sort of gift from the gods that would turn things around. Instead, every day of delay brought one crisis after another. The next came about when our scouts, the ones who managed to survive at any rate, came in the day after the Armenian Artavasdes left to report that the Parthians had allowed the Armenian army to leave unmolested. Later that day, a Parthian nobleman approached under a flag of truce, saying that he had a message concerning the fate of Polemon that he was ordered to deliver to Antonius and the ranking Pontic officer. The Parthian was allowed in camp, where Antonius had summoned not only the Pontic commander, but the other client kings, and they were all seated on a makeshift rostra made of shields, with Antonius sitting in the ivory curule chair that had belonged to Caesar. The Parthian was led into Antonius and the princelings' presence, where he informed them that Polemon was still alive and would be returned unharmed for a ransom of 2,000 talents. As Antonius and the others discussed this, the Parthian then made another announcement, catching everyone by surprise. He shouted at the top of his lungs that all foreign auxiliary troops that left the army would, like the Armenians, be allowed to leave unmolested and in fact would be given supplies and remounts to make it back to their respective kingdoms, should they require it. There was a huge uproar as Antonius leaped to his feet, screaming for the members of the Brundisium Cohort standing on guard to kill the Parthian, which they did, but not before the damage was done.

That very night, groups of men began slipping out of their respective camps, skulking away into the vastness of the Median wastes. Then, a few days after the Armenians left, a group of Pontic auxiliaries refused to take their turn foraging. It was only after one of the Legions in the Roman camp nearest to them was called out, marched to the Pontic camp to surround it, that they went. Not surprisingly, they did not return, but we all suspected that unlike the first groups, this one did not meet with an untimely end. It was at this point that Antonius called a halt to the foraging parties, realizing that one way or another he was going to lose any men he sent out. A week later, perhaps two weeks after we were informed of the fate of the baggage train, the inhabitants of Phraaspa decided to have a feast, the smell of roasting meat torturing every man in the army, creating such a crisis that we had to put guards on all the animals in order to keep the men from butchering the beasts, every one of which we would need to march out of there. The final blow came in late September, when without any warning, we awoke one morning to a thin blanket of snow on the ground. It had been growing colder with each passing day, but the sight of snow finally prodded Antonius into making a decision. Finally, the Primi Pili and Pili Priores were summoned to the *Praetorium* for a briefing. The question then was, where would we go?

The first thing I noticed when I walked into the tent was that there were only Romans present; not even the client kings were anywhere in sight, and as soon as we were settled in, Antonius explained why.

"What I'm about to tell you is for Roman ears only," he began. "Our days here are over. We can't take Phraaspa, not without the heavy siege equipment, and that little stunt the Medians pulled the other day with the feast tells me that they still have more food than we do. So we're leaving, but we can't just pack up and pull up stakes, or we'll have the Medians coming out of Phraaspa snapping at our heels, while having those greasy Parthian bastards swarming about our front." He paused to let us absorb what he had said, then took a breath to continue. "So I'm telling our auxiliaries that we're going on a foraging expedition, in force, and that they're to stay behind and continue the siege, and that once we've gathered sufficient supplies, we'll be returning." He gave a savage grin. "But we're going to be moving, and moving fast. I still have hopes of pinning that *cunnus* Phraates and his minion Artavasdes down and goading him into facing us in battle. If that does happen, and we're victorious as I expect, then we'll return and pick the auxiliaries up. If they refuse to face us, then we're going to continue marching to Artaxata."

There was a buzz as men talked excitedly, while for once Antonius was willing to let us carry on a bit before calling for silence.

"The only foreign troops that are going with us are the cavalry, because we need mounted troops and I trust them more than I trust those Eastern bastards, along with the slingers."

I saw heads nodding up and down in agreement with this assessment, and mine was one of them.

Antonius continued with his instructions.

"We're leaving a third of a watch before dawn, and it's absolutely crucial that you impress on your men that we'll be marching faster than they've ever marched before. Except for you veterans of Caesar's army, perhaps." He said this jokingly, and we laughed because it was expected. Turning serious, he continued. "You see how cold it's getting, so make sure that your men have every piece of cold weather gear in the top of their packs where they can reach it. Also, I've been warned that this snow is exceptionally wet, so make sure that their cloaks are greased properly. Finally," he said as his face turned grim. "As you no doubt know, we've scoured this country clean of every stick of wood, and what I've been told is that the country north of here beyond the point where we've already marched through is just as barren as here. There are going to be a lot of cold nights, and that means that men are going to be tempted to burn whatever they think will keep them warm." He leaned forward, putting his hands on his desk as he looked from one man to the next, making sure he had our attention. "Be sure that your men understand that if they burn any of their gear, whether it's their stakes, or the shaft of their javelins, they'll be flogged and executed on the spot, no trial, no questions. Do I make myself clear?"

We all either nodded or murmured our understanding, then Antonius dismissed us. We left the tent, each group of Centurions huddled together as their respective Primus Pilus issued his instructions.

No man slept that night as we prepared to set out before dawn, instead of our normal time shortly after first light, the plan being to steal a march on the Parthians. I walked through the Legion area, making surprise inspections, ensuring that the men were following Antonius' instructions to pack their warm clothing where it could be easily reached so we would not have to stop. Quite a few of the men needed to grease their cloaks, though only a handful of men like Vellusius, the old veterans from Gaul, had the fur-lined cloaks and the rabbit-fur socks that had been so valuable in the cold of the Alps. Naturally, I was one of the men who had these items, in fact having spares of each, so I sent a runner to bring young Gaius Porcinus to me. When he arrived, without saying a word, I handed him my spare cloak, along with two pairs of fur-lined socks.

His eyes lit up at the sight of the gifts, then he flushed, reluctantly shaking his head. "I'm sorry, Uncle Titus, I can't accept these gifts."

"Why not?" I asked, not hiding my surprise.

"Because none of the men in my section have anything like these. It wouldn't be right, and my friends might resent that you gave them to me."

I nodded thoughtfully, realizing that he was right. Nevertheless, this was one time I was not going to worry about the appearance of favoritism, as the image of my sister's face popped into my head, and I imagined what she would say.

"I understand, Gaius, but this isn't a gift, or a request. It's an order, and if your friends give you any grief, you can tell them exactly that."

I thrust the items at him. He took them reluctantly, but I could tell he was pleased. However, I was about to give him the harsh reality of what he was about to face.

"Gaius, you need to understand that this is going to be the hardest, most miserable experience of your young life," I said, studying his face as I spoke, and I was happy to see that he was listening intently. "We have to cover 500 miles to Artaxata, and you can be sure that the Parthians are going to be dogging us every step of the way."

He nodded in understanding, but I knew that he did not really comprehend, so I spoke more forcefully. "All it takes is one moment of inattention, where your mind wanders as you think about how cold you are, or how hungry you are and you lag behind a little, or you drop your shield a bit too far, and one of those Parthian horse archers will be watching and waiting for just such an opportunity. Then you'll either be killed outright, or you'll be wounded and that will be even worse because if you can't continue to march, you'll be left behind. And," I finished grimly, "if that happens you need to kill yourself before the Parthians get you."

I knew I was painting a bleak picture, but I wanted to ensure that my nephew did everything he needed in order to survive. I could see that he was indeed taking it seriously, his face mirroring my own.

Swallowing hard, he nodded as he replied, "I understand, Uncle Titus. I won't let you down."

"You better not," I joked. "If you die, I'll kill you."

Our conversation done, I sent him back to finish his preparations, while I continued my rounds. All over the three Roman camps, the same work was taking place, along with the camp where our cavalry lived. About a third of a watch before the appointed time, we pulled up our stakes, yet did not fill in the ditch as we normally did to reinforce the fiction that we would be coming back. Fortunately, there were no towers with our camps here so there was no need to burn anything. The Legions in the other two camps came marching to meet us since we were heading back to the north, then under the cover of darkness, we moved rapidly out of the valley, part of the Gallic cavalry leading the way. It was bitterly cold, though the snow was still wet, clinging to our feet and legs. I was thankful for the fur-lined socks on my feet, though I quickly realized that I would have to rotate the two extra pairs of socks that I had because it would not take long for them to become soaked. There was only a sliver of a moon, the eastern hills just beginning to be outlined as the sun came creeping up over the horizon, but even in the darkness we moved quickly, at least until the sun came up. As the world turned from black to gray, details becoming more visible, we saw just a short distance ahead what looked like a dark line coming across our path at an angle, before turning north so that it aligned more or less with our direction of march.

The sun finally peeked over the eastern hills to our right to illuminate the ground in front of us, and for the first time we could make out what had created the line. Stretching before us, on a front wider than ours, the ground was churned and chopped up, scarred by the thousands of hooves of the Parthian army. As soon as we reached this patch, men began stumbling over the furrows and holes in the turf, but as long as the ground remained frozen, it was not so bad. Unfortunately, that did not last long, as less than a third of a watch after the sun came up, the heat had completely melted the snow. Soaking the ravaged ground, it turned our path into a sticky quagmire, the mud sucking at our feet with every step. Since our goal was to close with the Parthians, we had no choice but to follow their trail, except where possible we tried to march parallel to it. However, we continued to move quickly despite the mud, though to compensate for our slower rate of travel, instead of our normal break we took only half that before setting out again.

It was just after midday when some of our Gallic cavalry came galloping back to the command group to report that the Parthian army had been spotted a few miles away. Antonius immediately gave the order for the army to form into an *agmen quadratum*, essentially a staggered series of four columns that form a huge square, with all of the Legion mules and slaves gathered in the middle between the columns. The advantage of this formation is that no matter what direction an attack comes from, the most that the men on the flanks have to do is to execute a right or left facing movement to meet the enemy head-on, while the Centuries and Cohorts at the head or rear of the column have to perform a pivot maneuver to get on line. But for every advantage there is a disadvantage, and there are a couple with the *agmen quadratum*; the first is that it requires a lot of room to execute properly. The second is the difficulty of maintaining the integrity of the formation, the correct spacing between the Legions being crucial in order to prevent a gap through which the enemy can drive to split the army, thereby threatening the baggage train in the middle. This was hard enough on open, level terrain, but stumbling over the choppy, muddy ground churned up by the Parthian horse meant that every man had to concentrate on each step taken.

Despite the challenge, we managed to march in good order, keeping our cohesion both within each Legion and the entire formation, although men stumbled while some fell heavily in the mud, giving their comrades a good laugh as they picked themselves up, covered in a combination of muck and horse manure. After another full watch, Antonius gave the order to halt and begin making camp, detailing two Legions along with the cavalry to place themselves as a screen between the rest of the army and the Parthians while the rest of us worked. The one blessing brought to us by the soft and muddy ground was that it made digging easier, the dirt flying as the men worked quickly to build the camp. As we worked, the Parthian army appeared as a black line on the horizon, slowly growing larger and more distinct until they drew close enough so that we could make out individual horses and riders. I know we had been told that the combined Parthian and Median army numbered no more than

60,000 men, but when you are looking at that many men just a few furlongs away, it is quite a daunting sight. The enemy made no overt move to attack us, in fact did not even send out their horse archers to harass us as we finished the camp. However, I believe that the presence of our slingers standing in loose array in front of the two Legions had everything to do with their inactivity. Instead, they seemed content to just watch us, clearly fascinated by how efficiently and quickly we built a marching camp in the face of the enemy, meaning that the ditches were wider and deeper than what we would construct if we were just on the march with no prospect of contact. The only thing missing from our camp were the towers, there being no wood available; in fact, there was not even enough for fires that night. Our work done, the men settled in to make themselves as comfortable as possible under the circumstances, while the other Primi Pili and I made our way to the *Praetorium* to find out what Antonius had planned. Turning the corner of our street onto the Via Principalis, I got the answer, in the form of Antonius' battle standard flying from the top of the *Praetorium*, the signal to all Romans that we would be offering battle.

"We're going to let these bastards think that all we want to do is go home," Antonius announced. "So we're going to strike camp, but instead of continuing north, we're going to turn back to the southwest as if we're heading back to Syria by the most direct route. The Gauls are going to act as a screen while we give every indication that we're heading home with our tails between our legs. But," he smacked his fist into his palm, "we're going to give these scum the surprise of their lives. To that end, the men have to be in battle order, and ready to drop their packs the instant the order is given. They're not going to sling their shields, they're going to carry them, and they're going to have their helmets on. I don't think the Parthians will expect anything when they see the men like this because it makes sense that we'd be prepared."

He paused to let us digest what he had said, then continued, "I expect that the Parthians are going to face across our direction of march in a crescent formation, at least that's normally what they do in these situations, with their cataphracts on the flanks and their archers in the middle. This is exactly what Hannibal did at Cannae, but this time, instead of us being sucked into the middle, when I give the signal, we're going to execute a facing movement, with half the Legions facing to the left and the other half to the right, and we're going to attack their flanks."

Men began shifting on their stools, murmuring to one another as each made his opinion known to the man sitting next to him. I was sitting with Corbulo on one side and Balbinus on the other. The three of us exchanged glances, but none spoke. While it made sense to go after the cataphracts, given that they posed the greatest threat to us now that we had learned that slingers could neutralize their archers, executing a double attack against mounted troops is a risky proposition under the best of circumstances. When the signal was given, the men would be expected to instantly drop their packs, execute a facing movement, then move immediately into an all-out sprint, all in an attempt to close the distance before the Parthians and Medians had a chance to react. Our own cavalry, along with our slingers, would have to engage the horse archers to drive them out of range while we were pressing the attack. One thing that we did have going for us was the nature of the cataphracts themselves. As I have said, over a short distance, a man can outrun a horse, and that task is even more possible when it is a cataphract, because the heavy armor on both man and beast make them ponderously slow when taking off from a standing start. Once they get going, they are formidable, but it takes them two or three furlongs to get up to full speed, and even then, they cannot maintain it for very long. Ventidius had shown us that if we could close with the cataphracts, they were actually easy to bring down with a sword thrust to the belly. Of course, as is always the case in battle, such things are more easily talked about than accomplished. Nonetheless, we all knew that this was our best and probably only hope of salvaging something from this campaign, not to mention making it possible for us to get back to Syria with the army intact. After dispensing with a few more details, we were dismissed to prepare our men for the next day.

Even for veterans, the night before a battle is anything but a restful time, the mind dwelling on all manner of things; from trying to remember what needs to be done, to all the things that can go wrong. For a Legionary who has never faced battle, it is the fear of the unknown that is the worst. Remembering what that felt like, I sent for young Gaius so we could eat our evening meal together. In doing so, I broke with a tradition of many years when I would dine with Scribonius, Balbus, and Cyclops. I confess that while I am not overly superstitious, it was in the back of my mind that I might have been tempting the Fates to exact revenge on me, though I was not sure for exactly what. Young Porcinus was withdrawn and quiet, a far cry from his normally inquisitive self, picking at his food, concerning me enough that I scolded him for it.

"It's bad enough we're on half rations, but when you don't eat what we do have, you're not going to be strong enough to throw your javelin past the first rank."

He managed a weak smile at my jest, but said nothing. Putting my piece of bread down, I studied him silently for several moments, trying to decide the best way to approach what I knew was bothering him. Finally, I opted for my favored tactic, the frontal assault.

"You're worried about tomorrow," I said, and after a moment, he nodded, looking away, red spots burning into his cheeks.

"You're worried that you'll shame yourself, and that you'll let your friends down, that you'll forget everything you've been taught to do." I suppressed a smile at the surprised look on his face. "And you're worried that you might die tomorrow," I finished, the spots on his cheeks spreading to the rest of his face as his feet began shuffling back and forth.

"Yes," he finally said in a quiet voice that clearly conveyed the huge burden he was feeling.

Leaning forward, I put my hand on his arm, causing him to look up and into my eyes. "Gaius, I would be much more worried about you if you said you weren't worried about any of that, because then I'd know you were either a fool or a liar. And I know you're no fool, which would mean that you were lying."

The look of relief on my nephew's face encouraged me to go further.

"Tomorrow, you're going to learn firsthand why your Centurions have pushed you so hard, and why they smack you with their *vitus* when you do something wrong. It's going to be the most confusing, terrifying, and exhausting day of your life to this point, but I'll promise you one thing; if you rely on your training, if you keep your head, and do what you're told, when you're told, you will survive tomorrow."

I grinned at him then.

"And you may find out that you actually love battle, like I do."

"Do you really?" he asked me, his face intently serious, catching me completely by surprise. "Do you really love battle?"

I sat back in my chair as I considered his question carefully.

"Yes, I do," I said slowly. "I'm obviously good at fighting. Nobody who's been in the Legions as long as I have isn't good at it, though I'll be the first to say that there's a healthy dose of luck."

"But did you always love it? And do you love it because you're good at it? How will I know if I'm good at it?"

As he asked these questions, I was remembering back to an eight-year-old boy who followed me everywhere, realizing that these were almost exactly the same questions he had asked me back then.

I shook my head, my mind going back to the very first battle back in Lusitania, when I had seen my first weapons instructor and Optio Aulus Vinicius incinerated before my very eyes, and how my own hubris had almost gotten me killed.

"No," I admitted. "I didn't always love it. In fact, after the fighting was over, I went and found a quiet corner and threw up my guts, and I was sure I never wanted to pick up a sword again."

Gaius looked at me in open astonishment, then shook his head, clearly having trouble believing what I was telling him.

"But then," I continued, "the next battle was easier, and I got better and better, because I kept practicing. Being made weapons instructor for my Century also helped because I would rather have died than let my friends down."

"I'll never be good enough to be a weapons instructor," Gaius said miserably, and I laughed.

"Probably not," I agreed. "But remember that I started training for the Legions when I was twelve years old. And just because you aren't an instructor doesn't mean that you can't be a good, even a great Legionary. But first," I reminded him, "you need to remember what I told you. Tomorrow is going to see you blooded, and the most important thing is that you shed the enemy's blood, not your own. Keep your mouth shut, your ears open, do what you're told when you're told, and you'll be fine."

I stood, then on impulse, I reached down to put my hand on Gaius' shoulder.

"I know you'll do your duty, Gregarius Porcinus," I told him, my voice gruff to try to hide my own swelling emotion.

Gaius looked up at me, swallowed hard, then responded in a clear, strong voice, "Yes, Primus Pilus. I will, I swear it."

I made the rounds of the Legion after the meal, able to move undetected because of the lack of fires, the only light provided by torches placed at intervals around the rampart, listening to the men talking as each of them went through their own individual pre-battle rituals. From what I could hear, morale was good, the men optimistic that they would be able to close with and inflict heavy damage on the Parthians, the rasping sound of blades being sharpened punctuating the conversations. As I listened, I heard some of the men discussing what I thought to be a good idea, which I passed on to all the Pili Priores, ordering them to make sure all of their men did what the originators of the idea came up with. Antonius had ordered that the men carry their shields instead of strapping them to their backs as they normally did on the march, but this presented a problem. How did a man hold his *furca* with his left hand and his shield at the same time? In his right hand, he would be carrying both of his javelins instead of just one as he usually did, both of which he would carry into battle to hurl at the enemy. The solution that these men came up with was to tie one end of a leather thong around the handle of the shield, with the other end tied in a slipknot around shaft of the *furca*, so that the shield dangled at their side, but allowed their hand to be free and hold onto the *furca*. When the order to drop their *furca* and pack was given, they would reach over with their right hand, holding the shaft of the *furca* just long enough to grab the handle of the shield with their left hand, then pull the knot, letting the weight of the pack pull the *furca* off their shoulder and fall to the ground. Naturally, as in most things, it was not quite as simple as it sounded, and I watched several men either drop their javelins as they tried to grab the *furca*, or more commonly, get smacked in the head by the shaft as it flipped over backwards from the weight of the pack. However, after some practice, I was happy to see that the men were able to make the transition quickly and without any further damage to themselves. It would only save a few moments, but I knew that if this operation were to be successful, we needed every one of those moments to achieve surprise. I thought about passing the word to the other Primi Pili about this idea, but decided against it, which proved to be a big mistake.

The next morning, we awoke to a blessing from the gods, who had seen fit to make it cold enough to freeze the ground and, as it became light, we saw that the day was overcast, making it unlikely that the ground would thaw out and become muddy. As expected, the Parthians, seeing Antonius' standard the day before and recognizing its meaning, had formed up in the crescent formation. Just as Antonius predicted, they positioned the mass of horse archers in the center, with the cataphracts divided into two wings. Also as expected, they were blocking our line of advance to the north, but instead of continuing that direction, the Legions suddenly executed a wheel maneuver, changing our direction of march from the north to the west, as if upon seeing our original line of march blocked, we were now taking the most direct route back to Syria. Once we changed directions, our cavalry and slingers moved into a screening position on what was now our right flank, interposing themselves between the Parthians and our main body. At the same time, the slaves driving the Legions' mules and wagons moved them to the far side of our formation so that there was, in effect, first a force of cavalry, then the Legions between them and the Parthian threat. To that point, everything was going exactly as Antonius planned it, with the next move expected on the part of the Parthians. Antonius was sure they would use their superior mobility to gallop to the west a short distance, where they would reestablish their blocking position, again in their crescent formation. That was when we would drive into the open side of the crescent, our cavalry attacking the horse archers and forcing them to fall back. This extra space would hopefully allow us to seemingly fall into the Parthian trap by advancing far enough so that the two wings of the cataphracts would be on our flanks. Following that would come the second order, with every other Legion facing to the right, dropping their packs to charge one wing of the cataphracts, while the remaining Legions would do the same to the cataphracts on the opposite side. However, Bellona is a fickle bitch.

While moving back into a blocking position was the tactically correct thing to do, the Parthian commander, not Phraates, who supposedly never led his men in battle but stayed well out of harm's way, clearly did not have much regard for doing the right thing. Instead, they remained in their original position, the only change being that the men turned their horses to face us, but it became clear that this commander knew what he was about. If we continued to march in our current direction, in just a short period of time we would put ourselves in a situation where we would have the entire Parthian army in our rear, whereupon they could either attack the Legions, or with us effectively out of the way, swing around to fall onto our baggage train. We had only one option, to press the attack, yet instead of being able to fall on both wings of cataphracts, while our cavalry pursued the archers, we could only engage their right wing. Meanwhile, if the cavalry and slingers went ahead after the archers, they would then have the left wing of cataphracts in a perfect position to fall on their rear. Despite the fact that our Gauls could outrun the slower cataphracts with little problem, the slingers would have no chance. However, if our cavalry tried to come to the aid of the slingers, they would expose themselves to the horse archers. Simply put, by not doing anything, and without firing an arrow, the Parthians had won this battle. The best thing we could have done at that point was to fall back on the remains of the campsite and rebuild it. Then Antonius and the command group could decide our next move. But Antonius was too desperate for a victory, so instead of doing the prudent thing, he showed every man in the army that he was not Caesar's bootlace.

"We're going to attack," the courier sent by Antonius told me.

"Attack?" I said incredulously. "Attack what, exactly?"

The courier could only shrug, then recited the instructions that Antonius had given him to pass to all the Primi Pili.

"On the *cornu* call, the army will execute the plan that the general outlined last night, except that every Legion will be assaulting in the same direction."

"Well, that's a relief," I snapped, pointing out into the open expanse to our left. "I think it would be a waste of time going that direction."

Again, the courier could only respond with a shrug, since all he was doing was relaying orders, and he clearly agreed with me.

"I don't know what to tell you, sir," he replied helplessly. "I'm just relaying the general's orders. Expect the order within the next tenth of a watch, as soon as the word's been passed to all the Legions."

I told him that I understood and acknowledged that I had received the order, while I sent my own runners to the Pili Priores to alert them. A few moments later, I heard a shout and turned to see Scribonius, standing at the head of his Cohort farther down the column. While I could not hear what he was shouting at me, I was positive I knew what it was, but all I did was put my hands in the air, thinking that there was a lot of that gesture going around right then.

"All right, boys, get ready," I called to my Century.

The situation was deteriorating rapidly, due to the fact we were forced to slow our march down to avoid moving past the Parthians too swiftly. I could not help but believe that the enemy knew exactly what was coming, as it seemed obvious from our actions. They still just sat on their horses watching us, and we were close enough to their right wing that I could see the men shifting about on their mounts, their heads turning as they talked to the comrade next to them. They were far enough away, however, that we could not immediately break into a run to close the distance, which would have exhausted us before we reached them. I took this as yet another sign that attacking was foolhardy at best, and suicidal at worst. Still, I knew that when the *cornu* sounded, we would assault the Parthians, no matter what. Taking several deep breaths, I waited for the sound that would send us hurtling after the enemy. For several more moments, nothing happened, and we were now in real danger of being too far to the side of the enemy wing. As it was, we would have to angle our approach to realign us with the Parthian right, and I wondered if Antonius realized that.

Finally, I heard the distant blast of the command *cornu*, the call instantly echoed by each successive Legion *cornicen*, until it was our turn, the horn blast giving the order to drop our packs, execute a right face, then launch immediately into the assault. I was happy to see that the thong idea worked, it taking only a couple of heartbeats for the men to ground their pack and turn to the right. Seeing them ready so quickly, I bellowed the order to advance, immediately stepping off towards the enemy. I was so proud of how quickly we were able to execute the maneuver that I completely forgot to check our alignment with the Legions on either side, at least until I heard Balbus call to me.

"Are you planning on attacking the Parthians with just us?"

That stopped me short and looking to either side, I saw that in fact the 10th was well ahead of the rest of the army. Fortunately, we were still a good distance away from the Parthians or they would have had the perfect opportunity to surround us and cut us to pieces. Calling a quick halt to wait for the rest of the army to catch up, I realized that in fact I should have informed the other Primi Pili about the method we had come up with, since it clearly meant that we moved more quickly than the other Legions. In a moment, the rest of them were abreast, then we resumed our advance. The Parthians continued to sit and watch impassively, seemingly content to let us close the distance before making their own move. In fact, they looked like a bunch of statues, except for an occasional toss of a horse's head or a sudden pawing at the frozen ground with a hoof, the animals betraying their riders' own tension. Suddenly, a man started tapping his javelin against his shield, which was quickly picked up by the others until first the Legion, then the whole army was punctuating every step, the cracking of javelin against the metal rim of shield drowning out every other sound. As we closed the distance, the racket we were making began having an effect on the Parthian mounts, and they started sidestepping nervously, tossing their heads. The closer we got to them, the more the horses became agitated, until a good number of them began rearing and plunging, with only the superb horsemanship of their Parthian riders keeping them from being pitched to the ground. Out of the corner of my eye, I saw our cavalry force moving to our right as we were advancing, I supposed to get out of our way when we began our charge, but suddenly, without any signal being given that I heard, they went charging headlong at the left wing of the Parthian army.

Just as quickly as that happened, I heard the *cornu* blast signaling the Legions to launch the attack, so I roared at the top of my lungs, "Up and at 'em boys," then broke into a run, heading for the waiting Parthians, the men of the 10th hot on my heels.

We closed the remaining distance quickly, and as had happened at the Cilician Gates, our speed caught the Parthians unprepared. At least that is how it appeared, because instead of fighting back, the heavily armored cataphracts turned to gallop off, their riders frantically whipping their mounts to open a gap. Without waiting for orders, some of the men stopped long enough to hurl their javelins at the retreating enemy, though without exception every one of them fell short, so I ordered the men to refrain from wasting their missiles. While we pressed the attack, our cavalry closed with the left wing of the Parthian army, but we could pay them no attention as we kept running after the cataphracts of the right wing, trying to close with them to inflict enough damage on them to send them back to Parthia. The cataphracts managed to stay just out of our reach, pulling up to give their horses a blow before trotting away again. Still, the Legions ran after them and I began to tire, struggling for breath, but not wanting to stop and show my age, instead forcing myself to keep running. Only after we covered at least three furlongs did we stop for a moment to catch our breath and when we did, instead of continuing their flight, the Parthians stopped as well. The moment I saw them doing so, I realized that they were not running away at all; they were trying to draw us out, the fate of Crassus flashing through my mind. However, the rest of the army kept pressing on, so I reluctantly ordered the Legion to follow and we broke out in a trot, not at the same pace as our initial pursuit, but neither were the Parthians moving with the same speed. Here and there lay the body of a Parthian, or one of their horses, but they were few and far between. Frankly, the results of what was supposed to be a decisive battle were nothing short of pathetic. Regardless, Antonius refused to recognize what was obvious to the rest of us and whenever any Legion showed signs of flagging, he would come galloping up on Clemency, alternately berating or flattering the men into continuing the pursuit.

For 50 furlongs, we followed the Parthians, the last 20 of them at a staggering walk as men paused long enough to vomit, their hands on their knees as they gasped for breath, before half-stumbling, half-running to catch up with their Century. Finally, after more than two parts of a watch in pursuit, Antonius ordered his *cornicen* to sound the recall, while directing the cavalry to keep up the pursuit as we marched back to our gear, then back to the remains of our camp. We were exhausted and demoralized, each of us knowing that we had not achieved our objective; in fact, when all was said and done, we killed less than a hundred of the enemy, and had taken all of 30 prisoners. The cavalry pursued the Parthians for more than ten more miles than we had, but were never able to close with them.

We made it back to the campsite, where all we had to do was to replace the stakes and erect our tents, which was a good thing, given how exhausted the men were. Antonius and the rest of the officers immediately locked themselves in the *Praetorium* to discuss and argue about what to do next, while the men sat in the growing darkness without even the comfort of a fire, holding their own discussions about all that had transpired. The men were decidedly downcast, their muttering going well beyond the normal grumbling, and after talking to the Centurions it was clear that the pessimism about our prospects permeated through the ranks. The one bright spot was that as light as the Parthian casualties were, ours were non-existent, at least in the Legions, though some slingers and a few of the cavalry had died.

"What was the point of that?" Balbus asked me when I stopped at his tent. "All we did was exhaust the men, and for what? Eighty-odd dead Parthians and thirty prisoners? At this rate, it'll take us three or four years to beat them, and that's only if we do this every day."

I could not argue with what Balbus was saying, but I felt obligated to offer some defense, though after a moment's thought, nothing came to mind, so I just shrugged.

"What next, do you think? Are we going to keep heading north?" he asked.

I considered this, then shrugged again. "I honestly don't know," I replied. "That's what they're talking about now, so I suppose we'll find out soon enough."

"Sooner than he decided to lift the siege, I hope," Balbus grumbled.

And to his credit, Antonius did make his decision more quickly this time.

"We're going back to Phraaspa."

I do not know why he acted surprised at the uproar that ensued as men began voicing their protests, either to each other or to themselves, but in voices loud enough that there was no way he could not hear. Antonius' face burned bright red, yet his voice was calm as he held his hand up for silence, his tone almost conciliatory, which I knew had to be hard for this man.

"I understand your confusion," he began, and I thought his choice of words was interesting, because the Centurions were anything but confused, though I supposed acknowledging that they were angry was not the smart thing to do.

"But we obviously haven't achieved what I'd hoped, so we'll need every man for our march to Artaxata. Besides, speaking politically, abandoning the auxiliaries would create innumerable problems. No, it's better if we go back and pick them up."

This last part seemed as if he were talking to himself, trying to convince himself that what he was saying was indeed true. For my part, I was wondering why it had suddenly become politically crucial not to abandon the auxiliary forces when it was just as vital to do so before we went off chasing the Parthians, but I put it down to just another example of Antonius' inconstancy.

"Going back to get the auxiliaries means that we'll be arriving in Artaxata even later," Vibius Spurius, the Primus Pilus of the 3rd Gallica called out. "We'll be eating cold rations, without fires at night, and if what we've been waking up to so far is any indication, in freezing cold. We can't afford to waste the time going back for the auxiliaries."

There was a loud chorus of assent at Spurius' words, my voice being among those agreeing with him. As far as I was concerned, the dice had been thrown as far as the auxiliaries, and although they were just a day's march away, the net loss of marching time would be almost a week altogether when the time we just wasted chasing the Parthians was factored in. Antonius stood listening to our cries of protest, but while he seemed almost apologetic, extremely unusual in itself, he refused to budge, so we returned to our respective Legion areas to inform the Centurions. They took it as poorly as we had, yet once an order was given, while I allowed the Centurions to vent their frustration, I expected them to carry it out as if it were their idea. However, my Centurions were all professionals and acted quickly to squash any sign of discontent with the men. Spending a cold night huddled in our tents, the men without warm clothing were forced to huddle together in order to preserve their body heat, while those of us lucky enough wrapped up, thanking the gods that we had them.

The next morning was bitterly cold, it being clear the night before, which always makes it colder the next day, though I do not know why. With every breath, the men exhaled a cloud of vapor that hung for a moment in the air before vanishing. It had been quite some time since I was exposed to this kind of cold, finding it difficult to climb out of my cot, the ache in my legs and back making me shuffle around my tent like an old man before I warmed up enough to move normally. It was now two days since we had gone running over the countryside after the Parthians, yet I was still feeling the effects of the exertion, something that never happened when I was younger. We broke camp, then began the march back to Phraaspa, our boots making a crunching sound with every step over the frozen ground. It was the coldest morning to that point, so the men had wrapped every bit of spare clothing about them, using spare neckerchiefs to wrap their feet while wearing their extra tunic instead of carrying them in their pack.

Despite the weather, we moved quickly, descending into the valley where Phraaspa was located, whereupon the vanguard came to a crashing stop again in the same way as when they first sighted Phraaspa, causing a ripple back along the column. Without any orders given, the rest of the army was forced to halt. We were right in the middle of the column so we could not see what caused the vanguard to pull up short, but it turned out that the command group was as caught by surprise, judging from the amount of shouting and gesturing going on between Antonius and his officers. I did not relish the idea of trotting a substantial length of the column to find out what was going on, yet I could see the Primus Pilus of the vanguard Legion approaching the Triumvir from the front. Whatever it was up ahead was sufficiently challenging or surprising enough that he did not feel confident continuing forward. Cursing under my breath, I began to make my way to the command group, despite no *bucina* call sounding. However, things were so confused I wanted to see for myself what was going on. I arrived in time to hear Antonius bellow at the Primus Pilus, which turned out to be Balbinus, to return to his Legion to push on. The Triumvir was clearly angry, his aides and even other generals suddenly finding reasons to be a good distance away from him as he raged, first at Balbinus, then seemingly to the gods.

"Where are the scouts?" he stormed. "Why didn't they warn me?"

Only Ahenobarbus seemingly had the courage to remind Antonius that he had ordered the scouts to pay attention only to the Parthians' location and not to the path ahead, since we were coming back to Phraaspa and the rest of the army. Antonius clearly did not want to hear what he considered to be excuses, as he and Ahenobarbus began bickering, while I took the opportunity to pull Balbinus aside to ask him what he had seen.

"All our hard work gone," he said grimly. At first I did not understand, my quizzical expression prompting him to explain. "Apparently, while we were gone, the Medians sallied out. They completely destroyed the ramp, and it looks like they whipped our auxiliaries while they were at it."

The valley floor around Phraaspa was a scene of destruction and devastation, just not in the way we would have hoped. Balbinus had been absolutely right; the ramp was thoroughly wrecked, down to its stone foundation, the dirt so painstakingly applied pulled off, now scattered about in big heaps. Some of the blocks had been moved out of position, making me wonder how the Medians could have managed to wreak such damage in such a short period of time as a normal sally would have taken. What we learned was that the Medians had so cowed our auxiliary troops that they huddled behind the walls of our deserted camps, refusing to give battle after their first defeat, thereby allowing the Medians to do a thorough job of destroying our work. The entire army was as angry as I had ever seen it, the men in my Legion just as vocal as the others in their rage and dismay at seeing weeks of work wrecked. Compounding the anger was the knowledge that we had come back for these men, despite our allies being oblivious to the fact that we had originally planned on leaving them to their own devices. Even without a nightly fire around each tent, men sat together like they normally did, shivering in the cold as they gnawed on a piece of boiled bacon or moldy bread, while the overwhelming topic was the perceived betrayal of their trust by the auxiliaries. As I wandered about on my nightly rounds, hearing the bile and vitriol spewed onto the collective heads of the auxiliaries by my men, I briefly considered pointing out that we had abandoned these men, immediately thinking better of it, mainly because I was angry myself. Still, I was as surprised as everyone else when Antonius announced his planned punishment for the auxiliaries as a result of their actions, or lack thereof, on the day in question.

"They are to be decimated," Antonius told a stunned audience of officers and Centurions.

This was not the first time Antonius had decimated; in fact, this would make the third time, the most recent being six years earlier when he and Octavian were contending for supremacy in Italia and some of the Legions had threatened to go over to Octavian. Once I thought about it, I could not remember any Roman general who had decimated his Legion more than once. Caesar had threatened to do it, but never followed through. Antonius was adamant, however, that the auxiliaries be decimated. Only when pushed by both the Centurions and his officers did he bother to explain why.

"The men," he said simply, prompting baffled expressions between the Centurions, forcing him to expand. "I'm not blind or deaf. I hear how angry the men are about having all of their work ruined, and I don't need an angry army at my back wanting to tear into the auxiliaries while worrying about a Parthian army in front of me. This should appease them."

I had little doubt that it would, though I could not help wondering how the leaders of the auxiliaries would feel, or their men for that matter. Apparently, Antonius was not particularly worried about having angry auxiliaries in his train. Nonetheless, the fact that Marcus Antonius was worried about the feelings of the Legionaries in his army was telling, though perhaps this is another thing only seen clearly when looking back through the years. When I returned to the men, they did not cheer the news as I expected them to, although most looked grimly satisfied. The punishment was carried out, and to our surprise, the comrades of the condemned men did not offer any resistance, even when men of the Brundisium Cohorts passed out the axe handles with which they would administer the punishment. Antonius had formed the army up in a large square, the Romans on three sides with the auxiliaries on the fourth. The lots were drawn among the troops of every nation represented, except for the cavalry and the force of slingers who had been marching with us, so that none could say that one group was favored over another. Not surprisingly, Herod's man put up the most argument, insisting that the only reason his men had not tried to stop the Medians was due to a lack of support and not courage on the part of his men. If they had gone out to try and stop the Median sally, he insisted, they would have been cut to pieces. Given my experience with Jewish fighters in Egypt, I actually believed the Jewish commander was telling the truth, but I was hardly about to voice that opinion. Nonetheless, Antonius refused to be swayed by the Jew's appeal, despite reportedly having a close relationship with the little toad who was their king. The condemned men were led out in nothing but tunics, their hands tied behind them, though they all walked out under their own power. The executions took place in plain sight of the watching Medians. I could only imagine what they were thinking as they watched their enemy killing their own, and in such a brutal manner as a decimation.

With that business done, we turned our attention back to our dilemma, which in some ways was as grim a prospect as the men facing decimation, because we faced death from exposure or starvation. Quite naturally, we all expected that now that we had joined back up with the auxiliaries, the order would be forthcoming to break down camp to start the march for

Artaxata. Instead, Antonius gave the order to repair the works, giving every indication that we were going to resume the siege. It is hard to describe the level of consternation and disbelief, not to mention confusion, when I relayed the order to the Centurions. Knowing as I did the likely reaction, I decided that I would pass the order to all 60 Centurions myself, rather than just the Pili Priores, enough of a rare event that the men were given some forewarning that the news was going to be big. When I stepped in front of them and they saw my face, they also knew it would be bad. Still, I do not believe that any of them in their wildest imaginings would have guessed what I was about to tell them. As difficult as it is to find a spot to hold a meeting of all the Legion's Centurions, it is even more difficult to find said spot where it is also out of earshot. Given the uproar of the Centurions, I was glad that I selected to take them outside the camp a short distance away. Not only would the men have learned of this development before I was ready to inform them myself, any nosy provosts would have had an earful of evidence to drag one of my Centurions before Antonius for inciting a mutiny. Fortunately, even if they had heard my men, there were so many similar meetings taking place that I expect that the army would have been without most of their Centurions if the provosts chose to make an issue of it. The men were similarly dismayed, but the brave or foolish few of them who voiced their displeasure got a taste of the *vitus* to remind them that their job was to obey orders, no matter how confusing they might have been.

It was the first real snowfall of the season that saved us, changing Antonius' mind, less than a week later. Those familiar with the country, like the Mardian guide, did admit that it was early for such a hard snow but insisted that it was a sure sign of a bad winter. The foraging had become almost non-existent, Antonius only trusting either the Gauls or we Legionaries to go out into the countryside, and we could not cover any territory on foot that was not already scoured and picked clean weeks before. We were not the only ones foraging either; the Parthian army was always present, just out of range of any missiles yet close enough that we could make individual men out distinctly. Between the two armies there was not a feather within miles, let alone a whole chicken, while any hidden supplies that the local farmers had tried to keep away from us to feed their families through the winter had their location tortured out of them long before. However, I suppose that an effort had to be made, for morale purposes if not for anything else, so one or two patrols went out every morning. That is when something quite curious started happening between the Parthians and our men, when they would cross paths on their respective foraging attempts. Normally this would occasion a skirmish between the two forces, very seldom inflicting losses on either side, yet for some reason, the Parthians began talking to our men, albeit from a safe distance. This is not as unusual as one may think; men are curious about those they do not know much about, whether they are enemy or not, so if the opportunity presents itself, they will talk to each other to learn more about their opponent. Men they will be perfectly happy to kill the very next moment, should it be so ordered or if the opportunity arise, but these Parthians were not asking questions as much as they were singing our praises. More specifically, those who could speak Latin would go on about how much they admired Roman Legionaries, commenting on our discipline and order, and how formidable in battle we were.

Increasingly, men were returning scratching their heads, eager to tell their comrades about how much the Parthians admired all that we were about, but it was only when it was men from my Legion and I got to hear them telling the whole story that it became clear what was going on. For, as many nice things as these Latin-speaking Parthians were saying about the rankers, they were saying as many, if not more negative things about our general. In fact, what the Parthians were doing was trying to sow discord and discontent among the ranks by lamenting that our unfeeling brute of a general Antonius was horrifically abusing the brave and noble men of the Legions, keeping us exposed to the elements without adequate shelter or fire. They also described in grisly detail what we could expect with the onset of winter, painting a picture of men being forced to choose between death by starvation or death by exposure. These encounters with the Parthians, when coupled with the news that we were resuming the siege, put the men into a state that I had never really seen before. They were not mutinous, but I believe that had more to do with their belief that if they mutinied, there was nowhere they could go than any sense of loyalty. The men were downcast to be sure, except that it went deeper than that, a sort of numbness of mind and spirit that comes when all hope is lost. While they still worked, still did their duties, the punishment list no more or less full than it was on any other day, there was a listlessness that could not be completely ascribed to the short rations. I for one, along with most of the other Primi Pili who shared my concerns, were worried enough about it to go talk to Antonius.

Fonteius was there to intercept us, blocking entrance into Antonius' private office.

"The general is in a meeting and can't be disturbed."

By common consent, I was chosen to be the spokesman of the Primi Pili in this matter, so I tried to hide my dislike of the man, keeping my tone respectful as I explained our concerns. To my surprise, he did not dismiss us, indeed looking quite concerned himself. He began pacing, looking at the floor in thought before turning back to us.

"If I tell you something that you could use that might give the men more confidence in what Antonius is doing, would that help?"

I exchanged a glance with the others, most of whom gave a slight nod.

"It certainly couldn't hurt anything to try."

This was apparently not what Fonteius wanted to hear, because he pursed his lips, then gave a sharp shake of his head.

"You'll have to do better than that, Pullus, if I'm to divulge what is a very sensitive piece of information to you."

"You want a guarantee that the men will feel better about whatever it is you're going to tell us?"

I was thankful that Balbinus uttered this and not me, though the point was not lost on Fonteius, who gave a small grunt to show his discontent, but relented.

"Fair enough," he said grudgingly. "The reason that Antonius resumed the siege has nothing to do with his belief that Phraaspa will fall, because in fact he doesn't believe that we can take the city before we run completely out of food."

Oh, he had a very attentive audience with that revelation, all of us suddenly listening intently for him to explain this statement. Clearly enjoying our shock and anticipation, Fonteius said nothing for the span of several heartbeats, until the suspense was too great.

"Well?" snapped Corbulo. "Are you going to explain or do we have to guess?"

"No, Corbulo, if you'll allow me to finish." Fonteius gave a small smile, clearly pleased at scoring some sort of victory over us. "The reason Antonius resumed the siege is because he has entered into secret negotiations with the Parthian king. In any negotiation, one needs leverage, and the prospect of us taking Phraaspa is that leverage. That's why it must appear as if we're intent on taking the city and why, if the morale of the army is as you say it is, the enemy will see what we're doing is just a ploy."

While I did not care to admit it, what Fonteius said made sense, at least as far as needing leverage to negotiate with any kind of strength. As I thought about it, I understood that any military man with even a basic amount of experience could spend a few watches watching the men and know that something was amiss.

The others apparently felt the same way, because Balbinus asked, "What concessions is Antonius trying to gain for us?"

"He's asking for the standards that were lost at Carrhae and with Statianus, as well as the return of the prisoners, but that's not his true goal. What he wants to get is a guarantee of safe passage for the army back to Artaxata. In fact, he's conferring with the Parthian envoy right now."

I confess I had forgotten about the men of Crassus' Legions taken prisoner at Carrhae some 20 years before, wondering how many of them were still alive and how brutally hard their lives must have been. I was saddened by the thought that they were expendable pieces in this game Antonius was playing. Still, if leaving them in captivity would buy my men a passage back to Artaxata, safe from harassment by the

Parthians, then I vowed I would make an offering to the gods to make their lives as comfortable as possible under the circumstances. I exchanged a look, first with Corbulo, who gave a slight shrug, then Caecina, who did much the same thing, as I snorted in exasperation at the lack of assistance.

Turning back to Fonteius, I made the decision for the group.

"We'll do what we can with what you've told us. Hopefully it'll be enough."

Fonteius exhaled sharply, gave a curt nod, then without saying anything more, he turned to leave us standing there. The rest of us left the *Praetorium*, not going ten steps before the moaning and complaining started. Despite the fact that it did not surprise me, I was no less angry to hear my peers carping about my agreement with Fonteius.

"You should have held out for more concessions." This came from Figulus, the Primus Pilus of the Deiotaran Legion.

If it had been from anyone else in the group, I probably would have suffered in silence. I did not like Figulus, considering him to be of a nature akin to the Primus Pilus of the 35th slaughtered with Statianus, a man who owed his rise more to his ability to be obsequious with his superiors than to his skills as a Legionary. The Deiotaran Legion was not a true Roman Legion anyway, being raised by the old King Deiotarus when he ceded his kingdom to Rome. Although they were trained and equipped the same way we were, they spoke in their tongue around the campfires and were just generally foreign. Now this man was yapping about something he had every opportunity to speak about in front of Fonteius but had chosen not to, so I rounded on him, truly angry. I was pleased to see him blanch, taking a step backward as I got in his face, snarling angrily that he had not seen fit to speak up when he had the chance, meaning he had better shut his mouth, only calming down when Corbulo and Balbinus pulled me aside.

"You don't want the men seeing this." Corbulo's tone was harsh.

Honestly, he was right so I immediately relented, though I refused to apologize. Apparently, it is not just the men who are on edge, I thought as we departed for our respective Legion areas to try to cheer the men with this latest news. It turned out to be a major miscalculation on my part, the only consolation being that I was not alone.

Assembling the men at the end of the day, shortly before dark, I told them what we had agreed on before we left the *Praetorium*, that the resumption of the siege was a strategy of Antonius to achieve a more favorable position for our march to Artaxata. Despite not saying it outright, I strongly hinted that he was in negotiations with the Parthians. After a brief discussion with the other Primi Pili, we decided to be as vague as possible on this point, not because of any worry about spies in our midst, but for the recent rash of conversing that had broken out between our foraging parties and their Parthian counterparts. If the negotiations were secret on both sides, we did not want to jeopardize them by the careless blabbering of a Roman Gregarius talking to some sympathetic Parthian. They were causing us enough trouble with their honeyed words about the rankers, along with the equally poisonous ones about Antonius. Even before I finished speaking, I got a sinking feeling in my stomach as I observed the men's reaction to what I was telling them. When one has spent as many years as I had at that point leading men, you learn to read the signs that are as plain to see as the concrete milestones on the Via Appia, telling you how your message is being received. It is a combination of subtle things, since men in formation are forbidden to speak and are standing at the position of *intente*, telling me now that trouble was brewing. There is a certain stiffness in their posture, over and above what is natural with being at *intente*. While we are trained to keep our faces impassive when in the ranks, it was like I was looking at the wax death masks of the patrician ancestors; the eyes blank, the mouths set in a manner that radiated their repudiation of what I was saying. I began to get desperate; my mind raced for the right combination of words that would appease the men and pull them from this funk, yet nothing I was saying seemed to have any effect. Finally, I concluded my remarks, and when the men were dismissed, they turned to walk to their tents without saying a word to each other, the usual banter and teasing completely missing. That more than anything told me that the situation was more serious than I had thought, and I could feel my stomach twist. Standing there watching them leave, the men of Gaius' Century passed by, none of them even looking in my direction, which did not surprise me. However, when Gaius walked just a few feet away, he resolutely stared at the ground, and he refused to acknowledge me when I called to him. For a moment, I debated making an issue of it, but knew it would just make things worse, so I said nothing, instead watching him trudge by. As I was watching my nephew, I sensed someone approach from the other side, turning to see Scribonius, who gave me a wry smile.

"Well, that didn't go well," he said lightly, and I had to laugh.

"Definitely not one of my better speeches," I agreed. Turning serious, I asked my friend, "What do we do now? I had really hoped that telling them what Antonius was up to would help."

"What, that we need to beg our enemies to allow us to march wherever we want to go, as if we were clients?"

I looked at Scribonius, completely surprised at the bitterness in his voice.

"Not you too?"

Now it was his turn to laugh, then he spoke ruefully. "Sorry, Titus, but that's just how I feel. I understand why Antonius is doing what he's doing, but that doesn't mean I like it. It just doesn't sit well to think that we have to negotiate with an enemy we've vowed to destroy."

I was ashamed to hear Scribonius' words, because it had never occurred to me that the men might look at things this way. For the first time, I wondered if I was losing my grip on my Legion.

The negotiations continued for a few days, until mid-October was upon us. Finally, some sort of agreement was reached. Diocles poked about, then reported that Phraates, apparently as worried about the coming winter as we were, had agreed to let us leave unmolested. However, he refused to surrender the standards or release the prisoners from Crassus' army. I was impressed; Fonteius told us that Antonius had planned on giving up the prisoners and standards in exchange for the promise of safe conduct, which is exactly what he had done. Diocles was clearly not as impressed, making no attempt to hide his skepticism. In fact, he was putting on such a show of it that I knew he wanted me to ask him his thoughts.

Sighing so that he knew I knew what he was up to, I asked, "Clearly you don't agree, so what is it?"

"What did Antonius gain, really? Phraates got us to lift the siege, and he doesn't give up the standards or the prisoners. All he had to do was make a promise not to molest us as we leave."

I considered this. When put that way, it did not seem like Antonius was quite as smart.

"And what happens if Phraates breaks his word?" Diocles continued. "He won't do it until we're well away from Phraaspa, and then he'll still have the standards and the prisoners. What's Antonius going to do about it except gnash his teeth?"

"If Phraates does that, he has no honor and the world will know it." Even as I said this, I knew how weak it was, making Diocles laugh at the idea.

"Somehow I don't think a Parthian king is going to be losing sleep over what the world thinks of his honor."

He ducked as I threw a shoe at him and he left my office, still laughing.

With the negotiations concluded, there was nothing keeping us at Phraaspa. Yet instead of giving the order himself, Antonius sent Ahenobarbus to us, which was not received well by either the Centurions, or the rankers.

"He can't even face us to tell us we're finally leaving this cursed place," I heard someone cry, followed by a chorus of agreement from the men around him.

I could only shake my head; Antonius could not seem to do anything right by the men. For the first time I had some sympathy for the Triumvir because he honestly seemed to be trying to think of the men's welfare. It took us a couple of days to break down the camp, preparing to leave. For the first time in weeks, the men seemed to have a sense of purpose and a bit of energy in their activities as they made the necessary arrangements. The people of Phraaspa lined the parapet of their walls to watch us assemble, then begin to march away, this time with the whole army, and they knew that they had for all intents and purposes beaten the army of Antonius. We were finally lifting the siege with nothing to show for it but a few less men and none of our heavy baggage. Antonius originally planned on taking us back the way that we had come to Artaxata, since the route was known by the army. Then the Mardian guide who was with the baggage train asked to see Antonius, informing him that there was a better route turning to the northeast before swinging around to the north. He insisted that this route had better forage. Most importantly, it had not been picked clean of wood for fires. He also warned Antonius that trusting Phraates to uphold his end of the bargain was folly, something that Antonius did not want to hear. As the Triumvir argued, how could he know who to trust between the Mardian who had, however unwittingly, guided the baggage train to such a disaster, or the king of the enemy army who had pledged his word that we could pass unmolested? To prove his trustworthiness, the Mardian offered to ride with his hands tied behind his back, his mount tethered to a guard's horse all the way to Artaxata, an offer that Antonius accepted.

Chapter 6- Retreat

We pulled out before first light shortly before the Ides of October, the 10th being given the vanguard position, a signal honor on the first day of a march. Nonetheless, I was not about to allow the men to bask in the moment, remembering Diocles' words about Phraates. Instead of the normal Century on the flanks, I sent two on both sides, one closer to the front and one to the rear so they could spot any attempt by the Parthians to cut through the middle of the formation. There were no Parthians anywhere in sight, which was unusual, as they had always been lingering about a mile or so away. However, it was not unexpected if Phraates was keeping his word, but I was still taking no chances. The wind was like a knife cutting through a man's vitals; before we marched a third of a watch, my face went numb, my hands tingling despite the fact I was wearing one of my extra pairs of fur-lined socks on them. Even with the cold, the men moved quickly, so by the end of the day we covered almost 30 miles without a Parthian showing himself.

It snowed again that night, so that when we awoke, there were several inches on the ground, the tents covered in white blankets of the stuff. Fortunately, it was cold enough that the snow did not stick to soak into the leather, though I wondered how long our luck would hold in that sense, remembering a time in Gaul when our tents became soaked from melting snow, overloading the mules. That time we had been forced to abandon some of our food supplies, but that was in a land where most of the time resupply was simple. There were still no Parthians anywhere in sight, so when we stopped at midday, Antonius gave the order that we could march in loose formation and not in our normal spacing that we used when enemy contact was expected. This was popular with the men, but not as popular with the Centurions because of the inherent risk if the Parthians did show themselves, along with the unwritten rule that allowed men to move among their ranks to talk to friends when marching in such a formation. Men are not allowed to move between Legions, but they can go visit their friend or relative in another Cohort. When a Legion is on the march and is stretched out, that means that a man might be a few furlongs away from his spot in formation. I saw this as another sign that Antonius was trying to appease the men, which was beginning to work, judging from the comments that I heard as we marched. Taking the opportunity as an excuse to march near Gaius, I did so by stopping to wait for Scribonius and his Cohort to reach me. Exchanging a few words with Scribonius for the sake of appearances, I then began walking slowly until Gaius' section caught up to me. His face was red and chapped, but compared to his tentmates, he looked decidedly warmer.

"Thank you for the cloak and socks, Uncle," he whispered to me, while I just nodded, not wanting to acknowledge his words lest I be overheard.

"How are you holding up so far?" I asked, which was a normal question a Primus Pilus would ask one of his Legionaries, meaning there was no need to lower my voice.

"Fine sir," he replied cheerfully. I felt a pang at his youthful enthusiasm. Still, he chattered on, oblivious. "It's colder than I've ever seen, but as long as we keep moving it's not a problem. What about the Parthians? Do you think they'll show themselves?"

"They've promised that they wouldn't bother us," I responded dutifully, hoping my voice was betraying what I truly meant. "And so far they've held to their word."

I could feel his eyes on me as I spoke and I knew that he was weighing what I said, along with how carefully I said it, hoping that he received the message I was trying to send him, which was that I did not expect the Parthians to hold to their promise. In that, at least, I was proven right.

It was on the third day, shortly before midday that we first ran into trouble, starting at a river crossing. At first glance, it was just a case of the river overflowing its banks on the far side. Nonetheless, the Mardian guiding us insisted that it was a case of sabotage by the Parthians, as he had traveled this road many times and had never seen the river behave in such a fashion. To his credit, Antonius took him seriously, so that after crossing the river, he gave the order to close the ranks back up, while having the missile troops shake out on either side of the column, though it took time for men to scramble back to their proper place in the ranks. It was this moment the Parthians chose to attack. It is difficult to describe how an entire army can suddenly appear as if conjured up by the gods when one does not understand how it happened himself, because even to an eye as experienced as mine, the land did not seem to offer enough undulation to hold so many men and horses. I suppose it is a tribute to the skill of the Parthians in their knowledge and use of the terrain, for they arose from seemingly flat ground to come charging in from all sides. One moment we were standing waiting for Antonius to decide what to do, the next there were *cornu* calls echoing up and down the column as Centurions bellowed out orders. I was doing a bit of thundering of my own, first commanding the Cohort, then the Legion to form squares by Cohort, the standard tactic for repelling cavalry. The 10th was located roughly in the middle of the column, with the thickest concentration of slingers on either side of us. It did not take long for the Parthian horse archers to feel the sting of those lead missiles that had worked so well for Ventidius, so they never got close enough to us to loose any arrows that posed a danger. Quickly turning their attention to what they perceived to be the weak spot in the column, they galloped around the auxiliaries, who had put themselves in even greater danger by lagging behind. This had been a problem since the first day of the march; the auxiliaries simply did not have the discipline or the stamina of the Legions, continually falling behind farther and farther every day. Now they were paying the price as the Parthians swarmed around them, the only protection for the infantry being whatever native missile troops were with their contingent.

The Pontics and Jews had men who carried sheaves of light javelins, much in the manner of the Numidian infantry. Essentially, it was only this that stood between the Parthians and their own comrades. Despite many of them falling to the horse archers, we also saw riderless horses galloping away from the rear of the column, followed by men clutching some part of their body, meaning that they were inflicting damage in turn. The javelineers of the auxiliaries managed to thwart the Parthian attack. Unfortunately, it was only for a few moments, because the enemy came rushing at the rear of the column again, clearly believing that this was the weak point. This time it took the Gallic cavalry to come to the rescue, just arriving from their advance position farther up the road. Again our allies managed to kill and wound a number of the enemy, despite taking a few losses of their own, yet before the Gauls could come to grips with the Parthians to do more damage, the enemy withdrew. As quickly as they had come, they disappeared, seemingly back into the ground, but obviously into the myriad hidden gullies and ravines that are part of the terrain. Suddenly the sounds of battle, the neighing horses, yelling men, *cornu* calls and of men wounded and dying was gone, leaving only the excited babbling of the army, underscored by the keening sound of the wind.

"At least we know what to expect now," was how Balbus put it, and he was right.

There had been a feeling of anticipation in the air around the army, building with every step we took, men waiting to see if the Parthian king would keep his word, and they would not have been Roman Legionaries if money had not changed hands the moment the first arrow flew. Fortunately, there was no more marching in loose formation, Antonius instead putting us into the *agmen quadratum* again, without any complaints from the men this time. We did not see the Parthians for the rest of the day, though like Balbus, I was comforted by the thought that we now knew what to expect. Little did any of us know that this day would be the best it would be for some time to come.

Crossing the river marked another change, besides the sign that the Parthians would do everything they could to stop us. While the land we passed through had some short but steep hills that had to be traversed, it was nothing compared to the rough and broken terrain we now found ourselves in. To be fair, the Mardian had warned us, though he insisted that while the country was more rugged, it also offered more opportunities for subsistence. In this, he was correct at least, at first anyway. Compared to what we had been through before, the land around us provided a bounty in the way of firewood, so that for the first time in weeks the men were allowed to have a fire at every tent, and not just for cooking. Next to food, nothing quite lifts a man's spirits as the sight of a warm fire in the night, except perhaps a woman, and I know that most of the men would have stepped over the most willing, beautiful maiden in the world to warm their hands at a fire that first night. It did not help matters that the weather was getting worse. It was about this point that the sick list began to become a real concern, if only because there was not much we could do for men who were ill from exposure and cold. The more rugged terrain also meant that our pace slowed considerably, meaning that the first three or four days, we managed barely 20 miles. We began losing men, stragglers who could not keep up and when they fell from sight of the rearguard, were never heard from again. Each morning before we set out, I would have to send my report to the *Praetorium*, and with every report there was a tale of men who would never see their homes again. I was losing an average of two men every day, and I knew that it was only going to get worse. So far, it was only men who had been sick, or men who injured themselves by tripping and falling over ground torn and gouged by tramping feet, the earth like iron from the freezing cold. Most of the time, men would be hauled to their feet by their comrades with nothing worse than a few bruises or cuts, yet sometimes a man would fall awkwardly, and those around him could hear the snap of a bone, followed by his scream of agony. If he was lucky, it would be an arm that had broken, but sometimes men would break their legs and if it was the big bone in the thigh, those men did not last long in the cold weather. Something about the body healing and trying to stay warm at the same time was too much for a man, so that even being carried on a litter by their comrades, they would usually die within a day or two. As I said, I knew it was going to get worse, yet when it did come, it was not from the cold or sickness, it was from battle, and it cost me a Cohort and most of a second.

The days passed in a haze of misery as we climbed steadily higher, always with the Parthians circling us like wolves after a herd of goats. Every moment of the day, we had to be on our guard, the terrain no help towards maintaining a proper *agmen quadratum*. One lapse of attention, where a Century wandered just a bit out of line because their Centurion was busy carrying on a conversation with his Optio about who had the duty that night and therefore did not follow exactly in line as he was supposed to, would cost someone their lives. Seeing this gap, a swarm of horse archers would immediately gallop in, loosing as many arrows as they could before the men got their shields up. Meanwhile, our slingers would run out from the center of the *quadratum* or the Gallic cavalry would arrive to drive them away. Scenes like this one were played out up and down the column, the need for constant alertness wearing on everyone, regardless of rank. Antonius spent part of every day circulating among the troops, getting down off Clemency to walk with the men, telling jokes while listening to their complaints. He never once displayed the haughty, cold-hearted, and mean-spirited Antonius that had gotten him in so much trouble with the men in Italia. Whenever he came to visit my Century or my Cohort, I made myself scarce, since it was not a good idea for me to be in a position to display my ambivalence towards Antonius. I appreciated what he was doing, yet I was suspicious of both his motives and his sincerity so it would not have been politic of me to find myself in a position where that distrust was on display. Young Gaius was quite taken with Antonius, however, and the evening after Antonius visited with the Second Cohort of the 10th, he was positively glowing. I remembered how Vibius had felt much the same way when we first encountered a much younger Antonius prior to taking ship for Britannia. Regarding my nephew, he seemed to be holding up well enough physically, yet I could not help noticing and worrying a bit at how tired he looked at the end of a day's march. Gaius' mental state concerned me more, as he seemed especially worn down by the constant threat of the Parthians hovering about the edges of the army, not close enough to hurt us immediately, but in a position to do damage if we made a mistake. That kind of tension wears a man down, even an experienced man. It was this tension that spurred a Tribune named Gallus to do something that almost got all of us killed.

I do not remember much about Gallus; he was just one of the many young Tribunes with the army who rotated through each Legion. Most of them were a damned nuisance, and if they did stick out in our memories, it was rarely for the right reasons. Nonetheless, I cannot totally discount what he tried to accomplish, while in truth the fault lies more with Canidius than with Gallus, since at least Gallus was trying to do something to relieve the constant pressure we all felt. Going to Antonius, he offered to lead a sally back to the rear of the column, where as usual, the auxiliaries were under the most pressure. They had been whittled down bit by bit every day, their numbers shrinking, leaving a trail of arrow-riddled corpses in our wake. Gallus asked for, and was granted, 3,000 auxiliary infantry and 2,000 cavalry to be formed up inside the square of the *agmen quadratum* at the rear of the column, ready for the next sortie by the Parthians. When it came, Gallus led his force out from behind the protective screen of the rearguard to tear into the Parthians, catching them completely by surprise. For the first time in days, there were more Parthian bodies on the ground than our own, making it understandable that Gallus would want to continue the killing, so he continued his pursuit of the Parthians until he was out of sight of the column. Canidius was commanding in the rear portion of the *quadratum*, so he sent a messenger on horseback galloping off to Gallus, ordering the Tribune back to the column. However, for reasons I never learned, Gallus refused. I imagine that like any young officer, he was anxious to make a name for himself, seeing this as his opportunity and he was not about to waste it.

Looking back, it is easy to see that this was just a ploy on the part of the Parthians, falling back in seeming confusion and disarray to draw an inexperienced and rash officer far enough away from the column to completely surround him and his men. The messenger somehow made it back to the column to report that Gallus was refusing to come back to the column, and that he was now surrounded, though he could still fight his way out. Canidius was naturally very angry; I do not know if he ordered Titius or if the quartermaster just went, but then Titius galloped back to the Tribune, whereupon an argument ensued. According to Titius, who returned by himself and in a blind fury, Gallus refused Titius' command to return to the column, despite the man grabbing two of the cavalry standards, pointing them back to the column in an attempt to exhort the troopers to return. Gallus had cited the fact that he asked Antonius for this independent command and therefore would only return on the commanding general's order, and not from any of his subordinates, no matter how high-ranking they may have been. In turn, Gallus exhorted the cavalry to stay with him, which they did. This was the moment on which everything that transpired turned, so who knows how differently things might have turned out if Gallus had obeyed, or if the cavalry had listened to Titius? Canidius should have immediately sent for Antonius, at the head of the column with the 3rd Gallica, who had the vanguard that day, but Canidius was like most Roman officers; worried about his own reputation and jealous of any man who threatened his authority. He was not going to appeal to Antonius over a junior Tribune's refusal to obey, so he sent yet another messenger back to Gallus, this time threatening a tribunal if he did not obey. It was too late, however, the messenger returning to report that Gallus and his force were now completely surrounded, cut off by a large force of Parthians, and forming an *orbis*. Again, Canidius had an opportunity to use the chain of command to inform Antonius, who was some four miles away farther up the column. Instead, he ordered two Cohorts of the Deiotaran Legion, marching on the opposite side of the *quadratum* as the 10th, along with a scratch force of cavalry of the outriders nearby to go to the aid of Gallus. When I saw just two Cohorts trotting back the way we had come, I thought about making my way to Canidius to suggest that if Gallus' force of 5,000 men were surrounded and overwhelmed, sending less than a thousand men, even if they were at least Roman-trained, did not seem prudent. I stopped myself, thinking how it was likely to be received if a Centurion lectured a general on tactics, and I have always regretted that I did not speak up. Although I know what his reaction probably would have been, I should have tried, given how things turned out. Instead, I stood watching the Deiotaran Cohorts trotting off to their destruction, not knowing I would be ordering some of my own men to do the same in a short while.

Since Canidius had not sent word of what was taking place behind the column, Antonius had no reason to halt, so we continued marching, knowing that if the rear of the army stopped, it would open up what might be a fatal gap in the *quadratum*. I walked over to Balbus, who was marching with his Century, but before I said a word, he shook his head, clearly knowing what was on my mind.

"Bad business," he said shortly. "I have a very bad feeling about this."

"So do I," I replied.

We walked in silence for a bit, suddenly turning at the sound of a commotion to the rear. I was forced to squint to make out the figures staggering through the rearguard and into the square, heading for where Canidius and his staff rode. As they drew closer, I saw that it was men of the Deiotaran Cohorts, about 20 of them, some of them still with their shields but most without, obviously discarding them to make good their escape. A couple of them had been wounded and were supported by comrades, but nevertheless they first made their way to Canidius to report. I saw him pull his horse up short, obviously agitated. Immediately after they made their report, he looked over to where the 10th was as I cursed under my breath, prompting me to start walking over to Canidius even before his *cornicen* sounded the call. When I got to him, the wounded men were lying on the ground being tended to by members of the army's *medici* who marched in the middle of the column with the baggage. Canidius tried to act oblivious to the sounds of the injured men moaning in pain as their wounds were bound, but I saw his eyes darting over to where they were as he talked to me.

"It's a bad business back there, Pullus," Canidius began, unconsciously echoing what Balbus had said just a short time before. "I need you to send two Cohorts back there and pull Gallus' fat from the fire."

"Two Cohorts?" I was clearly doubtful and made no attempt to hide it. "You just sent two Cohorts and look what happened to them."

"I'm not sending just you," he snapped, clearly irritated. "The Deiotarans are sending two more and I'm sending 500 cavalry as well, along with a thousand auxiliaries. That should be more than enough."

If he had not increased the number, I would have refused the order, taking my chances that I would be vindicated, given what was happening. However, he was sending twice the force that had just been repulsed. I saluted, but said nothing, returning to the Legion while deciding who to send as I walked. Balbus was standing waiting for me, but I waved him off, needing a bit more time to think. After a moment, I sent a runner to summon Servius Gellius of the Sixth and Gnaeus Nasica of the Tenth Cohorts to my side.

Over the last few years, I have had ample opportunity to think about decisions I have made, and there are few that haunt me as much as my choice of these two Cohorts, despite having never spoken of my true thoughts until now as I dictate this to Diocles. As Balbus had said, he and I had a bad feeling about what was transpiring behind us with young Gallus. I cannot honestly say where that feeling came from, other than more than 20 years and hundreds of battles and skirmishes worth of experience, yet I was almost certain that I was sending men to their death. With every order, there is the spirit and the letter of the order, and it is in that nebulous area in between where a Centurion's true influence lies. If I had been convinced that the situation was salvageable, or if young Gallus had been one of those few Tribunes that I considered had potential, I would have sent my Cohort, along with Scribonius'. However, the sum total of my experience and instinct for battle meant that I would instead send two Cohorts I could afford to lose without crippling the fighting capability of the Legion. Gnaeus Nasica, while performing his duties in a satisfactory manner, still had not redeemed himself for his betrayal of his Centurion Tetarfenus years before when we were on the Campus Martius, and this would be his chance to do something heroic. In a sense, I hedged my bet by sending Gellius, who had continually impressed me with his intelligence and quick grasp of a situation, so with that rationalization on my part, I sent for the two men. As soon as they arrived, I quickly explained the situation, then gave them their orders, pointing to where the other two Deiotaran Cohorts were forming up in the hollow of the square next to Canidius and his aides. They both saluted, but before Nasica returned to his Cohort to relay the orders, I called him back.

"This is your chance to make up for Tetarfenus," I told him.

While he said nothing, he nodded in understanding, then turned and trotted to his Cohort. The selected Cohorts moved quickly, leaving their packs in the middle of the square with the rest of the baggage, burdening the mules even further, with the plan to retrieve them later, then moved to the rear with the Gallic cavalry leading the way. The fighting was now taking place out of sight as we continued marching away, although remnants of the first two Cohorts and cavalry still came straggling back to the column. However, I had not yet seen Canidius sending a rider up to the head of the column to inform Antonius. I kept telling myself that my decision to send these two Cohorts was justifiable and the reason I did not send the Second Cohort and Scribonius had nothing to do with Gaius. Now, these many years later, I am not so sure.

A third of a watch passed with no sight of the returning party, while it was becoming impossible to maintain the *quadratum* because men of all ranks kept looking over their shoulders. I was as distracted as any of the men, straining my eyes to the rear, hoping that for once my instinct of a disaster was wrong. Finally, I spied a single figure growing closer and as he became more distinct I saw that it was a mounted man, whipping his galloping horse as if the Furies were after him.

"This can't be good," I muttered to myself as I watched him skid to a stop, spraying dirt everywhere.

He gestured wildly back to the rear and I did not need to hear him to know that Canidius' rescue mission had failed. Canidius turned, snapping an order, but I was already trotting over when his *cornicen* sounded the call. Somewhere along the way over, I made a decision, though I did not know it until the moment came. Canidius was visibly distressed, yet he tried to sound matter-of-fact, as if he were issuing a normal marching order.

"The attempt to extract Gallus isn't going well. This man," he indicated a Gaul, whose face was streaked with blood and was attending to his quivering steed, which had an arrow protruding from its rear quarter, "says that your two Cohorts and the Deiotarans have gotten themselves surrounded and are being pushed hard by the Parthians."

His inference that somehow my men had brought their predicament on themselves angered me greatly, but Canidius was oblivious as he gave me the order I was dreading.

"Detach two more of your Cohorts and send them back. That should be enough to tip the scales in our favor."

"No."

For a moment, he acted as if he had not heard, but I think that he was just so shocked he did not know what to say.

When I said nothing more and could no longer be ignored, he turned to look at me, his face now flushed as he snapped, "That wasn't a request, Pullus. Now do as you're told."

I had made my decision, and I was not going to be threatened or bullied.

"So they can be chopped up into bloody scraps like the first two?" I challenged. "I won't do it, General. It will take more than a couple of Cohorts to get those boys back."

"I didn't ask your opinion, Primus Pilus," he said tightly, clearly trying to keep a rein on his anger, but I did not care.

"Have you informed Antonius what's going on back there?" I shot back, happy to see him visibly flinch.

"I'm in command in this section of the column," he said stubbornly, yet I could see him wavering.

"If you send a courier to Antonius and he confirms your order, then I'll do what you say, and I'll go myself."

"By then it will be too late, and all your men will be dead," he shot back.

"General, they're probably dead already. I've seen how fast their archers can shoot, and if they're surrounded, it won't take long."

I suppose he saw that I was not going to be moved, so he snapped, "Fine. I'll find a Primus Pilus who will obey a lawful order."

He turned to his *cornicen* to sound the signal for the Primus Pilus of the 30th, who came trotting over from the opposite side of the *quadratum*. I turned to return to my Legion, but before I moved out of earshot, Canidius called after me.

"This isn't over, Pullus. Consider yourself on report."

"I'll be happy to make my case to Antonius," I called back over my shoulder.

I do not know whether my refusal to send two Cohorts had anything to do with it, but Canidius ordered four Cohorts of the 30th to head back to what had by now become a major battle, one that was falling farther and farther behind us, as the main column still continued to march. All of the men were now visibly agitated, calling to their Centurions that something had to be done to help their comrades, but we were just as helpless as the men and all we could do was tell them to shut their mouths. To make matters worse it began to snow, not hard, but it just compounded the misery and difficulty of an already bad situation.

Scribonius came running up, falling in beside me, something clearly on his mind. "Did you really refuse Canidius' order to send men to help?"

As often as it happened, I still was amazed at how quickly word travels in the army. When I had come back to the Cohort, I briefly told Balbus what had transpired. I confess I did not tell him to keep the news to himself, yet he could not have wasted much time in telling Laetus, who must have relayed the word back down the line for Scribonius to know so quickly.

"He wanted to send two more Cohorts back there to be chopped up," I answered, shaking my head. "I would have gone if he had sent all of us back there, but he keeps feeding Cohorts in piecemeal."

"It looks like it'll take a Legion to rescue Gallus," Scribonius agreed.

Despite his words, something in his tone made me turn to look at him.

I knew him better than anyone did, so I sighed, then asked him, "What's on your mind?"

He frowned as he tried to frame his thoughts, and as was his habit, he answered my question with one of his own.

"Did Canidius send word to Antonius yet? I don't see how he would keep marching if he knew what was going on back here."

I shook my head.

"I asked him the same thing and all he told me was that he was in command back here. Typical officer talk."

"So you think Antonius should be informed?"

"Of course I do," I said, almost angry that he should ask such an obvious question, but then I saw he had asked the question for a reason.

"Are you suggesting that I send word to Antonius myself?" I gasped, to which he shrugged.

"You're already in the *cac* up to your neck for refusing an order. I think that you should do something to even the odds against you. Canidius has the advantage of outranking you, but I imagine that he's scared to death of Antonius finding out that this has gotten so out of hand and he's trying to fix it before he finds out."

As usual, Scribonius made perfect sense when he explained things that way and in fact, I was chagrined that I had not thought to do it myself.

"No wonder you always beat me at tables," I said ruefully, signaling my runner, then reconsidered.

Primi Pili do not have mounted couriers like generals do, and even as swift a runner as my man was, it would take him almost a third of a watch to get to Antonius. However, I could send him on a shorter errand, so I pointed him to where a group of Gallic outriders were riding on our flank. I handed him a gold denarius, then told him to run to the cavalrymen, find one who spoke passable Latin or Greek, and bring him back.

"Tell them there's more waiting for whoever comes to us," I told him before slapping him on the back and sending him on the way. As expected, the gold gave him wings, and he sprinted across the broken ground to the Gauls.

"That's a lot of money for a simple task," was Scribonius' only comment.

"Like you said, my career is at stake," I answered. "It's a small price to pay."

The runner returned with a Gaul who did indeed speak Latin, though my interpretation of what was passable and the courier's apparently was quite different, but I was in no position to be picky. Giving him his instructions, and one gold coin with the promise of another, I sent him galloping to the front of the column. The four Cohorts of the 30th had gone trotting back the way we had come and like all the others, did not return intact, in fact was now stranded with Gallus and the original group or those who had gone to rescue him. I tried not to think about the fates of Nasica, Gellius, and all the men under their command, but it was impossible. That is perhaps the worst part at moments like this, not knowing exactly what is happening, though I cannot imagine knowing the truth of a man's last moments of pain and death are comforting. Yet that is the way the human mind seems to work; we would rather know the ugly truth than to be in the dark. One more group of bloodied, shattered men returned, some of these men from the 10th, who came staggering back to the comfort of their comrades. Among them was an Optio of Nasica's Cohort, one of his eyes a bloody ruin from a spent arrow that had just enough force to blind him for life.

"It was horrible," he gasped when he realized that it was his Primus Pilus standing before him, making a pathetic attempt to straighten his uniform and make himself presentable, which I stopped with a gentle hand.

"Tell me what happened," I said, not sure that I really wanted to know.

"There are thousands of the bastards. They were waiting for us and more just kept coming. They let us get to within sight of Gallus and his bunch before they descended on us like a pack of jackals."

He waved a hand helplessly, his one good eye filling with tears.

"Then it was like arrows were raining from the sky," he sobbed. "We tried to form *testudo*, but when we did, their cataphracts would come charging in before we could make a porcupine."

He had no need to expand on that statement; a *testudo* is nothing but raw meat to a lion, when the lion is cavalry. The porcupine is a *testudo*, with men thrusting their javelins out to discourage cavalry horses from barging into the *testudo*, except it takes an extra amount of time to get the javelins out. I bit back a curse, not wanting to shame the Optio, nevertheless thinking that perhaps a Pilus Prior with more ability could have gotten his men to work quickly enough to get a porcupine formed.

My fears seemed to be confirmed when I asked, "Did you see Gellius' Cohort?"

He nodded, replying, "They didn't get hit as badly as we did. They managed to get their porcupine set up, but I think that's because the Parthians concentrated on us."

I was not going to shame the man by pointing out that it was more likely the case that the Parthians chose the easier target, precisely because Nasica's men were slower in getting formed up and their javelins out than Gellius'. I patted the man on the shoulder, then called for medical help to attend to him.

Before he was led away, I asked him, "Did you see Nasica? Any idea what happened to him?"

He shook his head.

"The last I saw he was trying to rally the Cohort into an *orbis*. I got hit and fell, and the rest of the men were trying to make it to Gallus when I got separated. I played dead when the Parthians rode by, then I got up and gathered some of the other men and made my way back here."

I thanked him, assuring him that he had earned a commendation for having the presence of mind to lead men back to the column, despite his horrific wound. Fortunately, the loss of one eye does not disqualify a man from service in the Legions because I made a mental note to consider this man for promotion, if he survived without his wound turning corrupt and killing him by poisoning his blood.

I continued watching the rear of the column, walking backwards, and scanning the bleak countryside for signs of more men making their way back to the safety of the main body of the army, but the falling snow made visibility a problem. Suddenly, without any warning, beginning from the front of the column, a series of *cornu* calls came that signaled that not only were we halting, we were making camp. That was the first sign that my Gallic courier had gotten through to Antonius.

Canidius was clearly unhappy that we were stopping, because it meant that his time of handling the situation now a few miles behind us before Antonius was alerted was over. We passed Antonius on his way back to the rear, the Triumvir on Clemency, whipping him for all he was worth and I watched from my spot as he went skidding to a stop in front of Canidius, throwing dirt all over everyone standing nearby. He pushed Clemency almost up against Canidius' mount, the ensuing conversation punctuated by Antonius' furious gestures, while for a moment I thought he would strike Canidius, who pointed in my direction. Even as I was expecting Canidius to try and toss me in the fire, I felt my stomach lurch, but Antonius was clearly not interested at that moment and he went galloping back to the front where men were now preparing to make camp. He spared me barely a glance as he passed by, his mouth set in a grim line, Clemency frothing at the mouth from being run hard. The provosts were pointing each Legion to their part of the camp when Antonius reappeared, this time at the head of the 3rd Gallica as they ran double time to where Gallus and whoever was left were presumably still fighting for their lives.

Arriving at the designated spot, I put the men to work on their part of the camp, made more difficult by the absence of two Cohorts and the frozen ground.

Some of the men hacked at what would be part of the ditch, while others packed the spoil to make the rampart, the slaves assigned to the baggage train erecting the tents. To a casual observer it was the same as any hundreds of days spent on campaign. Only someone with an experienced eye would see the continual glances back in the direction from which we had marched, or hear the muttered conversations as the men speculated on what was happening. It was one of the rare times where men were not wagering on the myriad things that they find to pass the time; how long it will take a section to complete their part of the ditch compared to the next one, or whose tent was erected first. Neither was the normal bantering back and forth about long-ago escapades while in Damascus or Rome present. Everyone seemed to sense that if we averted a great catastrophe it would only be by the intervention of the gods, meaning that as soon as men were able, they set up their altars to their household deities, making offerings of their meager rations.

It was still daylight when the camp was finished and it was only then that the *bucina* at the Porta Decumana sounded the signal that friendly troops approached. Putting Mallius in charge of the Century and Balbus in charge of the Cohort, I ran to the back of the camp, arriving in time to see Antonius lead the 3rd Gallica and what was left of the Cohorts Canidius had sent out to rescue Gallus' force. It did not take any experience to see the horrific results of Gallus' foolhardy and ultimately reckless attack, as man after man was carried in on makeshift litters of javelins and cloaks, or on shields. After a moment of watching the procession of wounded being carried in, I came to the conclusion that most of the 3rd Gallica had been turned into litter bearers, bearing a cargo of human wreckage, making me turn away from the sight.

The Tenth Cohort of the 10th Legion ceased to exist that day, for all intents and purposes. Of its six Centurions, three of them were killed, including Pilus Prior Nasica, who from the accounts of the few survivors had at least attempted to keep his men together and fighting before he took an arrow through the throat. The Princeps Prior, Gnaeus Piso, and the Hastatus Posterior Gnaeus Corens had also fallen, their bodies left behind on the field along with Nasica and the other dead. Of the three remaining Centurions, only the Pilus Posterior Vibius Frontinus had minor wounds and would not require extensive care. The Princeps Posterior Aulus Scaurus had taken an arrow through his calf and another into his chest, but the missile had not punctured his lung or any other vital organs as far as the surgeons could tell, though he would be out of action for some time. The Hastatus Prior Aulus Varro had suffered a sword slash across his face from a cataphract, losing an ear and the sight in one eye. Of the 403 effectives in the Tenth Cohort that I sent out that day, less than 100 survived and of those, less than a third were unwounded. Of the 75 wounded survivors, 30 of them had wounds serious enough to need to be carried by litter, while seven of them would die the first night. The Sixth Cohort fared better, although not by that much, but the unanimous opinion expressed by every man of the Sixth was that Pilus Prior Gellius' quick thinking and calm under trying circumstances made the difference between their survival and suffering the same fate as the Tenth. Gellius survived, though he took an arrow through one forearm, while he had one Centurion killed, his Pilus Posterior, Titus Tullius, disemboweled by a cataphract's lance. Apparently, it took Tullius some time to die, for his men shuddered with horror when speaking of it. Of the remaining Centurions of the Sixth, none of them were unscathed, though only Gaius Capito the Hastatus Prior was seriously wounded, having had his left hand severed by a Parthian sword, meaning that as soon as we returned from campaign he would be retired. If he, and we, survive, I thought grimly as I surveyed the wax tablets that Diocles had prepared, tallying up the cost. Of the 416 effectives that marched out with the Sixth that day, 228 survived to return to camp, with more than 100 of these men wounded, perhaps 40 of them being litter cases. If I combined the Sixth and Tenth Cohorts, I still would not have one full-strength Cohort, I reflected, as I tried to decide what to do. My mind, however, was reeling from all that had transpired, and when I went to the *Praetorium*, my frame of mind was not improved. Gallus had somehow survived to be carried back to camp, despite his body being riddled with arrows and spears, some of which the surgeons could not remove without killing him instantly, but it mattered not, as he died that night. The original force of auxiliaries led by Gallus, both mounted and foot, being exposed outside the relative safety of the column the longest, were wiped out to the last man, the only survivors being in much the same condition as Gallus and dying soon after being carried back to camp. The four Cohorts of the Deiotaran Legion had suffered much the same fate as the Tenth, and were now a skeleton of what they were just a few watches before. The four Cohorts of the 30th, the men being relatively inexperienced and poorly led, suffered even more grievously, so that both the Deiotaran and the 30th were almost finished as fighting Legions. There were at least 1,500 Roman wounded, along with 2,000 auxiliaries, and about 1,000 cavalry wounded. Almost 3,000 men were left behind, dead on the field. The normal part of the *Praetorium*

R.W. Peake

used as a hospital was quickly overwhelmed, but the wounded could not be left outside exposed to the elements, or we would have even more corpses. The serious cases could not be carried to their own tents, since they needed to be placed where medical care was available. For some time, nobody knew what to do. The comrades of the wounded, the men who had not been called on to go out to slaughter, did their best to comfort and shelter their friends, standing over them and holding their own cloak above the wounded man in an attempt to shield him from the falling snow. Finally, someone came up with the idea of using the tents of those Cohorts, like my Tenth, who had been left out on the field and therefore would not be needing shelter any longer, to improvise an extension to the hospital. Given a task that they knew was vital to help keep friends alive, the unwounded survivors, along with those who had not participated in the battle worked frantically, dragging those tents designated for this endeavor over to the forum, where Antonius had directed that the shelter be erected. Tents were torn apart for the sections of leather that they provided, then hastily stitched backed together by the *immunes* who worked as tanners and leather workers into the new configurations, essentially creating several larger tents in which the wounded were sheltered. As with all things Roman, even in chaos there is order, as men were arranged by Cohort and Legion together in the same tent, unless they required more than one, which was the case with the 30th. When such activity is going on, the best thing a Centurion can do is get out of the way, letting the men who are actually doing the work get on with their jobs and just keep an eye on things to make sure the men do not slack, but I knew there was no question of that happening in this case. So I walked about just watching, until my men were settled into their spot before going to visit them, and it was while I was occupied in this task that I saw Marcus Antonius as he could have been and not as he was.

That night, Antonius seemed to be everywhere at once, circulating among the wounded with words of encouragement and praise. He spent time with the most seriously wounded, the men who were in the curtained area that we called Charon's Boat, which is designated for the doomed, whose life could be measured in thirds of a watch, praying over them and with those who were still conscious. To a man, none of the wounded blamed Antonius; in fact, they had as many words of encouragement for him as he for them. Normally, there is also a separate area for Centurions that have been wounded, but there was no room or time to set up the appropriate enclosure, so they were scattered among the rankers. I was sitting with Scaurus, conscious but in great pain, the poppy syrup reserved for men in greater agony, his chest now bound but still seeping blood through the bandage, when Antonius entered our tent. I watched as my men called to him, assuring their general that they would be up and about soon, ready to fight again and it was clear that Antonius was genuinely moved. He went into the Charon section of our tent, spending several moments inside before emerging, his eyes reddened. When he made his way towards where I was sitting with Scaurus, I was a bit apprehensive, wondering what he might say about my refusal to send more of my men out to slaughter. First, he stopped to share a joke with one of the men before walking over, looking down at Scaurus.

"Centurion. Scaurus, isn't it? What kind of nurse is Pullus? He taking good care of you?"

Both Scaurus and I were surprised that he remembered the name of the Decimus Princeps Posterior of the 10th Legion, but Scaurus managed a grin, replying cheerfully enough, "I've had better, sir. He's not as gentle as the Greeks."

"Well, at least you don't have to worry about guarding your backside around Pullus." Antonius grinned back at Scaurus, yet when he looked up at me, his eyes were anything but friendly.

"Primus Pilus, we need to talk."

I gulped but kept my voice steady, knowing there was only one answer expected. "Yes, sir. Now?"

He shook his head, heaving a sigh that seemed to contain all of the pain of every wounded man as he surveyed the moaning, suffering mass of men around him.

"Come find me in a third of a watch. I still have a few men to see."

I saluted, promising that I would find him and wondering if my career was finally over. Truly, at that point I did not much care.

I spent the time with the wounded, the last half of that in Charon, holding the hands of two men as they took passage in the boat. As many times as I had done this over the years, it never got any easier watching a man die. Next to the sexual act, it is the most personal exchange between two human beings. They both died bravely, Legionaries of Rome to the last, and it still makes me weep at the memory of seeing such brave souls wasted for nothing. I was spent, as if I had been in battle myself, but I had to put iron in my soul to face Antonius and at the appointed time, I went looking for him. Going first to the next hospital tent, the medicus there said he had left moments before and did not say where he was going, so I headed to the *Praetorium*. I do not know why, but I took the long way around, perhaps to gather my thoughts and regain my composure. Approaching a dark corner of the *Praetorium*, I heard a muffled cry, not an unusual sound in the camp that night, except that as I drew nearer, I realized that the figure from which the cries were coming was familiar. I stopped, unsure what to do. It was Antonius, huddled against the side of the tent, his head bowed with his *paludamentum* pulled around his face as he sobbed uncontrollably.

I shuffled my feet, but he did not seem to hear until I gave an awkward cough and I saw his body stiffen as he realized that someone was nearby.

"General," I called out hesitantly. "You told me to come looking for you, sir."

It took a moment for him to compose himself enough to reply, "Ah. Yes. Pullus."

He drew himself erect, and I saw his shoulders and massive chest rise as he took a deep breath before turning to face me, but I noticed he made sure to keep his face in shadows. For a moment, he said nothing, then he shook his head sadly, and I will say I was not expecting what came out of his mouth.

"Where did it go wrong, Pullus? What did I do wrong?"

I froze, not knowing what to say or do. If it had been Caesar, I would have answered him honestly, knowing that he would not hold my answer against me. However, this was Antonius, who was as changeable as the wind and I knew that brutal honesty was a huge risk to take with such a man. There was something about him this night, though, that was different, for I could sense that the pain and bewilderment he was feeling was real. The thought of Caesar encouraged me to follow his example when he crossed the Rubicon, as I let the dice fly.

"We should have turned back the minute we lost the baggage train," I said.

For an awful moment, I was sure that the dice had come up Dogs, because his posture stiffened. He stepped out of the shadows so that I could see his face, hard and unyielding, his reddish eyes staring into mine. Then, just as quickly, the moment passed and he slumped over, all the fight fleeing from his countenance as he nodded sadly.

"You're right. That was a huge mistake. But Artavasdes assured me that taking Phraaspa wouldn't be a challenge, that the defenders would crumble after just a couple of weeks."

"I don't think Artavasdes was ever on anyone's side other than his own, General."

"Just like every one of these Eastern *cunni*," he said savagely, spitting on the ground to emphasize the point. Turning back to me, he surveyed me for a moment before suddenly asking me, "You don't like me very much, do you, Pullus?"

"Not particularly," I admitted, cursing myself as the words came out of my mouth, thinking that it would serve me right if Antonius ordered my tongue to be cut from my mouth.

Yet, as I said, Antonius was ever changeable, because at this he threw back his head, laughing before surprising me further by reaching out to slap me on the shoulder.

"I would say that's an understatement," he said mischievously, and when he smiled at me, it was not so hard to see why so many of the men loved him.

Turning serious, he asked another question.

"Then why did you risk your career to warn me about what Canidius was doing at the rear of the column?"

I was astonished at the question, but it gave me an insight into how the men at the top of our world thought about things.

"General, just because I don't care for you personally doesn't mean that I'm willing to watch the army be cut to pieces. I wanted this expedition to succeed as much as any man, because I've never marched with an army that's been defeated and I don't want to start now."

"Don't go into politics, Pullus. You're much too honest for your own good," Antonius said lightly, before again turning to more serious matters. "But we are defeated, Pullus, as much as it galls me to say it."

I shook my head firmly.

"A setback isn't the same as a defeat, General. We're only defeated if we don't come back and try again."

"Maybe I was wrong about you and politics," he laughed. "I'll keep that in mind, and I'll swear to you now that we'll be back to avenge not just Crassus, but all the men that died today."

He looked at me thoughtfully then, not saying anything for moments as if he were deciding something.

"You no doubt know that Canidius is laying a large part of the blame for this debacle on you and your refusal to obey his order."

I had suspected as much, but hearing it spoken was still quite chilling.

"General, he wanted me to send two Cohorts out, after the first two didn't come back. It's my professional opinion that sending out just two Cohorts would have ensured them being chopped up like the first two. As it is roughly twenty percent of my Legion is gone, and I don't think having three Legions at sixty percent effectiveness would do the army any good right now."

Antonius looked puzzled.

"Two Cohorts? He said he ordered you to send five Cohorts."

I shook my head adamantly.

"That's not correct, sir. He ordered me to send two more Cohorts. If it had been five, and he had sent the Deiotarans as well, I would have gone myself, and that's what I told him."

His mouth set in a grim line as he nodded. It seemed to confirm something he had known.

"I know it's not correct. I already asked Frugi," he named one of the Tribunes on Canidius' staff, "and he remembers it as you do."

He began pacing, head down, clearly thinking.

"Still, he's a general, and strictly by regulation and custom his word is more reliable than that of even a Primus Pilus, or a Tribune for that matter."

I said nothing, not sure where he was heading so I waited for him to continue. I noticed he had a habit of rubbing the back of his neck when he was thinking, which he was doing now, still pacing. Finally, he seemed to reach a decision, turning to face me.

"But the simple fact is that I need you and the army more than I need Canidius. So this will come to nothing, and there will be no adverse entry in your record. However, I'm going to give you an ass chewing in front of Canidius the like of which you've never had before, even with Caesar. I have to throw him a bone. Understand?"

Indeed I did, and while I was not looking forward to the idea of a voice as formidable as Antonius' roaring at me, compared to the other possible outcomes, I was not likely to complain. With our business concluded, we went to our respective duties.

As I walked back to the Legion area, I grudgingly admitted that perhaps in some ways, Antonius could measure up to Caesar.

The dressing down happened the next morning, at the briefing just before the assembly that Antonius had called to address the army about the previous day's events. I stood at *intente* while Antonius roared and Canidius glowered, obviously unhappy that I was escaping with such a light punishment. I will say that Antonius was in fine form, inventing terms I had not heard, even from the time I was a *tiro* under Gaius Crastinus. From that meeting, I headed immediately out to the forum, which was packed with men standing jammed together, since so much of the space was taken up by the makeshift hospital tents. The sides were rolled up so that the men lying in the tents could hear what Antonius had to say. He mounted the rostra, wearing his scarlet *paludamentum*, instead of the black mourning cloak he had wanted to wear, but had been talked out of by Fonteius and Ahenobarbus, both calling it too much theater. Surveying the army first, he finally began to speak, it becoming clear very quickly why his funeral oration for Caesar was so renowned. First, he praised the 3rd Gallica for their resolute action in retrieving the remnants of Gallus' force, along with those who went to their rescue and failed. Turning his attention to the latter group of men, he was stern and uncompromising.

"What I witnessed as I led the 3rd Gallica to the aid of the fallen Tribune Flavius Gallus and his force was disgraceful! I saw men without any apparent wounds fleeing back to the safety of the column, discarding their shields and even their helmets in order to speed their flight! In doing so, you assured the fate of your fallen comrades, those brave men who did NOT flee.

Despite facing overwhelming odds, and yes, I admit that you were greatly outnumbered, but when has that ever stopped a Legionary of Rome, those men chose to stay and fight."

He paused, his cold eyes lingering on the Cohorts of the 30th, who had been the most egregious in this behavior and I was quietly thankful that my men had chosen to stand, with the majority of those who returned only doing so because they were seriously wounded, like the Optio who had lost an eye. Naturally, there were shirkers who turned to flee at the first opportunity, particularly in the Tenth Cohort, but there are ways to exact justice on men like that without any punishment ever being entered in the Legion diary. Hearing Antonius speaking, I resolved to make sure that happened sooner rather than later. Antonius' words were having an obvious effect, because the men he had singled out began crying out to him for forgiveness, one man even shouting that they should be decimated in order to appease Antonius. He listened impassively for a moment, then held up a hand as he shook his head.

"If there is any punishment to be meted out, let it be on my head. I am your general. I have led you to this place here in the wastes of Media. If there should be any punishment, let it be on me!" Turning his head skyward, he reached with both arms to the heavens as he called to the gods, "I, Marcus Antonius of the Antonian branch of the Julii, I have been favored more than most men by the gods, but now I offer myself in atonement for all offenses committed by this army. If you wish to punish this army for those offenses, let it be on my head! Jupiter *Optimus Maximus*, Mars, Bellona, and all other gods concerned with this endeavor, strike me down now!"

To a man, all eyes turned up, many of the men clearly expecting to see some sign, either in the form of a thunderbolt thrown down by Jupiter, or by a parting of the clouds and the appearance of the sun as a sign of his favor. Yet neither happened, even after several moments of waiting. After what seemed like a third of a watch, Antonius dropped his arms, turning his attention back to more earthly matters.

"We will not be marching today, in order to give the Centurions time to fill vacancies and for the wounded to have some time to recover. But tomorrow, we march, and I will tell you now that I pity any Parthian cur that dares to try and stop this army from marching to Artaxata!"

The men cheered at the top of their lungs, their spirits restored by their general, and despite my feelings towards Antonius, I was impressed. He was right, however; there was much work to do in order to set the Legion to rights.

The choice that faced me was what to do about the essentially non-existent Tenth Cohort. I had enough men in the Tenth Cohort to use to plump out the Sixth, making it a full Cohort, but that was not a real option because forming up with nine Cohorts was problematic in a number of the formations we used. On the other hand, fielding a Cohort of less than a hundred men was not viable either. Besides that problem, I had the issue of promoting Centurions into the slots emptied by death or by crippling wounds, as in the case of Capito. All of this had to be solved before we began the march the next day, since it was a long-standing army tradition that there are no unresolved issues before the army begins moving again after a battle. I suppose I should have counted myself lucky, since I did not have problems the scope of the 30th or

Deiotaran Legions, but I was not feeling that way as I sat in my tent, brooding over what to do. The First Century of the Tenth had less than a full section left, with its Optio dead, along with Nasica.

Finally, I decided to require the Pili Priores to give up twelve men from each of their Cohorts, along with the names of eligible candidates to fill the vacant Optio and Centurion slots. It was almost as if this was a new *dilectus*, but I did not have the luxury of time in making selections. Twelve men from each Cohort would require two close comrades from each Century because I did not want to separate men who had been together for so long. This would still put the Tenth Cohort at half-strength, suitable only for reserve duties and guarding baggage, but I felt it was the best I could do under the circumstances.

I called for Mallius and as soon as he arrived, I informed him that he was being promoted to Centurion, to take the post of Hastatus Posterior of the Tenth to replace the slain Corens. Naturally, he was very pleased, and I was sorry to lose him, but it was time for him to move up so I signed the warrant that he would take to the quartermaster to draw the appropriate uniform items from stores. I sighed as he left, thinking that was one that was done, but I had eleven slots to fill in the Tenth, and now I had to find an Optio for my Century. I worked through the night, the Pili Priores bringing me their list of names for both transfer to the Tenth and for promotion. I had to keep an eye out for the Pili Priores who tried to unload men who were problems, knowing that some of them would view this as a prime opportunity to quietly remove troublemakers in their Centuries and Cohorts, and in fact there were a few attempts to do as much, though not nearly as many as I thought there would be. I believe everyone involved understood the circumstances, knowing that while they might have helped themselves, it would be at the expense of the Legion as a whole, and by extension the army, and the army was in enough trouble without any extra help.

I promoted Frontinus to the Pilus Prior position while moving Scaurus up two spots to Pilus Posterior, with the idea that Frontinus would have to pull double duty with the help of the Second and Third's Optios, until Scaurus recovered. Varro had lost an eye, but had assured me from his litter that he would be fit to lead a Century, and in fact, that morning at the assembly he had been standing in front of the remnants of his Century with a bloody bandage across his ruined eye and ear. I moved him to the Princeps Prior slot, while from the Second Cohort came Scribonius' Optio Quintus Servius into the Princeps Posterior position. I filled the Hastatus Prior position from the Sixth Century with Gellius' Optio Decimus Aelius, who had distinguished himself in the battle. There were a number of *signiferi* positions open, but those were always left to the Centurions and men in the respective Century. I was thankful that, unlike the 30th and Deiotaran Legions, we had not lost our Cohort standards; losing some of our Century standards was bad enough. The Sixth did not take as long because I did not feel the need to pull men from other Cohorts, but I still had two slots to fill with the Centurions, since Capito would not be able to continue because of the loss of his hand. Taking Metellus' recommendation, I put the Optio from the Second of the Third, Aulus Cottius into the Hastatus Prior position then moved every other Centurion up, while from the Fifth Cohort came Spurius Macrinus to fill out the Sixth's Centurions. I was able to grab a third of a watch's sleep before I had to get up to supervise the breaking down of camp, the next challenge being what to do with the wounded.

The only good thing to come out of the debacle that had taken place two days before is that the gods had provided a means to transport the wounded with the horses and mules that were now spares because their riders and the sections of Legionaries whose burden they carried were dead. Despite having some wagons that had been designated for the *medici*, there were not nearly enough to carry all the injured. Wounded men who were able to ride were put on horseback, while men who were more seriously injured, still requiring to be transported by litter once the wagons were filled, were lashed between two mules. One man was lashed high on the animals' shoulders, the other suspended beneath him. I did not envy the man on the lower tier, but in most cases, the orderlies tried to put men who were still unconscious down there. Still, it had to be an extremely uncomfortable way to ride. Even doubling up with the casualties, several of the mules had to be overloaded so that there were enough animals to transport our wounded, since Antonius had promised the men that nobody alive would be left behind. Men were still dying of their wounds, while more would die along the way, but they would only be left when there was not a breath of life left in them.

As I was seeing to the men busily packing up, a runner came from the *Praetorium*, summoning me to attend to the Triumvir. I hurried to the headquarters tent, which is always the last tent struck when the army breaks camp. The men designated for the task were standing by, waiting for the command when I entered. Antonius was dictating the last orders to a scribe, while the rest of the staff was breaking down the desks, stools, and all the various paraphernalia that runs the bureaucracy of the army. Seeing me, he dismissed the clerk, then waved me over, returning my salute. His face was impassive, but his tone was not as unfriendly as it had been in the past when we spoke.

"Pullus, I want the 10th as rearguard today," he told me.

I froze, about to protest, then recognizing that given all that had transpired this was not the time to do so, said nothing. Instead, I merely nodded, sensing there was more, and there was.

"You can expect the Parthians to press hard because they have the scent of blood in their nostrils," he said grimly. "I'm going to post the slingers and the remaining javelineers with you as a buffer between your Legion and the Parthians as they seem to have the best effect against them."

This was a sound tactic, though it was not my place to say, but he was not through.

"However, I don't expect them to be able to hold them off for long. As I said, these *cunni* think that we're crippled and are going to want to finish us off. When they either overwhelm the missile troops or push them back through your ranks, they're going to be on top of you next. But I've come up with something that I think will give them a surprise."

He outlined what he had in mind. My respect for Marcus Antonius went up one more notch, and it was with more confidence in my general than I had ever felt before that I saluted him, promising I would carry out his orders in a manner that would do credit to him and the 10th Legion.

The Parthians were in plain sight as we pulled out, the army now beginning the long sweeping westward turn towards Artaxata. The men took the news of being the rearguard with an air of grim determination, every man losing a friend from the Sixth or Tenth Cohort, making them eager to exact revenge. As we waited for the rest of the army to begin the march, I called a meeting of all the Centurions, informing them of what Antonius had planned for the moment the Parthians came. Turning to Scribonius and Trebellius, I told them that they would be joining the First Cohort at the rear of the *quadratum*, both men nodded their understanding. With the instructions given, we formed up, then began to move out when it was our turn.

Before we had gone a mile, the Parthians descended on the remnants of our camp, intent on plunder, but unless they wanted some discarded odds and ends of dead men that their comrades did not want, they came away empty handed. With our cavalry keeping an eye on the Parthians, we marched facing forward so that we could make good time, saving the stage when we would have to move backwards for the moments when it would be needed. The slingers and javelineers were lightly armed and unencumbered with the load that the Legionaries were, meaning they were forced to slow their pace when we began marching uphill and the going was tougher. Ascending onto a plateau that extended for several miles, behind us the Parthians circled, silently watching, waiting for their chance. It came a few thirds of a watch later when the time came to descend the plateau, which could only be accomplished by squeezing into a narrow defile through which the *quadratum* would not fit. Therefore, the army was forced to compact itself into essentially a column of files of Legion size. As the vanguard proceeded down the defile, the rest of the column was forced to come to a halt, which is when the Parthians struck like a black wave, galloping their horses full speed at the rear of the column. The slingers began whirling their arms above their heads, waiting for the first of the horse archers to come within range, and when they did, loosed their lead shot. The missiles smashed into flesh of man and beast, except this time it only slowed down the Parthian charge, there being too many of them for our force of slingers to defeat singlehandedly.

Now the horse archers were in range, beginning their swooping circles as they fired at the slingers, felling some of them with their first volley. There were so many archers this time that it seemed as if it was impossible to see sky in between the arrows streaking through the air. Our javelineers began flinging their missiles, and while some found their mark, again it was simply not enough to stop the horde of enemy so it was not long before our men began taking the inevitable step backwards. With light infantry, however, they are trained not to take that step grudgingly. Unlike the heavy infantry who, when doing so, keep their faces turned toward the enemy, the more lightly armed men immediately turned to flee for the safety of their lines. The moment their retreat began, we knew that it would be a matter of a few heartbeats before they came streaming through our lines. Our missile troops were now running for their lives, though several of them did not make it, falling screaming to the ground with an arrow, or often more than one, sticking out of their backs. While we watched helplessly, the archers would gallop up to those men still alive, finishing them as they lay with their arms upstretched, clearly begging for mercy. I watched intently, not because I had any morbid curiosity or desire to watch men of our army die, but because to pull Antonius' tactic off, timing was everything. Once the archers finished the last fallen men off, they wheeled their mounts and without any overt signal began galloping towards where we were waiting for them. Turning to Valerius, when I judged the moment to be right, I gave the signal that the men had been told to expect, putting the core of Antonius' plan in motion.

What Antonius had outlined was a modified form of *testudo*, where we sacrificed mobility for defense, the plan being the creation of a wall of shields on which the Parthian wave would break and be severely damaged. The moment the *cornu* sounded the signal for *testudo*, instead of compacting our lines by Century, we maintained them, while the front rank of men kneeled as they brought their shield up in front of them. The second rank stepped between each kneeling man, placing the rim of their shield on top of the kneeling man's shield, while the third rank stepped between the men of the second rank, raising their shields high enough to set the bottom of their shield on the top rim of the second row before tipping them backwards at an angle. The fourth and final rank of every Century tipped their shields so they were held parallel to the ground, above the rest of their comrades in the front ranks, while the Cohorts on the side of the *quadratum* did the same thing. This meant that even when the Parthians attempted to overlap our lines, they were faced with the same line of defense. And this time, unlike the last, I sent a mounted courier that had been detached to me for my use, galloping to the front of the column to inform Antonius that the attack he expected was happening. Even when faced with this defense, the archers advanced to begin loosing arrow after arrow at us, but while some of the iron heads punctured the wall of shields, most glanced harmlessly off those held at an oblique angle. In fact, the biggest problem created by this hailstorm was the terrible racket it made as the missiles clattered against the wood, or sometimes made a clanging sound when the iron head struck the boss of a shield. The men, once they saw that they were relatively safe, began joking and making light of the whole experience. Despite my happiness to see them in such good spirits, I knew that it was not over, so I continually reminded the men that this was only the first phase of the plan, that the Parthians would not be content just to fire arrows.

After several volleys of arrows had no effect, the horse archers retired, shaking their bows at us in impotent rage, with our men jeering while making their own gestures at the retreating Parthians, something I was content to allow until some men took it too far, dropping their shields to free their hands to bare their backsides.

"The next man who does that I'll flay," I roared.

Men scrambled to pick their shields back up while I pointed out that they had done so just in time, the ground beginning to shake as between the retreating archers the cataphracts came thundering towards us, lances lowered.

"Steady on," I ordered, stopping some of the men in their tracks who looked as if they were about to move prematurely to spring the second surprise Antonius had ordered.

Clearly taking the sight of our men kneeling as a sign that they were exhausted already, since I do not believe the Parthians would otherwise have tried to attack our shield wall, the heavily armored horses were gaining momentum. The ground began vibrating with every foot that passed under their hooves. I had to give the command to hold steady twice more, until I judged the moment to be perfect. Turning to give the order, I had Valerius give a single blast on his *cornu*, instead of the normal signal for the porcupine. However, I had briefed the Centurions to expect this and all down the line I could hear their own commands ring out as the men in the first two ranks picked up the siege spears that they had been issued, then thrust them out, the wall of shields now bristling with gleaming iron points attached to stout wooden shafts. Unlike our normal javelin, the siege spear has a broad leaf head attached to a heavy shaft and it is not designed to bend like those that we throw. They are also two feet longer than the javelin, meaning they protruded from beyond the shields farther than if we had used our normal missile weapons. We had drawn the spears from the Legion stores when we were given the rearguard and now they promised death to the onrushing Parthians.

Some of the cataphracts managed to skid to a halt, but they were mostly to the rear of the mass of horsemen, the majority of the horses in the front ranks slamming into the waiting spear points because of their own weight and momentum. The broad iron heads punched through the protective armor that covered the chests of the beasts. All along the line men were shoved backwards, the mass of horseflesh meeting the resistance of the spears and shields, while above the thunder of hooves came the shrieks of animals in mortal pain and terror. Some of the riders were flung from the back of their mounts as if they were shot from a ballista, flying over the heads of the kneeling men and even the men of the second line. They came crashing down into the midst of our ranks, the men surrounding them thrusting down with their swords into the open faces of the Parthians' helmets with brutal efficiency. Parthians who were able to, savagely wrenched their wounded mounts away from the points of the spears, some of their horses staggering away from the danger, allowing their riders to dismount safely while others, maddened by pain and fear, galloped furiously away with their riders clinging to their backs for their lives. Many horses were unable to free themselves, their plight not helped by the mass of horseflesh behind them that only now was beginning to slow but still pushed forward. Hooves thrashed as the heavily armored horses toppled over on their sides, those riders quick or lucky enough to throw themselves free finding themselves dodging thrusts from the spears of men in the second rank whose point had not buried itself in a target. Many of the riders in the front rank, those that were not thrown to land among us, were trapped underneath the massive weight of their wounded beasts, and were at our mercy. The impetus of the attack was spent as quickly as it had built, so judging the moment to be right for the final blow, I had Valerius give the second single blast of the *cornu*, while I blew my own whistle for the men of my Century. Leaping to their feet, the men in the front rank turned to the side to allow the men of the remaining ranks to come hurtling through the gaps created by the action, clambering over the bodies of the horses and men of the front of the Parthian charge, stopping only long enough to end those cataphracts trapped beneath their mounts. That done, the men charged forward with a roar, intent on exacting vengeance for the men of the Sixth and Tenth Cohort.

"Kill these *cunni*," I snarled as I ran forward with my men, freed from the need to supervise and direct, finally able to kill with everyone else.

Just as we had at the Cilician Gates, we moved more quickly than the cataphracts could manage to wheel their mounts to flee, jumping underneath the bellies while thrusting up with our swords. The men who were still carrying their siege spears used them to go after the riders, three or four men surrounding one cataphract who would flail about with his sword or lance in a desperate attempt to fend his attackers off that invariably failed, whereupon another Parthian would fall screaming from his horse, pierced through every part of his body. It was complete mayhem and chaos, nothing but a gutter fight as men growled, spit, and cursed their hatred of this Parthian scum who skulked around us, refusing to fight in a manner befitting men. Only after we managed to kill a few hundred more Parthians did the men in the rear manage to move far enough away so that the Parthians closer to us were able to turn their own mounts to gallop to safety, leaving heaps of men and horses behind. My men stood panting, catching their breath after the short, furious fight. As soon as they recovered, I directed them to move through the bodies to finish horses and men, telling them to start with the horses first. I not only wanted the Parthians bastards to suffer, as always I felt badly for the horses that were given no choice in their fate. Some of the beasts were either unhurt, or only lightly injured, but had been taken to the ground by another horse next to them. These mounts were led back to the center of the column to be used as remounts for our cavalry. I put the slingers back out as a protective screen while we finished our business, but the Parthians wanted no part of us, at least for the time being, pulling a safe distance away to regroup. Hurrying the men along, I did not want to keep the column waiting, but they were experienced, stripping the bodies of anything valuable quickly. Within a third of a watch from the start of the attack, we were formed back up, ready to move again. Only this time the pile of corpses belonged almost completely to the Parthians, the men feeling that the deaths of their comrades had been at least partially avenged.

Once through the defile, we reformed in the
quadratum, but we had no trouble from the Parthians
for the rest of that day, or the next few for that matter.
They resumed their station at our rear, with riders
arrayed on either flank, stalking us as the column
plodded along, the weather turning worse every day.
Actually, it was more a case that it got bad and just did
not improve from one day to the next, the snow
beginning to pile up to make movement more difficult.
The more seriously wounded began to die off, the
decision being made that their bodies were to be
stripped of their tunic and armor, and most
importantly their cloak, at least those that were not
soaked with blood, for other men who still had a
chance of survival to use. Compounding matters was
that we were now down to quarter rations, bringing
out the worst in many men, with quarrels now an
everyday occurrence at the end of the day's march. A
large number of sections had sacrificed their grain
grinders, left behind after the disastrous battle in order
to make space for wounded comrades, because of all of
our equipment it is one of the heaviest items and takes
up the most space. Other sections chose to keep their
grinders, so they were now charging their more selfless
comrades exorbitant fees to grind their comrades'
grain. This was something I would not tolerate and as
soon as I discovered who the culprits were in my
Legion, I went with their Centurion to pay a midnight
visit to each of the ringleaders, putting a stop to the
problem quickly. One man in particular who was the
most egregious ended up with several broken ribs
when he fell repeatedly on his way to the latrine, yet
somehow he thought it wiser to keep himself off the
sick and injured list, which was filling with men who
came by their maladies more honestly. Sadly, not every

Centurion in every Legion took the same view as I did, I suspect because they were receiving a cut of the proceeds from the profiteers in their Century.

Additionally, men were developing deep, raspy coughs from inhaling the icy air, along with nosebleeds. It felt as if every breath was composed of thousands of tiny, razor sharp knives that you drew into your lungs. Some of the weaker men became feverish, so that as quickly as one litter would empty due to a wounded man succumbing to his injuries, it would fill with a shaking, delirious one. Still the Parthians did not attack, but neither did they go away, continuing to plod along at the same pace as our army. Occasionally, the more ambitious among them would come swooping in to loose as many arrows as they could manage before our cavalry would arrive to drive them off. They very seldom hit anyone, yet every so often, there would be a lucky shot, with a man falling to the ground to writhe in pain, calling for help from his comrades. At the end of every day, the distance we covered would measure a little less than the day before as the men steadily weakened, yet somehow they summoned the energy to fight amongst themselves over a few kernels of grain. Once camp was established, the Centurions did not have time to rest as they ran from one fight to the next, trying to break things up before men got seriously hurt, but they were not always successful. In the Fifth Cohort, a man stabbed his close comrade to death because he was convinced that the man who was his closest friend in the Legion since they were *tiros* was hoarding his grain ration and not sharing it. When it turned out that he was wrong; a thorough search of the man's belongings having turned up not a single kernel, the offending Legionary was so distraught that we did not even have to bother to go through the trouble of a tribunal, as he fell on his sword. Tragedies similar to this were happening in every Legion, as boon companions quarreled as they never had before over any loot, no matter how valuable it may have been, this time over a piece of moldy bread. I must say that Antonius did his best to stop the men from killing each other, though he did not do much to stop the profiteering. However, I can see how it would have been next to impossible for the commanding general to do much when some Centurions were determined to hide it from him. Even the very ground over which we marched seemed to be conspiring with the elements and lack of food, the terrain becoming even more broken and undulating. Nonetheless, the Mardian had to that point at least been correct about the availability of firewood. If it were not for the fires at night, even more men would have died, yet despite the warmth, roughly one man a day from each Cohort was succumbing to the elements or lack of food. Our progress was marked by the pale, naked corpses of Legionaries and the few auxiliaries who remained, so that if one chose to look behind the army, they would see the air dotted with vultures and other carrion birds circling above. I wondered if they had ever eaten as well in this land that seemed to have nothing of sustenance in it besides us.

Through it all, Gaius Porcinus was irrepressibly cheerful, despite clearly suffering as much as any of his comrades. His face was drawn, the skin on it peeling off from the constant abrasion of the icy blast of the wind, yet there was always a smile on his face whenever he saw me. Although I suspected it was for my benefit, his attitude did more for me than he knew, because I was suffering more than I ever had on any march. My old chest wound would tighten up during the night when I tried to snatch a couple watches' worth of sleep so that I had to have Diocles' help to put on my armor every morning, unable as I was to raise my arms above my head. My body ached as it never had before, and despite the fact that it was no different from any of the other men, in the past I had never seemed to suffer as acutely as the others. Now that I was, it was very hard to cope with, greatly affecting my frame of mind. I became extremely short-tempered with the other Centurions, until finally Scribonius came to me one night. We had long since run out of wine, so all I could offer was water, but at least it was heated up and felt good going down. He sat in silence for several moments, eying me over the rim of his cup, until I finally set my own down to stare hard at him.

"What's on your mind? Spit it out instead of looking at me like a Suburan whore sizing up a prospect."

Pursing his lips, he seemed to consider what he was about to say carefully. I suppose he had good reason to do so, though I did not recognize it at that moment, snarling at him to speak up or get out.

"You're being . . . difficult," he said finally.

"Difficult? What does that even mean? Am I supposed to give each of you a hug goodnight and tuck you in?"

He laughed, and even as sour as I felt, I had to grin at my own wit.

"No, Titus, we don't expect you to tuck us in." The smile left his face. "But neither do we expect you to snap our heads off over things that are hardly worth getting angry over."

"So I'm a little short-tempered lately." I knew I sounded defensive, but I could not seem to help myself. "I can't always be levelheaded and sweet as honey."

"Nobody is asking that of you, Titus, but you know as well as I do that I'm talking about something else entirely."

He leaned forward, looking at me intently as he spoke. "I know this march is the hardest we've ever been on, and we've been on some bad ones, but I never once have seen you react to the pressure the way you have these last few days. So tell me, what's going on? Is it because you're worried about Porcinus if he gets sick?"

"That's part of it," I admitted, for it was a topic that occupied my thoughts more than it should have.

"Then what else? What has you so raw these days?"

"I'm getting old," I blurted out, both relieved and horrified that I had finally managed to utter aloud what had been gnawing at me.

I could feel the heat rising to my face at this confession of weakness, yet it had been quite some time since I had felt so insecure, and there was no person other than Scribonius that I would have dared to discuss this with. However, I was not prepared for his reaction, which was to burst out laughing, throwing his head back, opening his mouth wide. Now the blood in my body was pumping, as I gripped the cup so tightly that it might have shattered, yet Scribonius was enjoying himself too much to notice. Truthfully, I was as bewildered as I was angry, and not a little hurt. Finally, he wiped his eyes, then looked at me, still chuckling.

"Oh, Titus! You're not *getting* old; you ARE old."

This was not going at all as I had thought it would. I expected a reassurance from my friend that it was all in my imagination, that I was as good as I ever was, so I waited, hoping that this would be forthcoming from Scribonius. I was to be disappointed in one sense, but as ever, Secundus Pilus Prior Scribonius was a man of surprises.

Seeing my face, he shook his head, then said, "Titus, what's happening to you happened to most of us years ago. You tire more easily, you have aches in places you never had them before, you can't see as well as you could. Am I right?"

I nodded.

"How old are you now?"

I no longer worried about the long-ago secret of my enlisting a year early. It turned out Scribonius had known from our initial training, when Vibius had told him. The fact that Scribonius never divulged to me that he knew until I told him revealed more of his trustworthiness than any oath he could have taken, no matter how sacred.

"I'm about to turn 42 in April."

Now he nodded, replying, "I'm 45, about to turn forty-six, and I started noticing more than five years ago. Balbus is 47, and he told me that he's been going steadily downhill for ten years. And Cyclops?"

There was no need for him to expand on Cyclops, for his decline was plain and sad to see. This would surely be his last campaign, whether he chose it to be or not, and I fervently hoped that he would make the decision voluntarily.

"You're just going through what everyone else has been going through for the last few years. It just started later with you because . . . well, because you're Titus Pullus, hero of the 10th Legion."

He grinned as I grinned back. It was only then that I noticed that he was missing a couple teeth, while more were broken off. I do not mean to say that I had not noticed before, it is just that its implication only hit me at that moment, comprehending that this was yet another thing that I had escaped, since I still had all of my teeth and they were still in good shape. Then I felt the grin flee from my face.

"But I'm not everyone else," I said glumly. "I'm the Primus Pilus. I can't be like everyone else."

"And who says that Primi Pili aren't allowed to grow old?" he asked gently.

I knew that he was right, but truthfully, I wanted to feel sorry for myself, so I was unwilling to accept the wisdom he was offering.

"Not me," I said firmly. "Even if other Primi Pili do, Titus Pullus doesn't."

I could tell I was trying Scribonius, because his voice was tinged with impatience as he sighed and said, "Titus, you should thank the gods that it's just starting now. No mortal man can cheat the gods of their due, and you may be many things, but you're not a god. You're not immortal."

And that was the kernel of it, right there. As much death as I had been around, and been involved in, as many people who I loved that were taken from me, deep in the darkest, most secret part of my being I believed that I was truly blessed by the gods, that I could not die. I do not think I am unique; in fact, I think most people have that belief, yet for whatever reason, it was dispelled at some earlier point in their lives. And for equally obscure reasons, I had never come to that moment of realization and recognition that I was indeed like every other human, until that march in Parthia. As I thought about it, I recognized that even at moments when I was sure I was about to die, as at Mutina, when I almost did, there was a spark in me that denied that this was even a possibility, while the fact that I survived only reinforced that belief. Now, sitting in a tent with the wind howling, making the leather walls shudder and shake, I was forced to acknowledge the truth in what Scribonius was saying. We sat in silence for several moments, then I shrugged.

"You're right. But that doesn't mean I have to like it."

Scribonius laughed again. However, this time I joined him, and we toasted each other with our cups of tepid water.

"To aging gracefully," he said.

"Never," I shot back.

After our talk, my mood did not improve, necessarily, but I was careful to keep my temper in check, so that soon enough the men were no longer scrambling to hide whenever I came along.

There is a saying in the army that the best way to ensure that things will get worse is to declare that it is not possible for it to happen. We were still supposedly days away from the Aras River, which marked the boundary between Media and Armenia, where Antonius assured us that Artavasdes would be waiting for us with supplies. Why he thought the Armenian king who had abandoned us when the baggage train was destroyed would do so I could not determine. The mountains were completely covered in snow, rearing above us even higher than we already were. Then, after crossing a nondescript ridge to descend into a broad mountain valley, the landscape altered. Where before there was sufficient scrub brush and stunted trees to supply firewood, now we had entered a land where it seemed that it was picked clean of anything remotely flammable. The men did not notice at first, dazed and deadened to the monotony of putting one foot in front of the other as they struggled for breath, while dreaming of warm loaves of bread drenched in olive oil. In fact, I did not notice either; it was young Gaius who first brought it to my attention when I made one of my several trips ostensibly to check on the Second Cohort. The men in Gaius' Century had long since seen through the pretense, but they were unlikely to bring it up to Gaius. This was not because they were worried that Gaius would complain to me if they gave him any grief about it, but because Gaius was so well liked that they were happy to see that the Primus Pilus cared enough to check on him. Of course, I did not learn this until later; as far as I was concerned, the men were oblivious to my real purpose, blithely accepting my fiction. Now, Gaius was not smiling, which was unusual in itself.

He had a puzzled frown on his face, obviously so perplexed that he made no attempt to keep his voice down when he spoke. "Uncle Titus, do you notice anything strange?"

I followed his gaze out into the bleak countryside, now covered in a thin blanket of white, with drifts piling against the base of the rolling hills, filling the gullies that are a feature of the land that we were marching through. At first, I did not see anything remarkable and was about to make him point out what he was referring to, grumbling to myself that my vision was getting worse with each passing day. Then something registered in my mind, telling me that there was a problem, but at that moment, I did not know what it was. Whirling around to look on the opposite side of the column, I trotted a few feet to the side to look ahead. My heart felt as if it were being squeezed by an invisible hand; there was not a speck of vegetation in sight, at least nothing sufficient to start and maintain a fire.

Moving quickly back to his side, I whispered urgently to him, "Yes, I see it too. There's no wood. Now listen to me, Gaius. Say nothing about this right now. If the others notice, then so be it, but don't point it out. I need to get up to the general and find out if this guide is taking us someplace where there's wood and this is just something we're passing through."

He nodded his understanding, yet there was no hiding the worry in his eyes.

"This is very bad, isn't it, Uncle?"

There was no point lying to the boy, but I could not find the words, so I just nodded, then went trotting up the column to find Antonius.

When I found Antonius, his face was wrapped with a scarf so that only his eyes showed and he was deep in conversation with the Mardian guide, who was assuring him that we would at most be one night in a stretch of land where there was no firewood.

"One night?" I heard Antonius roar, despite his voice being muffled by the scarf. "One night in this and the rest of the wounded will die, as will the men with fever!"

The guide, who I had learned was named Cyrus, shrugged helplessly.

"It is only this stretch, Marcus Antonius, and if we were down there," he gestured to the south, down the slope of the mountain range we were traversing to the lower elevations, "we would be in open territory and would be nothing but walking targets for the Parthian arrows."

What he was saying was undoubtedly true, as there was a wide, open valley with no cover, perfect terrain for the Parthians. Still, it did not make what Antonius said any less true either. Antonius gave a growl of frustration, turning to me.

"What do you want?" His tone was less than friendly, but I did not hold it against him.

"You're talking about it, and I know what's facing us, General. What I need to know from you is what you want the Centurions to tell the men."

I saw his brows come together, a sure sign that he was about to explode in anger. Fortunately, the moment passed and he shook his head wearily.

"That's a good question, Pullus." He thought a moment, then said, "Tell them the truth. Tell them what Cyrus just said, that we'll go without tonight, but there'll be wood further along the march. Make sure they understand that the hardship they'll suffer tonight is still better than the alternative."

I saluted, making my way back to the Legion, refusing to do the smart thing by just waiting for them to march by, as it would smack of weakness. Calling the Pili Priores over, they reported that some of the men had noticed what Gaius had pointed out to me. Telling them to spread the word as Antonius had ordered, I returned to my Cohort to do the same. Despite our assurances, it was clear that the men were worried, so that for the first time in a few days they were interested in surveying their surroundings as we continued the march. That night in camp, the men were forced to either eat what baked bread they had squirreled away, which very few had, or gnaw on raw grain. Thanks to Diocles, I still had a partial loaf left over, as he was always vigilant about husbanding our resources. Also, because of my fondness for meat, I always got a portion of whatever animals were slaughtered after they had died, which of course did not help when there was no fire. Most of the meat went to the auxiliaries, since the Legionaries generally disdained eating mule and horsemeat, even under the most extreme circumstances. In fact, they would only do so under direct orders, which for some reason Antonius had yet to order. The rumor around camp was that we would be going to barley the next day, which I knew to be fact, making the mood in the army sink lower watch by watch and furlong by furlong. The only way we could keep the sick and wounded alive that night was for men to volunteer to wrap up with one of them to share their bodily heat, though we had no shortage of volunteers, as these were friends and comrades. I was not sure how much longer this spirit would remain with the men; it had been my experience that there was a certain point where men stopped thinking about their comrades and started worrying about themselves to the exclusion of everyone else. I had not seen it happen often, but when it did it was ugly and with the Parthians skulking about, it could spell the destruction of the army.

It was that night that the price of what wheat was available reached its all-time high. Diocles reported to me that men were paying 50 sesterces for an Attic quart of wheat, while other men were digging up the few plants growing around camp and eating them, whether they knew what they were or not. Very few men got any sleep that night, myself included as we sat huddled and shivering, talking through the night, afraid to go to sleep because of the danger of freezing to death. It was one of the few times that men did not mind, and in fact sought walking posts on guard duty because it was the best way to keep from freezing. The men on stationary posts were not so lucky, and when the *bucina* signaled it was time to rouse ourselves to begin breaking down camp, three men were found frozen to death, still standing at their posts. Their Optio, who should have been walking posts to check on the men, had been huddled with a couple of other Optios, keeping warm. He was immediately busted back down to the ranks, but his sentence of flogging was suspended, as it would have undoubtedly killed him. Despite deserving it, Antonius' grip on the army was slipping so he did not want to inflame the men further by giving the order. This incident happened in the 7th, and Caecina tried to change Antonius' mind about the flogging, arguing that it would in fact help morale because the Optio's actions had led directly to the death of some of his men. Still, Antonius was not willing to take the chance, suspending the sentence. From my perspective, it was the kind of situation that no matter what Antonius did, he would be condemned by one portion of the army; while the men might indeed applaud his decision, the Optios and most of the Centurions would not. This was the state of the army, with at least another ten days to the Aras River.

The next day saw another skirmish between the Parthians and the army, this one taking place between the remnants of the Gallic cavalry, along with some of the Galatian horsemen who still survived. The attack was fended off with light losses on both sides, but the need for constant attention, with the sudden flurry of activity when the alarm sounded signaling an attack taking place somewhere in the column, was taking its toll. Also, contrary to what Cyrus said, there was no wood after that day either, so consequently there were more deaths by freezing. Men who had never spoken a cross word to each other were now quarreling constantly, with these arguments now just as likely to break out in the middle of the march as they were once we settled into camp, another sign that discipline and morale was breaking down even further. The 10th was not immune, and neither was my Century. Before the midday stop one day, I was alerted by the sounds of men shouting behind me. Running down the formation, I found two men rolling on the ground, their packs lying where they had dropped them, their friends making no attempt to separate them, instead shouting encouragement as they snarled and pummeled each other. So far, neither had tried to pull a weapon, but I knew that unless I intervened, it was only a matter of time.

"On your feet," I roared, yet for the first time that I could remember, I was completely ignored, at least by the two combatants.

The other men stopped cheering to look at me warily, but I was more concerned with the two men as I strode over closer. By this time my new Optio, a man named Numerius Lutatius, had arrived from the far end of the column, and I pointed to one of the men, telling him to grab him while I took the other. Reaching down, I grabbed the man by the collar and was hauling him to his feet when, without looking back, he turned, taking a wild swing. If it were not for my height it would have caught me full on the jaw, but instead hit me in the chest, right on my old wound. Lightning flashes of intense pain shot through me, my knees buckling for a moment, while there was a roaring in my ears, the white landscape growing dim. Somehow, I know not how, I managed to keep my feet, my head gradually clearing and I saw that I had not lost my grip on his collar. The man had realized by now what he had done; he stared at me wide-eyed with fear because it is an automatic death penalty offense to strike a Centurion. I recognized the man, causing my knees to go weak again; it was Vellusius, one of my original tentmates from the first days of the 10th Legion. The other man was in the grip of the Optio, while all of their friends were standing as if they were the sentries who had frozen to death the night before. I could feel all eyes on me as they waited to see what I would do. While I stood there, unbidden by my conscious mind the faces of those first comrades sprung up before my inner eye. Calienus, our first Sergeant from whom I had learned so much, and whose woman I had taken after his death; the twins we called Romulus and Remus, their real names Quintus and Marcus Mallius; Marcus Atilius, whose execution I had ordered when he was found with three dead civilians during winter quarters. There was Spurius Didius, the bane of my early years in the army but for whom I had developed a grudging affection, simply because he had survived for so long, until the loss of a leg had forced him from the Legion. I even thought of Quintus Artorius, the weakling who was the first to be weeded from our midst. Then, there was Vibius Domitius, oldest but no longer dearest friend, living a life of peace and quiet, or so I hoped, despite all that had taken place between us. All of these men were dead or gone, so that now only Scribonius, Vellusius, and I remained. And here was Vellusius, staring at me, his lips moving in what I assumed was some silent prayer and I knew that I could not have him executed. I had done that once, because I had no choice, and if I were to follow the regulations and customs of the armies of Rome since long before any of us could remember, he would be the second. However, over the years I had learned that sometimes it was just as important to ignore the regulations as to obey them. My chest was throbbing and truly I was still angry, so ignoring the pain, I hit Vellusius with an open-handed slap, drawing my arm back as far as it would go, putting all of my power behind it, hitting him on the side of his head. His feet flew up in the air as he sailed several feet backwards and I have to say that it was satisfying to see the result of what I could still do when I put my mind to it. Even with an open hand, he was out cold before he hit the ground.

Breathing hard from the exertion and the pain, I turned to point at the other combatant, still in Lutatius' grip, commanding, "You're going to carry Vellusius until he wakes up. Understand?"

He gulped, but nodded his head.

Then, I turned to walk back to the front of the column, calling over my shoulder as I did, "Tell Vellusius when he wakes up that he hits like a girl."

I was happy to hear the men chuckling as I left.

Without wood to heat the water, eating snow was a death sentence because it froze a man's insides, so as much of it as was available to us, it was still the same as being in a desert. The Centurions had been diligent about forcing men to conserve water, but the barrels were still down to the dregs while men's skins were sloshing with every step as they were being drained a little at a time. Toward the end of the day that I broke up the fight, outriders returning from their futile attempts at foraging reported that they had been approached by Parthians, either waving a flag of truce or with their bows unstrung as a sign that they meant no harm. They claimed that after the last repulse, the men of the Parthian army had agitated to make it clear to Phraates that they saw no chance of breaking our *quadratum* and that they were suffering as much as we were and wanted to go home. To that end, these Parthians informed our foragers that their army was turning away, returning back to Parthia while only the Medians, in whose land we were still located, would be following us for just two or three more days to make sure we were indeed headed for the Aras River. News like that cannot be kept from the men of an army, word shooting through the ranks as quick as Pan, the excited chatter of the men at least occupying them and keeping them from dwelling on their current misery. I was not as easily moved, thinking back to all the treachery that had been an integral part of this campaign, but I did not wish to dampen the men's hopes.

We passed another night in misery, at least physically, although the thought of the Parthian army quitting their pursuit kept the men warm in spirit. Even so, the next morning dawned to another row of bodies. The wounded were still dying, although some men had actually managed to recover enough to leave their litters to rejoin the ranks. Unfortunately, for every such man there was at least one who had taken ill and now occupied the recently vacated litter. The most bizarre and tragic of these were some men, including a half-dozen from the 10th who dug up one of the native plants that turned out to be not only inedible but poisonous, except it was not quick-acting. The men who ate of this plant, both root and leaves, were first robbed of their senses, to the point that many of them stumbled about dragging rocks from one part of the camp to the next, only to then grab the same rocks and return them to their original position. When friends tried to stop them, they became extremely agitated. The affected men were taken to see the medical staff, who gave them the normal antidote for poison, which is unwatered wine, yet the antidote had the opposite effect intended. These men without exception died in agony, frothing at the mouth before convulsing in their last moments. In the space of moments, I lost six men from the Legion; in total I had lost more than 200 men just to illness and exposure. Combined with the men I had lost in the battle with Gallus, the losses of the 10th Legion now totaled more than 600 men, but the worst was still ahead.

As I recall, it was the next day that another unusual event occurred, the appearance of a Parthian nobleman named Mithradates, who was escorted into camp at the end of the day's march. He claimed to be a cousin of the traitor Monaeses, the Parthian who Antonius had rewarded, in turn repaying Antonius and the army with treachery by being the main leader of the Parthians, finally being positively identified by some of Antonius' officers who knew him by sight. This Mithradates told Antonius that, as they had done before, the story told by the Parthians of leaving to return home was a ploy to throw Antonius off his guard. The problem confronting Antonius was the lack of water exacerbated by the lack of wood to heat snow, so he had been seriously considering going down off the mountainside to the lower elevations, but Mithradates insisted that this was exactly what Monaeses wanted us to do. That was where the Parthians were waiting, he insisted, and if we went down there we would share Crassus' fate, which was perhaps the most compelling thing he could have said to Antonius, because it was no secret that he worried about sharing that disgrace. Antonius immediately called a council of his officers and the Primi Pili, seemingly sincere about wanting our input, yet another sign that he was worried. Cyrus agreed with Mithradates, but also admitted that here on the side of the mountains water was nowhere to be had, except for a river a day's march away. I looked askance at Cyrus, remembering that he had promised that there would be wood for fires on the route he had set us on. Being fair, he had been right for the first few days, and I was not present when he pointed Antonius this direction. He may very well have warned Antonius that the wood would run out, and as I thought about it, I believed it was likely that this was a piece of information that Antonius had not wished to pass along to the men. So I tried to keep an open mind as he spoke, but there was no need, for first Ahenobarbus, then Titius, Fonteius, and finally Canidius, who had studiously been avoiding me since the Gallus battle, all voted to stay on this route. Either still not satisfied, or more likely wishing to seem to be willing to listen to the Centurions, Antonius polled each of us, though none of us were about to speak out against what the generals had already voted for, besides which it did seem to be the best option.

"How much water do your men have left?" he asked each of us.

When it came to my turn, I informed him that most men were down to perhaps a quarter skin each, while the Legion reserve was less than two barrels. Most of the other Legions were in the same shape, and from that information, Antonius made his next decision.

"We're going to steal a march on the Parthians, since I believe Mithradates that they haven't given up yet," he announced, hands on his hips as he stared at the parchment on which a rough map of the area had been drawn.

"Cyrus says it's a day's march to this river." He pointed at a line on the map. "We're going to march through the night and take advantage of the Parthians' reluctance to fight or move at night."

I was not watching Antonius as he spoke; I was concentrating on Mithradates, wanting to see how he reacted as Antonius talked. I thought a saw the faintest glimmer of a smile on his face when Antonius reached the part about the Parthian reluctance to operate at night. It was true that this was accepted as an article of faith among all levels of the army and that to this point they had never given any indication that it was anything but the truth. I wondered what this oily, tricky Eastern nobleman had up his brocaded sleeve, but the decision was made and I did not speak up.

The men were nearing the end of their tether, so that telling them to break camp just a matter of a full watch after they finished it created a tense situation throughout the army. The men of the 30th in particular had to be physically encouraged to break their tents down and pull up their stakes, while there were scattered outbreaks of similar behavior, even in my Legion. My Century obeyed with alacrity, and without the sullen attitude that some of the others' displayed, but I cannot take credit for it. My actions with Vellusius, when I had chosen to take action unofficially over such a serious offense, turned out to have benefits I did not expect, not least of which was that it was Vellusius who was enforcing discipline among his comrades. He had avoided me after our run-in, while truthfully I had other things on my mind, but finally he worked up the courage to approach me as we finished packing for our night march, encouraged no doubt by the darkness. Standing awkwardly at *intente*, he waited while I ignored him for several moments as I dictated something completely unimportant to Diocles. The truth was that I was still angry with him because he had inflamed my old wound even worse than before, but Vellusius, knowing the game, made no move or sound. Finally, I grudgingly rewarded his patience with a curt nod.

"Well?"

Clearing his throat, he began shuffling as he searched for words, but I was not in the mood for hemming and hawing.

"Pluto's cock, Vellusius, you've been standing there for half a watch and you haven't thought of what you want to say?"

Despite the gloom, I could see his head drop in what I assumed was embarrassment, then he said quietly, "I'm sorry, Primus Pilus. I was just thinking of Atilius."

The mention of that name from our shared past froze me. I turned slowly to face him, not sure what direction his thoughts were taking, but sure that I would not like it.

"What about Atilius?" I asked, hoping that my tone conveyed what dangerous waters he was swimming in, but I was not prepared for what came from his mouth.

"I was just thinking that by rights I should have joined him."

I confess that I had forgotten that he and Atilius had been close comrades, it was so long ago. He continued speaking, his voice having that dreamy quality when someone is looking back through the years.

"I suppose that would have been appropriate, seeing how he . . . you know."

I did indeed know, but saw no need to say anything.

"Pullus, I've known you as long as any man in this army." He said this with the pride a man takes in seeing one of his close friends who had achieved success so I did not begrudge the use of my name. "And I know how much your career means to you. I know that you not only had the right by regulations, but you had the right by what I did to do a lot worse than you did to me."

I saw his few teeth gleam in the moonlight as he reached up to touch his jaw gingerly.

"I still can't chew. Not that there's anything to chew on."

Unbidden, a laugh escaped from me, secretly pleased to hear that I had not lost my punch.

"Anyway." He turned serious. "I just wanted you to know that I'll never forget what you did for me, and I won't let you down again."

"See that you don't," I replied softly, then leaned over him, using my favorite trick of my height to reinforce my point. "Because I expect more from a man trained by Gaius Crastinus."

Clearly relieved, he smiled at me, took a step back, giving me a perfect salute.

"I will not, Primus Pilus. I swear by Mars and Bellona."

I had many, many troubles with the men of the 10th for the remainder of my time with the Legion, but never again did I have a problem with the First Century, because of Vellusius, and that first night was an example of his influence over his comrades.

We began the march with only the moonlight shining down on our path. In anticipation of fresh water, I ordered that the Legion reserve be distributed among the men, but it was so small that it was less than a cup per man. We could not move as quickly as we did during daylight, but the moon was full that night, so we were able to march at close to the same pace as during the day. Even during the short time we were in camp, men had died for one reason or another, and as I looked back I could see their pale, naked corpses almost glowing in the moonlight and I wondered if the vultures came at night. There is no way for an army of the size of this one, even as shrunken as it had become, to move with any stealth at all, but so confident were our officers in their belief that the Parthians would not march at night, they gave no orders to muffle our march, so there were no bits of cloth wrapped around clinking pieces of metal, nor did the horses have their hooves muffled. We were near the front of the column this night, just behind the vanguard and the command group, so Antonius was a frequent visitor as he trotted up and down, exhorting the men to march as if they were with Caesar, as he put it. The only time he mounted Clemency was to go farther to the rear, but the rest of the time, he marched on foot, making his rounds, talking to the men, but his magic was not as powerful as it had been. The men were exhausted, they were hungrier than most of them had ever been; we had gone on barley rations the day before, running out of even raw wheat to chew on, and now they were thirsty as well. All of this added up to an army that would not be mollified by Antonius' jokes or pretense that he was one of them. While the men appreciated his sharing of the hardships on the march, none of them were unaware that when camp was made, he slept under fur, and was still eating better than the rankers.

Mile after mile passed under our feet, despite the rugged terrain, figuratively flogged on by Antonius, who I must admit was a paragon of energy and courage that night. Men were staggering, their normal load now becoming almost too heavy for them to bear, while I was doing little better. A few days before, Diocles made a surreptitious visit to the doctors attached to Antonius' staff, and with my gold had paid a pretty price for a small stoppered bottle that supposedly contained an elixir that gave a man energy and vitality under the direst circumstances. The Greek doctor claimed that it was a concoction developed by one of Cleopatra's court physicians to be used by Antonius himself, and was supposedly the reason he was the seemingly inexhaustible fount of energy he had been on this campaign. I had to admit that he did seem to be indefatigable, yet to that point I had not used the elixir, for a variety of reasons. However, that night found me in the baggage train looking for Diocles who, as if reading my thoughts, had kept the bottle with him instead of packing it in my baggage. Without a word being spoken, he handed it to me, and I drank some of the contents, almost gagging on the vile taste. Trotting back to my spot in the column, for some time nothing happened and I was cursing the Greek for cheating us. Then, I noticed that it seemed to have gotten brighter, as if the moon's light had somehow increased itself, while my legs did not seem to be as heavy as they had been. More importantly, the pain in my chest eased, in fact almost disappearing as the miles went by, the army rumbling along. The moon was sinking towards its resting place, the men now clearly staggering, many of them falling and more than one not getting back up. Their comrades would stagger over to check on them, sometimes able to revive them, pulling them to their feet, then taking their pack while the stricken man recovered, but all too often they would check the man's pulse, shake their head, say a brief prayer, then immediately go through their friend's belongings to take everything of value. They also would strip the man of his cloak, tunic and whatever other piece of warm clothing he might have been wearing. After we had one incident where it turned out the man was not dead, that he had just fainted and then was left to die, I forced the Optios and Centurions to stand over each man to ensure that he was beyond hope.

The disintegration that I had been concerned about was happening, as men stopped worrying at all about their comrades to focus on their own survival, to the exclusion of everything else. While I was feeling better than I had felt in weeks, the army was falling apart around me. The sky was just turning pink when our scouts reported back that the river was in sight and without needing any urging, the men picked up their pace, finding last reserves of energy to close that final bit of distance to water. The horses and mules, smelling the river, began fighting their riders and the men driving them, so that it was not much longer before the baggage train threatened to push the army into the water as animals obeyed their own inner voice that demanded they survive. The vanguard reached the river and men, despite the cold, went plunging into the water, which ran clear and deep, looking as inviting as any water I had ever seen. Just as they were doing so, a series of *cornu* calls came relaying from the rear, announcing that the Parthians were attacking.

Disproving the long-held belief that the Parthians did not operate at night, they had in fact been stalking us when, just before the sun rose, at a point where they judged that our men were at their most exhausted, a force of horse archers came dashing out of the gloom. It was Corbulo and the 4th that had the rearguard during that march and I have no doubt that the attack was repulsed because that crusty old bastard was the man holding the line. Despite their fatigue, after marching what turned out to be 30 miles through the night, the men of the 4th held off the Parthian attack, taking not insignificant losses in the process. After perhaps a half-dozen attempts, the Parthians broke off their attack, but the myth of Parthians not fighting at night was destroyed forever. While Corbulo was involved with the Parthians, the men in the front of the column were drinking their fill of the water, whooping with delight, smiling for the first time in weeks. The men of the 10th were pushing their way towards the water when one of the first men to take a drink suddenly clutched his stomach, then began violently retching, the recently ingested water spewing from his mouth along with the rest of his stomach contents. Within a matter of moments, every other man who drank from the river was violently ill, but still my men pushed forward, oblivious to the obvious danger. Before I could stop them, some of them dropped to their stomach to begin drinking. It was utter chaos until Antonius came galloping up on Clemency, leaping down to begin dragging men away from the riverbank. Between the general and the Centurions, we were able to establish some semblance of order but not before we had dozens of men violently ill. In between bouts of vomiting, they complained that their thirst was worse than ever. There was no chance of continuing the march, and while we were worried that both man and beast would be driven mad by the presence of water they could not drink, we had to take the risk, hoping that the example of men stretched out holding their guts and moaning would be enough to deter them. Orders were given to erect the tents, without building a full camp to allow the men someplace to rest out of the wind. The *medici* did what they could for the men taken ill by the water and, while most recovered, about a half-dozen men, probably already weakened, died. Then, Mithradates came to Antonius, saying that there was another river not much farther along, that this river would not only provide water that he swore was potable, but Phraates had been forced by his men to promise not to pursue beyond it. I cannot speak with any assurance as to Antonius' frame of mind at this point, yet I think he was so desperate to believe this ordeal was coming to an end that he accepted what Mithradates said with such pathetic thankfulness that he gave the Parthian some of his golden dinner plates, with which the Parthian skulked off as his reward. Some of the men saw him leaving loaded down, and I am sure that is what gave them the idea for what was to follow, with Antonius' decision providing the spark.

I was called to the *Praetorium* not a third of a watch after I lay down on my cot and I was as unhappy as the rest of the Primi Pili, all of whom looked in a similar state as I felt. Antonius and his generals were waiting for us, Antonius looking impatient while his generals looked as grumpy as I imagined as the rest of us.

"Mithradates has given me information that changes things quite a bit," he said bluntly. "I know the men are tired, but I also know they're thirsty and being camped next to a river that they can't drink from isn't making things any easier."

I shot a glance at Corbulo, who was standing next to me. He eyed me back, then shook his head, clearly not liking what he was hearing either.

"So we're packing up and we're going to continue on the march to the next river. Once we're across that, not only will there be water, but the Parthians won't pursue across the river."

Even knowing it was coming, it was no easier hearing the order. Nevertheless, none of us disputed it, knowing that when Antonius was this way, there was no arguing. We dispersed to our Legion areas to rouse the men.

Aside from that dusty day at Pharsalus those many, many years ago, that day was the closest I ever had men under my command come to mutiny. It started with the Centurions, who I summoned all together. What I had to say was met with a sullen silence, the men refusing to meet my gaze, none of them moving for several moments. I scanned the faces, at first trying to gauge where each man stood, then with more and more inner desperation, I started looking for a friendly face, but there were none to be found. Even Scribonius, Balbus, and Cyclops refused to meet my gaze. I had never felt so isolated and alone as I did at that moment.

Then, feeling the slow coil of anger tightening in my stomach I took a step forward, saying softly, but loud enough to be heard by all of them, "I just gave you an order. I don't like it any more than you do, but those are the orders we've been given. Are you really going to shame yourselves and the 10th Legion by refusing to obey this order?"

None of them answered, but I saw some heads drop or turn away as I looked their direction. Then, Scribonius stepped forward, and without saying a word, walked towards his Legion area, Balbus turning a moment later to where his Century was located. Whatever resistance was left melted away, as the rest of the Centurions turned to walk to where their men were laying in an exhausted stupor, with the shouting beginning, though the challenges were not over. Rousing Valerius, I commanded him to give the signal formally for the Legion to break camp, then Lutatius and I began walking through our Century, opening the flaps of the tents when the men did not show themselves quickly, and they were exceedingly slow to get up and start the business of packing up. Some tents I had to go back to twice and when I did, I used the *vitus*, but still the men moved slowly. They began packing in sullen silence, which was unnerving, making me extremely nervous, though I was determined to act as if nothing was amiss. Then I saw Vellusius circulating among the men as they were packing, exchanging a whisper here and there. As if by some magic, the men suddenly began working at their normal pace. While they were not bantering and complaining as they normally did, they were moving in a manner that no Centurion could find fault with, and I silently thanked my old comrade. Unfortunately, things were not going so smoothly in the other Cohorts, and it was Pilus Posterior Gnaeus Aureolus of Glaxus' Ninth Cohort who came running.

"Primus Pilus, Pilus Prior Glaxus requests your presence in his Cohort area. Some of the men are refusing to break camp."

"How many?" I asked.

I could see him gulp, before he said, "Almost all of them."

Hurrying with Aureolus, I found Glaxus along with the other four Centurions standing facing a group of men who were congregated in their Cohort street. Significantly, none of the men were doing what they were supposed to be doing, while the Centurions were looking nervously over their shoulder for my arrival. Glaxus was snarling curses and threats at the rankers when I walked up, but while none of the men were saying anything back to him, neither were they showing any inclination of changing their minds. Walking past Glaxus so I was between the Centurions and the men, I stood with Glaxus standing just off of my left shoulder. I was facing my second showdown in less than a third of a watch, yet this had the potential to be much more serious business than with the Centurions, because this was a Cohort of some 400 men at that point. If they succeeded in their refusal, it was a sure bet that there would be other Cohorts who would follow their lead, and I would have the full Legion in a mutiny. Scanning the men, who were now beginning to shift nervously, I was able to identify what was bothering me. There were at least three Optios standing with the men and as I turned back towards the Centurions to look more closely, I saw that there were at least two Centurions who had slightly separated themselves from the others. The Hastatus Posterior of the Ninth was a man named Laberius, and he and the Princeps Prior, Voconius was his name, were the two who seemed to be trying to send a signal to the men that they were on their side.

Putting that aside for the moment, I turned back to the men, asking in a reasonable tone, "Who speaks for you as a group?"

There were several looks of surprise, telling me that this had not been a planned event and they had not thought things through very well. Some of the men turned towards the Optios, but at my appearance, they had been trying to surreptitiously edge to the back of the mob. I could see that there were indeed some men who were continuing to work, though most of them were now gathered in front of me, and I repeated the question. Finally, one of the Optios was shoved forward, as I kept my face a mask, not willing to show my contempt and disgust for who they had selected. He was a tall, thin man with a pockmarked face and a weak chin. His name was Numerius Sacrovir, and he was one of my mistakes in promotion. As a ranker, he had shown promise and initiative, or at least so I thought, but I had been suspecting for some time that he was recommended based on his contribution towards his Centurion's purse. He had all the characteristics of a budding Celer, my old nemesis from the first enlistment of the 10th, a man who had his eye on the main chance and never did anything for any reason other than his own profit. I still had been unable to determine if Glaxus had been gulled as I had, or if he had a few coins dropped in his purse, but that was for another time. Now, this puffed-up little turd had chosen the wrong side while I was forced for the moment to converse with him as if he were my equal.

Sacrovir approached with a fixed smile on his face, but I could see his eyes darting about as if wanting to be somewhere else. He saluted properly enough, which I returned, then waited for him to speak, discomfiting him even more.

Finally, he said, "Primus Pilus, the men are tired."

I nodded sympathetically, saying loudly enough for all to hear, "As we all are, Optio. But you can see that the men of every other Cohort," I waved my hand to indicate all the work going on around us, "who are as tired as all of you, are doing their duty. Or are you saying that for some reason, the Ninth Cohort has reason to be more exhausted than any other?"

Sacrovir may have been a lot of things, but he was not stupid and he immediately saw where I was going, as did most of the rest of the men, who began looking about nervously. They were counting on the men in the other Cohorts following their lead as soon as they saw the Ninth stop working, but their Centurions had immediately recognized the threat on their own and stepped in, one way or another keeping the men in their Cohorts on their tasks.

"No, Primus Pilus, we're not saying that we have any more right than the others," Sacrovir replied, licking his lips as he thought hard on the best way to retrieve something from the situation. "But we have rights," he insisted. "The rights of every Roman citizen to be treated fairly."

Now, I never remembered that as being a right of Roman citizens who were serving as Legionaries at all, but I was not going to argue the point.

"And with those rights come responsibilities," I pointed out. "Not to mention the responsibilities you have as Optio."

This struck home, as he blinked rapidly, then glancing over his shoulder, he stepped closer to me to whisper, "I never wanted this, Primus Pilus. I was trying to convince the men to get back to work when you showed up; that's why I was in their midst."

I choked back a laugh at the bald-faced lie. Nevertheless, the fact was that I wanted to end this as quickly as possible before someone higher up came poking about, so I accepted this as if it had come from the mouth of a Vestal Virgin.

"Then you're to be commended, Optio Sacrovir, not censured."

He brightened visibly, his manner becoming conspiratorial. "Look, Primus Pilus. Give me a few moments with the men and I'll get them back to work. The only thing I ask of you is your guarantee that there will be no reprisals, officially or unofficially," he emphasized, confirming again that he had a clever streak, "and we'll make sure that our Cohort doesn't delay the Legion in joining the march."

He was making awfully big promises and I confess that part of me wanted him to fail, yet more of me just wanted to get this over with. I was not lying when I said that the rest of the Legion was just as tired as the men of the Ninth, including the Centurions, their Primus Pilus perhaps more than any of them. I nodded, telling him that he had my word before turning away from each other to return to our respective sides. Glaxus was standing, waiting for me, still red-faced, but I did not know if it was from anger or embarrassment. I was sorely disappointed in my former Optio, and I suppose my face reflected that feeling, because he would not look me in the eye.

"What happened, Glaxus?"

He shrugged, mumbling that he did not know and I had to rein in my anger, this being neither the time nor the place to dress Glaxus down. All I said was that we would talk later, and I was happy to see that my tone left him white-faced and shaking. Turning about, I saw Sacrovir approaching, yet even as he was walking closer, men were dispersing quickly to pick up where they had left off.

Saluting first me, then Glaxus, Sacrovir said crisply, "The Cohort realizes that while they have legitimate grievances, they went about expressing those grievances in the improper manner, and for that they humbly seek the Primus Pilus and Pilus Prior's pardon."

"The pardon is granted, as promised," I replied, returning his salute. Mentally gritting my teeth, I kept my tone as pleasant as I could manage as I finished, "Good work, Sacrovir. I'll be keeping my eye on you."

The sallow-faced man beamed with happiness at my words. As I turned to return to my other tasks, I thought grimly, but not in the way you think, you little bastard.

With that crisis resolved, I returned to find that the rest of the Legion was almost finished, while at least Sacrovir was good to his word, the Ninth only delaying us perhaps another sixth part of a watch, so that we still managed to slot into our spot in the column before the delay was noticed. What made me feel a little better was that similar scenes to what happened with the Ninth were taking place all over the camp, as men pushed to their limit and beyond refused to move until their Centurions used a combination of threats and bribes to get them going. Nevertheless, the army began rumbling along again and we took some small comfort in the fact that we had made the Parthians rouse themselves, and more importantly their horses, who had to be as tired as we were. However, it was only a third of a watch into the march when we took our first break that it became clear the men were truly dead on their feet. Men collapsed, falling fast asleep, and that included Centurions, who normally were responsible for checking on their men while staying on their feet to show the rankers that they were impervious to fatigue. I was weaving about as if I had been drinking, so that when the signal to resume was given it took an extra several moments to get the men roused and on their feet, while not all of them were able to do so. In my Century, I got a frantic call from Lutatius, who was standing over a man in the third section, a veteran of Gaul and Pompey's Legions, one of the oldest men in the 10th, who was laying with his head on his pack, his mouth slightly open. His name was Memmius, but he was called Felix for his renown at games of chance, though when I saw the tongue hanging limply out of the side of his mouth, I knew that his luck had finally run out. The men of his section were clustered around him, shivering in the howling cold, their sorrow showing clearly through their own fatigue, for Felix, like Vellusius, had been one of the unofficial leaders of not just the Century, but the First Cohort. I knelt, taking a gold coin from my purse, which I placed gently in his mouth, then clamped it shut. I said a brief prayer to the gods, asking them to accept this good man. When I finished, his comrades knelt to begin to strip him, as this had become our standard practice, but I stopped them.

"No, we're not going to leave him naked and cold out here," I commanded.

"But the Parthians will just strip him themselves," Lutatius pointed out.

"Probably," I agreed, and they will probably take the coin as well, I thought, "but I think they're just as tired as we are, and when they see Felix here left like this, I think they'll see a great warrior and respect that we honor him."

I knew no such thing, but I had seen the desperate sadness in the men's eyes and I wanted to give them something. Turning away to walk back to my spot in the column, Lutatius followed me a short distance until he was out of earshot of the men.

"How many more men do we have to lose this way?" he whispered.

"As many as it takes to get across the Aras, I suppose."

It was the only thing I could think of to say.

We continued in this manner for another full watch, until Antonius was forced to recognize that he was marching with an army of men more dead than alive, whereupon he called another halt, this time having the men make a proper camp and not just erect tents. I know he meant this as a signal to the men that they could look forward to a good rest, but there is a fair amount of work involved in building a marching camp, so that men who were already exhausted were now forced to hack and dig into the frozen ground to create the required ditch and rampart. The men had passed from their normal phase of grumbling and complaining about the work that comes with being a Legionary, through the sullen silence. Now they were openly angry and close to outright mutiny. Ironically, I did not have any trouble with the men of the Ninth, but now whatever *numen* that inhabits the souls of men that makes them defiant had passed through the Third and Seventh Cohorts. It began with Metellus' men, more specifically with the Century of the older brother of my new Optio, Gnaeus Lutatius, the Hastatus Prior. This time I was not summoned, as Metellus handled the problem himself by beating the ringleader to a bloody pulp, making him even uglier than Metellus himself, which was quite a feat. With the Seventh, I was not so lucky, as Marcius himself came looking for me, his anger and distress clear in his body posture as he stalked up to me.

"The bastards," he spat. "The ungrateful, mutinous bastards. They threw down their tools and are saying they won't do any more. That they're too tired."

I knew how they felt; I was almost overcome with a huge weariness that felt as if a boulder were pressing down on my shoulders and was driving me into the ground. The thought actually crossed through my mind of simply throwing down my *vitus*, taking off my helmet with the transverse crest I was so proud of, and just walking away from it all, but I shook it off to begin walking with Marcius to his Cohort area.

"I need to warn you, Primus Pilus, that there's a Centurion involved."

"Who?"

"Macrianus."

I cursed bitterly. Servius Macrianus was the Princeps Prior. He had always been one of the good, steady Centurions, one I had been mentally marking as worthy of promotion. Now his actions not only put his promotion in serious jeopardy, but more importantly, for a man the quality of Macrianus to take such a step meant that my hold on the Legion, and Antonius' hold on the army, was growing more precarious, almost by the moment.

Macrianus was standing calmly, with the men of his Century clustered around him, as well as what appeared to be most of the Cohort, some of them standing in the partially completed ditch that was their section of the camp. As I approached, I saw the Hastatus Prior, Vibius Geta, seem to take a deep breath, then take a clear step away from the rest of the Centurions, going to stand beside Macrianus. Unlike the situation with the Ninth, and adding to my trouble, was the presence of every Optio standing with the men.

I shot a furious glance at Marcius, hissing, "Did you just forget to mention that all of the Optios are with the men too?"

Marcius gave a helpless shrug. "They weren't when I left; they were still with us. I guess when Macrianus sided with the men they did too."

Marcius' admission was telling, pointing to yet another issue I would have to address when we got back to Syria. I did not have to ask who spoke for this group, as it was clear that Macrianus was the leader, but there was no defiance in his posture or in his voice when he spoke.

"Primus Pilus, first I want to say that this is in no way aimed at you or your leadership of this Legion. This is a protest against the treatment of men who have been forced to endure conditions against all reason. We should have called off this campaign the moment we lost the baggage train, but our general," he did not mention Antonius' name, his bitter tone making it clear who he meant, "so lusted after a conquest of the Parthians that he ignored all military logic. Now, we're forced to pay for it, and the men have had enough."

I paused as I thought about my answer, because he was absolutely right, in every respect. Finally, I said as much.

"I agree with you completely, Princeps Prior Macrianus."

I took a small satisfaction in the reaction of Macrianus and the men, this statement clearly not what they were expecting. They had the mulish set to their faces of men who were fully anticipating more threats, just from a higher rank, which I recognized would get us nowhere, Macrianus not being a man to be cowed.

"You're absolutely right in your assessment," I repeated. "But where does that put us now? Saying that the jug was broken by carelessness doesn't mend the jug, though it might make its owner feel better."

Pausing as if gathering my thoughts, instead I was gauging the men's reactions. All I wanted to do at that point was to plant the first seed of doubt, then make it grow. I was somewhat satisfied as I saw some men murmuring to each other as they took this in, though most of the men's expressions had not changed.

Continuing, I said, "So we agree that we shouldn't be here, but neither can it be argued that we are here. Therefore, I put the question to you; what would you have us do now?"

This was a tactic I had used before, and I could see that Macrianus was not expecting to be asked his opinion. For the first time he looked uncomfortable, as I had hoped. Now, all eyes turned to Macrianus, waiting to hear his response.

Shaking his head, he replied slowly, "That's not for me to say, Primus Pilus. But something must be done about this. Men are dropping dead as if they are flies. I lost four men from my Century in the last day alone!" Suddenly, his eyes filled with tears, the very real anguish clearly heard in his voice as he cried, "And we're dying for nothing! We aren't even able to die with a sword in our hands, facing those bastards who stalk us like wolves about a fat herd of elk!"

His head dropped as he stopped speaking, clearly unable to continue. In his face, I saw the pain of a true leader of men, raging at his helplessness in caring for them and protecting them from the whims of the generals. I understood his frustration, in fact completely agreed with everything he said, making me resolve at that moment to do whatever I had to in order to protect Macrianus from the consequences of the stand he had taken, because he was doing so for the purest of motives. Without thinking, I took a step forward to put my hand on Macrianus' shoulder, but my grip was gentle, holding no censure.

He looked up at me in surprise, as I said quietly, "I understand your pain, Macrianus, because I feel it too. But how does not completing the ditch and palisade help protect the men from the Parthians?"

"I would rather my men die with a sword in their hand, even if it's in the camp, than drop dead digging a ditch," he said bitterly. Turning, he gestured at the perimeter of the camp, forcing me to look about for the first time. "Besides, do you think we're the only ones who are done with all this?"

I immediately saw that he was right. As I gaped in amazement, I saw that far from being the only part of the camp where work had stopped, it was more a case that the men working or finished with their section of the camp were in the vast minority. I had never seen anything like the sight before me now; a partially dug ditch, next to spots where it had not even begun, punctuated by places where the ditch and rampart was finished. Clearly, the entire army had endured enough, so I made my decision right then and there.

"You're right," I said finally, looking back at Macrianus. "Your men are done, and so are the rest of the men, at least of the 10th. All I ask is that you erect your tents, and agree to a watch of fifty percent, because I have a feeling that the Parthians are going to see this and want to take advantage of it."

Without making any attempt to wipe his eyes, Macrianus stood back, saluted, then said loudly, "As you command, Primus Pilus. We'll make sure your orders are carried out."

Then he turned back to the waiting, expectant Cohort, explaining what had happened. Marcius was standing there open-mouthed, unsure of what had transpired, but when I told him, his jaw gaped even wider.

"So, we're not making a marching camp?" he asked uncertainly, to which I shook my head.

"Macrianus is right. I'd rather take our chances fighting the Parthians than watch men die from digging a ditch."

I turned away to head to the *Praetorium*, grimly determined that I would make Antonius and the generals understand that not only their careers, but their lives depended on his decision.

The men of the Brundisium Cohorts had survived more intact than the regular Legions because of the lack of duties like making camp, and because they had yet to participate in any battle against the Parthians. Still, their ranks were thinned from starvation and exposure and they were clearly nervous as they clustered around the *Praetorium* tent. It was from one of them that I learned they had been forced to erect it themselves when the Legionaries assigned to the task refused. The mood was incredibly tense and when I stepped inside the tent, there were a number of bodyguards standing about, which was also unusual, but this was an unusual day. The other officers were huddled around Antonius, whispering to him urgently, as at least four other Primi Pili were milling about as well, obviously here to inform him of the mutiny of their Legion, or at least part of it.

Spotting Balbinus, I walked over to him as he gave me a grim nod, his usual sardonic humor missing from his voice as he said, "Half of my Legion has quit on me. How's yours?"

"Two Cohorts," I said, "but it could just as easily be the whole Legion, and I'm worried that it will be unless Antonius does something."

"Like what?" Balbinus asked, but I could see he was genuinely asking, clearly as much at a loss as I was. "They're not asking for money. They just want this to stop."

I nodded in agreement. "I know, which is why I think the best thing that Antonius can do is just ignore what's going on and let the men rest. I got my mutinous Cohorts to agree to set up their tents in exchange for staying at half alert the whole night. Like I told them, whether you're dead of exhaustion or dead because the Parthians can walk up and cut your throat while you sleep, you're still dead."

Balbinus grunted, rubbing his chin. "What did they say to that?"

"That they'd rather die with a sword in their hand than a shovel."

"I can't blame them," he replied frankly. "I'll tell you this Pullus. I've never been this tired, this cold and this hungry, all at the same time."

"Nor I," I agreed. "And I can't blame them either, and that's what I'm going to tell Antonius."

"Better you than me," he gave a barking laugh, slapping me on the back as he wished me luck.

Whenever I talked to Balbinus I always remembered the conversation that led me to believe that he was one of Octavian's agents, guarding my tongue when talking more than I did around other men, though at this particular moment it seemed pointless. Approaching Antonius, he looked worse than I had ever seen him. Gaunt, haggard from lack of sleep, he kept running his hands through his curls, which seemed to grow grayer with every day. He looked at me through red-rimmed eyes, reminding me of a bear I had once seen at a bear-baiting at some festival long ago; wounded but still dangerous, viewing anything around him that moved as a possible threat.

"What do you want?" he snapped. "Are you coming to tell me that the 10th is disloyal too?"

"They're not disloyal General," I said evenly. "They're exhausted, and they've reached the end of their tether."

"And I haven't?"

He made no attempt to hide the anguish in his voice. In that moment I saw all the crushing disappointment and bitterness that was grinding at him every step of this retreat.

"Haven't I shared every step of the march with the men? Haven't I suffered through the same weather, the same hardships?"

"Yes, you have," I agreed. "But they're just men, and you're Marcus Antonius."

The Triumvir usually was mollified by honeyed words that put him on a level above other men. This time it had no effect.

"And Marcus Antonius is just a man too! Why do they insist on seeing me as if I'm some sort of a god when I'm just like them?"

Because you have been beating the drum of divinity every chance you get, I thought but did not say.

"That I can't answer, General," I lied. "But what I can tell you is that at least the 10th has no desire to usurp you or threaten you in any way. They just need to rest."

"How can they expect to rest without camp walls to protect them?" interjected Fonteius.

If Antonius had not been nodding pathetically in agreement, I would not even have bothered to answer the man, given that he held no official position of rank in the army other than advisor to Antonius. What he was really asking was how he could expect to sleep while he worried about Parthians from the outside and our own men from the inside. In answer, I repeated what I had told Balbinus. This did not make any of the men standing about feel any better, but that was not my concern.

"General, the men will be fine after a night's sleep and some rest," I assured Antonius, then amended, "at least as well as can be expected under the circumstances. They'll be strong enough to get to the Aras River, and if indeed the Parthians stop their pursuit, that will solve a large part of the problem. They're worn down from the need for constant vigilance every step of the march, every day of the march. Once that's removed, things will be better."

"Mithradates swore on the lives of his wives and children that it was so," Antonius cried.

He sat heavily in his ivory curule chair, putting his head in his hands and saying nothing for several moments. Finally, he looked up at me.

"So what is it that you're asking for exactly, Pullus?"

"That you give me assurances that there will be no punishment or retribution of any kind for the men not finishing the camp," I replied.

Fonteius sputtered in protest, but Antonius wearily waved him silent.

"Fine," he said shortly. "Let them get their rest while I stay awake all night, worrying. They won't be punished." He sighed. "I suppose they deserve that much."

They deserve that and more you bastard, I thought savagely, but I was determined that I would do nothing to threaten this concession, instead saying nothing other than a thank you, turning to leave before Antonius brought me up short.

"Pullus."

I turned, and he gave me a smile that was both grim and unpleasant at the same time.

"I'm assigning the 10th the rearguard tomorrow. As you say, the sooner we get to the river, the less time your men will have to spend at it."

I opened my mouth to protest, but knew it would do no good. Instead, I saluted, then stalked out.

The next few thirds of a watch were a nightmare for Antonius as he alternately worried about the Parthians and his own men. The Parthians had proven that their fear or dislike of operating at night was a myth and with no walls to guard the camp, had perhaps their best opportunity to destroy us once and for all. I think the fact that they did not proves that they were as tired as we were, though none of us knew that at the time. The other Primi Pili had adopted the fifty percent alert status that I had, so that men either stood shivering at their post or walking up and down the Legion streets, hunched over in their *sagum* against the cold. I think that having men walking about contributed to what happened, because it gave the troublemakers the opportunity to move about the camp at night that they normally did not have. However, what put the idea in their heads was the sight of Mithradates making off with Antonius' gold plates. From that, the opulence and value of Antonius' table setting grew in value with every telling, men adding jewel-encrusted cups, and pitchers carved from ivory to what supposedly graced his table. Even in the most desperate of times, there are men whose primary motivation is greed, despite it putting their lives at great risk. It was a group of these men who took advantage of the extra activity in the camp to sneak into the *Praetorium* and into the room that was both a meeting room and the officer's mess. That room was directly adjacent to the general's private quarters, where Antonius was lying on his cot, trying to sleep when he heard noises from the next room.

Antonius' immediate thought was that the Parthians had infiltrated the camp, so calling on the *de facto* Primus Pilus of the Brundisium Cohorts, a man named Rhamnus, he made the man swear to kill Antonius, then take his head and hide it so that it would not suffer the same fate as that of Marcus Crassus, whose mummified remains still stare sightlessly across the Parthian wastes from the ramparts of Phraates' capital. Rhamnus promised, then he and other men went to investigate to find that it was not Parthians, but some of our men, their hands full of Antonius' tableware. They were quickly subdued and held for tribunal, but there was more mischief afoot, as other Legionaries took the same opportunity to sneak into the tents of some of the generals, namely Canidius and Ahenobarbus, stealing various articles, which were never recovered.

The whole camp pulsed with a restless energy that night, any real chance of sleep made almost impossible by the cold, the keening of the wind, and the low mutter of voices as men talked about things that one's imagination turned into all manners of sinister plots. More likely, finding it as hard to sleep as the officers and Centurions, they were talking of home, and things like fresh-baked bread still warm from the oven, or women they loved or wanted to, but at least that night, there were other possibilities that made it hard to sleep.

I had chosen not to tell the Centurions of Antonius' little gift to the 10th until the next morning and I am glad I did not, given their reaction. The men did not take it much better, muttering angrily, but a night's sleep had restored them to a point where they did not outright refuse. I think the prospect of reaching the river, with the hope of safety once across was sufficient enticement for the men, so they packed up willingly enough before waiting for the rest of the column to move out. As we did so, an extraordinary thing happened, presaged by an excited buzzing of talk and I frowned as I turned, about to tell men to shut up when I saw none other than Antonius, walking among the men, his *paludamentum* swirling in the morning breeze. And as much as I hated the man at the moment, I have to say he was magnificent, wearing his golden cuirass with the snarling lion's heads, their silver-capped fangs glittering in the growing light. He was the laughing, joking, Legionary's Antonius, acting as if he had not spent the night before huddled in his tent worrying about Parthians and mutiny.

"Boys, this is the last day, I swear upon my ancestor Hercules Invictus. We make it across that river, and the Parthians will give up. But," he turned serious, his voice pitched high so it carried to all the men of the Legion, "they know this is their last chance and they'll probably throw everything they have at us. That's why I picked the 10th to stand between them and the rest of this army. Can I count on you?"

The ground shook with the roar of the men as they shouted their pledge to this general who just the day before they were cursing with every breath. I could not help shaking my head in admiration at how quickly he could change his nature, and how quickly men would forgive him his lapses and mistakes. And he was not finished, as he held his hands up to wave the men to silence. In an instant before where there had been thunderous noise, now there was dead silence.

"There is one last thing I must ask of each of you," he said somberly. "And that is your forgiveness."

I felt my jaw dropping, and as I glanced about, I saw that most of the men shared a similar expression.

Antonius continued, "I have made many, many mistakes on this campaign, and they've been costly ones. Men have died because of those mistakes, men who were your friends, comrades, and perhaps even relatives." He scanned the sea of faces, all of them registering the sadness and suffering that his words evoked. "But know that I made those mistakes honestly, that at all times I was trying to achieve victory for the glory of Rome, and for the glory of its Legions. We've been turned back, this time." His mouth twisted into a bitter grimace as he finally publicly acknowledged what we had known for weeks. "But this is a temporary setback. We will return, and we will avenge every death, and every humiliation these Parthian scum have forced us to endure. This, I also swear by Jupiter Invictus."

The men did not cheer this, as it did not seem appropriate, and Antonius did not seem to expect it. Then, without another word, he was gone in a swirl of scarlet and gold, leaving us dazed in his wake. Of all the generals I have marched with, I understood Marcus Antonius the least; he was always surprising me at times when I was sure he had no more surprises left.

The Parthians attacked almost immediately after we set out, but it was more of a probe of our defenses than a serious attack, which we were able to fend off without any loss. With remnants of the slingers and javelineers, perhaps a third of their original number among the rearguard, along with about half the Gallic and Galatian cavalry, their horses reduced to little more than walking bags of bones. For the first time in what seemed like months, the men were moving with a sense of purpose, though I know not why; we had been teased with promises before, only to have them crash down on our collective heads. Perhaps it was Antonius' words and his own conviction that convinced the army. Whatever the cause, the army moved like it was the first day, but despite appearances, we were a shell of what we had been on that first morning at Zeugma. Shortly before the first break of the march, the Parthians came again, this time in larger numbers and with more conviction to their attack than the first. I ordered the men into the formation that Antonius had suggested the first time we were on rearguard, the men in front kneeling while holding their shields perpendicular to the ground, though the Parthians were not fooled into thinking the men were doing so out of fatigue this time. A few moments after we formed the *testudo*, they ceased their volley fire of arrows, but not before we suffered a few casualties. Most of the time an arrow does not kill a man outright, at least at first, because our armor and helmet keep the points from penetrating deeply, while only the extremities are exposed. However, the wound can fester and corruption can spread from it, and if that happens, it is a horrible, lingering death of stench and fear as your body rots from within. Fortunately, most of the time, an arrow only wounds. Nevertheless, there are times where a combination of luck and skill converge, as an archer manages to send his missile to the one vulnerable spot in the few inches from the base of the throat to just below the forehead, and on that day, one of those Parthian bastards was both lucky and good. After a volley strikes, there are curses and yells of pain, or laughter from men who dodged the missile meant for them, followed immediately by calls for the *medici*. Most of our clerks doubled their duty by acting as litter bearers, while the rest had some sort of medical skills learned on the battlefield, so they helped provide immediate care to wounded men to supplement the *medici*. Diocles was one of the latter, spending time with his countrymen who were physicians, and it was Diocles who came to find me, his tunic drenched in blood. At first, I thought he was wounded so I ran over to meet him. My concern must have been clearly written on my face, because he assured me that it was not his.

"Master, I think you better come with me, quickly."

"If you hadn't noticed, I'm a little busy," I said crossly, then after looking more closely at his face, I realized he would not have come if it had not been important.

A surge of panic shot through me as I thought of young Gaius.

"What is it?" I asked, saying a quick prayer to the gods that my nephew's name not come out of his mouth, but when he did speak the name, it was almost as bad.

"It's Cyclops. He's been hit, badly. I don't think he'll survive more than a few moments."

I ran over to the Eighth Cohort, where a number of men were clustered around a figure on the ground and as I approached, I saw the feathered shaft of an arrow protruding from the man's throat. Then I saw the scarred, one-eyed visage of my mentor, tutor, and former brother-in-law, husband of my dead sister Livia. He was making awful, choking sounds as blood pooled in his throat, despite one of the orderlies doing his best to swab the blood out of his mouth as I knelt down beside him.

"What are you doing?" I said, angry that the orderly did not seem to know what he was about. "Turn his head so the blood will drain out."

"No!" The voice came from behind me and it was Diocles, who also knelt, putting a hand on my shoulder. "I'm sorry, Master Titus, but to do that will kill him instantly. The head of the arrow is lodged in his spinal column. Turning his head will sever it completely." He turned his head to the side and whispered to me, "He's paralyzed from the neck down as it is."

"I can hear you, you little Greek pederast." The voice was a choked whisper but clearly recognizable as that of Cyclops', and while he could not move his head, I saw his good eye looking over at us.

I turned to him, forcing a smile, but I could not hold it for more than a heartbeat before I burst into tears.

"I suppose that tells me what I need to know," he said wryly, which only intensified my grief. "I would slap you if I could," he continued, then began to choke again, forcing the orderly to swab more blood from his mouth. I did not know what to say and I was afraid to touch him, but I tentatively reached for his hand, wanting to offer some sort of comfort.

"It's all right, Titus. I was tired," he said as his breathing became more and more labored. "I'll be with your sister. And I lived long enough to see you become the Legionary I knew that you could be."

I wanted desperately to say something, anything to tell this man how much he had meant to my life, but the words would not come because I was crying too hard and at that moment I did not care who saw me. He took one long, gurgling breath, then it rattled out, making a noise that I had heard so many, many times before, his spirit fleeing his body to cross Charon, to find my sister and walk with her in happiness and light forever. I was oblivious to everything around me, as other wounded men were attended to, the Centurions shouting orders to return to marching formation as the Parthians receded out of range. All I cared about at that moment was making sure that Cyclops was not left behind, and I wiped my eyes before I stood back up, the men around me refusing to meet my gaze, not wanting to embarrass me further, though I was past caring.

Turning to Diocles, my voice did not sound like my own when I told him, "Make sure that he comes with us. I'm not going to leave him behind for these cocksuckers to defile."

Without waiting for an answer, knowing that it would be obeyed, I returned to my spot in the middle of the *quadratum*, as the march continued.

"The river has been sighted!"

The word flashed down the column, the men letting out a faint, tired cheer at the news, but we were not out of danger by any measure, which I continually stressed to everyone around me. My mind was numb from the death of Cyclops and now the habits instilled over the years stood me in good stead as I did everything from memory, mouthing words that I had spoken gods know how many times before. The march was still taking place in good order, the men learning to adjust for the rough and broken terrain, the Parthians still lurking just two or three furlongs away. What we did not know was exactly how far the river was. Was it spotted by the vanguard, or by the advance party of scouts and engineers? That was a difference of miles, so I was expecting at least one last push by the Parthians, so I tried to focus my thoughts on this fact and not on the death of Cyclops. At some point,

Scribonius came trotting over to walk beside me for a few moments, but he said nothing, which was the best thing he could have done. Just having him next to me helped, then with a squeeze of my shoulder, he returned to his spot.

Word filtered back that the vanguard was within sight of the river, starting the most nerve-wracking and dangerous part of any operation, a river crossing under pressure from an enemy. To help with the rearguard action, Antonius dispatched the rest of the cavalry to the rear, and on arrival they immediately moved into a protective cordon between the 10th and Parthians, who were forced to withdraw even further back, despite giving every appearance of gathering themselves for one last attack. The wounded and sick were brought up from the center of the *quadratum* to be forded across the river first, including some of my men injured in the last Parthian attack. In many ways, these men were the luckiest, being wounded so late in the campaign, as I do not believe that riding a bouncing litter strapped between two mules was any easier than carrying your pack under your own power. I suspect that at least as many men died from the jostling, jarring ride; opening wounds and damaging internal organs over the rough terrain as the cold and infection. But there is something that is as crucial to the morale of an army as a full belly and a warm cloak, and that is taking care of wounded or sick comrades, because in the back of every man's mind is the certainty that it could happen to them, and if it did, they wanted to know that their officers cared for the unfortunates among us. The men of the 10th, sensing that at last the end might be near, were almost back to their normal, bellyaching, bantering selves, as friends called to each other, reminding them of wagers made about who would survive the campaign.

"No money better change hands yet," I ordered, knowing from bitter experience what happened when men did such things, cursing them to fall short of their goal, sometimes by mere feet or moments.

Keeping my eyes fixed on the Parthians, I watched with growing concern as they drew themselves together, creating a larger and larger mass of horsemen directly across from the center of the rearguard, bringing their men off the flanks. There was something different about what they were doing that I could not identify, not remembering seeing them act in this manner before, making me even more nervous. Turning to Valerius, I had him blow the signal for the Pili Priores, who came trotting over from their respective Cohorts.

As I watched them approach, I was assailed by a number of thoughts. They all looked exhausted, which was to be expected, but it was how gaunt they all were that struck me, as if I had not really seen them every day for the last months and was just laying eyes on them after a long absence. We do not have mirrors in the army, although I knew some of the more vain Centurions kept polished brass discs in which they could see their reflection, but I was not one of them, so when I looked down at my own body, I gasped in surprise. I had noticed that my armor was chafing me more than it had in the past though I had not thought of it much, yet now I looked almost as skinny as Scribonius, at least the Scribonius before the Parthian campaign. I am not being vain when I say that I did not have much fat on my body, though I had noticed as I got older my waist had thickened some, but now all that had melted away. What was more distressing was that a great deal of muscle seemed to have gone with it, though I am sure that it was not quite as dramatic as I thought when I first looked at myself at that moment.

My disturbed train of thought was interrupted by the arrival of the Pili Priores, whereupon I pointed out at the Parthian army, now a solid mass of horsemen gathered directly across from the center of our vanguard, with only a few scattered outriders arrayed along each flank. When compared to that large a group, our remaining cavalry looked decidedly puny in comparison, and I quickly realized that the Gauls and Galatians would be swept aside as if they were not there.

"I don't like the looks of that," I announced. "I've never seen them concentrate that way before, so look alive because I'm sure they have some surprise in mind and that we're not going to like it."

"I think they might be forming a wedge," Nigidius spoke up.

He did not talk often but when he did it was usually something sensible, and I felt a chill run up my spine as I realized he was probably right. It had been a topic of conversation many cold nights; why the Parthians, with all of their experience with mounted tactics, had not at any point so far used the massed weight of their cataphracts in a wedge formation. Not that we complained about it, but it was puzzling, because that was the one thing that we all feared about the cataphract. When they attacked us in a line formation, no matter how tightly packed they were, we had proven we could defeat them, in at least 17 different engagements in this campaign alone, not counting our time with Ventidius. Yet, they had never attempted to attack us in a wedge formation until, it appeared, this last moment.

They sent the archers forward first, in a series of waves, each one composed of several hundred archers galloping across our front, firing one arrow after another in an almost endless stream. Their first targets were our cavalry and slingers, and with the cataphracts lurking nearby, I saw no point in wasting any more of the horsemen. Additionally, there were no longer enough missile troops to do any damage to such a large force, so I ordered Valerius to sound the recall for both groups. The cavalry retreated up the sides of the *quadratum*, while the missile troops came running between our lines, heading for the river without so much as a glance back over their shoulders. Then the horse archers turned their attention to us, swooping down into the attack. The sound was horrific as most of the missiles clattered off shields, though inevitably some men were struck, and the orderlies kept busy dragging the wounded out of the line to be tended to.

I moved from one spot to another, crouching under the safety of the shields as I called out encouragement to anyone bothering to listen. This onslaught lasted for several moments, but our *testudo* as usual frustrated the vast majority of the missiles fired at us, though the shields of the men in the first two ranks were quickly riddled with arrows. Men cursed bitterly at the sight of their ruined shields, knowing that the cost of replacing them would come out of their pay, and this campaign had been completely bereft of any opportunity for loot. The horse archers finally gave up their assault, peeling off to the sides of the Parthian formation to reveal a gleaming mass of armored horses and men. Now I was faced with a choice that I did not want to make, for once again I realized that this attack by the horse archers, futile as it was every other time in breaking our formation, had a different design this time. The front ranks of Legionaries facing the Parthian cataphract charge that seemed inevitable would be doing so with shields weakened and made more cumbersome by the amount of arrows protruding from each of them. We train relentlessly with the shield, but not with arrows attached to them and I cursed the cunning of the Parthian commander, the traitor Monaeses, if rumor were true. My mind raced as I tried to calculate if I had enough time to pull the men out to replace them with fresh Cohorts and if I did, who they should be. Making my decision, I snapped out the orders for the men of the Fourth, Fifth, and Seventh Cohorts, who had borne the brunt of the arrow attack, to be replaced by my Cohort, along with the Second and Third. Valerius blew the command for relief, as I called to the Centurions of my Cohort, pointing to the Parthians, telling them to hurry. They needed no urging, the controlled chaos of Cohorts relieving each other beginning immediately. This was obviously what the Parthians were waiting and hoping for, because as soon as it became apparent that we were exchanging places, the higher-pitched sound of their bugles carried across the frigid air and they began moving forward.

What I was gambling on were two things; the superior training and discipline of the Legions in making moves of this nature, along with the slow start of the cataphracts when beginning a charge. They needed more time to get to the full gallop, which was in our favor. As I shoved my own men into place, who were in turn dodging the men of the relieved Cohorts, I surveyed the front, grimly satisfied that we would be in place in more than enough time to face the cataphract charge. Then Balbus ran up to ask me a question that chilled my blood.

"Primus Pilus, what about the siege spears?"

I had been too smug in congratulating myself for outwitting Monaeses; in my haste and fatigue, I had forgotten to relay the order for the men of the retiring Cohorts to pass the relieving Cohorts the siege spears that had been so effective in crushing every Parthian attack since the 10th used them the first time. I saw some of the men who had the presence of mind to make the exchange on their own, but it was not nearly enough, while the maneuver was too advanced to try to correct my mistake, an error that was going to cost men their lives. Frantically, I ran along the rear of my Cohort, shouting at men who had grabbed a spear to pass it to the front, as Scribonius and Metellus, taking my lead, began doing the same. The cataphracts had now increased their pace to the trot, giving us no more than a few heartbeats, which the men could plainly see for themselves, making for a mad scramble as the long and bulky weapons were handed forward to the men that needed them. Once every spear was passed forward, I ordered the men to advance them, not waiting for the last moment as I had in the past, my heart sinking when I saw that only perhaps every other man in the front rank had received a spear, with none in the second rank. It would not be enough, the Parthians advancing to the gallop, the ground shaking as the formation, now clearly a wedge, came thundering towards us.

"Jupiter *Optimus Maximus*, protect this Legion, soldiers all," I said, the first time I myself had ever uttered the Legionary prayer.

The first man in a wedge formation is either suicidally brave, desperate to redeem himself or to make a reputation, because they are riding into an almost certain death, not only from the men facing him, but equally from the weight of his own comrades pushing him from behind. As I watched the distance rapidly closing, I saw the man at the point of the wedge slightly veer from his original path. Looking over to where he seemed to be headed, I could tell that he was aiming at the seam between the First and Second Cohorts, right where Scribonius was standing just behind the front two ranks with his *signifer* and *cornicen*. He stood there calmly, talking to his men in an oddly soothing tone, as if this was nothing more than an exercise back in winter quarters. With the gap only 50 paces, the Parthians lowered their iron-tipped lances, and knowing what was coming, I could barely stand to watch. Without a pause, the man at the point of the wedge, shouting the war cry of Parthia, smashed into the front rank, veering his horse a matter of inches to avoid the point of a siege spear, the point of his own lance skimming over the top of the first man's shoulder, full into the face of the man in the second rank. The iron tip ripped through then out the back of the man's head, showering his comrades with blood and brains, the armored chest of the Parthian mount smashing into the shield of the first man to send him hurtling backward. In the space of a heartbeat, the first Parthian had punched a hole in our formation, the men immediately behind him slamming into the Legionaries on either side, also sending them flying backwards. Fortunately, the fraction of a delay between the first man's impact and the second rank gave my men time to either bring their shields up or dodge the lances of the second rank, but still their massive weight pushed deeper into our own formation.

Scribonius had drawn his sword and despite the chaos and screaming madness of the charge, had the presence of mind to step nimbly aside as the momentum of the mount of the first Parthian carried him into the third rank of our formation, still knocking men over. Leaping over the body of the dead man in the second rank who had fallen directly in Scribonius' path, my friend made a perfect lunge at the Parthian, taking advantage of the man's split-second fumbling when the mounted man dropped his lance to try pulling his sword. The point of Scribonius' weapon found the one weak spot in the cataphract armor, other than the unguarded face, his blade punching into the Parthian's armpit, deep into his body. Blood gushed out of the man's mouth as it opened in shock, his eyes registering the surprise that always seems to come to men at the moment of their death, before toppling from the saddle. The horse was still there in the middle of the formation, and being trained for war it started to rear, the smell of blood in its nostrils as its hooves lashed out, one of them catching a man full in the face, splattering his nose and dropping him like a sack of grain. The third and fourth rank of the Parthian charge had smashed into our formation by this point, fully engaging the men of the First and Second Cohorts, as the added weight of the extra horsemen helped to push the Parthian charge even deeper into our ranks. In a matter of just moments there were only two more lines left between the Parthians and a breakthrough. Running over to the threatened point, out of the corner of my eye, I saw the figures of other men coming forward as well, and when I looked over I saw that Nigidius and Trebellius had gathered men who still carried the siege spears and were bringing them back into the fray. I had lost sight of Scribonius in the fighting, as blades flashed upwards to meet Parthian lances punching forward, their iron heads flickering as they probed for weaknesses in men's defenses. The solid thudding sound of metal on wood told me that most of the men were managing to parry the lunges, though there were a number of cries in our own tongue that meant that some were not.

Keeping my eye on one large Parthian in particular, his oiled beard streaked with gray telling me that he was an experienced warrior, I pushed through the mass of men, stopping long enough to pause by the first Parthian's horse, wounded but still lashing out with all four feet and biting any man within reach. The next time he reared, I stepped in quickly, grimacing at what I knew I had to do, thrusting my finely honed Gallic blade up into the horse's unprotected belly, giving a tremendous yank upwards with the blade, disemboweling the horse. It let out a heart-rending scream, collapsed to its knees, blood gushing from his belly and mouth, then rolled over, knocking a couple of my men off their feet.

"Next time don't let it get so far into the ranks," I snarled at men before looking back around for the older Parthian.

I spotted him; he was wielding his long curved sword with terrible effect. Before I could close with him I watched him cleave a man's arm off at the shoulder, the severed vessels spraying bright red blood directly into the face of the Roman next to the wounded man, blinding him and forcing him to fall back as he tried to clear his vision. The Parthian, seeing an opportunity, spurred his horse deeper into our midst and raised his blade to strike down at the blinded man.

"No, you don't!" I roared at him as I used the prone body of a man, I do not know if he was friend or foe, as a launching point to throw myself at the Parthian, my shoulder striking him in the midsection, the combination of my momentum and bulk carrying him from the saddle.

I had violated the first and most important rule of fighting by leaving my feet, yet I was so angry that I did not spare it a thought. We fell heavily, with me landing on top of the Parthian, driving the air from his lungs, coming out in a whooshing sound that smelled as foul as a sewer, and in one of those moments of strange clarity that come in battle, I looked into his opened mouth to see that most of his teeth were rotting. He was dazed, but he had not lived this long by luck alone, clawing at my eyes as I tried to bring my blade up to drive the point into the base of his throat. His fingernails raked my face and I turned my head, causing one of his fingers to fall into my own open mouth. As my own teeth were still in good shape, I bit the finger off, feeling the bone and gristle grinding against my teeth. He let out a scream that almost shattered my eardrums, jerking his hand back, giving me the opening I needed, and I brought the blade up between us then drove the point downwards. With his good hand, he pushed desperately against my own holding the sword, fighting with the strength of a man who knew his life was measured in breaths, but even as weakened as I was, I was still too powerful, the blade driving inexorably downwards. Our faces were a hand-span away from each other, our eyes locked together, both of us oblivious to all that was going on around us in our own private death struggle. After what seemed an eternity, I felt the blade punch into his body, his eyes widening in shock as the strength suddenly drained from him and with the release of pressure against my arm, the point drove the rest of the way home, crunching through bone to bury itself in the dirt. For the second time that day, I heard the rattle of a man's last breath, as he mouthed words that I assumed to be a prayer to his gods. I lay on top of him for several heartbeats, during which time any Parthian could have speared me through the back like a frog, but as I regained my breath and senses, I saw that my men had formed a protective cordon of shields around me and the dead Parthian. Climbing to my feet, I pulled the blade out as I gave thanks to the men, who grinned and waved a salute before turning back to the fight.

In the few moments I was involved in my private battle, more Parthians had smashed into the rearguard so that everything was a confused mass of horses, men and flailing weapons. The only thing that could have made it more confusing was the presence of dust, but thankfully, the weather precluded that problem. Horses were screaming in mortal terror and agony, men were cursing in their respective tongues, others were calling for help or making a prayer to their gods as they drew their final breaths, or at least believed they were. The men who had come with Trebellius and Nigidius were using their siege spears to push the mass of horsemen back from the rear ranks of the formation, but the Parthians were still feeding men into the charge. Looking to either side of the *quadratum*, I could only stand there, desperately considering what to do. I thought of pulling the Cohorts guarding either flank, but a moment of examination told me that it was not possible because the horse archers had moved to either side and were even now peppering the men with arrows to prevent just such a move. Searching about, I did not see our cavalry nearby, since they would have been able to run the archers off. Instead, we would have to turn the attack back with what we had, but to be safe, I summoned my runner to inform Antonius that we were being hard pressed. With that done, I returned my attention back to the fighting, seeing that it was not going well for the First and Second Cohorts. The Third was not being pressed as hard, though the rear of the Parthian charge had begun shifting its point of attack to hit the ranks of Metellus' men. As my mind digested what I was seeing, I had the first glimmer of hope that we would be able to turn this attack back. Despite understanding the Parthian commander's decision to devote some of his men to pinning the Third down, this had been an all-or-nothing attack, and those horsemen now occupied with Metellus could have been the difference in punching through. The problem with a cavalry attack if it does succeed in piercing the lines is in their speed and mobility; they would be falling on the rear of our men more worried about crossing the river than the threat from Parthian cataphracts well before any warning could be sent. By siphoning off some of his strength, the enemy had given us a chance, and that was all that I asked.

Moving back towards where the fighting was fiercest at the original point of attack, I saw the issue was still in doubt. The cataphracts were packed into a large pocket bulging into our lines, a black mass of danger and death, desperately hacking and pushing against my men, who were pressing back with equal fervor in an attempt to contain them. In the midst of the chaos, I saw Centurions' crests, and I could make out the distinct voices of each of them as they exhorted their men to kill as many of the enemy as they could. I do not know if the Parthians have a counterpart to a Centurion, but there are certainly officers, and though I could not understand them, I could tell that they were doing much the same. This was a battle of wills, Parthian against Roman, one side intent on destroying, the other intent on surviving. In our case, the best way for us to survive was to kill as many Parthians as possible. To help in that effort I rushed back in, realizing I had done all I could do at that moment as a Primus Pilus and now my sword was of more value than my *vitus*. Shoving my way past some of Nigidius' men who had helped my Cohort thrust a small group of cataphracts back that had broken from the main body, I used my height to reach up and grab one of the

Parthians around the waist, yanking him from the saddle. He had not seen me coming, yelping in surprise as he fell to the ground, but before he could make another sound, one of the men armed with a siege spear lunged with it, punching the point into the man's unprotected face. The Legionaries next to the man with the siege spear reached out, grabbing the reins of the horse, but it sealed its own fate by doing as it was trained to do at such moments by rearing and lashing out. One of the animal's hooves caught me across the back as I was advancing past, almost taking me off my feet, knocking the wind out of me.

Normally, I did not like killing animals, but I snarled, "Kill that fucking thing," an order the men obeyed immediately, using their spears.

I continued pushing past my men, who had regained the normal rhythm of our way of fighting, at least as much as it was possible in such a mess of a fight, holding onto the harness of the man in front of them while waiting for the Centurion's whistle to make an exchange.

Squeezing between the files, I continued to move up towards the thick of the fighting, as I heard someone call out, "Look there, boys. The Primus Pilus is going up there to whip those bastards by himself."

There was an ironic cheer from the men around him, but I did not bother answering, my eyes fixed on the sight of what I was looking for. Up ahead I could see the taller transverse crest that could only be Scribonius and his Cohort. My heart, which had already been hammering, started to pound even more urgently as I saw him and a group of his men completely surrounded by Parthian horsemen, all of them intent on collapsing the fragile pocket of men gathered around Scribonius and the Cohort standard. For an enemy army, killing a Centurion is a feat that gives a man enhanced status and the right to brag around the winter fires when warriors gather. Taking a Cohort standard on top of that means a reward from their king or leader second only to the taking of a Legion standard. Now, both were under threat, so I increased my pace, trying to push my way up to them, thinking to rally some men to cut our way through. Even as I was doing so, I saw the flash of a Parthian blade as it rose into the sky, then in seeming slow motion slash down. An instant later, Scribonius' transverse crest disappeared, followed immediately by an anguished cry that carried clearly above the din of the fight.

"Scribonius is down!"

Time seemed to stand still, the image of that moment frozen forever in my mind. The Parthian who struck the blow was raising his sword in triumph, shouting his own joy at accomplishing the feat of striking down a Centurion of Rome. The other Parthians around him, their faces partially obscured by their helmets were shouting their joy as well, yet underlying it all was a low, growling hum of anger and despair that was coming from Scribonius' men. Unbidden, without thought, something issued from within me as well, a howl of rage as for the first time in many years I felt the surge of madness that was like the return of a long-lost friend. It was that raging joy I had first experienced on a dusty hill in Lusitania when Vibius, Scribonius and I were marching in the Second Cohort under Gaius Crastinus, and were surrounded by a force of Gallaeci greatly outnumbering us. It was on that occasion, when they made a nighttime assault on our hill that a power that I can only attribute coming from Mars himself filled my body, making my sword sing, as according to all who saw it, for I have no real memory of the actual deed, I single-handedly destroyed the attack. For my actions, I was awarded my first set of phalarae and more importantly, first came to the attention of our general, Gaius Julius Caesar.

Now, that power was coursing through my veins again as I pushed through the rest of the men surrounding the knot of Parthians that were in turn threatening to overwhelm Scribonius' men and the Cohort standard, which still stood, defying every Parthian attempt to snatch it. I reached the first Parthian who, to be fair, was distracted by the cries of triumph from his own comrades, only at the last moment even realizing that death was coming for him. Twisting desperately in his saddle, he flailed wildly with his sword, a blow that I knocked aside with my own blade, not even feeling the impact. Reaching out with my free hand, having dropped my *vitus* at some point and contrary to my normal practice of not picking up a shield from a fallen man, I plucked him from the saddle. The Parthian saddle has very high cantles, fore and aft, so that a frontal or rear impact will rarely unseat the rider, yet from the side is where they are vulnerable, so that is where one could apply force, from either side, as I did on this occasion. My rage was such that I was able to hold the man up with one hand, though he was also small for a Parthian, then as he dangled in the air, I ran him through with my sword. The blade, forged in Gaul that I had paid so much for, punched through his thick armor as if it were not there. He gave one small shriek, going limp as I threw him to the side much the same way a child will discard a toy of which he has grown tired. The men around me grabbed the reins of the man's horse, but fortunately for the beast, it did not try to fight, therefore being quickly led out of the battle. Continuing my push forward, I was intent only on reaching the Cohort standard where I knew Scribonius was lying, refusing to allow myself to believe that he had been anything but stunned. Getting to the spot where our men were facing those Parthians, I saw that there was one layer of horsemen turned outwards, protecting the rear of the cataphracts intent on destroying the remnants of Scribonius' men in order to capture the standard. I must confess that at this point I had not allowed myself to think about the fact that Gaius was somewhere in there, afraid that the very thought would freeze me into inaction. That is what I tell myself now; perhaps it is the truth, yet it is just as likely that I was reveling in the feeling of warmth that this madness bestowed on me by Mars gave me, as it seemed as if it had been forever since I was warm, in any sense of the word. One Parthian, still carrying his lance, spotted me, given that I am hard to miss, spurring his mount forward to push against the shields of our men surrounding him, jabbing above their heads at my face. He was quick, I will give him that much; I felt the breath of air whisper against my cheek as I moved my head to avoid his lunge, but before I could react with a counter-move he had pulled the lance back. Do it again you bastard, I thought, and we will see who the better man is. As if reading my thoughts, I saw the man give a savage grin behind his helmet as he made another lunge, the point of his lance moving towards me at unbelievable speed. Now, I was never as fast as Vibius, who was simply the quickest man I have ever known. Nevertheless, for a big man I move fast, so as quick as that Parthian was, it seemed to me as if he was moving underwater, the point of his lance whistling past my left ear as I moved to the right with a purpose. I clearly remember thinking that this was for Cyclops as I reached up, grabbed the lance with my left hand, then twisting my body, gave a huge yank on it. If he had been an experienced warrior he would have simply let go, but in that small moment when our eyes met before he made his second lunge I had seen he was a young Parthian noble. Clearly intent on making his name known among his people, he paid for that desire with his life. As I said, the Parthian saddle being what it is makes it extremely difficult to unseat a man when pulled from front or rear. Still, it is not impossible and I am a very, very strong man, especially when Mars' power is coursing through my body. It was the inexperience of the young Parthian that kept him holding onto his lance, and because of that, he went sailing over his horse's head and over mine for that matter, though I had to duck, to land in the midst of some very angry Roman Legionaries behind me, who promptly cut him into pieces. I did not even bother worrying about the Parthian's horse, moving past it so quickly that even if it was so inclined, it could not have struck me, having already learned my lesson.

I was into the second rank of Parthians, despite still having a distance to go to reach the Second's standard. Not missing a step, I ducked underneath the slash of a Parthian's sword, then without any hesitation, punched the point of my sword up and into the horse's belly, twisting my body with all my strength, ripping down through the midsection. Offal and blood burst out and down onto my arm, but I was beyond caring, intent on only one thing at this point. The horse let out an almost human scream as it staggered sideways, hitting the mount of the man next to him. Both Parthians were suddenly thrown from the backs of their horses, one mount dying while the other, trying to cope with the smell of the death of one of its own kind, jumped away and tried to turn back towards what it thought of as safety and home. I did not worry about their respective fates, knowing that the men behind me would dispatch them, so that before the enemy horsemen were aware of what was happening, I was now among the Parthians facing the ever-shrinking knot of Second Cohort men. Before any of them could turn to address the new threat to their rear, I reached up to pull yet another man from the saddle, punching my blade through his face before he even knew that his death had arrived. I was close enough now that if I looked between the horses' legs I could see the men of the Second, though I could not make out any man's face, but I did not need to see faces to know that it was my nephew who was standing over the body of Scribonius and next to the *signifer*, surrounded by Parthians.

There is no way to describe the sensations and feelings that crackled through every fiber of my being at seeing Valeria's only son, sword in hand, facing the Parthians. Where my body had been running hot, as if I had a raging fever, just as quickly as it had come it was now replaced by a surge of ice running through my veins, making me feel every one of my 41 years as I tried to make my way to the standard. At the same time, a fierce sense of pride surged through me at the sight of my nephew, standing as a Roman should, sword in hand, spitting defiance at his enemies with his last breath. However, I was determined that it would not be his last so I lunged, slashed and parried my way through the last group of Parthians between me and Gaius. I do not know how many of the enemy I killed in those moments, so focused was I on reaching him and Scribonius. Finally, after what seemed like a full watch but was probably only a matter of several normal heartbeats, I reached Gaius, calling to him and immediately regretting it. He was inexperienced enough to turn his head at the sound of his name and it was only a desperate lunge on my part that saved him from a Parthian lance through the face, my blade knocking it aside. Instead of hitting him, the point caught me high in the shoulder, breaking a few links of armor, cutting into my skin, though not deeply.

I let out a string of curses, then growled at him, "Keep your eyes front, damn you, or I'll gut you myself."

His young face flushed red, but he nodded before turning his head back toward the enemy. Scribonius was lying at the *signifer*'s feet, face down and I could see that his helmet had been cleaved almost in half, my stomach lurching at the sight, but I could not pay any more attention. Quickly surveying the situation, I saw that Scribonius' Optio was still on his feet, with about three sections of men with him that were separated from the dozen men surrounding the Cohort standard by a double line of Parthians, each line facing the opposite direction. Whirling about, I looked for one man in particular, then I saw that Scribonius' *cornicen* was down and unconscious, causing me to curse again. Grabbing the whistle hanging at my neck, I began blowing the same pattern of notes that the *cornicen* used to signal an attack, hoping that the fact that I could not change pitch would not confuse the Optio. Fortunately, he was a worthy Optio for a Pilus Prior in the Second Cohort, a post I had once held, so that after just a couple of blasts I heard him bellow the command to attack.

With a roar, his men started pushing against the line of Parthians facing them, while I turned to the small group of men with me, shouting, "Follow me, boys! Do this for Scribonius!"

Leaping over his body, I launched myself at the nearest enemy, and it was young Gaius who was next to me as we pushed forward. Without a word spoken between us, we both set our sights on the same Parthian, a thick man with closely set eyes that were almost crossed, though it did not seem to hinder his ability to see since he immediately divined what we were up to. Gaius approached from one side, I from the other, our blades held in the first position while Gaius gripped tightly to his shield, and I was struck by the thought that I should have picked one up. Instead of turning his horse to one side or another, he jammed his spurs viciously into his horse's flanks, causing it to lunge forward, aiming the horse towards me, while simultaneously striking down at Gaius. I leapt aside, the shoulder of the horse barely grazing me and though I could not see because my view was blocked by the bulk of the horse's body, I heard the clanging ring of metal on metal that told me Gaius had successfully parried the blow. Now it was the Parthian's turn to be on the defensive and with a man on either side, his fate was essentially sealed. I made a lunge that he was able to parry with a glancing sweep of his sword, then underneath the horse's belly I saw a pair of hands, one holding a sword, reach out and grab hold of the Parthian's boot, suddenly yanking upwards. The man's face registered the shock and surprise as he came toppling towards me, but despite grabbing the horn of his saddle and keeping his seat, it did not matter. The point of my blade punched under his free arm, and before his heart had stopped beating, I pulled him from the saddle to dump him on the ground. This was yet another moment for which I was thankful for my height because it allowed me to look over the pommel of the Parthian's saddle, just in time to see one of the remaining cataphracts turning towards Gaius' unprotected back.

"Behind you," I shouted, pushing the Parthian horse aside with every ounce of strength in my body.

Fortunately, Gaius was blessed with the reflexes of youth, spinning quickly while bringing his shield up as he had been trained, so that the Parthian lance bounced harmlessly against the boss. One of the Optio's men dispatched the attacker from behind, and like his predecessor, he also toppled from the saddle. I became aware that there were more empty saddles than men still atop their horses, and while the animals were still a threat themselves, they were not as formidable without their riders. Standing on tiptoe to see that the men of the First and Second Cohorts had surrounded pockets of Parthians, I could also tell that while the fighting was not over, the attack had failed. Turning my attention back to the matter at hand, I was in time to see young Gaius and one of his comrades wrestle another Parthian from the saddle, then my nephew's sword arm drew back, thrusting home with a perfect stroke, killing his enemy. The situation was still a confused mess, riderless horses alternately milling about nervously, or with the better trained or more aggressive ones, rearing and lashing out at every attempt made by a Legionary to grab its reins. There were still a fair number of cataphracts clustered in small groups in the midst of our formation, but they were now more concerned with getting away than trying to break through. The largest concentration of Parthians was still located where the original assault had hit our lines to penetrate the deepest, the survivors of the initial charge now completely surrounded and isolated from their own comrades, but I decided they could wait until we eliminated the last of the Parthians around the Second's standard. Gaius had begun to move towards another small group of Parthians. Before he could get away, I moved quickly, grabbing him by the collar.

"You're my runner now," I commanded, and he opened his mouth to protest, but just as quickly shut it when he looked at my face.

"I've lost enough today," I said quietly. "I'm not going to lose you too."

With the immediate crisis over, I resumed my role as more of a supervisor of the action than being involved directly in it, making sure that Gaius stayed next to me wherever I went. Lutatius had been directing the Century in my absence, yet given their spot at the far right, they were not as hard pressed as the other Centuries. The Fifth and Sixth Centuries, under Asellio and Vistilia respectively had borne the brunt of the First's fight and were still mopping up the last resistance in their area. Parthians were now trying to cut their way free, no longer intent on destroying us but now wanting only to live, giving them a desperate courage. Our men were equally determined to make these Parthians pay for all of the suffering incurred at their hands, making the fighting bitter and bloody, but our men were also tired and weak from hunger. As much as we tried to prevent it, a large number of cataphracts were able to extricate themselves to gallop away, despite leaving a pile of corpses behind, along with more horses. All that I have described above took at the most a sixth part of a watch from the start to the point where I sent another runner, young Gaius as it turned out, to report to Antonius that the situation was in hand, the crossing now secure. As much as I had been exposed to it, the sudden silence following a battle was still unnerving, this time being no exception. Turning about, I surveyed the carnage, my mind a blank as I tried to absorb what my eye took in. There were mounds of corpses but if one looked closely, one would see that the mound seemed to be alive, as it was, men not yet dead pulling themselves out from under the pile. Most of them would be seriously wounded, although there were a few who had perfected the art of falling into a heap of bodies, pretending to be dead as the battle raged, tucked away in what is ironically one of the safest places on the battlefield. At least until after the fighting when men begin to search the piles for wounded friends, enemies, and loot. The combination of the moaning wind and the wounded made the most lonely sound imaginable, while men searching through the fallen for friends alternately let out cries of joy at finding them alive, or shouts of despair when they were not. If it was a Parthian they found wounded, they ended his misery with a quick slash across the throat. In short, it was a typical after-battle scene and it was not until I took a step, feeling the shaking in my knees that my mind began to come back to the present. I had been transported across the world to scenes of other battles, of moments I had spent walking the field looking for friends, but now I forced myself to come back to the present, knowing that there was much to do. The first task was one that I did not want to perform. Nevertheless, I squared my shoulders before I walked to where the *signifer* of the Second Cohort was kneeling, next to his standard planted in the ground. I did not need to look to know by whose side he knelt, walking over as I did with my heart in my throat. The *signifer* looked up to see me approach before turning to look back down and I saw his lips moving. It seemed as if my worst fears were confirmed as I was sure he was saying a prayer for the dead. Then to my utter shock he laughed, making me quicken my pace, intent on giving him a dressing-down that he would not forget about the propriety of expressing mirth when saying a prayer for the dead, especially when it was my best friend. I was a few paces away when the body next to the *signifer* moved, an unmistakable sign of life, in the form of a hand that appeared to be waving at me. I ran the last few feet to look down into the smiling face of Sextus Scribonius, albeit a face completely covered in blood to the point where one would think he was a triumphant general parading in Rome.

"What are you looking at?" His voice was surprisingly strong for a dead man.

Once again, my knees threatened to buckle, though this time in relief, so to avoid further embarrassment, I hurriedly knelt beside him.

"How on Gaia's earth are you alive?" I gasped.

"I've been wondering that myself," he replied wryly, reaching up to touch the huge gash on his scalp, wincing as his fingers probed the wound. "All I remember was the sight of that Parthian meat cleaver coming down, and I thought that was it. The next thing I know Publius here is pulling my helmet off and babbling like an idiot."

"I thought he was dead too, Primus Pilus," Publius' face was streaked with tears, but his smile was wide and bright with relief. "And he would have been too, if it hadn't been for Porcinus."

Both Scribonius and I looked at Publius sharply, exchanging a glance.

"What do you mean, Publius?" Scribonius asked.

"Well, sir, when you went down, I was occupied trying to keep one of those Parthian bastards from grabbing the standard. That just won't do. You know how I feel about the Second Cohort and nobody is going to take . . ."

Before I could, Scribonius interrupted gently, reminding Publius of his original mission, clearly used to the man rambling.

"Right, sir, sorry. Anyway, since I was busy, there was nobody able to do anything when another Parthian with a lance tried to spear you. He was aiming right for the gullet, and he would have had you too, if Porcinus hadn't come out of nowhere." His eyes widened as he continued, both of us listening attentively. "Honestly, sir, I don't know where he come from. But right before that lance ended you, he took a swipe at it with his sword and cut it in half like it was a twig. Oh, that Parthian was mad enough to bite through nails." He chuckled at the memory. "But it was young Porcinus, sir, sure as I'm sitting here. He saved you, no doubt about it."

"It sounds like someone has earned himself his first decoration, and a big one at that," a new voice spoke from over my shoulder, and I whirled to see Marcus Antonius sitting astride Clemency, looking down at us.

As bad as Scribonius' wound looked, it was like most scalp wounds, which bleed profusely without much real cause. His helmet suffered most of the damage, absorbing the brunt of the blow so that his skull was unbroken. He had a nasty gash that separated a large section of his scalp from his skull, but that could easily be stitched back up. Antonius ordered his personal physician to attend to Scribonius, the general following Gaius back after my nephew delivered my message. The men had to work quickly to gather the wounded and on Antonius' order, the dead were also collected to be carried across the river, so sure was he that the Parthians would not follow. He had ordered that the hospital tents be erected on the far side, where the sick and wounded were now gathered, and we sent our own to join them. Scribonius refused to go with the rest of the wounded, and in truth, I was so relieved that he had survived that I was not inclined to argue.

The Parthians had once again retreated out of range, while our cavalry patrolled between them and the rest of the army as men slowly moved across the waist-deep river. We put the recently captured Parthian horses to use transporting the freshly wounded; the dead were carried by their comrades the remaining distance, other men carrying the packs of the litter bearers. No Centurion had to urge the men to move quickly now that the end was in sight. Some men even began singing a marching song, a sound that had not been heard in weeks, and I stood next to Antonius astride Clemency as the men marched by.

"That's the spirit boys," I called to them as they passed. "The Aras River is just ahead."

I believe I said that at least twice before Antonius interrupted me.

"Pullus, what are you telling them that this is the Aras for?"

I looked up at him in surprise.

"Because that's the name of it, isn't it? That's the river where we cross into Armenia."

He stared down at me, giving me a strange look that I could not interpret, his lips pressed into a thin line, his brow suddenly furrowing. Then with a jerk of his head that I should follow, he turned Clemency, moving several paces away. When I rejoined him, he had his back turned towards the men, so I matched his facing.

"Pullus, this isn't the Aras River."

I looked at him in shock, not sure I had heard him correctly.

"But that's when the Parthians were going to stop pursuing, when we crossed the Aras."

He shook his head, and now he looked embarrassed.

"That was true, until Mithradates informed me that they would call off the pursuit before that, here at this river. I don't even know the name of it. It's more a stream than a river anyway," he said absently, looking back in the direction in which the men were headed.

"So, Artavasdes isn't nearby?"

For this was the second part of the reason that the men were so energetic, the Centurions fueling that enthusiasm, because Artavasdes the Armenian had sworn to make up for his cowardice in leaving us when the baggage train was destroyed by waiting with fresh supplies of food and forage for the whole army once we crossed the Aras River.

Again, Antonius shook his head.

"No, Pullus. The Aras is still another week's march, but we won't have to worry about the Parthians."

He stiffened as another thought occurred to him. "Who else among the Primi Pili thinks this is the Aras?"

Now it was his turn to be shocked as I replied, "Every one of them that I've talked to. We all thought that this was the Aras River."

My mind was reeling with the implications of what he had told me, not least of which was the question of how the commanding general could have let a detail this important slip by and not inform us. I suppose that we were at least partly at fault for making the assumption that the river we had been told would mark the end of Parthian pursuit was the same where Artavasdes was meeting us, yet it showed me how little communication was taking place between the command group and the Centurions the last few weeks.

"Well, don't tell the men until they're across the river and we're safe. We're going to make camp for the night, though I know it's still early and we could go a few more thirds of a watch, but the men need rest."

Without another word, he turned to gallop back towards the river, his head bowed, obviously lost in thought. I could only mutter a curse under my breath before turning back to the men, who were still marching by and singing. I had detailed the Seventh to be the last Cohort of the rearguard across the river, so I joined them as they approached the riverbank, keeping my eye behind us at the Parthians who were edging a little closer as the army contracted on this side of the river. The main body of the enemy reached the site of our fight, men dismounting to search among their own dead, though if they were looking for wounded they searched in vain since we had made sure to leave none behind. I saw some of the dismounted men pulling at their beards or ripping the sleeves of their garments, which I had learned was their sign of grief. I supposed that just like our army they had friends and even relatives who were part of that last charge against us. When you see men acting with such sadness at the death of someone close to them, it is hard to view them as an enemy, though in the case of the Parthians, it was not so difficult. We had bloodied them, but they had made us suffer in a way that no other enemy had and particularly with the death of Cyclops, dead just a few thirds of a watch by this point, my hatred of the Parthians congealed into something that still sits inside me like a bitter lump of lead to this day. Finally, it was just the Seventh and the cavalry on this side of the river. As custom befits, I resolved to be the last Roman across. The first men of the Seventh had just entered the water when one Parthian came galloping closer, waving a flag of truce. The Gallic commander snapped out orders to several of his men and they went thundering towards the Parthian, surrounding him before bringing him closer.

I turned to Marcius, who was standing next to me, telling him to continue on.

"Primus Pilus, are you sure that's wise? They're treacherous bastards."

I could not help laughing at Marcius' words, patting him on the shoulder as I said, "That they are, Marcius, but if I can't handle one of those treacherous bastards, I don't belong in the army anymore anyway."

Whereupon I faced about to meet the Parthian, still surrounded by Gauls, each of them with his hand on his sword, looking very much as if they wanted the Parthian to try some trick, but he was no fool. He was about my age, with piercing black eyes and wind-tanned leathery skin, each wrinkle earned, much as mine were. He sat, regarding me in silence for a moment, while I stood, watching him calmly, determined not to speak since he had been the one to approach.

Finally, he spoke in passable Latin. "You are a Centurion, yes?"

"Yes."

I was not much in the mood for a conversation.

"You are very large for a Roman, are you not?"

"I suppose." I shrugged. Clearly expecting more, he waited, then seeing I was not a willing partner, he smiled, displaying surprisingly even, white teeth.

"You don't like me, do you, Roman?"

"Why don't you get off that horse and find out?"

Now he laughed, shaking his head. "No, I do not believe I will do that."

He turned serious.

"My King has ordered me to tell you that in tribute to the valor of Roman arms, the army of Phraates, King of Parthia, will not pursue you beyond the river which you have just crossed."

"As a tribute to our valor?" I asked sarcastically. "More like you were tired of losing men."

The smile disappeared from his face and his horse, sensing its rider's agitation, began making small hops sideways, causing the Gauls to tighten their grip on their swords.

"You have lost as well, Roman. You would do well to remember that," he said tightly.

Taking a breath, he regained his composure, the smile returning, but it was easy to see that it was forced.

"However, I was not sent here to quarrel, just to assure you that you will not see the army of Parthia again."

"Are you a betting man?" I asked him suddenly, catching him completely by surprise.

He looked at me for a moment before he replied cautiously, "I have been known to place a wager."

"There is one sure wager you can make with your Parthian friends," I said. "You can bet that we will be back again. We have unfinished business here."

His face darkened, but his tone was even and under control when he replied, "And you can wager with YOUR friends that we will be here, waiting for you, Roman." He then made an exaggerated bow and said, "When that happens, Roman, I look forward to meeting you again. My name is Monaeses."

Without another word, the man who had led the Parthian army so skillfully jerked his horse around and galloped off, followed for a short distance by the Gauls.

The Gallic commander looked down at me with amusement and said in heavily accented Latin, "I think you made him angry, Primus Pilus."

"I have a way of doing that," I told him, in his own tongue, then turned to wade across the river.

It was another tense night in camp, because we were forced to tell the men that this was not the Aras River and none of us were willing to trust the Parthians. However, there were no major disturbances, no Parthians trying to slip across to do mischief. The next day, men rose in the bitter cold, packed up, loaded the wounded and ill on the litters, then resumed the march. Scribonius was sporting a white bandage wrapped around his head, yet other than a headache did not seem the worse for wear. Word of young Gaius' actions quickly spread through the Legion and I had sent for him the night before, after the camp was settled in. He showed up still in his blood-spattered uniform, hollow-eyed and clearly exhausted, moving jerkily as his brain struggled to stay alert. I immediately had him sit down, sending Diocles to find some clean rags with which he could wash.

"I'm sorry we don't have any wine, and I can't heat water for you."

He shook his head and said woodenly, "It's all right, Uncle."

He was gazing at a point off into space, a look that I knew well because I suspect that I had displayed a similar one in the past, many years ago after my first hot action.

"So, is it what you thought it would be?" I asked quietly.

He started at the question before his eyes slowly focused on me, and he did not answer, just shook his head slowly.

"Legionary Porcinus," I said in my official voice, "as Primus Pilus of the 10th Legion, I commend you for your valor in saving the life of Secundus Pilus Prior Scribonius. Your actions reflect the highest honor of the Legions of Rome, and the 10th Legion in particular. You will undoubtedly be decorated, and since there were numerous witnesses, the probable decoration will be the Grass Crown. As you know, there is no higher individual honor that a Legionary, or citizen for that matter, can attain."

I stood and he automatically rose from his chair, coming to *intente*. Weaving as if he were drunk, I ignored this as I stepped forward to offer my hand. He took it, and we stood for a moment, two Legionaries of Rome.

Then I released his hand and without any thought, I reached out, grabbed him to me, hugging him fiercely as I whispered, "But as your uncle, and you the only son of my much-loved sister, don't ever scare me that badly again."

I do not know if it was the words or the action, but it was as if a dam burst, and he began sobbing, his head buried in my chest. We stood there for I know not how long and it suddenly became as if I were holding Vibi again, who I had only seen as a small boy, all the fierce love a parent has for his child rushing back, and I realized that I loved young Gaius as if he were my own son. I felt tears coming from my own eyes, feeling the ache of the loss of Cyclops, the scare of almost losing Scribonius, the fear I had felt when I saw young Gaius standing alone against the Parthians, the misery and cold and hunger of the past weeks, all rushing at me at the same time, until we were both sobbing. I am not sure how long Diocles was standing there or how much he saw, but when I spotted him I released young Gaius to guide him gently back to his chair before waving him over. Despite having no wood, somehow Diocles had managed to heat a basin of water a bit, so that while it was not hot, it was not ice cold. Dipping a cloth in it, he gently began to wipe Gaius clean. None of us spoke as Diocles worked, but I could see Gaius slowly relaxing, his tear-streaked cheeks regaining some color, his breathing becoming more even. Diocles finished cleaning Gaius, whereupon I waved him to leave us.

When he had gone, I asked Gaius, "Do you want to talk about it?"

Gaius said nothing for several moments, then he burst out, "Oh, Uncle Titus. It was horrible!"

He buried his face in his hands and began weeping again. Slowly, in fits and starts, he began describing his first true, hard-fought battle.

"It was complete chaos and confusion once the Parthians pushed three or four ranks deep into the Cohort, and it was only the Pilus Prior who kept us together," he explained. "There were men who started to turn and run, but Pilus Prior Scribonius just acted so calm that they were too ashamed and they stopped and fought. But that's why the Parthians were able to get so many horsemen into our midst."

He shuddered as he recalled the carnage. While he did not know it, he had given me a valuable piece of information, because I had been puzzled how the pocket had grown so quickly once the Parthians slammed into our lines.

"I saw one of my best friends killed today," he said quietly. "Otho helped me a lot when I first came to the Legion, showing me what I needed to do in order to do things the way they're done in the 10th. Now he's dead. Gone, just like that." He snapped his fingers.

"I would say you get used to it," I told him. "But that would be a lie. You don't get used to it, you get . . .

numb to it after a while. You grieve for the friends you lose." I was thinking of Cyclops as I spoke. "But you put the memory of them in a special place in your mind, and you don't think of them, except on special occasions."

He looked at me, his expression unreadable, asking me suddenly, "Uncle, how many friends have you seen die like this?"

I exhaled sharply, feeling like I was being punched in the gut, but I could see there was no malice in the boy's question, no desire to open old wounds. Just the curiosity of a young man trying to learn how to cope with that which it is essentially impossible to cope.

"Too many to count, Gaius. Too many to count."

Seeing that was all the answer he was going to get, Gaius sat quietly for a moment.

"Uncle, can I tell you something? When I saw you fighting today, I have never, ever seen anything that terrible. You killed anything that stood before you, as if you were the god Mars himself. I saw firsthand why you're a legend in the army."

I was not sure how to respond to what Gaius was saying; how do you tell someone that you are sure that a god is working through you?

"It's a gift, Gaius," I said carefully. "A gift of the gods, that comes to me at moments of great danger. But it's a dark gift, and I wouldn't wish it on anyone, because there's a heavy price that comes with that gift."

He considered this, only nodding and not commenting directly.

Instead, he asked, "Can I tell you something else? Something that may seem strange and might make you think differently of me?"

I stared at him for a moment, trying to think of what it could possibly be.

"Yes," I said slowly. "Whatever you tell me here, you're telling me as your uncle. It will go no farther."

"As much as I hated everything that happened today, there was a part of me that . . . liked it as well. I've never felt so . . . alive."

He seemed embarrassed by the admission, yet I am glad he was too absorbed in his own thoughts to hear my sigh of relief, for I had been in fact thinking the opposite, that he would tell me that he had no desire for the army and wanted out.

"It is a puzzle, isn't it?" I asked in a light tone. "How can something so horrible be so alluring at the same time?" I shook my head. "I don't know. And Gaius, I'll tell you this. If you ever discover why that is, please tell me so I'll know as well."

We were back on the march the next day and after spending the first half of it looking over our shoulders, keeping scouts near the river, we began to breathe easier, finally believing that perhaps the Parthians would not be coming after us any longer. However, the news that this was not the Aras dampened the relief we might otherwise have felt, prompting something somewhat strange to take place with the men, the focus of their anger shifting from the Parthians to Artavasdes the Armenian. Despite the fact that it was not the Aras, meaning therefore we were not in Armenia, there was still a strong sentiment among the men that he should have been present with all the foodstuffs and warm clothing that he had supposedly promised. With every passing mile, the men's anger grew, until there was a clamor throughout the army to attack Artavasdes as soon as we came into contact with him, then take the supplies, rather than rely on his charity.

"If it hadn't been for him taking his own cataphracts and archers away, we'd have been able to beat those bastards in one battle," Vellusius declared to me as I walked beside him at one point, his comrades nodding vigorously or calling out their agreement.

Vellusius was not the brightest spark in the fire, as we said, yet when it came to battle, I trusted his judgment.

"How do you figure that?" I was genuinely curious.

"It's simple, Primus Pilus," he said seriously. "As good as we are, we can only defeat the Parthians when we're on the defense, but once we beat them back, we didn't have the heavy cavalry and horse archer troops we needed to pursue them and finish them. We needed to fight fire with fire, and when that bastard Artavasdes left with his men, we lost the chance to finish them once and for all."

It was the kind of profound military wisdom that only comes from hundreds of skirmishes and battles, of being part of every one of them to see the results of lapses of judgment and mistakes made, of the tragedy of hesitation or the disaster of rash action, and Vellusius had seen more than his share of all of it. I knew he was right, as did all of the other men of the army, which helped fuel their rage at Artavasdes, but it was also that the suffering of the sick and wounded was not over. Despite the fact we were safe from the Parthians, we were still exposed to the bitter cold and wind, the wounded were still bouncing along on litters, tearing open the gashes of some of my men wounded the day before, causing more blood loss. Inevitably, some of those men succumbed to their wounds, while men stricken by a cough and fever also continued to die. Our supply situation continued to be extremely critical, even the profiteers suffering, as the entire army was down to barley. The only other positive note was that we were now entering into country that showed signs of supporting scrub vegetation and trees that would supply firewood, meaning there was at least a prospect of having enough wood to make bread, rather than chewing the raw kernels of grain like the men had been doing. For my part, my stomach was growling at the thought of eating from a haunch of one of the mules that would go lame on the march that day, and I suspected that more of my comrades would be partaking of meat than on previous occasions. We passed the first day on the safe side of the river with no sight of the Parthians, making camp and spending the night without incident. The foraging parties had scrounged enough wood for cooking fires, not for warmth but eating bread, even if it was made of barley instead of the raw grain, cheering the men immensely. Meanwhile I enjoyed my stringy piece of mule haunch as if I were once again sitting at Cleopatra's table.

Some things were looking up, but I had some sad duties to attend to, as I had to tally up the final butcher's bill of wounded and dead, then make a number of promotions and changes in the Centurionate. Despite Scribonius surviving, his Princeps Prior Titus Cipius had taken a Parthian lance through a lung, dying on the field. Two Optios, one in the Second Century and one in the Fifth Century had also been killed, while in my Cohort, my Hastatus Prior Gnaeus Asellio was on a litter with a wound to his belly, and barring some intervention from the gods, was going to die. Vistilia's Optio had also been killed. The Second Cohort had lost 22 dead, had 18 litter cases, with 31 walking wounded, out of 398 effectives, though the Second also had more than twenty sick litter cases yet to recover, or to die. The bulk of the First's casualties were with the Fifth and Sixth Centuries, both of them being next to the Second

Cohort where the attack was centered. The Fifth Century had 58 effectives moments before the attack began; by the end of the battle they had seven dead and 13 men wounded, five of them on litters with one of them, Asellio, almost certain to die. The Fifth also had eight men sick on litters. Vistilia's Century had been in slightly better shape beginning the battle, with 63 men standing in line, but they had suffered the most casualties, with 11 men killed and 20 wounded, nine of them litter cases. The Third Century suffered a half-dozen casualties with one man killed, while in this battle the First and Second Centuries had escaped with only a couple of wounded, none seriously. With Diocles' and the other clerk's help, a freedman Greek like Diocles named Perdicas, I tallied up the reports, signing the wax tablets before giving them to Perdicas to take to the *Praetorium*, then stretched out on my cot to get some rest as I thought about the choices I had made to replace the lost Centurions. I had moved the Pilus Posterior of the Eighth into Cyclop's spot, then taken the traditional route of moving everyone in the Century up one slot. Into the Hastatus Posterior slot, I promoted Cyclops' Optio, Vibius Pacuvius, who Cyclops had spoken of highly on multiple occasions. I left the promotions in the Second Cohort to Scribonius because I trusted him implicitly and he had selected his Optio, a man in appearance as unlike Scribonius as it was possible to be; where Scribonius was tall and spare, Quintus Fronto was built like an amphora of oil with arms and legs, but while he looked fat, he was immensely strong. He was swarthy in complexion, with black, wiry hair and he perpetually looked in need of a shave, yet Scribonius had seen something in him that frankly I had not, because Fronto would not have been my first choice, despite acquitting himself well in the previous battle. While Asellio still lived, I could not appoint or promote anyone into his slot, but I had definite ideas about who I would choose, wondering how much uproar there would be as I fell asleep.

By the middle of the second day, Antonius was reassured enough that the Parthians would not come swooping down on us that he allowed us to march in open order, with men again able to move among Cohorts. The cold was growing steadily worse, until those men who had either not brought or been unable to fashion warm weather clothing were now paying for it with the loss of appendages to frostbite. Most commonly, it was toes, first turning white as the man lost feeling in them, before gradually turning black, then just snapping off when he tripped over a rock. There was no pain when it happened, the man looking down in surprise at the cracking sound as his foot struck a stone or some other obstacle, but I had seen before what happened when the men got warm again, knowing they would be in agony. Some of the men insisted on picking up the blackened toe, putting it in their purse until it started to stink or they got bored with it. Other men were not so lucky, and I noticed that men with proud, protuberant noses seemed to number most prominently among these unlucky souls whose noses went the way of some men's toes, leaving gaping, ugly holes. Even without any pain, these men were horrified, as were their comrades, so that men checked each other's noses religiously every day, looking for the telltale whitening of the tip that signaled the beginning of the trouble. I was never in any danger, thanks to my supply of fur-lined socks and my habit of keeping a scarf wrapped around my face, the ends tied behind my neck, yet not all of the men in the Century were so lucky. The most unfortunate lost all of the toes off one, or in a few cases both feet, and once they were gone they could no longer keep up with the pace set on the march, having to be transferred to a litter, and would be out of the Legion when we returned to Syria. It turned out that the Parthians had served a useful purpose, for without the need to be on watch constantly for a sudden attack, the men could now focus all of their attention on their misery, so that now the sullen mood was never far away. The second night we reached an area where there was enough wood for fires to do more than cook; we could at last have heat for most of the night, but this forced a decision, made by Antonius on the advice of his personal physician, that all Primi Pili were summoned to the *Praetorium* to hear.

"We have a choice to make," Antonius said, his face grimmer than what was normal for him those days. "We can either have fires, but only for men whose limbs are whole and are not suffering from frostbite, or we have no fires for anyone."

Not surprisingly, there was a huge uproar, all of us leaping to our feet to protest. It took a moment for him to quiet us down, something that would have never happened just three months previously, but much had changed.

"I'm no happier about it than you are, but let my physician explain."

He turned and motioned to the bearded, older Greek man who had tended to Scribonius.

"If you allow men whose appendages have been afflicted with frostbite to thaw those appendages out, they will suffer horribly, so much so that it is highly unlikely that any of them would be ready to march in the morning."

"What are you on about?"

This came from Corbulo who, like all of us, was a shell of the man he had been at Zeugma. Still, the fire continued to rage within him, his voice still as strong as ever.

"Imagine that you have had a toe, or finger, or a nose severed suddenly," the Greek replied calmly, clearly not intimidated by a Primus Pilus, which I could understand with Antonius as a patient. "You would feel great pain, no?"

We all agreed with this, some like Corbulo more grudgingly than others, he clearly not fancying the prospect of telling men that they would not finally feel the warming flames of a fire this night.

"The reason these men do not feel that pain is because the tissue surrounding where the appendage has been lost is still frozen, and as long as it remains frozen, they will be able to function at their current level, whatever that may be. But when that tissue starts to thaw, feeling will return, and that is when the pain of losing that appendage will be felt."

"Some of the men have lost several toes and fingers," someone pointed out. "They'll be in more agony than a man who's lost just one."

"So we should deprive other men of their first chance to warm their backside?" Corbulo was grumbling, but that was the nub of the problem.

"That's what we need to decide," Antonius announced, looking uncertain, and it was clear he was looking to us for some idea of what to do. "You tell me what the mood of the army is, today. Given all that's taken place, will there be the danger of a mutiny?"

"I would say definitely yes if we tried to keep all of them from using the fires to warm themselves," I answered this, while the others nodded their head.

"They're not going to like the idea of their friends who have frostbite not being able to sit next to them, but given the choice of staying cold for their sake or keeping those men away from the fire, I think they will say 'Fuck 'em,'" Caecina announced, to which there was general agreement, though some were not quite as certain about it.

Myself, I thought Caecina was probably right, but I would also not have been surprised if they did choose, and that is when I had the idea.

"Why not put it to a vote?"

All heads turned at me in surprise, and I could see men like Corbulo grimace at the idea, but others nodded thoughtfully.

"Vote?" This came from Rhamnus, the commander of the Brundisium Cohorts, who was always invited to these meetings, much to the disgust of the other Primi Pili. His tone was scoffing, and since I already despised him, it did not take much to anger me where he was concerned. "This isn't the forum. It's not an election, it's the army."

"And what exactly would you know about the army?" I growled. "How many of your men have frostbite? How many of your men have been killed or wounded, for that matter?"

"My men have performed the duties they've been given," he said defensively, his eyes darting about, but there were no friendly faces.

"And how many have frostbite?" I continued to press.

"Only one or two," he admitted. "But it's not their fault that they have better warm weather clothing."

"And it's not my men's fault that they don't," Caecina shot back, appearing to be as angry as I was. "I have at least 200 men in my Legion alone who have frostbite, but they're still marching and making camp every night. When's the last time your men have dug a ditch, or have they ever done that?"

"Enough," Antonius said, not with the roar that I would have expected, but with a weary tone. He stood up from his curule chair, running his hands through his hair as he paced, while we waited. "Pullus is right," he said finally. "Let the men decide for themselves whether they restrict the use of the fires to men who don't have frostbite, or do without entirely."

He turned away, waving his hand in the air as he walked into his private quarters.

"Let me know what's decided."

The men voted to have fires, the afflicted men prohibited from coming within ten paces of any fire. Nobody was happy and I sensed that men would weaken seeing their comrades suffering in the cold, outside the circle of warmth.

"If any man with frostbite is found within ten paces of the fire, he and all of his tentmates will be flogged," I warned them.

I could feel their hard stares, but they said nothing. However, that night something totally unexpected happened. The men with frostbite were huddled in their respective tents, while their comrades sat about the fire, soaking in the warmth that only flames lapping about a log can bring, the first exposure to such a luxury they experienced in more days than anyone could remember. Then, without a word said, slowly the men around the fires stood, yawned and stretched, then went to their tents. Before a third of a watch had passed, the fires were still blazing brightly about the camp, a sight that I had not realized how much I missed until I gazed down the Legion streets, yet barely a soul could be seen still seated by the fire. The men of the 10th could not bear to let their afflicted comrades suffer alone, so rather than warm themselves, they returned to their tents to sit huddled and shivering together. It was Gellius who first came to my tent, calling me outside, pointing to the eerie sight of a Roman military camp with barely any men sitting by their fires, as only those men who were on guard duty were walking up and down the streets. After inspecting the Legion area and seeing that the whole Legion was involved, I called Perdicas out, sending him all around the camp. About a third of the watch later, he returned to report that much the same thing was happening throughout the army. It was one of the most stirring things I had ever seen in all my years in the army, even with Caesar in Gaul. If one stood and just listened, you could hear the low hum of conversations as men talked in their tents, but instead of the laughter that usually punctuated the evening air, there was the sound of quiet sobbing. While I did not go to any tent to pry and see what was taking place, I believe that the crying men were the afflicted, overcome with emotion at this simple demonstration of solidarity and brotherhood that none other than a fighting man can understand.

The next morning, nothing was said, by anyone, yet for the rest of our march to the Aras, although we had wood for fires, they were only used for cooking and lighting the camp perimeter and streets in the normal manner, the men disdaining them for any other purpose. The only exception was for the wounded, who were brought out of the hospital tents on their litters, arranged around the fires for a few thirds of a watch, including those frostbitten men who had lost all of their toes. Their howls of pain could be heard throughout camp as feeling returned to their extremities. I think this contributed to the men's resolve in helping their less fortunate comrades who were still mobile to stay away from the thawing heat until we were at a point where they could go through the excruciating process without the threat of being left behind on the next day's march.

Men were still dying, succumbing to the harsh conditions, some still dropping dead on the march, particularly among the auxiliaries. As little as I cared for the auxiliaries, with the exception of the slingers and cavalry who had proved their value, it was still disheartening to see how they had just melted away. There were little more than 500 men from each nation's contingent left, the survivors looking more dead than alive, staggering as they put one foot in front of the other, their heads down. I could not blame them for not being conditioned to such hardships as we were. Being fair, I know that they did the best that they could and that Antonius treated them poorly in many respects, but they were not my concern. If it came down to a choice of feeding Romans or feeding auxiliaries, to me it was and is a simple choice. We do the bulk of the fighting, while we also do most of the work when building camps, roads, and anything else that a general can dream up during a campaign. To my mind, that gives us the right to the lion's share of everything; food, wine, women and loot. However, there was no plunder on this march. In fact, most of the men had lost money, since each Legion's savings fund had been locked in strongboxes on one of our designated wagons in the baggage train. All that money was now in the purses of the Parthian army, another reason we hated them so passionately. I had lost a fair amount of money as well, and while I normally did not think much about such matters, believing that the gods would either give or take away whatever I accrued as they saw fit, it was worrying nonetheless. I was fairly certain that I still had the requisite 400,000 sesterces deposited with Caesar's old bankers that would elevate me to the equestrian order, and I had sent a good sum to Valeria for safekeeping. I suppose it was a natural progression that I began thinking about whether it was time to retire after this campaign, and it was this idea that occupied me for the rest of the march to the Aras River.

Perhaps the only thing that Antonius got right in the entire campaign was his prediction of how long it would take to reach the Aras once we crossed the river where the Parthians stopped pursuing. A week to the day, we topped a ridge to look down at a silvery ribbon crossing our path, while men began shouting for joy as the word that the sight before our eyes was indeed the Aras. As a river it was not much, but what it represented could not be of greater importance, and as we drew nearer I could see a small group of horsemen just on the other side of the river, clearly waiting for us. A halt was called, the order being met by groans and cries of frustration, but Antonius had experienced enough Eastern treachery to be cautious, so he sent one of his lower-ranked and less valuable Tribunes galloping down to the riverbank to determine the reason for this party waiting for us. A few moments later, he came galloping back and the march resumed, so I sent Diocles up to find out what he could. He returned to tell me that the party had been sent by Artavasdes of Armenia, with the usual flowery assurances that we were honored guests and how overjoyed Artavasdes was to see that we had marched out of the wastelands of Media.

"I would love to gut that bastard," I growled, and Diocles laughed.

"That's exactly what Antonius said." He turned sober. "But he also said that he can't do that, not yet. We need Artavasdes' good will, and we can't afford to fight our way through another country in the shape that we're in."

I knew Antonius was right, but it did not sit well, so instead I grumbled about Armenians in particular and Easterners in general.

The army crossed the river, and as men reached the far bank, many of them fell to their knees to give thanks to the gods, while others actually kissed the ground. As relieved and happy as I was that we had reached the river, there was a nagging suspicion in the back of my mind that somehow we were not done yet, so I restrained my enthusiasm. The wounded and sick were transported across first, where they lay in their litters watching as men clasped hands, hugging each other. If there had been wine and food, it could have been a festival day judging by the way men were acting. Antonius gave the order that we would settle in for the night, despite having a few thirds of a watch left in the day. We made camp, and as we were working, a train of animals led by the same party that was waiting at the river arrived laden with grain and wine. The Armenians said that this was just the beginning, that more supplies would be coming, and these would be carrying olive oil, dates, fodder for the livestock, along with all manner of delicacies. This actually presented more problems than it solved, because there was not enough in this first train to feed the whole army, but after a quick discussion, it was decided that there would be enough for the sick and wounded, the men having no objections when they were told. The only decision made that was not popular was the joint one about continuing to keep the frostbitten men away from the fires.

"Not until we reach Artaxata," Antonius declared. "It's just a few days more and there we can rest before we head for Syria."

We all understood his reasoning, but none of us particularly liked it. Neither did the men, though they obeyed readily enough. Fortunately, enough good things had happened that the Centurions did not have to sleep with one eye open that night, as the men just grumbled about the order. The smell of baking bread, made with real wheat and not barley, was more of a torment, as men found excuses to suddenly go visit a sick or wounded comrade. There was a crowd of men around the hospital area just standing there, taking deep breaths through their noses, sucking in the aroma and salivating. I did not see the point in torturing one's self, but there was no harm in it, and most men did not begrudge their wounded and ill comrades this luxury, probably because they knew that the next day, or day after at the latest it would be their turn. As further events transpired, I was always somewhat puzzled how we did not receive any warning about what was coming, but I suppose it was because the medical staff knew what they were doing and did not allow the sick and injured men to gorge themselves, so they had no ill effects.

The Armenians were good to their word, as that first train was just the beginning, while the next days as we moved towards Artaxata saw a seemingly endless procession of trains carrying food, forage, medical supplies, and even warm clothing arriving to meet us on the march.

"Where was all this when we were starving in Media?" Balbus asked as we watched the third train of the day arrive to join us.

"Sitting in Artavasdes' warehouses," I said grimly. "Waiting for the moment when we needed it most, but also when he could deliver it without risking anything."

"I really want to gut that bastard," Balbus replied, and I laughed, slapping him on the back.

"There's a lot of that going around."

It was about a day out of Artaxata that things started going badly for some of the men. Their bodies, having become accustomed to deprivation, now reacted violently to the surfeit of food in their systems. Unlike our medical staff and the wounded, none of the Centurions had the knowledge to supervise their consumption. This meant that men who had been surviving on a quarter of barley bread a day, with no oil to go with it, suddenly had full loaves of wheat bread and all the oil they could consume with it, their bodies almost immediately rebelling because of it. I believe that the dates in particular did not help, but men were starved for anything sweet, their time in Syria making them fancy dates as one of their favorite sweet things. At first, it was more a source of amusement for comrades who had not yet been afflicted, as men suddenly bolted from the formation to run to some spot a distance away to relieve their aching bowels. However, it quickly stopped being a laughing matter; by the time we were in Artaxata more than a quarter of the men were stricken, while it quickly became apparent that trying to prevent the men from gorging themselves was a task beyond the capacity of the Centurions to control. It became so bad that a number of men died, literally shitting their guts out, or so it seemed, and only after seeing men who had survived a march as horrific as this one die from essentially eating too much did the men start to restrain themselves.

Artavasdes was waiting for us in Artaxata, greeting Antonius as a long-lost comrade, a greeting that Antonius was no less effusive in returning, though he had described in graphic detail what he wanted to do to Artavasdes at some point in the future. Watching the two, one would never believe that either had a hateful thought towards the other, but I suppose that this is just part of what it means to be high born. It was at Artaxata that Antonius finally allowed us to honor our dead properly, holding a formation, both to remember them and to award decorations to the living. When on the march, there are seldom opportunities to view the army in its entirety, so it was not until that formation that the true scope of our losses was plain for all to see. The army was 24,000 men fewer, 20,000 gone from the ranks of the Legionaries and auxiliaries, and 4,000 from the cavalry. Those were the dead; there were still half that number bed-ridden and a fair number of these men would die as well in the coming days and weeks. More than half of the men who had died did so from illness and not battle, and given the fact that we had never had a widespread plague sweep through the army, it was this number that was most disturbing.

It was not all a sad occasion, since I was able to witness Legionary Gregarius Gaius Porcinus win the Grass Crown for his actions in saving Secundus Pilus Prior Sextus Scribonius in the eighteenth and final action against the Parthians at the river. I had never experienced the surge of pride that ran through my body as I watched him stand at *intente* while Antonius and I, acting in my capacity of Primus Pilus, made the award. I held the simple grass crown, woven together using the tough, dried strands of the local grass, on a silken cloth of Tyrian purple, standing to Antonius' left, who took it, then placed it gently on Gaius' head after reading the citation describing his actions. Gaius stood with his helmet under his left arm, as custom dictates that the grass crown be placed on a bare head, but then he was entitled to wear it around his helmet the rest of the day. From now until he dies, he is allowed to wear it on all official occasions in which he participates. His eyes were shining, clearly as proud as I was, a far cry from the shaking, hollow-eyed boy who sat in my tent the night that it had happened, and I was reminded how resilient the young truly are. Servius Gellius also received a set of phalarae for his actions that disastrous day when the Tenth Cohort was lost and Nasica was killed. No number of decorations could completely erase the sour taste in our mouth of how the campaign turned out, but with full bellies and warm fires, the mood of the men was considerably improved.

After a week at Artaxata, Antonius released the client kings, along with the remnants of their auxiliaries, who began dispersing to their respective countries. Artavasdes, still trying to ingratiate himself back into Antonius' good graces, invited Antonius and the army to winter at Artaxata, but Antonius, sensing the mood of the army and I am sure having had his own fill of Eastern duplicity, instead demanded that Artavasdes open his granaries to us so that we could stock up for the remaining march back into Syria. In a rare moment of foresight, he also demanded that the citizens of Artaxata surrender their supplies of firewood they had lain in for the oncoming winter. Artavasdes was not happy, yet he also knew better than to argue with an army that hated him planted just outside his walls, so with his most false Eastern smile he graciously agreed to that which he had no choice in anyway. He also offered up his entire supply of rolling stock so that supplies and men who could still not walk could be transported, though very few of them were the solid Roman wagons that we were accustomed to, but lighter carts. While they were better suited to travel through the rugged terrain of Armenia, they could also transport only two men lying side by side, or a few barrels and bags of supplies. Still, compared to what we had on the march out of Media, it was a huge improvement. All of these additional luxuries; the supplies, the wood, and the carts, put the men in relatively good spirits for the final leg back to Syria. Also, while we were in Artaxata, Antonius sent a message to Cleopatra, urgently ordering that she come with supplies and most importantly, money to Syria. Having done all he could do to continue our march in the best possible manner, Antonius gave the order to break down camp, load the sick and wounded, to begin heading for Syria. We all felt that we had survived the worst that could be done to us as far as the enemy and the elements, and we were right, but only on one count.

To get back to Syria, we first had to cross through the mountain range of which Mount Ararat is the central feature. The rock of the mountain itself was barely visible, so covered in snow and ice all the way down its slopes that the original shape of the mountain as we saw it earlier in the year was hidden. The lower ridges that flank Ararat and run in an east-west direction were equally covered, although there the snow was not so deep. Antonius, determined to take the shortest route possible back to Syria and believing that the men were inured to the hardships of winter at this point, ordered us to cross over the series of ridges, using the passes of which our guide knew. Artavasdes had offered his own guide, but Antonius was not about to trust that Armenian snake, so Cyrus was paid handsomely to continue to lead us on our journey. We originally viewed those small carts supplied by Artavasdes with some disdain, but on the rough terrain, climbing through the icy patches that covered what was barely more than a goat track that they called a road in this part of the world, they proved their value. Still, the footing was treacherous, so that we began losing men who made a careless step, or who walked a short distance away to relieve themselves thinking they were walking on solid ground, only to find in the last heartbeats of their life that they had chosen a snowdrift with nothing to support it underneath, whereupon they would plunge, screaming, hundreds of feet to their death. There would be a shout of alarm, the column would stop for a few moments before resuming, the comrades of the men cursing and weeping at the loss. As often as we warned the men not to trust the appearance of the ground around them, deaths of this nature were a regular occurrence, happening several times a day. Despite the fact that we had recuperated somewhat during our time at Artaxata and the men were stronger now with regular rations, this last section of the march was brutally hard, the sounds of men panting for breath as they climbed up the seemingly endless series of ridges, drowning out any attempts at conversation, save for a quick order or warning.

Then, the first blizzard struck while we were still negotiating a particularly difficult pass that only the vanguard and the command group had passed through. In moments, the visibility was so bad that men could only see the rank immediately in front and in back of their spots, the wind blowing what felt like icy needles into our faces, howling so loudly that a man could only be heard if he bellowed at the top of his lungs. The *medici* tried desperately to keep the wounded protected, but the wind was so fierce that it ripped the coverings that had been rigged over each cart into shreds, or they were blown away completely, disappearing into the swirling white. I was as blind as any of the men, forced to feel my way back along the column, keeping my footing, trying to avoid stepping off into the void by keeping a hand on the rock wall that lined one side of the road, as I yelled at men to do the same. Having them do so meant that it destroyed the integrity of the marching formation and that men would be crowding each other in their move to grab the rock wall, but at that moment, it seemed like the lesser of two evils. I would rather have had the men milling about like cattle than see more of them fall to their deaths trying to march in a straight line. Even with my scarf tied tightly around my face, the small area of exposed skin around my eyes burned from the blast of icy snow, as if my skin was being scoured by a piece of lava stone. With every passing moment, the track we were following was becoming more obscured, the progress of the men slowing to a few shuffling steps, followed by a pause as someone tripped and fell. If they were lucky, they fell straight down and were able to struggle to their feet. However, if they took a stumbling step in the wrong direction, there would be a shrill scream that briefly pierced the din of the howling blizzard before things returned to what had become normal, men continuing to grope blindly forward. For one part of the watch, then two, we struggled through the pass, knowing only when we reached the top by the change in direction of the slope. Ice had crusted on my eyebrows, the weight of it threatening to close my eyes. Yet after several swipes to clear it away, only to have it return in moments, I finally gave up, just enduring it, even as it dangerously limited my vision. The men were similarly covered, looking like icy apparitions, every particle that struck them seeming to cling to their cloaks, scarves, and bare skin as they continued to struggle to keep moving. I kept shouting at men that stopping meant death, yet their fatigue mounted, the Centurions forced to begin using the *vitus*, striking some men repeatedly before they roused themselves to take another step. The time for a break came and passed, because we knew that we could not allow the men to rest as long as the blizzard continued unabated, so we struggled on. Men like me, mostly veterans of Gaul, who were lucky enough to bring at least one pair of bracae, the leggings made of wool worn by the Gauls obviously fared better than men who did not, clumps of ice forming on their bare legs, and I knew that we would have more cases of frostbite before we were done. Finally, the wind began to abate, the visibility becoming slightly better, enough so that I could have the Centurions perform a head count, starting with the Third Cohort, which on this day was directly behind us. I held a brief meeting with the Centurions of the Cohort, learning that every man was accounted for.

Dismissing the Centurions, I made my way down to the next Cohort; on this day, the Second Cohort was next in line, since I always mixed up the order of march when there was no prospect of shaking out into battle formation. When I reached Scribonius, the greeting froze in my throat when I saw his eyes above his scarf, clearly reading the alarm and pain in them. My heart seized, knowing that only one thing could put that look in them. When he pulled down his scarf to speak, I staggered back a step. Scribonius grabbed my arm to steady me, pulling me to the side.

"Titus, I can't find Gaius."

There are moments in time that are so painful, so terrifying that they must be locked away in a box in your mind, never to be opened, and that moment standing there with Scribonius is one of those moments. The same sense of loss and searing pain that came with the deaths of Gisela, Vibi and Livia struck all over again as I felt my knees buckle, only Scribonius' strong grip preventing me from shaming myself in front of the men.

"Titus, listen to me. There's something else. One of his tentmates is missing as well."

I looked at him dumbly, not caring or understanding why he was telling me this. Seeing that I did not comprehend, he tightened his grip on my arm, shaking me.

"Don't you see what that could mean? He might not have fallen down the slope. He could just as easily have stopped to help his tentmate. And the man he stopped to help is Vulso, who's recovering from frostbite and has been struggling to keep up."

I struggled to try to accept Scribonius' optimism as a possibility, but it was difficult to think of anything other than what seemed to be the only real explanation for his disappearance. Telling Scribonius to continue the march, I stayed to wait as the next Legion marched by, hoping that he would be straggling, but it was almost impossible to tell men apart because they were all wrapped up and covered in ice, so that after a bit I gave up, pushing my way back up the Legions. I was close to exhaustion by the time I arrived back at my spot in front, my legs feeling as if they were filled with molten lead, but luckily we were now on the downhill leg, while the storm was abating. My mind was completely absorbed with Gaius' disappearance, so I barely registered the *bucina* call that we were making camp on a wind-swept plateau barely large enough for the whole army to fit, with yet another high ridge to the south beckoning as the main challenge the next day.

It was only when Balbus came trotting up to me, clearly puzzled that I was not snapping out the normal set of orders as I went to the command group to determine what our duties would be that I realized I had not been paying attention. He had not heard that Gaius was missing, so when I told him the reason for my distraction, he did not seem to know what to say, standing awkwardly and not speaking. Truthfully, I did not know what to say either, so I gave him curt instructions as I went to find out what we were doing, where I was informed that we had the guard duty. Men normally loved getting guard duty when it was time to make camp, just not when it was so cold, when working kept a man warmer than standing at post. For me, it did not make much difference as I just walked around supervising, but this day was torture because all I could think about was how I was going to write Valeria to tell her that her only son had survived battle, in fact winning the highest award a Legionary can earn, only to slip off an icy slope to his death by accident. I had not been so despondent since the death of my family many years before, and I stood huddled against the cold, feeling as empty of life as I imagined Gaius was, broken and cold, lying in the bottom of the snow-choked ravine along the road over which we had just struggled.

Once the camp was completed, I took the opportunity to stand on the rampart along the Porta Decumana, looking back in the direction that we had come, ignoring the biting cold. I sensed a presence, turning to see Scribonius, who said nothing, just standing next to me for the rest of the time I stood, waiting. Finally it became dark, so I turned away, heading to my tent, this being one of the few times I was looking forward to sucking down as much wine as it took to rob me of my senses. Scribonius told me that he would stay and wait, but I do not believe I thanked him in reply.

It was one part before the third watch, when we would be relieved and the men would be able to go to their tents, which the Legion slaves erect as they stand guard, finally able to warm themselves and make their meal. I had been drinking since coming to my tent; Diocles having heard the news and anticipating my demands, was waiting for me with an amphora and cup. However, no matter how much I drank, the image of Gaius alone in the cold would not leave, so I sent Diocles to find one of the Greek doctors to buy, borrow, or steal a sleeping draught. I knew that I would suffer for it in the morning, as the few times I had used such concoctions I had been staggering in a fog most of the next day, but I did not care. So I was alone when the Princeps Posterior of the Fourth Cohort, Gaius Didius came to my tent. With Diocles gone, he apparently stood in the outer room of my tent, which served as the Legion office, not sure what to do, before finally slapping the leather curtain that served as my door. Thinking it was Diocles, I growled at him about why he was bothering to knock but then, sensing that it was someone else I looked up to see Didius standing there, a strange look on his face. Thinking that he had heard about my nephew and had come to offer his condolences, I shouted at him to leave. Still, he refused to move, so I began roaring at him, jumping to my feet to rush at him, intent on beating him within an inch of his life. Didius stood his ground, enraging me further and I had drawn my fist back, intent on crushing his face when the words he was shouting at me finally sank in.

"Primus Pilus, Gregarius Porcinus has been found!"

He was brought in by the cavalry patrol that always rode as outriders. Because of the narrowness of the road, instead of riding on the flanks they had been far behind the rearguard, and the only reason they found Gaius was because one of their horses shied suddenly when a snowdrift began to move. Jumping off to investigate, they found a barely conscious Gaius, along with the unconscious tentmate that Scribonius had reported missing along with Gaius. Scribonius was right all along; the tentmate Vulso, one of the older men in the Century had slipped on his frostbitten feet then hit his head, and would have fallen to his death but Gaius was immediately behind him, grabbing Vulso before it happened. They both slid partway down the slope, until Gaius was clinging to a patch of bare rock with one hand while clutching the unconscious Vulso around the waist. This was during the height of the storm, so none of the other men saw either of them, nor did they hear Gaius calling for help. By the time Gaius managed to struggle back up to the road with Vulso, the army had passed them by. Not knowing what else to do, Gaius slung Vulso, who had a fractured skull, over his shoulder, then followed behind the army. He finally collapsed about two miles short of camp, but before he lost the last of his energy, he dug out a hollow in the snow, laying his spare cloak over the hole. That last action undoubtedly saved both their lives, though it did not stop either man from getting frostbite, Vulso's original case becoming more severe while Gaius' was fairly minor. They were taken to the hospital tent and I rushed over immediately to find Gaius sitting up on a cot, with three of his tentmates sitting around his bed beaming down at him, all of them clearly as relieved as I felt. My nephew, his face raw but glistening with some ointment, saw me standing there and smiled, but it quickly fled at the sight of my face.

"Leave us," I snapped to his friends, who had only noticed me standing there when Gaius looked over, scrambling to their feet.

They fled, leaving an anxious looking Gaius and his uncle glowering down at him. I gave him the full treatment, not saying a word for what had to seem like a full watch to him, before I finally spoke, "I thought we had agreed that you wouldn't scare me anymore."

I tried to keep my voice stern, but I found it hard to get the words out without choking on them. I knew I should be angry, and I did want to put a scare into the boy, yet I was just so relieved that I suddenly felt so weak in the knees I was forced to sit down heavily on one of the stools next to his bed, hearing the legs crack under my weight.

"I'm sorry, Uncle Titus," Gaius said quietly.

I shook my head, sighing, not knowing what to say.

"It's just that Vulso and I are close comrades since Otho died. He and Otho had been together since they were *tiros*, but since I was new I had never selected a close comrade until then."

I started; I had not known that, but I supposed there was no reason for me to know.

"How is Vulso?"

Gaius looked over at his comrade in the next bed, head heavily bandaged, mouth open, his nose already black, a sure sign that it would fall off.

He was still unconscious and from the look of him, he would never regain consciousness, but Gaius did not have enough experience in these matters, so he replied hopefully, "I think he'll wake up soon. The doctors don't think so, but I told them that he was talking some while I was carrying him."

"That's a good sign," I agreed, knowing that it meant nothing, yet I could not take that hope from him, not after he had risked his life for his friend.

"They said that I can be released in a day or so."

Gaius grimaced, moving his feet under the blanket as the feeling returned to them. I stood, looking for an orderly, and when one came near I told him to go get poppy syrup, but Gaius put his hand on my arm.

I looked down as he shook his head. "No, Uncle, there are men here a lot worse than me and they're not getting poppy syrup. I don't need it."

He was right, but I hated seeing him in pain, though I knew that I was violating every rule of the Centurionate by showing him favoritism. I decided that I had done enough damage so I made ready to leave, bidding Gaius a restful night, thankful that he was alive to have one.

We resumed the march by climbing the next ridge and though there was no storm, the footing was still treacherous, meaning more men fell to their deaths. The toll from the previous day's blizzard on the sick and wounded was horrific, as men already weakened were exposed to the blasting wind and snow. More than a quarter of the litter cases died from the storm, while the lot of the survivors was not any easier in the coming days, and despite the fact we did not have another blizzard, they were succumbing at an alarming rate.

Asellio had not died as quickly as either I or the physicians had thought, in fact giving appearances of recovering, then without warning he developed a searing pain in his side, followed by a high fever then within just a few thirds of a watch he was dead. I had delayed the announcement of my decision until he was dead out of respect for him, but when I told the others that I had decided to move Macrianus into the First Cohort in his spot, there were some hard feelings. In Macrianus' old spot I promoted a man named Appius Pilatus, another younger Optio from the Fourth Cohort who was on the list of candidates for promotion when a slot opened up. I knew I had my work cut out for me with Macrianus, Marcius being too weak a leader for a man as strong-willed as Macrianus, but I saw a great deal of potential in him. First, I had to keep an eye on him and get to know him better. The army was still reeling from the blizzard the day before, and wisely, Antonius did not push the men hard, knowing that to do so would put all of the men back into the same condition they were in when we staggered into Artaxata. We only covered perhaps 15 miles that day, but they were brutally hard miles because of the terrain. When we made camp, we learned that even more of the wounded had died on the march. Gaius was allowed to come back to the Legion, still limping from his frostbite though the physicians told him that as long as he kept his feet warm that he should not lose any toes. He was warmly greeted by his comrades, while Scribonius could only smile and shake his head as he recounted the scene when he came to visit me that night.

"They truly love him, Titus. And I tell you this, he may not be the swordsman you are, but he's every bit as brave."

"Braver," I replied, and it was not just a proud uncle talking, for I did not think I would have struggled so hard to save a man who was not a lifelong friend like Vibius, or someone I had marched with for many years.

Gaius had been in the 10th a little more than a year now, and he had just become close comrades with Vulso, but he risked his life without hesitation. We sat in silence for a bit, sipping our wine as I reflected on what it was in a man that would spur him to such actions for someone he did not know all that well.

"Keep an eye on him, will you?"

Scribonius nodded, knowing how worried I was. Finishing his wine, he returned to his men.

Another bout of bad weather descended on the army and while it was nowhere near the fury and bitterness of the blizzard, it was enough to kill even more of the sick and infirm. It got to the point that the men began to think that the train of carts and mules bearing litters was cursed, so they did whatever they could to avoid showing themselves for sick call, held every morning before the march, and then again in the evening after camp is made. The frostbite cases still continued, except that now men refused to complain, trying to cover up any sign of affliction. However, most of the time they would begin limping so badly, then start falling behind, giving them no way to hide. Scribonius was true to his word, keeping an eye on Gaius, who seemed to make at least a partial recovery, limping only slightly, no doubt helped by the second pair of fur-lined socks that I ordered him to wear. After another day, we finally passed out of the worst terrain. While the route still climbed over rolling hills, it was not as severe and fraught with danger as what we had just passed through. The men sensed that at least the marching would be easier, even if the weather conditions were not, so spirits improved somewhat. Men were no longer falling to their deaths, it was true, but there was still danger. Legionaries who had somehow managed to stay healthy for the entire campaign finally broke down, becoming ill, developing hacking coughs that produced great gobs of mucus, accompanied by ever-increasing fever. Making it even more difficult to shake was the loss of appetite that kept men from eating enough to keep up their strength. In short, men were wearing out, and every morning it seemed there would be a cry of alarm and anguish when a man's tentmate went to rouse him, only to find that he had finally given up. Even I developed a cough and started running a fever, but with Diocles around to tend to my needs, watching over me like a mother hen, it did not cause me more than a mild discomfort and some tough days on the march. Several of the Centurions were stricken as well, with a couple even forced to risk the curse of riding in a cart when their fever became so high that all their senses fled from them. More of the sick and injured continued to die, their weakened condition making it easier to succumb to the constant wear and tear of the march. Some men recovered sufficiently to leave their litter to return to the ranks, though they were in the minority.

Antonius left the army about this time to head for the coast, to a port called Leuke Kome, where he had directed Cleopatra to come with the aid he demanded. Men looked at each other with a knowing leer and wink, joking about the power Cleopatra held over our general. It was late November when we finally reached Samosata again, except this time we were not there to take the city while Antiochus, having reconciled with Antonius, offered up a portion of his supplies to help replenish our stores. Ahenobarbus was left in command by Antonius, which Canidius did not like at all, spending most of his time in staff meetings making snide comments about Ahenobarbus' decisions, providing a great deal of entertainment for the rest of us. There is nothing we lower classes love quite as much as seeing the upper classes picking at each other; their petty squabbles and jealousies are fodder for full watches of discussion around the fire. It was Ahenobarbus' decision that we spend a week at Samosata, his goal being to reduce the rate at which the sick and wounded were dying, and it did help to allow them to rest. The weather was still cold but had lost its bitter edge so the men did not have to walk about wrapped from head to foot, while the single brazier in my private quarters was enough that I could wear just my tunic.

We marched out of Samosata with our spirits almost restored, as a number of the sick and wounded managed to recover enough to return to their spot in the formation, though we still had a large number in the litters. Samosata marked the end of the more challenging terrain, then just a few days later, the weather softened to the point where men only wore their cloaks early in the morning. Now we all knew it was just a matter of putting one foot in front of the other all the way to Leuke Kome, the men beginning to sing again as they swung along in their mile-eating gait. We crossed Syria quickly, the army needing no urging to put as many miles in every day as they could manage, almost as if they could smell the ocean breeze. For the first time in months, men began talking about the future in hopeful terms, though their enthusiasm was tempered by the fact that they would not have any loot to shower on whores and amphorae of wine.

I was so fully occupied with running two Centuries at once that I had little time to spend with Gaius, only seeing him during the march when I would be passing from one Cohort to the next. I would make sure to spend a few moments with him, and I was happy to see that he was fully recovered and had not lost any toes. His close comrade Vulso was not so lucky; he had already been suffering from frostbite when he suffered the blow to the head and Gaius had rescued him, so the exposure he had endured coupled with his head injury was too much, and he died shortly after Gaius rescued him. Gaius now needed to find another close comrade, but while he had been the new man a few months before and nobody was eager to team up with him, the combination of the gaping holes in our ranks and Gaius' proven bravery ensured that he was being wooed by men on a daily basis. His reaction was equal parts flattered and bemused, as he discussed with me the merits of each prospective candidate as we walked. I teased him gently about being so sought after, but told him that he needed to pick a man who would help keep him alive when things were tough, and I was not just talking about in battle. I had a strong suspicion that Antonius would be letting the men run rampant when we finally arrived at Leuke Kome, relaxing discipline in an attempt to erase the memories of what was ultimately a failed campaign. I believed that would help, but I also knew that Antonius would have to find a way to come up with a bonus of hard cash if he wanted to keep the army loyal and willing to march into Parthia with him again. For I had no doubt that Antonius held every intention of returning, because now he had two reasons for revenge.

Despite Phraates dangling promises that he would return the standards lost by Crassus, not only had he not done so, but he had gained another with the loss of the baggage train. I wondered if Cleopatra was on her way, and how long we would have to wait before she arrived with all the things that Antonius had demanded she provide. Marching in a southerly direction, we bypassed Damascus to the west, passing through the valley where Heliopolis is located, so I suppose it was natural that my thoughts turned to

Miriam, knowing that she was relatively nearby. We had started to attract camp followers almost from the moment we crossed into Syria, the women only staying about long enough to learn that there was precious little hard cash to be had, except for those few men who had been profiteering and selling grain at exorbitant prices when it was scarce. And there were even less of these men still marching, as it seemed that a disproportionately large number of them had suffered a variety of accidents during our retreat, ranging from slipping off the icy trails to tripping over a tent rope at night. Normally this is not fatal, but for these men it seemed to cause broken necks with amazing regularity. I believe it says more than any other single example about the state of the army and the tenuous grip that Antonius and the officers had on the men that not one of these accidents was ever investigated. As gratifying as it may have been, it was also concerning to me, for I was sure that things were only going to get worse when we finally stopped marching.

Chapter 7- Respite

We arrived in Leuke Kome (modern-day Jiyeh, Lebanon) in early December, but early winter in that part of the world, that close to the sea, was as close to paradise that it was possible to get compared to what we had just been through. Antonius had spent the time waiting for us having a camp prepared, so for the first time in months, we did not come to the end of a march and immediately start working. There was a sense of unreality as we marched through the Porta Praetoria, seeing that this was no marching camp, but a proper winter camp with huts instead of tents, the men and officers still having a hard time comprehending that it was finally well and truly over. Our training and discipline had us move without thought as we marched into the forum, where Antonius was sitting astride Clemency, turned out in his gold and silver armor with the snarling lions, waiting for the remnants of what had been the largest army in Roman history.

The 10th reached its spot right of the line, where we waited as the rest of the Legions moved into their accustomed spots. From my vantage point, I had a clear view of Antonius. As I watched him stare down at us, I became aware that he seemed to be weaving slightly in the saddle, causing me to examine him more closely. Despite looking essentially unchanged since he departed our company, I could see, if I squinted, the telltale puffiness around his eyes, along with the sallow cast to his normally bronzed skin that indicated he had been drinking heavily. However, when he spoke, his voice was strong and his speech not slurred in any way.

"My soldiers," he began, and I was reminded how Caesar always referred to us as his comrades, something Antonius never did. "I welcome you to Leuke Kome. This will be where you spend the winter, and....." before he could finish a majority of the men broke out in a chorus of groans and boos, as I braced myself for an Antonian explosion, but once again he surprised me, giving the men a wide smile as he held up his hands for silence. The men quieted down, then he boomed, "You don't think that I would let you spend a winter here alone, do you? I have sent for every whore in Damascus, Tyre, and Antioch to keep you company during your long watches of leisure. They should be arriving any day."

I saw his mouth continue moving, but I do not know what he said since his words were drowned out by the deafening cheers of the men. He waited for silence and once the men calmed down, he finished what he was saying. "And you don't think I'll let you entertain company dry, do you? I know some of you will need all the help you can get to woo even a whore, so the wine is already here."

His jibe was greeted by a roar of laughter, followed by another raucous cheer. He let the men go on for a bit, then his face turned serious, and that was enough to quiet the army.

"Tonight, when you sit by your fires and begin your well-earned rest, I ask only one thing of you. Take a moment to remember those of us who are not here with us in the flesh, but will always be with us in memory."

It is hard to describe how quickly the mood of an entire army of men changed with those words and I know that while it was not Antonius' intent, he evoked a sense of guilt as men chastised themselves for being able to laugh and think about all the debauching that they were going to do. To his credit, Antonius saw the reaction that his words had provoked, so he hastened to soften the blow.

"While you're taking that moment to remember your friends, I also ask that you take a moment to forgive me, your general. For I have failed you, and there are no words I can muster that will adequately convey my deepest sorrow and regret for the mistakes that I have made during this campaign. While I acted with the best of motives, having the earnest desire to avenge the defeat of Marcus Crassus and the loss of seven Legion standards, and more importantly to free those poor wretches who have been in bondage to the Parthian scum for these last 20 years, what matters is that we were turned back. But I swear this to each of you, that this was not a defeat but a setback, and that we will have our vengeance upon the Parthians, not just for Crassus now, but for all of the men we left behind!"

He was roaring at the top of his lungs by the time he finished, with the men roaring right back with their approval. The noise continued for several moments as each Legionary added his own promises to the one made by Antonius, for there was not a man left who had not lost a friend. Antonius dismissed the army, calling for the Centurions to meet with him in the *Praetorium* as soon as we dropped our gear and made sure the men were seen to. The dismissal was the official signal to the army that it was over, that they had survived. Men immediately began weeping and hugging each other as they made their way to their new quarters. I spied Gaius among a group of Second men, and I called him over.

I did not embrace him, instead offering him my hand, telling him, "You've not only survived your first campaign, Gregarius, you've exceeded even my expectations. Congratulations." I could not resist giving him a wink, and he beamed back at me.

"Thank you, Primus Pilus. I'm just happy to have survived."

"So am I." I grinned at him. "Your mother would have flayed me alive if you hadn't."

For once, the atmosphere in the *Praetorium* was relaxed and almost convivial, as the Primi Pili congratulated each other for still being among the living, and for leading their respective Legions through what we all agreed had been the most physically difficult campaign any of us had ever been through.

"Of course, none of us are getting any younger," Corbulo pointed out. "That had to have had something to do with it."

"Speak for yourself," Balbinus retorted. "I'm like a good Falernian. I get better with age."

Antonius entered and we all came to *intente*, which he waved off, telling us to take our seats. Ahenobarbus, Canidius, and Titius sat in the front row, along with the senior Tribunes, the rest of us sitting in the subsequent rows. Antonius sat down behind his desk and now that I was closer, there was no missing the fact that he had been drinking. Before he spoke, he shuffled through the wax tablets that each Primus Pilus had brought containing their strength reports. As he read each one, the furrows on his brow deepened, and I braced myself for the coming storm, but Antonius did not seem to have much bluster left.

He just looked at us, asking in disbelief, "Eight thousand? We lost another 8,000 men from Artaxata? How is that possible?"

That very question had been the subject of much discussion among all the Primi Pili and their

Centurions, and it seemed as if each of us had our own idea.

He looked first at Ahenobarbus, and, while I could not see his face, I could see him shift uncomfortably as he stammered, "The conditions were too much for the sick and wounded, Marcus Antonius. They succumbed to the conditions."

"But we didn't have 8,000 in the litters," Antonius protested. "There were no more than 5,000 when I left the army."

Ahenobarbus could only shrug, as Antonius looked over to where we were sitting, his expression clearly beseeching one of us for an answer. None of us spoke for several moments. Finally, Caecina broke the silence.

"There were no more than 5,000 men in the litters at any one time," he agreed with Antonius. "But men were getting frostbitten or coming down with pneumonia as quickly as men were dying from their wounds or whatever illness they had. The litter wouldn't even get cold when they dumped a dead man before another man was put in."

I believed that this was exactly what had happened as well, yet hearing it spoken aloud did not make it any less distressing. Antonius listened, then sat back, giving a soft curse in disgust and resignation, which we took as a sign that he accepted Caecina's explanation. However, this was not the end of the bad news, which Antonius discovered when he opened the next tablet. Reading it, he let out a gasp.

"We're losing another 3,000 men because of frostbite?"

"Those are just the men who have lost either their entire foot or their big toes. Or more than two toes on each foot," Ahenobarbus said. "Or men who have lost their thumbs, or more than two fingers of their right hand. Men who have lost their noses or ears are allowed to stay under their standard."

It may sound peculiar that a man losing a big toe would no longer be fit for the army, but apparently, the big toe is a requirement for a person to be able to walk normally, and I can certainly attest that any man I saw missing a big toe could not walk without a severe limp. Antonius sat looking dumbly down at the tablet, as if by a sheer force of will he could alter the numbers staring back up at him. Of course, he could not and neither could we. We were all struggling with the scope of the loss, as overall the Legions had lost four of every ten men, either dead or, like the men with severe frostbite, no longer fit to march. Some Legions were a little better, some a little worse. While the 10th had fared a bit better in terms of illness or frostbite, we had been in three engagements, including the one when the Tenth Cohort was wiped out, so we more than made up for it with battle dead. Antonius put his head in his hands as he struggled to cope with the realization that he had lost almost half his army, yet had nothing to show for it.

"Antonius, what do you intend to do about paying the men some sort of bounty?"

I silently thanked the gods that it was Ahenobarbus who asked the question that I knew was on everyone's minds, as all the wine and whores in the world would do no good if men did not have the money to pay for them. Most of the men had lost a significant portion, if not all of their savings with the loss of the baggage train.

Antonius looked up slowly, his eyes unfocused as he replied dully, "I plan on getting the money from Cleopatra to pay the men a bonus of 400 sesterces."

Corbulo, Caecina, and I exchanged glances at the mention of the sum, and I knew we were thinking the same thing, that this might not be enough to appease the men. Four hundred sesterces was a little less than a half year's pay, but while the men should also be receiving their back pay, most of the men of the veteran Legions had lost much more than that from their savings accounts.

"Maybe the wine and whores will keep the men in line," Caecina whispered.

I hoped he was right, but only time would tell. A few other matters were discussed, including Antonius' decision that for at least the first month we were in winter camp there would be no drilling or training of any kind.

"I want the men to stay drunk for this first month. I want them to swim in the ocean, to eat their fill, and to forget about all the horrors that they've seen."

I was torn on hearing this; while I appreciated what Antonius was trying to do, giving the men the license to run rampant for a month would make it extremely difficult to get them back under control when the time came. We were dismissed to go back to our men, and as we left the *Praetorium*, I voiced my concerns to the others, but they did not seem to be particularly concerned.

"So we have to stripe a few backs." Balbinus shrugged it off. "It's worth the risk, in my opinion."

Corbulo and Caecina clearly agreed, nodding their heads at Balbinus' words, so I decided to drop the matter and worry about it when and if it came.

The whores started arriving the next day, as Antonius had promised, while the wine flowed freely. The only work that the men did was the cooking of their meals, their laundry, and other small tasks that could not be avoided. The rest of their time was spent in debauching and revelry; I do not believe that the majority of them spent a full watch sober. Gaius tried to resist his comrades' insistent attempts to get him as drunk as they were, but it is a hard business treading the straight and narrow when all one's friends are trying to make sure you crawl in the gutter. By the end of the first week, I spied him arm in arm with some of his tentmates, weaving down the street on their way to the series of huts that Antonius had set aside for the use of the whores, who were still streaming in from all points of Syria. The men alternated their time between trips to the whores, basking on the beach soaking in the warmth of the sun, playing seemingly never-ending dice games, drinking bouts, and sleeping. For the first several days, things were peaceful between the men, even when they were from different Legions, as I believe everyone was just so relieved that they had survived their ordeal that the usual animus that inhabited some men that made them so eager to fight their peers was dormant. That could not last forever, and by the second week, fights were beginning to break out between the men, though they were still relatively few when compared to a normal winter camp.

As time passed, the other Primi Pili and I began to form the opinion that the hardship and misery that the men had shared had formed among them a bond that we did not see normally, even after some of our toughest campaigns. We came to the conclusion that the brutally hard conditions of the march were so horrific that the normal rivalries and arguments rife in a winter camp were viewed as petty and unworthy by the men. The Centurions enjoyed themselves just as much as the men, all of us secretly relieved that the burden of disciplining the men was temporarily lifted, and we were as openly jubilant that there was no training schedule to maintain as the rankers were. We maintained only a skeleton group of Centurions on duty, one from each Cohort, with the only requirement I imposed being that the men had to be sober while on guard duty. Like the rest of the men, I had an itch that only a woman could scratch, but I found the experience supremely unsatisfying, so two weeks after we arrived at Leuke Kome, I sent Diocles on an errand to Damascus. I began to count the days when I expected to see my servant and friend return to camp with the woman who had been haunting my dreams with him. Our general was clearly experiencing the same sense of anticipation, but the major difference between us was that I did not stay drunk and carry on like a lovesick fool.

Antonius had taken to waiting for Cleopatra down on the dock, even having a couch brought down so that he could lounge on it while he swilled wine, looking seaward. When darkness or the weather forced him to his quarters, he greeted every visitor with the same question.

"Is she here yet?"

For a short period of time after the army arrived, he made at least an attempt to give the appearance worthy of the general commanding the army, yet with every day that passed without any sign of Cleopatra, or any word of her whereabouts, he put less and less effort into maintaining that appearance. Finally, he gave up altogether, stopping bathing and shaving, while I do not believe that he spent one sober moment in those weeks waiting for the queen of Egypt. Even those of us who did not care for Antonius had no desire to witness the spectacle of one of the most powerful men in Rome reduced to such a state, but even after Ahenobarbus went to talk to him about the display he was putting on, he was oblivious.

In fact his only question to one of his most loyal generals was, "Is she here?"

At first, the men were too absorbed in trying to see exactly how drunk they could get, or how many whores they could go through in a day to pay much notice. As time passed and men got bored, they picked back up with their favorite activity, after wine and women of course, gossiping about their general. It did not take long after the men began sniggering about Antonius and his pining for Cleopatra that the talk turned to the more serious matter of the bonus that the general had promised. Somehow he had managed to scrape together enough cash to pay the men a portion of their back pay, enough that they could pay the whores and buy more wine once the supply that Antonius provided had run dry, which did not take nearly as long as I believe Antonius had anticipated, and gamble, of course. Now that those funds jingling in each man's purse was running low, the grumbling was not long in following. I suppose that Antonius, as drunk as he may have been, was acutely aware of this, fueling his desperate question. It did not help matters that the section of beach that the men frequented was in plain view of the docks, so they could see Antonius slouched on his couch, draining cup after cup of wine as he stared out to sea.

Finally in early Januarius, the man whose job was to stand in the tower positioned on a small knoll a few yards away from the warehouses fronting the dock shouted that he spied a vessel approaching. This was a common occurrence, but fairly quickly he relayed that this was no ordinary merchant ship, that it was much larger than that. I was resting in my quarters when I heard a man running down the street shouting the news, although I did not rouse myself, as this happened a few times a week and had always proven to be a false alarm. In truth, I was in as much of a state of anticipation as Antonius was, because I had received no word of the whereabouts of my own precious delivery and I was beginning to feel serious doubt that Diocles had been successful in his mission. It was a matter of a third of a watch later that I heard a voice that sounded as if it belonged to the same man, this time shouting that the approaching vessel had been positively identified as belonging to Cleopatra, and that she was leading a convoy of ships. Moments later, men were out in the streets, shouting to each other, their voices clearly happy at the news that Antonius' wait, and by extension the army's, was over.

Ironically, Antonius was not in his usual spot to hear and see what he had been waiting for these past weeks, forcing Cleopatra to disembark and proceed to his quarters. She did not make the same kind of entrance as when she was first summoned by Antonius, but a queen like Cleopatra is unable to do anything silently, so that as she walked, surrounded by her Nubian bodyguards of course, she developed a tail of followers. Most of them were Legionaries, none of them wanting to miss an opportunity to gawk at this creature that held their general in such thrall. It still makes me smile to think of the open disappointment and astonishment as some of the men got their first chance to view her up close, without all of her royal regalia and the thick makeup she wore for formal occasions. They would never get the chance to spend time with her or hear her talk like a Legionary one moment, then be as sweet as honey the next. When I heard that she had arrived it was not long before I wondered if I would ever get a chance to spend a moment with her, but it was only a passing thought. I was more concerned that she had brought the needed supplies, and most importantly, the money with which Antonius was going to pay the men their bonuses, because with every passing day they were becoming more restive. As important as this may have been, I found it hard to pay much attention to all the goings-on around me as I was maintaining a vigil of my own, though I did not stay drunk or sit on a couch facing the direction of Damascus.

Scribonius, Balbus and I spent the evenings as all old soldiers do, clutching our cups of wine while reminiscing about battles fought, a good part of that time talking about comrades lost, each of us feeling the loss of Cyclops in our own way. He had never talked much, but he had been the fourth member of our private little club, and we felt his absence keenly. The other two men knew that I was awaiting my own delivery, but they could also see that I was losing hope with every passing day so they did not make my despair a matter of fun, for which I was thankful. I was happy to see that both men were filling back out, gaining the weight back that they lost during the bitter campaign. For my part, I was finding it difficult to do the same, as my normal appetite did not return, due in no small part to the fact that Diocles was not around to make sure that I ate properly. But the major cause was because I was no less lovesick than Antonius was, and it was at least good to see that the appearance of his queen restored him somewhat to his former vigor.

Cleopatra had brought all that Antonius required, so that no more than two days after her arrival, a formation was held where the general paid the men the remainder of their back pay, along with the promised bounty of 400 sesterces. It was not much compared to the men's expectations when they had first set out, all of their heads filled with the fabulous tales of the riches of Parthia. As the men stood in line to receive their cash, I was reminded of Gaius Crastinus and how he had been looking forward to fighting the Parthians, claiming that their soldier's armor was chased with gold and the hilts of their swords encrusted with precious jewels. I had believed Crastinus at the time, so much so that in fact after our first battle under Ventidius, I examined several of the bodies of the Parthian dead, but did not find any sign of such riches. I chuckled at the thought of what Crastinus' reaction would have been if he had lived to see the drab iron plating and plain wooden hilts of the Parthians we killed.

The Centurions below the first grade received a bonus of 800 sesterces, while those of the first grade received a thousand. The Primi Pili like me received a bonus of 1,200 sesterces, and while I understood the men's envy and grumbling that I received three times the amount they were given, what they did not see was how much of that money went back into the Legion. When the wine supply was running low before we received our monthly stipend for the purchase of more, the replenishment of stock came out of my purse. When there was a feast held that was not on a festival day mandated by the priests and augurs, such as the one that had become an annual tradition that honored our victory at Alesia, the expenditure was borne by me and the other Centurions. Therefore, I did not feel guilty when I took the money, knowing that the men would be seeing a good portion of it again.

A week after Cleopatra arrived, I was sitting in my quarters, reading a recently acquired scroll, irritated that I had to hold the thing almost at arm's length to read the tiny, cramped script, wishing that Diocles was available to help me work out some of the more difficult words, it being written in Greek. I had learned to speak the language many years before, but learning to read it had been a long and painful process consisting of many nights with Diocles sitting at my side like a disapproving tutor, helping me sound out words while correcting my many, many mistakes. My literacy in Greek was also something that I kept secret from everyone except Scribonius, who was fluent in the language in both written and spoken form, since a Centurion who did such things was subject to suspicion from both the men in the ranks and the upper classes, though in some ways things had changed. When I was a young boy, what I was attempting to do in elevating my status was next to impossible, but the civil wars had wrought huge changes in our society, mainly because the ranks of the knightly class were so thinned by proscriptions, fighting and assassinations as rivals took advantage of the overall lawlessness to even old scores. Now, Octavian being the prime mover among them, the upper classes were opening the doors to men they considered worthy of moving into the vacated ranks and I planned on taking advantage of it, despite being keenly aware that I lacked the formal education of even the merchants who were my rivals for advancement. So I struggled at my Greek and I was absorbed in this task as I sat in my quarters, cursing as a shadow fell across the scroll as someone entered, blocking the light.

"There better be a good reason for someone to enter my quarters without knocking," I snapped, not bothering to look up.

"I thought I had a good reason, but perhaps I was wrong. Would you like me to leave, Titus Pullus?"

The words were spoken in Latin, but with an accent that betrayed a Syriac heritage, the voice soft and melodious. In truth, I had never heard a song sung in all my days that sounded quite as sweet as those two sentences. I swung about and stood up, my heart hammering against my ribs as I viewed the small woman, draped in her drab brown gown, still with her traveling cloak wrapped about her thin shoulders. She looked exactly the same as when I had left her, though she was clearly tired from the long trip, her large brown eyes staring up at me, her full lips curved in a teasing smile. Diocles was standing just behind her, beaming at me, but I only had eyes for Miriam, and without saying a word, I came to her, enveloping her in my arms before kissing her long and hard.

The gods are fickle, it is true. But they have their moments of kindness, and it was only through their machinations that Miriam and I were reunited. After we had spent some time alone, I called for Diocles to thank him for bringing Miriam to me. He ended up staying for dinner as he and Miriam told me all that had happened in his quest to find her. Miriam had not been in Damascus. As I had feared, Hashem did not take my leaving without marrying Miriam well at all. Despite Miriam making light of it, I could tell that whatever took place between them had taken its toll. Naomi was caught in the middle, but she had no choice other than to back her husband, and while Hashem did not throw Miriam out, he made her feel unwelcome, so Miriam had chosen to leave. She had no other family in Damascus, meaning she was forced to go stay with a cousin in Chalcis. That had not worked out well, as he had tried to force himself on her, making her stay at Chalcis less than a week. Then, using some of the money I had left with her, she paid her way as part of a merchant's caravan returning to Antioch. The merchant's wife always accompanied her husband on his trips, which I suspected was to keep an eye on him, so Miriam had a female companion and despite the differences in station, the two women became friends. On their arrival in Antioch, Miriam stayed in the merchant's household, ostensibly to work as a domestic, but ultimately to act as a companion to the merchant's wife.

When Diocles arrived in Damascus, Hashem refused to talk to him, and while Diocles did not speak the Syriac dialect that Hashem did, he got the distinct impression that Miriam's brother-in-law was not asking after my health when my name was in his mouth. Diocles had chosen an inn near the market, where he was sitting in the downstairs room where the meals are served, brooding about what he was going to do next, when Naomi found him. Through a mish-mash of Latin, Greek, and the gods know what else, she managed to let Diocles know where Miriam had gone, though she had now been away for several months. Naomi had not heard from the cousin and therefore did not know that Miriam had left, so Diocles traveled to Chalcis to find an uncommunicative cousin who refused to even acknowledge that he knew Miriam. Diocles had reached a dead end, but thanks to a nosy neighbor bearing the cousin a grudge, he learned that Miriam had left on the caravan. However, the neighbor was not sure of its destination, giving Diocles three possible destinations in Antioch, Laodicea, or Tripolis. My servant and friend, being the smart fellow that he is, and knowing that all three were on the coast, reasoned that his best course of action was to go first to Antioch in the north, then work his way south since he would have to head in that direction anyway. However, Antioch is a huge city, with caravans coming in from all directions, but again my little Greek had learned one important piece of information, that the merchant in question specialized in pottery of the type produced in Chalcis. Asking around, he learned that there were perhaps a half-dozen such merchants, so he went from one to the other until he found the correct one. The merchant's wife was not happy about losing Miriam, but she was also a woman who remembered what it was like to be young and in love, so she bid Miriam a fond farewell as my woman climbed aboard the docile mare that Diocles had brought along with him.

As I sat listening to them alternately tell their part of the tale, it was easy to see that the two of them had picked their conspiracy to control me back up right where they had left off, but I was of an age now where I did not mind. I was just happy to have them both back with me, and we spent that evening telling stories and laughing. During the course of the evening, I realized how much I had missed this woman from my life; I had been so sure that I would never love another as I loved Gisela, and while the feelings I had for Miriam were subtly different, they were just as powerful as they had been with my wife. The only thing I was sure about was that I was not willing to have more children, so a part of me did worry that this would cause trouble between Miriam and me at some point in the future. However, I was determined just to enjoy the moments we were sharing and I gave a silent thanks to the gods that Diocles had been so persistent.

With all the outstanding matters disposed of, both personal and professional, the men settled down, their restlessness and uncertainty soothed by the production of the promised bounty. Cleopatra's presence, while comforting to Antonius, served to open the old wounds of rancor and bitterness between his generals, none of them making any attempt to hide their resentment at Cleopatra's inclusion in their council meetings. As the matters being discussed were political and not military, we were exempt from attending, for which we were all thankful. While entertaining, watching the bickering was also disheartening because it reminded us all of the rancor and hatred that had led us to kill each other in such huge numbers. It helped that I had other matters on my mind, none of them martial or political, instead wholly concerned with the happiness I felt at having Miriam back with me.

Leuke Kome was a small town, so I was forced to pay a goodly sum to rent her an apartment that was not a complete hovel, but I did not care. I took to spending most of my time outside the camp, coming in for the obligatory formations in the morning and evening, or to take care of the necessary business of running the Legion. The rest of the time, I was otherwise occupied, and I did not see anything wrong in having young Gaius as a guest to dinner most evenings, since we were outside camp. Once he got over his initial shyness around Miriam, they became good friends as well. Although I never had confirmation, I suspect that the cabal against me added another member, as it seemed to happen with astonishing regularity that if one of them brought up a subject, the others would then add their own thoughts at different moments. Naturally, they all claimed innocence, saying that just because all three of them agreed on something it was not proof that they were conspiring. I soon gave up fighting about it; it is the wise general who knows when the numbers are not in his favor and makes a tactical withdrawal with his forces intact.

Scribonius and Balbus were frequent guests, but it was the addition of Macrianus to our table that I know surprised the others. In the time I had spent with the younger man, the suspicions I held about both his potential and his headstrong nature were confirmed, as we had already butted heads over a couple of matters concerning the men. Although I appreciated his devotion to the rankers, from my perspective he had not achieved the separation necessary that gave a Centurion that ability needed to send men to their deaths while still being able to do their own job. However, if given the choice, I much preferred my Centurions to be like Macrianus than those men who had forgotten what it was like to be in the ranks, viewing their men only as a source of labor, or worse, a source of extra income. I am ashamed to say that while I tried, it is impossible to weed such men completely out of the Centurionate, which is why I chose instead to spend time with those like Macrianus, hoping that they would then rise through the ranks to be put in a position at least to control the predations of baser men. Macrianus had a quick wit, with a tongue that tended towards the sharp, which I appreciated and enjoyed as long as it was under the right circumstances. All in all, we were a merry bunch, passing the long winter watches in good conversations.

Despite our attempts to keep politics out of it, we were Romans, most of us anyway, and there is no way to keep Romans from talking politics at some point. Most of our speculation focused on Antonius' prospects and how damaged they were when the news of Parthia and the disastrous campaign reached Rome and Octavian's ears. We knew that Antonius had sent back dispatches claiming great victories, but that was early on, and no matter what he said now, too many men who would tell a different tale were being sent back to the mainland of the Republic. If it was just a handful of men who had lost their feet or hands, or suffered some debilitating wound, it would have been one thing, but thousands of men were being removed from the Legion rolls, and some of them had opted to brave a winter crossing with the few captains willing to take the huge risks in return for the huge reward of being the first across the sea. These Legionaries that survived the crossing would be telling anyone who would listen about all the disasters that had befallen Antonius and the army. Even accounting for the exaggeration that maimed men put on the face of what had happened to them, there was no way to disguise the scope of the disaster. The men who would be sailing later would only serve to corroborate the stories of the early arrivals, so Antonius had a matter of weeks before the backlash began.

"He's buggered, well and truly buggered," Balbus declared. "Octavian is going to use this to finish Antonius once and for all."

I looked over at Scribonius, wanting to see what he thought, but while he said nothing, I could see he agreed with Balbus.

"So what do we do about it?"

I had decided to ask the question that I knew was rattling around in each head, knowing that none of us wanted to come out on the losing side. Balbus gave a sidelong glance to each of us, as the question was ostensibly aimed at him, before shrugging.

"I don't know there's much we can do right now. The moment's not right because nothing has happened."

"Hopefully we'll know when the moment's right," Scribonius answered, and I did not pursue the conversation any farther.

Fortunately, as we learned later, for the time being Octavian did not choose to make political capital out of our misfortune, indeed going along with the fiction perpetrated by Antonius, who declared that he had subdued both Media and Armenia. Antonius claimed that it had never been part of his strategy to conquer Parthia in this campaign, but to first ensure that the two kingdoms bordering our Eastern foe were pacified and not a threat. It was a sound strategy, except we all knew that it was nothing but a fiction, that it had never been part of Antonius' plan to do anything about Media, while Artavasdes the Armenian had been a supposed ally, though none of us considered him as such. In fact, the rumor started circulating that we would be marching to chastise him with the next season.

Despite Octavian choosing not to challenge Antonius' version of events, even when it became obvious to anyone with a set of ears that the Parthian campaign was anything but a success, neither was he willing to send Antonius any aid. He even went so far as to forbid Antonius from recruiting in Italia as was his right, Caesar's heir sending a snippy letter saying in effect that seeing how Antonius had won the great victory that he claimed, he hardly needed to raise more troops. He also used Antonius' supposed victory as an excuse not to hand over the four Legions he promised his colleague as part of the trade for ships called for by the Treaty of Tarentum. Antonius did not learn of this until early March, and when he called us together, he was livid, in my mind justifiably so.

"That sneaking, conniving little cocksucker Octavian is trying to stop us from rebuilding the army," he snarled, throwing the scroll that I assumed contained that news down on his desk.

He leaned forward, his heavily muscled arms taut with his suppressed rage as he glared at each of us in turn, as if daring us to agree with Octavian's perfidy. I could not help shooting a glance at Balbinus, yet he looked as angry as the rest of us, because Octavian had put us in a very difficult spot. We had already been informed that we would be doing things in the manner first practiced by Caesar, not reenlisting the Legion as a whole but instead finding replacements to fill the empty spots. However, we had planned on having boatloads of new *tiros*, preferably from Hispania like the bulk of the Legion, or at worst from Italia. Now we were being told that we would have to scour this side of Our Sea for Roman citizens, and we did not have a moment to lose in doing so. Although we are all on the same side, when it comes to recruiting, other Legions are viewed as the enemy, so I had to scramble to send recruiting parties out to the African provinces to find suitable men before the other Legions. That is why I wasted no time in selecting the men who would be in the recruiting party. Deciding that the best and only person to lead the *dilectus* was Scribonius, I invited him to dinner that night, making sure that it was only the two of us, with Miriam, of course. The minute he entered the apartment and saw the table set for just three people, he knew I was up to something, and his expression turned wary.

"I never could fool you," I admitted, hoping that by being frank with him that this would ease the tension.

I had Diocles offer him some wine, then waited for him to take a few sips before I broached the subject.

"I need you to do something for the Legion, Scribonius."

He gave me his thoughtful frown, saying nothing, clearly waiting for me to continue. I proceeded to explain what needed to be done, and he listened carefully, still not speaking. When I was finished, he considered, before giving a resigned shrug.

"When do you want me to start?"

"Tomorrow," I told him, but before he could protest, I reached over to refill his wine cup.

"But tonight, let's just drink and talk."

I do not know what prompts such moments, whether it is the stars aligning in a certain order, or if the gods decree that this be the day when all mysteries are revealed. Neither do I know what force put the words in my mouth, or if I simply put the same words I had uttered so many times before in a slightly different order, thereby unlocking some door in Scribonius' heart.

Whatever the case, when I asked as I so often had before for Scribonius to tell me of his background, treating it as something that had developed into a joke, I could have been knocked over by a breath when he set his cup down, gave a slight smile, then said simply, "All right."

Of all the momentous events that happened that winter for me personally, that still ranks as one of the most memorable, the night that Sextus Scribonius told me where he was from and how he had come to join the army.

"I was the son of a knight, and we were members of the first class of the Claudii" he began. "The third son, but my father was very wealthy and had more than enough to set each of us up." Scribonius' gaze had turned inward, as Miriam and I sat spellbound, while out of the corner of my eye I noticed Diocles had crept into the main room where we ate our meals and was sitting in a dark corner, clearly as interested as we were.

Scribonius looked up, his eyes turned towards me, a sad smile on his face.

"He was like you in many ways, Titus. He was extremely ambitious to advance the fortunes of his family, and to that end, he spared no expense in our education. We three boys had our own tutors but naturally, it was my oldest brother Marcus who was being groomed for the Senatorial order. My father had done very well, and he was very close to the million sesterces needed to elevate the family into the Senatorial class. We would still have been plebeian of course, but nowadays there are mostly plebeians actually serving in the Senate anyway."

He sipped from his cup before continuing, "Oh, how I looked up to Marcus! He was ten years older than I was, but he was a wonderful older brother. He didn't torment me the way so many older brothers do, and was always there to protect me from the older boys. He could do no wrong in my eyes."

He heaved a great sigh.

"But then he fell in with Catiline. There were two types of men in the upper classes who flocked to that demagogue, one type being young idealists like Marcus who wanted to change things so that more people of the lower classes had a voice. And then there were the men heavily in debt who could have given a rotten fig about the poorer classes and only cared about Catiline's promise to cancel debts. I was 19, and I never questioned Marcus, or any of his friends, for that matter, about what Catiline was really up to. He had made his reputation in the Social Wars militarily, and he was quite the figure in his toga as he walked about inciting the mob. Honestly, I didn't care about any of it. As long as Marcus was involved, I wanted to be part of it as well.

"So when Marcus said he was joining the army that Catiline was forming up, under that bastard Manlius, I made it clear that I was joining as well. Our family wasn't politically important enough for Catiline to use us for what he had planned in Rome; that was for men like Cethegus, Publius Cornelius Lentulus, and men of that stature. The young firebrands who hadn't yet made their name in the *cursus honorum* were all sent down to fill the ranks of Catiline's army, which Manlius was commanding. He had been a Primus Pilus in one of Sulla's Legion, or so he claimed. Now, as I look back, I'm sure that he was never higher than a third grade, and certainly had never even been a Pilus Prior. But he was a right mean bastard, and he had some of his veteran friends put us through training."

He paused, shaking his head at the memory, while I had one of my own, as I remembered that Scribonius was one of the *tiros* like Vibius and me who clearly had some sort of military training. Ours came from Cyclops back in Hispania, but now I was learning how it had been for Scribonius.

"But when you're young, it's all a great adventure. Marcus was made a Tribune, but I was too young so I was in the ranks, though I didn't mind because it wasn't like a real army camp. It was like a big festival at night, where we were allowed to mingle freely with men who were supposed to be our officers. I have to laugh now at the idea, but the mess it created when the fighting started wasn't funny at all. Yet at that moment, it was great fun, and we would spend the nights talking about what Catiline was trying to do. I suppose that's when I started to see what this revolt was really about as far as most of the men were concerned, at least the men in the ranks. Most of them were Sulla's veterans, and they were bored, or they were broke, or they were both. They laughed at the boys like me, but they weren't cruel to us. The more I heard, the more I wondered if we had made the right decision, and one night I went to Marcus and suggested that perhaps we should reconsider, but he wouldn't hear of it.

"You see, when we had left Rome, Marcus and my father had a huge fight, and my father, as *paterfamilias*, forbade Marcus to go. He said that it would end badly, and that the family's prospects would be ruined because Catiline couldn't win since too many powerful men were aligned against him. Cicero was only the most vocal, but there were men who were infinitely wealthier and more influential who felt threatened by Catiline. It wasn't until I was older that I learned that in the end; it was all about money and the old order preserving itself. My father saw that immediately, but Marcus called him an old fool who was too bound to the past to see that change was inevitable."

Scribonius gave a small, sad laugh.

"Marcus was half-right at least. Change was inevitable, but it wasn't going to be Catiline who brought it about. Anyway, my father told Marcus that if he left, he was disowned, but Marcus didn't care and he left that night."

Miriam frowned. She had been listening raptly, but now she was moved to ask a question.

"What about you? What did your father say about you joining Marcus?"

Scribonius' face took on a pained expression as the memory evidently stabbed at him like a dagger.

"He didn't say anything because he didn't know. I don't think it ever occurred to him that I would disobey. He didn't forbid me because he didn't know I was interested or involved, and in truth to that point I wasn't, not really. But I sneaked out of the house that night, after Marcus left like the man he was. He made no attempt to hide what he was doing, announcing to everyone in the house that he was leaving to join Catiline. He even made the pronouncement that, like the men of Sparta, he would either return victorious with his shield or on it."

I could see the tears forming in Scribonius' eyes, but his tone was mocking as he raised his cup in a salute.

"But not me. No, I left like a thief, after my father had fallen asleep. I never said a word; I didn't even leave a note. I just...left. And met with Marcus, who was waiting for me with some friends at the Capitoline Gate where we made our way to the camp in Etruria. So when I went to Marcus to suggest that we should go back home, that maybe this hadn't been the glorious undertaking that it had been made out to be, Marcus got very angry with me. I know now that it was his pride, because I could see in his eyes the same doubts that I had, but there was no way that he would admit that my father had been right, so we stayed there in camp.

"And there we played at soldier, waiting for word from Rome that Catiline's part of the plan had begun. I never knew what the plan was, at least until later. If I had, or more importantly, if Marcus had, I don't believe that things would have turned out the way they did for the both of us."

Every time Scribonius' cup looked as if it were empty, I would reach over to refill it, not wanting to break whatever spell had fallen over him. I had learned more about Scribonius' past in the last few moments than in all the years I had known him, and I wanted to hear the whole story. Scribonius drank about as much as I did, but despite his consumption that night, he was not slurring or rambling as the drunk tend to do. It was as if he had decided that he needed to unburden himself at long last and he would not stop until he had.

He took another deep gulp before continuing.

"Then, word reached us of the letters to the Allobroges, and how Catiline's offer to ally himself with Gauls, our ancient enemies, had turned the people against him. Well, you know the rest. Catiline barely escaped with his own life, but a number of the conspirators were sacrificed by Catiline to enable him to escape with his skin, at least that's how I saw it. Catiline came to the camp, and he gave a rousing speech, I'll give him that, but out of the 10,000 men gathered there, all but about 3,000 of them left. Of course, Marcus was determined to be one of the 3,000, while a number of the friends we had come with went skulking back home. I wasn't going to leave Marcus' side, but I wasn't happy about staying. Then Catiline gave orders to break camp, and we started marching. Supposedly, we were headed to Gaul to go into exile there, but when we heard that, almost all of Sulla's veterans flat out refused to go, saying that they hadn't joined with Catiline to spend the rest of their lives with a bunch of smelly barbarians."

He gave a rueful laugh.

"Little did I know that the first part of my career in the real army I'd be doing that very thing. Anyway, when Catiline learned that if he were to go to Gaul he'd do it by himself, he then resolved to avoid battle until conditions were more favorable. That's what he told us anyway, but now I know he was just stalling for time and praying for a miracle. Then the patricians finally got their forces together and they sent Caecilius Metellus and three Legions down from the north. We marched south, but Antonius' kinsman Hybrida and Marcus Petreius were waiting for us. Well, you know, Hybrida and Catiline had been colleagues when they both ran for Consul so he hoped that Hybrida would be unwilling to face him, and even if he did, he wouldn't fight hard. He was wrong, but you know that too."

Now Scribonius' face tightened as he began reliving that day. I shot a quick glance at Miriam and

Diocles, who were both sitting spellbound; Miriam with elbows on the table, chin in her hand, gazing at Scribonius with glistening eyes. Diocles had barely moved a muscle, still sitting in the darker corner of the room, but if Scribonius had even seen him, he gave no notice. My friend was now staring down into his cup, frowning in the manner he always did when he was thinking.

"They call it a battle, but it was hardly that. I know that now, having been in more than a hundred of them, but that day, I had never seen anything that confused, heard anything that loud, or witnessed anything so terrible. We couldn't array ourselves in proper wings, not and have more than one line anyway, but Catiline did what he could with what he had, I suppose. I was put in the center, and Marcus was the Tribune in command of my Cohort, but you know how that is. One of Sulla's veterans was really in charge, and I honestly don't believe that Marcus would have done a worse job. He either completely forgot or panicked and never blew the whistle for the relief, so the men in the first rank were forced to keep fighting until they were exhausted. The other side didn't have that problem; they had Centurions who knew their job, so they kept the shifts short and the men fresh. It was just a matter of a few moments before our men were so tired they couldn't lift their shields, and you know what happens then. They were cut down, and in the confusion of men falling and the men behind them trying to get around their bodies, well, it was just a huge mess. I was fourth man back, and I was scared out of my wits. I kept looking over at Marcus, who was trying to rally the men, but he didn't have any more experience than I did at that point. Oh, he had gone to the Campus Martius and done his exercises like I had, but you know, Titus, that it's not nearly the same fighting as an individual as it is to command a Century or Cohort. It wasn't a question of bravery, at least on Marcus' part, but he didn't have a chance. I watched as the men around him were cut down, and I tried to break free to get to him, but by that point we were all crushed together as we were being herded like lambs to slaughter."

He stopped to take another huge swallow of wine. Now the tears were flowing freely, yet his voice was still steady.

"It happened like it was in slow motion, kind of like when they're first teaching us the movements by going through each motion one step at a time. I saw Marcus, his sword in his hand, and he was fighting a pair of men and they sucked him in, just like we're trained to do. The man he was engaged with started falling back, making a good show of being close to cracking, so Marcus pressed in, thinking he was about to make a kill. He didn't even see the blade that cut him down from his unprotected side, but I did. I remember opening my mouth to scream a warning, but nothing came out. I watched him die and there was nothing I could do about it."

I do not know why, but what affected me more were not Scribonius' words; it was the matter of fact way that he was speaking, as a professional Centurion giving an after-battle report, except that I could see by his face how painful it was, and I felt tears coming to my own eyes. Without thinking, I reached out to put my hand on his shoulder, telling him gently that he did not have to continue.

"Yes, I do," he replied calmly. "I've never told anyone about this, and it's time for me to let it out of my soul."

I could only nod my understanding as he continued.

"I don't remember the next few moments after Marcus fell. My next memory is suddenly running, along with the remnants of the men of the center as all we cared about was fleeing with our lives. Of course, that's when the real slaughter begins, but I've always been fleet of foot and it served me well that day. I ran, and I ran, and I ran. I don't know how far I had gotten by the time I stopped to take a breath, but I was in some deep woods, and I was all alone. Before I did anything else, I stripped off my armor, threw away my helmet, my javelin, sword, everything. I wanted nothing to do with armies or fighting or killing as long as I lived, I was sure of it. Once I was stripped to my tunic, I suddenly became very, very tired and all I could think to do was to lay down and sleep, but before I did I walked a short distance away, as I didn't want to be seen anywhere near my armor. I found a hollow in a large tree that was just big enough for me to curl up in, so I crawled in and went to sleep. I slept the rest of that day, and only woke up after it was dark when I heard men shouting. As I came awake, it took me a bit to remember where I was and how I had come to be in a tree hollow, which is when I remembered what happened to Marcus, how he was dead and that I'd never see him again. Somehow, I convinced myself that it had all been a dream and that I had managed to flee out of the camp, that if I returned I would find Marcus alive and well. I was about to head back in that direction, but then I saw a line of torches. I realized that they were from Hybrida and Petreius' army and they were hunting down survivors, so I crawled back in my hole in the tree. As they got closer, I could hear them shouting when they flushed a man out from wherever he was hiding, and then I would hear a scream, and I knew that another man had been cut down. I hadn't thought it possible that I would be more scared than I was earlier that day, but now I was terrified almost out of my mind. Every muscle in my body was trying to force me to get up and run, yet somehow I managed to keep my head enough to realize that my best chance was to stay put in my spot. The line of men passed me by, and one of them was no more than ten paces away from me, but he never even looked in my direction.

"Once they passed by, I got up and made my way back in the direction of the battle. I had to stop and hide on several occasions as more men came by looking for survivors, so it was the middle of the night by the time I made it back to the spot. The bodies had all been stripped and looted, and they were in great piles waiting to be thrown in a pit, and I think it was at that moment that I realized that it had been no dream and there was no way that Marcus was alive. I couldn't get close enough to try and find his body because there were men going through all the piles of clothes while others were gathered around fires, getting drunk. I could hear them bragging about how many men each of them had killed, and I was gripped by a terrible anger. It took everything I had to keep from charging at the nearest group and try to kill as many as I could before I was cut down. But there was something inside me that stopped me, and I'm glad I didn't. Seeing there was nothing I could do to retrieve Marcus' body, I decided to slip away."

He paused again, while his listeners sat there, trying to absorb what it must have been like to be in his place on that night, knowing his brother's body was about to be defiled, for there is nothing worse to a Roman than to be buried in the ground. Even with many of the people that are now part of the Republic doing so, we consider it barbaric. We only did it to fellow Romans when there was no other choice, or to insult their memories, and it was clearly the second reason that the victors of the battle against Catiline had in mind with the enemy dead on the field.

Scribonius was clearly tiring, his voice growing hoarse, but he seemed intent on continuing, so we let him talk.

"I headed north, not really knowing where I was going, but not really caring."

"Wait," Miriam interrupted, clearly puzzled.

"Was not the battle north of Rome?"

Scribonius looked at her with a mixture of respect and amusement.

"I see that Titus has been teaching you about our geography," he replied. "But to answer your question, yes, the battle was north of Rome, and I went north from that."

"But why would you not return to Rome to your father to let him know you at least were safe, and what had happened to your brother?"

"For one thing, it wasn't safe," he said quietly. "Up until Caesar, Romans were not much for forgiving her enemies, and I was afraid that if I returned to my family, I'd put them in danger. Besides, I was too ashamed." He gave another sad shake of his head. "I couldn't face my father and tell him that I had been unable to protect my brother. So I didn't want to go anywhere near Rome. I lived by what I could steal from farms, but at first I wasn't very good at it, and I took a few beatings."

He laughed at the memory.

"But it only took a few of those before I became very adept at sneaking into barns and granaries to grab the odd chicken and handful of grain. I got so good that I could actually get into a farmhouse, if there were no dogs, that is. I made my way to Cisalpine Gaul, and there I took a job herding cattle."

He turned to me then, saying, "You know how the Gauls love their cattle. Well, I learned more about cattle than I ever wanted to know. It was brutally hard work. Remember, I had never done any kind of manual labor before, other than the exercises we took on the Campus Martius, and of course wrestling bouts and the like. Still, I survived and became stronger, but I knew that I had to keep moving, so I never stayed very long in one place. Then, I was hired to help move a herd from Cisalpine Gaul to Hispania, driving along the coast. When I got to Corduba, I decided I was far enough away from Rome that I was probably safe, and I decided to stay. I was there almost a year, where I was working as an apprentice to a metalsmith when the *dilectus* was announced."

He shrugged.

"So I joined the 10th Legion, and that's where I met this huge oaf." He gave me a playful cuff on the arm, which I returned with a little more force, knocking him sideways. He rubbed his arm, glowering at me. "Must you always prove you're stronger than everyone?"

"Yes," I said simply, then we both began roaring with laughter.

Miriam watched us with a bemused expression, and I imagined that she was having a hard time understanding how Scribonius could go from so sad to laughing uproariously in the space of a few heartbeats.

She shook her head at the two of us, then asked Scribonius, "Did you ever let your father know that you were safe?"

Scribonius stopped laughing immediately, his face growing long again.

"Not for a long time, no."

"So he thought you were dead as well?" she asked crossly.

My friend's face reddened slightly as he replied defensively, "I can't defend my actions. I was too ashamed to begin with, and besides, I wasn't exactly enlisted in the Legions in the most legal manner."

He shot a mischievous glance at me.

"But then I wasn't the only one, was I?"

I laughed as Miriam shot me a quizzical glance, and I told her I would explain later.

Scribonius' statement had aroused my curiosity, so I asked him, "How did you get a member of your family to swear the affidavit to join?"

Scribonius shrugged.

"Same as you, I paid someone to lie for me. I had a long-lost uncle who did it for a hundred sesterces."

I whistled; while that was not much money to either of us now, I could imagine how hard it was to scrape that together for someone like Scribonius who was probably making two sesterces a week. Then, another thought struck me, something that had been niggling at the back of my mind for many years that Scribonius' story had awakened and brought to the forefront.

"Do you think Caesar had anything to do with the Catiline conspiracy?"

For that had been rumored for as long as I could remember, even before I joined the army. He certainly had not been shy about defending Catiline before he actually revolted, while at the same time he made what some would call mealy-mouthed, but was at the least half-hearted protests at his subsequent actions. Nothing was ever proven and it obviously did not damage Caesar's political ambitions, yet much like his rumored affair with the Bithynian king Nicomedes, it had hung about him like a bad odor. Scribonius was clearly surprised by my question, not answering immediately, his frown returning.

Finally, he asked me, "Do you remember the day we were addressed by Caesar the first time, back in our training camp in Hispania?"

Indeed I did, clearly recalling the moment in my mind's eye. It had been one of the biggest moments of my life to that point, though I did not think so at the time. I know that I have built it up that way in my mind over the years, given all that happened.

I nodded in answer to his question, so he continued, "I don't suppose you remember our conversation, where I said that he looked familiar?"

I did, but just barely. "It was when he took us on our first long march, wasn't it? He gave us a speech, then marched our legs off."

We both chuckled at the memory, then Scribonius turned serious.

"Well, it took a while, but I finally remembered where I had seen Caesar before. Shortly before the battle, after Catiline came from Rome, Caesar came to meet with him. I had guard duty at the Porta Praetoria when he rode in and that's the first time I laid eyes on him."

While it was interesting, I did not see that it was damning and I said as much, but Scribonius shook his head.

"There's more. Marcus was in the *Praetorium* and he told me about it later. He said that he heard Catiline arguing with someone who told Catiline that he had gone too far with what he had planned in Rome, that it wasn't what they had agreed on. Marcus said that whoever it was sounded extremely angry, as if someone subordinate to him had botched his orders."

"That sounds like Caesar," I said. "Did Marcus see him?"

"No," Scribonius admitted. "He just heard the argument and when it sounded like they were leaving Catiline's quarters, he made himself scarce."

"So you don't know for sure that it was Caesar talking." Even as I said it, I knew how weak it sounded, and honestly, I do not know why it mattered. Caesar was dead now nine years and was beyond any mortal man's reach, but for some reason it seemed important that his name not be soiled any more than it already had been. I suppose that it was a mark of how much I was still Caesar's man and always would be.

"No, I don't know for sure, Titus. But truly, does it matter one way or the other? You asked the question. I'm sorry if I didn't give you the answer you wanted or expected."

I could see that he was upset, so I let the matter drop.

Thankfully, Miriam still had her own line of questioning to pursue.

"So your father never heard from you again?"

Miriam was clearly not going to let go of this topic, as Scribonius heaved a sigh, shooting me a glance. All I could do was give a helpless shrug, smiling an apology.

"He never saw me again, that's true. But I did let him know that I was well and was happy."

He looked over at me. "Titus was with me, in fact."

I could not hide my surprise.

It was on our first visit to Rome, when we had come to march in Caesar's triumphal parades. Scribonius had taken me about the city, showing me the sights and given me a tour of the neighborhoods. When we reached the lower section of the Palatine, where the houses are spacious and well maintained though nowhere near the luxury of the mansions near the top of the hill, Scribonius had stopped across the street from one house in particular. He did not say anything, while at the time I just thought he had paused for a brief rest because we had been walking about most of the day. In truth, I was not paying much attention, being busy looking around, so I obviously missed him walking quickly across the street to place a small scroll in the tiny niche next to the postern gate that was used for messages. Only that night many years later did I learn he had done so, and that the house we stopped across from had been his childhood home.

"I wrote a letter to my father, telling him that I lived, that I was doing well, and that I was sorry for what I had done. I told him how Marcus had died, that he died well, facing his enemy, and I begged his forgiveness," he said quietly to Miriam.

This clearly gave her some comfort, then she asked Scribonius, "Did you ever hear back from your father?"

Scribonius nodded. "I did. He told me that he forgave me, that I was welcome to come home, as by that time all the repercussions from the Catiline conspiracy had long since died down. But I had found a home in the army, and I was happy. Besides, my brother Quintus had stepped into Marcus' shoes, so I would still be the third son. Quintus had not only filled in for Marcus, he also stepped into my shoes and clearly found they fit him perfectly, but that's a story for another time. Here in the army, everything I accomplished I did on my own, for myself and nobody else."

He looked over at me. I found myself smiling, realizing how thankful I was that he had made that decision to stay, though I was curious about his remark concerning his brother and his role, but that could wait.

Scribonius, with five other Centurions and a half dozen Optios, left the next morning, boarding a coastal ship I had hired that would sail west to Egypt and the African provinces. Scribonius would go to Alexandria, our goal being to find Pompeian veterans who were bored, since the Legions left behind in Egypt by Caesar years before had fairly recently undergone a new enlistment. We needed men, which was certainly true, but because of Octavian's refusal to allow the agents of Antonius that were left behind in Italia actually to do their job, we were now pressed for time if we were to renew the campaign as Antonius had planned. That meant that I only wanted raw youths as a last resort, so the men of the *dilectus* were under strict instructions to that effect. Scribonius would have one Centurion and Optio, while the rest would go to the African provinces to visit the small veterans' colonies established by Pompey Magnus. These men would be long in the tooth for a full enlistment, but they would not be needed for a full term, and frankly, I was desperate. If given the choice between an older man, who may not be as strong and fit as a younger one, yet on whom I did not have to spend much of my Centurions' time training, I would go for the more experienced men. That was in the future, however; until they returned there was not much to do, though I did begin a light training schedule for the men.

We set up the stakes, beginning with the basics, something that was met with much grumbling and complaining, but I did not care. The fact was that we had not fought once as a Legion in quite some time, only a few Cohorts seeing any real action, and like any skill working with the sword requires constant repetition. Even I had fallen off with my own training regimen, so the first few days back with my exercises were excruciating, as once again I was reminded of my age, remembering a time when I could take two or three weeks off then pick back up as if I had not missed a day. Most troublesome were my old wounds, particularly the one I suffered at Munda, making it so I could barely lift my arms above my head at the end of the day. My only consolation was watching men much younger than me staggering back to their huts, moaning and complaining about the aches, pains, and the bruises they had earned. I knew from long experience that the harder the Centurions pushed the men now, the better their chances were when the *cornu* gave the order to fight for real, while I also knew that behind all the grumbling the men understood that as well, and I was happy to see them work hard. The other Legions were beginning their own training regimens, meaning it was not long before the natural spirit of competition blazed openly between the men, each Legion trying to outdo their comrades in other Legions. The air was filled with the sounds of men working at the stakes or running around the camp singing, while other men, on punishment, alternately dug holes then filled them in or performed some other menial but unpleasant tasks. It was back to normal days in winter camp in all respects, and we were so busy that we barely noticed that Antonius and Cleopatra were packing up to leave.

My first indication that our general was departing was when the Primi Pili were summoned to the *Praetorium* and I saw the stacks of crates and baggage that signaled that a move was underway. I asked Corbulo but he was as mystified as I was; only after we went nosing about did we discover that Antonius and Cleopatra were taking her barge back to Alexandria.

Ahenobarbus was stomping around, snarling at anyone nearby, clearly unhappy at Antonius' decision.

"How we're supposed to plan a campaign with him lolling about with his queen in Alexandria I have no idea," he fumed.

I have to say that I agreed, though I knew better than to speak, even if it was in support of what Ahenobarbus was saying. I had learned the hard way that the upper classes always looked out for each other, so I pretended to study the stack of requisition forms I had brought with me. Fonteius emerged from Antonius' private office, concern clearly written on his face as he called to Ahenobarbus, motioning him to a corner where they talked in whispers. I saw Ahenobarbus stiffen at whatever Fonteius was telling him, then after another exchange turn to walk off, head down as he absorbed whatever he had just heard. Fonteius then waved us into the office, so we filed in, then found seats in front of Antonius' desk.

The general was looking better now that Cleopatra was attending to him, but I was somewhat taken aback by the appearance of the queen, who was sitting on Antonius' right. She was dressed simply, for a queen at any rate, her hair pulled back in its usual style, though she looked as if she had lost weight, her face having a pallor underneath the cool olive complexion that I did not remember seeing before, and she looked tired. Nevertheless, she favored me with a bright smile that caused some surprised looks from the other Primi Pili, even garnering a sharp glance from Antonius, and I could feel the flush all the way to the roots of my closely shorn hair. I took a perverse pleasure in Antonius' obvious irritation that his consort had shown me a sign of favor, but it also made me nervous, knowing that I would bear the brunt of my fellow Primi Pilis' rude conjecture once we left this office.

"I'm leaving for Alexandria in the morning," Antonius told us, adding unnecessarily, "along with the queen. I have matters that must be attended to in the governing of the provinces of the East. I expect to find the Legions fully manned and trained when I return."

Saying no more, he stood as a signal that we were dismissed, then before any questions could be asked we were ushered out by Fonteius. I looked over my shoulder and Cleopatra gave me a wave of farewell. For some reason, I was saddened by the thought that I would never see her again, which proved to be wrong. Now, after all that transpired, I wish I could have had a moment to speak with her privately, despite having no idea what I would have said. Perhaps I would have thanked her for listening to a poorly born soldier's tale of woe, but more likely, I would have just mooned about. And even if I had, I know that it would not have altered all that was going to happen between us. I suppose that is why I have such fond memories of that moment, because it was the last time the queen and I would ever be on friendly terms.

We did learn one thing about what Fonteius and Ahenobarbus were whispering about in the corner. In the ever-shifting sands that are the politics of the East, yesterday's enemy is tomorrow's ally, which was what was happening now. Artavasdes the Median and his former ally Phraates had a falling out, so that now Artavasdes had sent embassies to Antonius proposing that we join forces. Ignoring the rumor that the reason for the falling out had been about the division of booty taken from the baggage train, Antonius accepted the offer, realizing that having his own force of cataphracts and archers would be vital to success. Now, the question was when we would finally be marching, since none of us had a good feeling about the possibility of Antonius returning in time for campaigning this season. As is normal whenever an army our size stays in one place for any length of time, the nearest town grows dramatically, Leuke Kome being no exception, more than doubling in size as the whores, winesellers, tricksters, conjurers selling fake potions, and whoever else looking to make a few sesterces descended on what had been a sleepy port town. Dozens of new buildings were thrown up, many collapsing almost as quickly as they had been constructed, squashing whoever was unlucky enough to be inside. Sometimes it would be men from the army, while one time it was three of mine who were sitting in a wineshop drinking, when the roof and upper floor collapsed on top of them. I could not help reflecting on the irony of surviving all that these men had been through, only to die sitting at a table. Soon enough, there was the almost inevitable outbreak of sickness, so that even more men were lost to a bloody flux that swept through the camp. By this point, the men of the 10th were accustomed to my almost obsessive demand for cleanliness, the Centurions and Optios conducting a daily inspection to make sure the men bathed every day, so the 10th did not suffer nearly as badly as the other Legions. The men had slowly recovered from their ordeal, although some still limped and always would because of a missing toe, but as long as they could keep up on the march, none of the Primi Pili cared if there was a slight bobble in the ranks as they marched by.

Now all that was left was the integration of the new men that Scribonius and the *dilectus* would be sending back, so I settled down with Miriam to wait, falling into a routine of domestic life that I had not enjoyed in many years. We were in our own little world, but there was a wider one, particularly on the other side of Our Sea, where events were taking place that moved Antonius ever closer to a confrontation with Octavian.

However, that is all of my tale that I will tell for now, gentle reader. There are still many matters pertaining not just to me, but to the fate of our beloved Republic that must be resolved, as Rome changes from one thing to another, becoming a new form of government that the world has never seen. Most importantly, the struggle for who would become the First Man in Rome between Antonius and Octavian is yet to be resolved. And it is with some pride that I claim my small role in all that is about to transpire, both for me and my fellow Legionaries. But I am old and I tire easily, so I must pause again to refresh myself, ever mindful that I still have one last duty to perform, one that can only be told by me, Titus Pullus, a Legionary of Rome.